Lighthouse Reef

A Pelican Pointe Novel

VICKIE McKEEHAN

beachdevils
PRESS

Lighthouse Reef
A Pelican Pointe Novel
Copyright © 2013 Vickie McKeehan

This book is a work of fiction. The characters, incidents, and dialogue are drawn from the author's imagination and are not to be construed as real. Any resemblance to actual events or persons, living or dead is entirely coincidental.

beachdevils
PRESS
ISBN-10: 0615797776
ISBN-13: 978-0615797779
Printed in the USA

Cover design by Vanessa Mendozzi
Pelican Pointe map designed by Jess Johnson

Visit the author at:
www.vickiemckeehan.com
www.facebook.com/VickieMcKeehan
http://vickiemckeehan.wordpress.com/
www.twitter.com/VickieMcKeehan

For all those who wage their
war every day against cancer,
for all those who support
them, and for all those who
ultimately kick its ass

And for Johnny, an inspiration to us all

Don't miss these other exciting titles by bestselling author

Vickie McKeehan

The Pelican Pointe Series
PROMISE COVE
HIDDEN MOON BAY
DANCING TIDES
LIGHTHOUSE REEF
STARLIGHT DUNES
LAST CHANCE HARBOR
SEA GLASS COTTAGE
LAVENDER BEACH
SANDCASTLES UNDER THE CHRISTMAS MOON
BENEATH WINTER SAND
KEEPING CAPE SUMMER (2018)

The Evil Secrets Trilogy
JUST EVIL Book One
DEEPER EVIL Book Two
ENDING EVIL Book Three
EVIL SECRETS TRILOGY BOXED SET

The Skye Cree Novels
THE BONES OF OTHERS
THE BONES WILL TELL
THE BOX OF BONES
HIS GARDEN OF BONES
TRUTH IN THE BONES
SEA OF BONES (2018)

The Indigo Brothers Trilogy
INDIGO FIRE
INDIGO HEAT
INDIGO JUSTICE
INDIGO BROTHERS TRILOGY BOXED SET

Coyote Wells Mysteries
MYSTIC FALLS
SHADOW CANYON
SPIRIT LAKE (2018)

No man is rich enough to buy back his past.
Oscar Wilde

Lighthouse Reef

A Pelican Pointe Novel

VICKIE McKEEHAN

Welcome to Pelican Pointe

Prologue

The waves crashed up against the rocks. The wind whipped in gusts while a slice of moonlight trailed along the sand, glistening like silver. On the deserted stretch of beach, three young men huddled in front of a campfire they'd built up trying to stay warm in the chilly, damp night air. Two were brothers—the other an older tag-along already of legal age they'd talked into buying beer and cigarettes in the neighboring town of San Sebastian— where you could purchase liquor if you were twenty-one.

But San Sebastian was farther inland and it didn't offer the Coast Highway to tour up and down cruising for chicks, especially in the summertime, or during spring break when babes wearing string bikinis were as common as surfboards. Oddly, that was usually the best time of year to pick up hitchhikers, too.

Not four hours earlier, the trio had set off an alarm on Main Street when they'd broken a window to get inside Ferguson's Hardware store. Their plan had been to rob old man Ferguson, take whatever cash they could find. Who knew Ferguson had gone and installed an alarm system? Probably something the son had come up with to impress his old man, a step toward progress, signaling a change in ownership one day in the not too distant future. Something to show the town he deserved the cushy job he'd fallen into as daddy's right-hand man.

After all, nepotism ran strong in this shitwater of a town, didn't it? Fathers turned the reins over to their sons to inherit the business, whatever the business happened to be. It was a practical matter, a legacy that had held its own ritual for years and would continue to do so for future generations.

Future generations? What a joke that was. Like anyone with a brain would stay in Pelican Pointe their whole life and hope to have a future here.

Flames rose higher on the fire as they took turns tossing more driftwood onto the pyre hoping to make it more like a bonfire.

"Why do you want to do that?" the younger one asked. "We're just attracting attention to ourselves."

"Shut up," the older brother barked. "Didn't we just gather up all this wood? It's freezing out here in the mist. Besides, I call the shots. Don't forget that," he warned as he chucked another log into the blaze, making the tips of the flames shoot up higher, as if trying to reach all the way to the top of the bluffs where the lighthouse sat high atop its craggy perch.

Up to now, the discarded beer cans that littered their feet were the only true indication the three had been drinking. But as they got drunker—they also got more surly—and louder. Nasty tempers began to clash as they always did between these same companions and flare like rockets on the Fourth of July.

The youngest, barely sixteen, spared a glance in the direction of the young teen girl they'd tied up earlier and placed close to the fire. Her eyes told him she looked scared to death. Not an hour earlier, his brother had stuck a gag in her mouth to shut her up and keep her from screaming. "What should we do about her?"

The older brother didn't take long to think about it. "Let's take the bitch up to the lighthouse. Whaddya say we go up there and have ourselves some fun. We'll put it to her good and hard. No one will hear a thing."

"He's right. The longer we stay down here on the beach, the more we risk somebody could come along and spot us," the tag-along agreed without much hesitation.

"But shit. How do we get the bitch up there? You feel like toting her all that way?"

"Hell no. We'll stick her in the back of my pickup while we make our way through town. That way it just looks like it's the three of us same as it usually does."

"Then let's do it."

"I'm in. How do we choose which one of us goes first though? Should be the oldest that gets first dibs, dontcha think? Since that's me—"

"No. No different than the way we always do things. I go first, then my little brother. You last."

"Why does it always have to be your way?"

"Because it's my damn truck that's why. Now shut the fuck up and help me get this bitch loaded up. Anymore crap from you—?"

"Okay. Okay. No need to get your panties in a wad. How much do you think she weighs?"

"How the hell should I know! The three of us should be able to handle her though." With that the oldest brother went over and pulled the terrified girl to her feet. He brought out the knife he carried and stuck it to her throat. He looked into the blonde's brilliant-blue eyes and wondered what it would be like to watch the life go out of them. He'd been thinking about it a lot lately, reading about it, too. Tonight he had his chance to see what it was like for himself. He just had to bring the others around to his way of thinking.

"Grab her feet," he ordered the tag-along. To his brother, he yelled over the sound of the wind and surf, "Open up the tailgate."

"What about the fire?"

"We'll come back. For what I have in mind, this won't take that long at all."

Chapter One

Present day
Somewhere over California

Logan Donnelly was so close to a part of his past he could almost smell the California coast. He was pretty sure that was impossible at twenty-five-thousand feet. But the minute the plane had crossed into California airspace, it seemed to Logan, a weight had lifted.

As he glanced out the window of the sleek jet just as it bumped into a nasty pocket of turbulence that had his stomach lurching, he decided if he didn't get this phase of his life out of the way once and for all, he would never be able to move forward to do what he wanted in his work.

He'd put off coming to Pelican Pointe long enough. But since he'd made a promise two decades back, it was past time he kept it.

He'd traveled literally thousands of miles to get here. It was true he'd spent his early years drifting from one place to another to learn everything he could about his craft. When he'd been a budding, eager artist just starting out, he'd tried living in San Francisco for a time just to stay closer to his roots. But it hadn't taken long for the wanderlust to nip and bite and he was off to try a new place. For a time Los Angeles had offered the distance he needed. But in the end, the City of Angels hadn't worked out any better than the City by the Bay had. While both offered merits, each in its own way, neither had worked for Logan, at least, not for very long.

Instead he'd packed up the tools of his trade and headed to the Big Apple where he'd worked and lived in a sparse loft he'd renovated in Greenwich Village with his own two hands. It had taken him twenty months of sweat equity to get it livable. And after spending a few more years there, he'd left the U.S. behind altogether for places like Athens and Paris and more recently Rome.

God's truth he'd seen the world, lived in many different places. But now he could admit he was tired of bumping elbows in the crowds of major metropolitan cities, any urban city. He didn't want to spend another minute breathing exhaust where it seemed as if the noise never stopped. He yearned for the quiet and the solitude where the press would leave him alone for five damn minutes— without asking some stupid question about his work or his failed relationship—which meant he could no longer blame his lack of inspiration on his pressure-packed, high profile marriage to Brazilian model Fiona Perez.

Thank God and all that was holy his lawyers had finally persuaded Fiona to sign the divorce papers three months ago.

He looked down at the evidence of that. The cast on his right hand was simply one indication of the errors in judgment he'd made. It had taken him way too long to admit that, even though he'd known it within the first ninety days he hadn't made a move to correct it. Especially since Fiona Perez possessed a right hook more like an Irish boxer with a temper to match. Her frequent mood swings often reminded Logan of a meth addict on an overload of speed, which wasn't that far off the mark. If Fiona ever downed anything other than diet pills, if the woman ever bothered to eat something besides baby food, it certainly hadn't been during the thirty months and twenty-five days Logan had spent married to the manipulative witch.

Not to mention, Logan was convinced that Fiona Perez had lived a past life where she'd ruled earth with an iron fist, where she'd been crowned the queen of bitching and moaning early on. Secretive and cagey, getting the truth out of the woman had been damned near impossible. In those first ninety days of what should've still been the honeymoon stage, he'd caught Fiona in lie after lie. It didn't matter if it was something major like money, or something as trivial as a dinner party, the stories she propagated became an embarrassment to him. It didn't matter to Fiona what subject she found important enough to fabricate. She'd lie about something as insignificant as what she'd done that day to pass the time right down to her age, which happened to be five years older than what she'd admitted to.

The final straw had taken place in a villa outside Rome when he'd discovered she'd taken out a five million dollar life insurance policy on him *and* his work behind his back. That night had been the turning point. He'd finally reached his limit and kicked her skinny, bony, lying ass out of his life then and there for good. At two in the morning he'd phoned his lawyers and instructed them to file divorce proceedings.

Two weeks after that, Fiona had found a way to sneak back in. She'd picked the lock on his studio, pilfered a marble statuette he'd just completed that had been commissioned by the Italian government, and then gone bat-shit crazy with it. She'd crept into his bedroom in the middle of night, armed with the statue and started beating him in his own bed. Before he could wrestle her to the floor, she'd cracked open his skull, and broken two bones in his wrist.

The gash in his head had taken sixteen stitches to close. However, his *right* wrist, the one he used predominantly to create, to earn a living, had suffered tendon damage along with cracked bones that had taken way too long to heal. He supposed he was lucky his hard head hadn't been equally impaired. Otherwise he might be dead right about now instead of embarking on a new phase of his life. It hadn't seemed to bother Fiona in the least to learn that the breaks she'd caused had resulted in Logan having to undergo two major surgeries already.

Even though Logan had filed charges, Fiona Perez had simply packed up and fled Rome, flown back to her native

Brazil where the authorities couldn't or were unwilling to get at her and haul her ass back for prosecution.

The doctors still weren't completely convinced Logan would ever be able to use his right hand with the same kind of dexterity he'd had before.

No, for Logan, it was past time to get away from his messed-up lifestyle of the past three plus years and move on to another chapter. In fact, he was looking forward to fixing up the lighthouse he'd just bought in an online auction. Since the entire spot had spectacular views of the Pacific Ocean, his goal was to turn it into his studio. A new place, a new environment in a small town where he could hopefully recapture whatever was missing in his life sounded almost like heaven to Logan.

Because somewhere during the last thirty-six months, he'd lost his passion for what had once been his reason to get up in the morning. He hoped to Christ he could get it back—and soon. His agent had already told him the galleries were losing patience with the "genius" he'd once been. Which was a crock, he thought now. He was the same damn person he'd been a dozen years earlier when the critics had dubbed him a talent to be reckoned with, whatever the hell that had meant.

Coming back to his native California had to be the best place to start.

When the Challenger 600 reduced its air speed to descend, when the pilot announced to his only passenger that he needed to prepare for landing in Santa Cruz, Logan briefly wondered if what he was doing wasn't foolish, even irrational. He was well aware he was at a crossroads of sorts. But if he couldn't come to terms with his past, how could he ever hope to move forward into the future?

Plus, he'd had his fill of high maintenance women, enough to last a lifetime. No more marriages for Logan Douglas Donnelly. He'd vowed to live the rest of his remaining years—whether fifteen or fifty—without ever taking another trip down the aisle again.

And because he was fed up with the intrusive paparazzi's stupid questions they always managed to ask, he hoped the little town of Pelican Pointe could provide some privacy. If not, his first order of business would be to install a gate at the end of what was now his own road to keep people out.

Using this opportunity, he planned to do something to change the direction his life had taken. Since he intended to make the most of it, Logan didn't want to waste more time.

If it also paved the way to keeping the promise he'd made to his grandmother, then he might rack up bonus points for that, too.

In that next instant, he heard the landing gear drop down. The pilot nosed the jet through wispy clouds until Logan could make out one of two runways. He caught a glimpse of ocean, then mountains before he heard the bump of wheels making contact with the tarmac at the little Santa Cruz airport.

Once the pilot lifted the door and Logan descended the steps, he had a brief urge to get on his knees and kiss the California ground, even if it was nothing more than asphalt. It had been twelve years since he'd set foot on California soil. But by the time someone pointed him in the direction of his waiting pickup, a four-door, champagne-colored F-150 Ford, luckily the temptation to make an ass out of himself had completely passed.

He flung his garment bag over his shoulder and headed in the direction of the truck. As the rest of his luggage, the tools he'd brought, and other personal belongings were transferred from the belly of the chartered jet then loaded into the pickup, he spotted a Native American man, wearing civilian clothes, walking his way. Logan assumed the man was Ethan Cody. It had to be Cody because the deputy sheriff was the only one who knew he'd be here at this time and place.

The two men eyed each other before Cody held out his hand in welcome. "Logan Donnelly?"

"And you must be Deputy Cody," Logan assumed, reaching out his good left hand to awkwardly take Cody's extended right. "How's the newest addition to the Cody family?"

Ethan stared briefly at the cast on the man's broken right wrist and hand. But at the question about his four-month-old son, he grinned from ear to ear. "Nate? Nate's outstanding. He's gained another ten ounces since his last checkup. Kid eats all the time."

Logan picked up on the man's body language. "What's up? I mean I'm glad to have a welcoming committee but a little surprised at the gesture."

"There's something...uh...I probably should've mentioned it before now. It's why I decided to meet your plane. We need to talk. What happened to your hand?" Ethan finally asked. "Won't it be a little difficult to remodel a lighthouse with a broken wrist?"

"It's a long story," Logan answered while studying the other man. "That's why I'll have to hire help...locally. What's this about, Deputy?" Logan asked, about the time he saw Cody scrunch up his mouth.

Ethan shifted his feet. "Uh...there's something you need to know." He scratched his chin looking more uncomfortable by the minute. "I'm no longer a deputy, not since the first of the year."

"I see...the book thing? You could've said something in the email," Logan grumbled.

"I should have," Ethan agreed. "But to tell you the truth, I felt like it was something I needed to tell you in person once you got here, especially since you'd already made up your mind to buy the lighthouse."

"Then I need the name of the guy taking your place."

"Man by the name of Garver, Dan Garver. Been a deputy for about three years now, green and inexperienced as they come, but a decent enough guy. Not only that, Pelican Pointe is new territory for him. Dan hasn't even moved into town yet. But he will once he grows tired of making that long commute back and forth in traffic every day from Santa Cruz to come in and handle disputes."

Not much Logan could do about the turnover or what had already taken place so he simply nodded and grunted. But Ethan still seemed uncomfortable. "What else is on your mind?" Logan asked.

Ethan ran a hand through his raven-black hair he'd taken to wearing even longer than he had when he'd been a member of law enforcement. "You needn't bug Garver about anything. For one, the guy knows nothing about your particular case. Do you remember my brother Brent? He's still county sheriff. If you want, I'd be happy to take you over there now, sit down with him and go over the case file. But...nothing has really changed since our last email. And since I no longer have access to—"

"You want me to meet with your brother?" Logan surmised. "Not a bad plan. It's just—"

"What? You want to do it another time?" That surprised Ethan. "You seemed eager enough in your emails."

"I do appreciate the offer, but right now, I'm so beat I can't think straight. After landing at Kennedy this morning from Rome, I hopped a charter here. I haven't slept in almost..." Logan looked at his watch. "Twenty plus hours. I don't even think I can manage to stay awake on the drive to the B & B tonight. So if it's all the same to you, if the offer still goes, how about I check into a hotel here in Santa Cruz for the night, grab some shuteye, go in first thing in the morning, sit down with Brent then? That way I have a chance to get my thoughts together. Right now, they're scattered as hell."

"Sure. That'll work. He's aware you're here now and will have the file all ready to go. But again, I emphasize, nothing's changed in all these years."

"Yeah, I know." Logan took out a rubber band from his jacket pocket, neatly ran his hands through his thick shoulder-length chestnut mane, bunching it up. He threaded the strands through the band, and then wound it tight into a neat ponytail. "But maybe I can change that."

"Look, I know how you feel—"

Logan held up a hand. "Stop right there. Unless you've been holding back something personal in your emails, you couldn't possibly know how I feel."

"Okay, you're right. I don't *know*. But you can't expect after all these years to show up and answers will fall into your lap."

"The answers certainly haven't fallen into the laps of law enforcement, now have they?"

Ethan sucked in a frustrated breath. "After all these years, I'm not sure what you're looking to find. But promise me when you go poking around, and I know you will, you won't get a case of the stupids."

"Right now, my only claim to stupid includes buying a lighthouse and getting hyped because I think I can refurbish it to the way it was. Just ask the Lighthouse Restoration Commission. Even they aren't so sure about me. But you're probably right. After all, what could I possibly turn up after all these years that law enforcement hasn't?"

Logan's sardonic tone didn't go unnoticed by Ethan. "Just use common sense. That's all I'm saying."

"I'm here to restore what I hope to make into my home and studio, nothing more."

"Sure you are. If you plan to spend the night, you'll want the best place Santa Cruz has to offer."

"I thought I'd try the Brinkerhouse."

Ethan laughed at that. "They tore down the Brinkerhouse more than a decade ago. These days it's The Portola. Do you need me to draw you a map?"

"I guess I do."

But about that time Ethan slapped Logan on the back. "By the way, how does it feel to be back in California?"

"Right now…exhausting."

"How does it feel to own a lighthouse?"

"I'm a California real estate owner...and that feels...like I've finally come home."

Pelican Pointe buzzed with the news. Some damn fool had gone and thrown hard-earned money away on the Smuggler's Bay Lighthouse. The same lighthouse that hadn't worked since Kennedy sat in the oval office.

Not only that, but rumor had it old man Hartley, the town's only lawyer, had finally gone senile and hired himself a replacement, a woman that didn't even have a regular law degree but one she'd earned over the Internet.

At the Hilltop Diner, a throwback to a 1950s malt shop, both events had given the longtime residents something to mull over. While they sipped coffee and dug into Margie Rosterman's homemade cherry pie, they wondered what the hell the world was coming to.

How could anyone think bringing back that dilapidated lighthouse was a good idea? In tough economic times like now what idiot would throw away his hard-earned cash on something so ridiculous? But then rumor had it that the guy that bought the place was some hippie artist with hair down to his ass and wore a gold hoop earring in his left ear. That's probably why he didn't know squat about finances. He certainly didn't know anything about the town since the idiot man had bought it in an Internet auction put up by the Coast Guard.

And how could anyone in town rightly trust having their wills drawn up by a ditzy woman who didn't know a classroom from a computer, or a bequest from a codicil?

The whole thing had tongues wagging from Ocean Street to Main. Ever since Kinsey Wyatt had first checked into the Promise Cove B & B three weeks earlier and waltzed into Pelican Pointe hoping to sweet-talk Hartley into a job, the townspeople hadn't been able to stop talking about the two newcomers, one of whom hadn't even set foot in town yet.

But Kinsey Wyatt had. She'd heard all the scuttlebutt. In fact, Aaron Hartley, her new boss, had come clean about it her first day on the job. But today, he'd handed her the brand-new, shiny nameplate with black lettering that sat on her desk and read "Kinsey Wyatt" engraved at the top and "Attorney At Law" underneath. Kinsey had waited a little more than two weeks to get it. Since she'd just started her third week of employment, she was still settling in.

It had taken her three interviews, which meant three trips down from her native San Francisco Bay area to convince the old lawyer she knew enough about wills and trusts and deeds to fill his shoes once he decided to hang up his shingle.

But after living here for a couple of weeks now Kinsey was convinced Hartley had finally relented for one simple reason. He'd given her the job because he hadn't been able to persuade any other seasoned attorney, or newly graduated law student for that matter, to relocate to Pelican Pointe.

The reason she'd been hired didn't matter much to Kinsey. Because she'd worked too long and too hard to get here, she had decided weeks earlier to accept the stingy salary Hartley had offered her though and tough it out. The money would barely cover the rent. But who else would she find willing to give her a chance to practice law in the State of California with a degree from an online university?

Because of the paltry paycheck, Kinsey had already decided to fill out an application at Murphy's Market to supplement her income. Murphy's needed a cashier and that was one thing Kinsey knew how to do with her eyes closed. Since she'd worked for one of the local Bay area grocery store chains since the day she'd turned sixteen, Kinsey was good with customers. Not only that, she knew how to work hard, knew something firsthand about making ends meet.

At twenty-eight, Kinsey Wyatt had seen her share of tough times. Born to a single mom who had worked her butt off as a housekeeper for the Nob Hill crowd in the Bay area, Kinsey grew up learning how to stretch a dollar.

In fact, growing up with a mom like Ellie Wyatt, Kinsey had learned a lifetime of frugal habits. When Ellie wasn't scrubbing out other people's toilets, sometimes for twelve hours a day working as a domestic, she picked up odd jobs cleaning office buildings at night. It wasn't unusual for Ellie to put in an eighteen-hour day. In those early years, Ellie always brought her daughter along to work with her, at least until Kinsey had started school. As Kinsey grew older, mother and daughter might work until midnight only to get up to do it all over again the next day.

During those early years, Ellie Wyatt had taught her daughter one thing. Rely on no one but yourself. Because Ellie believed in being her daughter's role model, she practiced what she preached. She avoided getting mixed up with men. Of course, that mantra was mostly due to the fact that Ellie had never quite gotten over losing her heart to what she often referred to as the no-good, married son of a bitch who'd fathered her little girl. She'd never asked or received a dime of child support from the court system either. But then, Ellie couldn't very well get a dollar out of a dead man. Not since the lying bastard had been killed in a car accident almost six months to the day after Kinsey had celebrated her first birthday.

That meant raising her daughter alone fell on Ellie's shoulders. Even if it was damned near impossible to do that on a maid's salary, especially in pricey San Francisco, Ellie Wyatt had managed to survive and so had her daughter. They hadn't even owned a car—until one of the families Ellie had faithfully worked for over the years rewarded their housekeeper—by leaving her a beat-up, old Ford Fairmont in their last will and testament. Kinsey had been thirteen at the time and remembered full well how they had celebrated when the estate lawyer had handed Ellie the keys. They'd climbed into the Ford and driven up and down the streets of their Tenderloin neighborhood until well past dark, stopping only to fill up the tank with gas and treat themselves to chocolate sundaes.

In reality, the day-to-day struggles of mother and daughter might have been what contributed to how close the two were. That's why when Ellie had been diagnosed with breast cancer in Kinsey's senior year of high school, Kinsey had put her dreams of one day going to San Jose State and getting into law school on the backburner.

In place of that, Kinsey had crammed her days with college prep and advanced placement courses figuring she'd be able to head off to college after her mother beat the big C. But when Ellie's illness dragged on and on, and bills mounted, Kinsey stayed on at the grocery store. She also picked up odd jobs to make up for the fact that Ellie worked less and less as the disease progressed.

Kinsey had to settle for sandwiching a sometimes sixty-hour work week into a community college closer to home. Being closer allowed Kinsey the flexibility to get Ellie to and from chemo therapy treatments, countless doctor appointments, and group support sessions. Even with everything happening, Kinsey managed to earn her Associate's Degree in record time, and take whatever courses she could find online to finish out a four-year degree.

But it still didn't get her into law school.

Never one to give up—Kinsey stumbled across another in-road to get where she wanted to go—she could enroll in law classes online. Once she learned that the State of California would let her take the Bar exam without an actual four-year degree from a traditional university, she had another goal. Even though online law degrees didn't count in the eyes of the American Bar Association, if Kinsey could pass the California State Bar, she could practice law—by the back door method. She studied night and day and took every law course the online colleges offered. Then to her surprise, on her very first try, Kinsey Wyatt did what many law school grads couldn't do. She passed the Bar. In order to practice law though, she had few options. One was to set up her own law office. Since her finances didn't allow for such grand plans, if she could find someone to take a chance on hiring her, it would be a good way to gain valuable hands-on experience.

It wouldn't be easy. But then nothing had ever been easy for the Wyatt women.

Six days after learning she'd passed the Bar though, she'd had to bury her mother. During that last year of her mother's life, Ellie Wyatt had put up one helluva prolonged battle with the disease, which unfortunately had also racked up medical bills that resembled the national debt.

For the past year, every dime Kinsey had earned and scraped together had gone to paying off the doctors and hospital. She wasn't done, of course, but Kinsey came from a work ethic that rivaled none.

So if she had to get three jobs here in Pelican Pointe to survive, that's what she would do. If she had to stand on her head every day to convince Aaron Hartley she could write a will, she'd do that as well.

In fact, when she got off work this afternoon, she intended to stop by Murphy's to fill out that application. It wouldn't be the first time she'd held down two jobs to make ends meet.

With the nameplate, front and center, sitting prominently on her desk for everyone to see that happened to walk through Aaron Hartley's front door—and there had been plenty of curious townspeople come to check her out—she felt like she'd finally arrived.

Even though Kinsey had only been in town a little more than three weeks, she was still staying out at the Promise Cove B & B, which was getting expensive. Finances dictated she couldn't stay there indefinitely. She wanted a place of her own anyway. Despite the fact Nick and Jordan had given her a major discount, the bill each week still strained her bank balance. Since her goal was to find a little house to rent close to town so she could walk to work, she had to watch her pennies.

Thanks to Hayden Cody, the woman who ran Hidden Moon Bay Books and was married to the former deputy sheriff, Ethan Cody, Kinsey had a lead on that score. Since Ethan was now a published author, he'd given up his job in law enforcement several months back to stay at home to write full time and help with the couple's new baby boy, Nate. And according to the new mother, the Codys were actively looking to move into a bigger place. Kinsey hoped she could talk them into letting her lease their little house. The Cody house not only offered a view of the water glistening off Smuggler's Bay, it was the cutest little bungalow on the block.

If the Codys changed their minds, there was one other empty house available just down the street from Hartley, on Landings Bay. It had belonged to a woman whose body had been found last year floating in the ocean. Since Aaron handled the probate, Kinsey had the inside track on what the Carr family planned to do with the house. But her boss had already indicated—twice—that Sissy Carr's family intended to sell the property, not to rent it out.

That left Kinsey back to square one when it came to finding an affordable place in town in her price range she could rent.

"Want me to get out the can of Pledge so you can polish that thing?" Aaron Hartley teased from outside her "office," interrupting Kinsey's train of thought.

Her "office" consisted of a small alcove with no door directly across from the man's own study located inside Hartley's place of residence, a Tudor style house that doubled as his business. It was anything but a typical home office setup. Aaron had furnished the little space with a pedestal desk, a laptop, a bank of waist-high filing cabinets filled with forty years' worth of client information at her disposal, and a skinny credenza which held a collection of her own set of law books. Kinsey not only felt completely comfortable here, she felt like she'd fallen into her dream job.

When she looked up at her seventy-eight-year-old boss, she couldn't help feeling a little intimidated. Despite his repeated efforts to try to make her believe his mind was slipping, she knew better. The man could recite business and personal law backwards and forwards in his sleep. His knowledge of estate planning would be a go-to source for years to come.

"Not yet," Kinsey tossed back in a playful tone. "But if I find any smudges on it, I'll know who to blame."

"You really are proud of that thing, huh?"

"I certainly am. Some people told me I'd never practice law. Look at me now, I just wrote up Murphy's will. After work, I'll drop it off for him to sign." Should she mention the cashier application she intended to fill out? She decided to wait. No sense upsetting the waters until it was a done deal.

"That's considered company time," Aaron pointed out, feeling a little guilty at the low salary he'd given the girl because so far his new employee exhibited nothing short of a go-getter attitude. For two weeks there had been nothing she wouldn't tackle. Plus, he had to admit her knowledge of personal law had surprised him. "You make sure you add that to your time sheet."

"It's no biggie," Kinsey acknowledged.

Aaron nodded in approval. If the girl worked out, and he planned to see to it that she did, she'd soon own his practice. He'd already run a detailed background check on Kinsey Wyatt. Everything she'd told him in her three interviews had turned out to be the solid gold truth. Her work ethic aside, she'd had a rough go of it for years.

If the girl worked out, if she continued on the same path, Aaron Hartley intended to make sure Kinsey Wyatt finally caught a break.

Chapter Two

Once Logan reached the city limit sign of Pelican Pointe, he veered off the Coast Highway and into the business district. He knew what the town looked like. But out of curiosity he reduced his speed to thirty or so and crawled along Main Street. Just as he suspected, it hadn't changed much in two decades.

The Community Church still sat on the corner with its red and gold stained glass depiction of Jesus with the cross in the background. Logan had spent more than a few warm Sunday mornings, especially during the summer months, sitting inside that building, counting every piece of the stained glass to pass the time. If anyone ever asked him, he'd be ready. There were three hundred and thirty-two pieces to be exact. His butt had been parked on one of those pews, sweating like everyone else without a fan and no air conditioning, while he added and subtracted whenever he lost count. Surely, long-winded Reverend Whitcomb had to be dead by now.

Logan recognized the heart of downtown, the First Bank of Pelican Pointe, Murphy's Market next door. Knudsen's Pharmacy, Ferguson's Hardware, The Snip N Curl, and The Hilltop Diner along with tidy little bungalows nestled here and there lining both sides of the road. At the four-way stop, Logan made a left onto Beach Street and drove past Wally's Pump N Go, which if memory served, used to be Pierce's Service Station, owned by Jimmy Pierce. Some years back after suffering a heart attack, Jimmy had turned the day-to-day operation over to his son, Wally, who also happened to be a first-rate mechanic like his father. Once again, the torch had been passed from father to son. Logan knew because he'd done his homework. He might not have kept up on every detail through the years, but since he hadn't been able to work because of his injured hand, that didn't mean he couldn't research all he needed to know.

Even though he didn't have the keys yet to the front door, he might as well take a swing by his property, get a look at the work he had to do. He intended to remedy the key thing as soon as he got settled in at the B & B and located the lawyer handling the paperwork. His own attorney had already wired the money for closing. All Logan had to do was locate an address over on Landings Bay that belonged to the sole lawyer in town and put his John Henry on the title and deed to make it official.

He took a right on Ocean Street, drove past the pier, a bait shop for fishermen, a T-shirt shop for tourists, and McCready's, the closest Irish pub for a hundred miles. Logan continued north for almost a mile, the grade changing to a gradual incline. When he made a left on a twisty, narrow lane the locals affectionately called Make-Out Pointe, he knew he was close. Since the Coast Guard had abandoned the property in 1961, couples from fourteen to forty had used this spot for daytime picnics or nighttime rendezvous. As long as you brought a flashlight with you to guide the way through beach grass, low scrub and pine, you were pretty much assured a secluded spot and plenty of privacy.

Logan slowed to fifteen miles an hour taking the hairpin turn with caution as it wove farther back toward the craggy cliffs, high above Smuggler's Bay. The Ford-150 bumped along a slice of gravel road before coming to a stop. The view might not have been as spectacular as the Riviera or that in Monte Carlo, but the buildings and the land belonged to him.

He stuck his head out the truck's window, turned his attention to the building. It looked a lot more run-down in person than it ever had in the auction photographs. In fact, it dawned on him the federal government had more than likely used images from four decades back.

Because he expected the worst—a person couldn't buy an eighty-year-old structure and not expect a major renovation—Logan took note of the damage with a certain degree of resignation.

He'd accepted the fact he'd be in for a lot of work. Besides, when it came to working with his hands, it wasn't really a hardship. After all, when he'd first walked into his Greenwich Village loft it too had been in a sorry state before he'd gotten his bare hands on the inside and worked miracles with the wood and metal. Since he felt even more passionate about this renovation, Logan couldn't wait to get started. He had no doubt that bringing the lighthouse back to its former glory—or as close to it as he could get—would provide the bump he needed to get his creativity back on track.

The spring sun glistening on the water had his mind wandering to all the things he needed to get done today. He had supplies to order, workers to hire, and eventually to find a permanent place to live. But topping the list right this minute was getting a good look in person at the piece of real estate that was finally his.

Logan got out of the pickup, inhaling the familiar smell of fish, craned his neck to look up at the sixty-foot octagonal concrete tower that hadn't functioned as an actual beacon since 1960. The thousand-square-foot tower room at its base had long since given way to rust damage and rotted wood. Logan peered through the filthy windows making mental notes along the way.

Built in 1935 as part of the WPA under Franklin Roosevelt, the official address of the little two-bedroom keeper's cottage read 14 Lighthouse Lane. At some point the plaque had dropped off leaving behind the imprint on the masonry. Probably discarded in some trash pile right along with the sign at the front of the lighthouse, Logan decided.

Walking around the structure, he took out his phone to take pictures of broken patches and gashes to the sandstone to study later. As soon as his cast came off, he couldn't wait to get his hands on all that stonework. After he'd done the three-sixty once, then twice around the base, he looked out over Smuggler's Bay. For a minute a wave of nostalgia moved through him before he could tamp it down. He remembered swimming here as a young boy. In fact, he wasn't prepared for the memories of another time assaulting his brain.

When tears tried to gather in his eyes, he took off his Oakleys, blinked the water back. He stood for a minute trying to get his emotions under control. At the sound of a car engine pulling in behind his truck, he brought himself out of the past and back to the present. Annoyed at the intrusion, ready for battle at what he thought might be the media showing up, Logan whirled around to see a tall, caramel-colored brunette crawl out of an ancient, silver Nissan Altima.

Unless the paparazzi had taken to one helluva downgrade in car rentals, he assumed this was not the dreaded press. Logan had one solid moment of raw nerves jitter inside the wall of his stomach before he braced for what he considered to be an invasion to his privacy. But the woman kept heading straight for him with a smile as wide as Smuggler's Bay all the while clutching a file folder in her hand. Her long, straight hair billowed around her shoulders in perfect layers. He sucked in a breath just watching the way she walked in her open-toed, sexy-as-hell heels. With her free hand, she waved cheerily in his direction as she continued to advance on him

Once she got within two feet he noticed her eyes first. Her Heidi Klum, brown flecked, hazel eyes met his. He ought to recognize the similar features since he'd met the model two years earlier at a Paris fashion show inside the Carrousel du Louvre where Fiona had insisted on dragging him.

Locking on those hazel orbs now, he had a tough time focusing on her cheery voice and what she was saying.

"Hi! I'm Kinsey Wyatt. I work with Aaron Hartley, the attorney handling the sale for the lighthouse. If you're

Logan Donnelly, I brought the papers by for you to sign along with the keys." The woman's voice was as sunny as a warm day in August.

"How the hell did you know I was out here?" Logan barked over the sound of the waves crashing up against the cliffs. "I've been in town for less than two damn minutes."

Kinsey frowned. The man might have eyes as green as clover to go with a thick mass of flowing, chocolate brown hair that tipped his shoulders—but he was beyond rude. That pretty face with the devilish dimple on his chin didn't make it right either.

Okay, artists could be temperamental so she'd give him a pass—this time. Plus, he was a client. Sort of. So she put a little extra syrup in her tone, reminding herself she was good with people. "Ethan Cody said he saw you turn the corner in town and called the office, suggested I might want to head out here to catch you. He thought you might want to go ahead and sign the deed, get the keys."

She widened her smile, softened the lilt of her speech a bit before adding, "You might as well get used to small town ways. I know I've had to do the same. I've only been here three weeks myself."

Logan's first layer of tension dropped away. There was something about the face, the smile, the all-American-girl look that came together in a cheerleader froth of bubbly. Too bad he wasn't interested in cheery or bubbly. History told him you couldn't trust either to run true. But curiosity got the better of him. "You've only been in Pelican Pointe less than a month?"

"Originally from the Bay area. San Francisco born and raised. In fact, I'm still staying out at Promise Cove myself. Have you met the Harrises yet? You'll love Nick and Jordan. They said they were expecting the infamous Logan Donnelly yesterday." She tilted her head, looked up at what had to be a six-three build. "But you spent last night in Santa Cruz. Do you plan to stay at the B & B or commute from the big city?"

Logan rolled his eyes and cursed under his breath. "If I answer that question, is there anything sacred that isn't for public consumption around here?"

Kinsey got the gist, not just surly, but guarded as well. Years of checking groceries, dealing with the public on a daily basis, made her an expert in studying a person's body language and how it related to mood. This particular man seemed to have a chip on his shoulder the weight of a California redwood. She lifted a shoulder. "Probably not. But then I'm still trying to fit into small town America." As the breeze kicked up, almost blowing the folder out of her fist, she pointed out, "It's a little windy. Where do you want to sign these? I have the keys here to the cottage. We could get inside out of the wind. Or get it done in my car or yours?"

"The keeper's cottage is a mess. Might as well crawl inside my truck," Logan muttered as he opened the passenger truck door for her. As she climbed inside, he noted the professional attire. The black pencil skirt that showed off long, tanned legs, the sleeveless white shirt revealing a pair of toned arms. He forced that pull of attraction to all but evaporate. He refused to even stick a toe in her particular direction. But he'd be a dead man with no beating heart if those huge hazel eyes didn't lure a man into the deep part of the ocean without an oxygen tank.

They both settled into the front seat of the Ford. "I'll have to thank Mr. Hartley for being thoughtful enough to send his secretary all the way out here for curbside service." At what he considered a compliment, her smile vanished, her friendly face turned to stone.

"I'll need to see some form of identification," Kinsey informed him.

A minute ago she'd called him by name, acted as though she recognized him. Now all business, he dug out the piece of paper from the California DMV he'd gotten just that morning. "I'm supposed to get the plastic version in two weeks."

"That's standard," Kinsey uttered as she went over the document, scouring it for mistakes. When she handed it back she advised, "Legally that isn't an acceptable form of ID, as there's no photo for me to verify. But I believe I can make allowances."

He watched as her long slim fingers with perfectly manicured nails finally opened the manila folder on her lap. Without saying a word, she took out a pen from her skirt's side pocket and handed it over to him, which he gingerly took in the fingers sticking out of his cast. Awkwardly, he gripped the barrel, pointing it at the paper.

"Will you be able to sign?" Kinsey asked.

"I'll manage," Logan mumbled as he began to read line by line the legal description of the property. There were already several clear little sticky pieces with red arrows on the tips adhering to the paper indicating where exactly he should put his signature. But just in case he missed that, Kinsey curtly pointed to each one and reminded him, "Here. Here. And here."

It was a fairly simple transaction since Logan had paid cash for the place. With his broken hand, it took him longer than usual to sign, but as soon as he'd finished the process, he handed her back the pen.

She immediately dumped two brass keys onto the loose fingers sticking out of his cast. She patted the manila folder. "I'll give you copies for your files tonight when I get to the B & B, how's that?"

Before he could say anything, Logan heard another vehicle pull up, this time a faded red Nissan pickup almost orange in color. It screeched to a halt in the gravel as if the driver had trouble braking and parked next to the woman's beat-up ride.

Logan watched from his rearview mirror as a young kid, who looked to be about eighteen, got out and waved to the woman who was already sliding out of his truck.

"Who is that?" Logan asked.

"No need to keep snarling at everyone, Mr. Donnelly. That's Troy Dayton, a highly skilled local carpenter. He's probably come out here to see you about a job."

Logan noticed her face soften, considerably, when she greeted the young teen.

"Hi Troy," Kinsey said to the lanky man when he walked up. "How've you been? Did you have any luck over in San Sebastian at that construction site I told you about?"

Troy shook his head as the wind blew back his curly white-blond hair. "I appreciate the lead, Kinsey. But it didn't pan out. They already had a full crew hired by the time I got there." He stuck out his hand in Logan's direction and spotted the cast. "Looks like you need a right-hand man," Troy noted. "That's why I stopped by. Thought maybe you could use a good carpenter. I wanted to be the first one here, Mr. Donnelly. I'm the best around. I've got my own tools, my own transportation." He threw a thumb in the direction of his little truck. "She don't look like much but she runs. And I do good work."

"How old are you?" Logan wanted to know.

"Twenty. I know I look young, but I'm not kidding when I tell you I know my way around carpentry work. Ask anyone in town, they'll tell you the same thing. And besides, I've been working during the summers since I was fourteen on all kinds of construction sites from here to Santa Cruz my uncle, Derek Stovall. Plus, you hire me, you'll get him, too. He does wiring, hangs sheet rock, and installs plumbing. Take your pick. Work's hard to come by around here. He's been looking for a job, same as me, since the first of the year. We both could use the work."

"Well, I've got to head back to the office," Kinsey said interrupting Troy's pitch. "We secretaries have such a busy life we hardly have time out to socialize or eat lunch. You know how it is, I'm sure. Anyway, back to my workstation," she muttered with a little salute. "Good luck Mr. Donnelly, Troy."

And with that, Kinsey Wyatt stormed back to her Nissan.

Logan's brow creased as he watched the woman clomp away on those heels. So did Troy. "Wonder what that was all about?" Logan groused, truly perplexed at the woman's change in disposition.

"Huh," Troy said flatly. "That *is* strange. Kinsey's usually sunny as a tulip. Wonder why she referred to herself as a secretary?"

"Doesn't she work for Hartley?"

"Sure, but Kinsey's an attorney like Hartley," Troy replied, scratching his chin. "In fact, rumor has it old Hartley's thinking of calling it quits, retiring his practice. Got Kinsey down here from the Bay to take care of the town's legal stuff once he closes his doors."

"Ah," was all Logan said, realizing that probably explained the huff. Couldn't say he blamed her. He supposed he'd have to apologize at some point.

Since Troy wasn't privy to the byplay between the two before he happened on the scene, the young man pressed Logan, "What about that job? I'm dependable and know my way around a remodel."

"If you've got references, let's talk."

While Troy listed a few previous employers off the top of his head, Logan pointed out, "You know I'll have to check those, right?"

Troy nodded. "Sure. I know that. They'll check out, you'll see."

"Good. I could really use someone in a couple of days to help me start setting up all my equipment out here."

Troy grinned. "I'm good at setting up equipment."

Logan liked the kid's enthusiasm. "I hope so because there's a lot of it." Logan threw out an hourly wage to test the waters. "Does that sound like something you'd be—"

Troy's eyes grew wide and he didn't let Logan finish. "I'll take it. And thank you. You won't be sorry."

Logan looked at the kid almost bouncing on his toes. He wanted that to be true because he really needed someone he could rely on. In a town where there were too many prying eyes and wagging tongues, the fewer people that knew his business, the better off he'd be.

Chapter Three

Kinsey fumed the entire six blocks it took her to drive back to work. As she turned onto Landings Bay then pulled into the driveway, she decided Logan Donnelly was an arrogant jerk. Why had the stupid man just *assumed* she was Hartley's secretary? And secretary? Ha! Shouldn't men as worldly as "the sculptor" live in the twenty-first century? Didn't he know that the word secretary was an outdated term? Nowadays people generally used administrative assistant when they talked about the support of management. Did she look like a secretary? she wondered as she pulled the car into Hartley's driveway.

Why couldn't he have at least *assumed* she was a paralegal? After all, paralegal more aptly described her job duties over the past several weeks since Hartley hadn't yet assigned her any of the harder stuff to do like taking care of the town's legal issues. She hoped it was only a matter of time.

While crossing the lawn to the front door, she glanced down at the way she was dressed. Maybe the skirt wasn't new but it was in good shape for a thrift store purchase. Maybe the blouse *was* a little too casual for an attorney—but the days were heating up—and Hartley's house wasn't air-conditioned. As she tromped into the hallway and slammed the door shut, she decided it couldn't be helped. She couldn't very well put on the same designer suit every day that she'd worn to nail the job. The Donna Karan outfit she'd splurged on to wear to the interview had cost her a small fortune. She couldn't duplicate that kind of expense this soon into the job.

She'd have to improvise.

Maybe there was a used clothing store nearby where she might at least add one more professional outfit to her meager wardrobe that might make her look more—tailored. The thing is she'd need to find more than one getup to stretch out over five workdays. Since the black skirt was practical, she might be able to wear it twice, if she changed out tops. Even with wearing the suit and the black skirt a couple of times each week that still didn't fix the problem of what to wear the other days.

No, one dress wasn't the answer. A step in the right direction, maybe, but she'd still have a hole to fill. Why hadn't she thought about slowly building up her wardrobe before she took the job?

The answer to that was money, right along with the fact that she'd worn a store uniform for too many years to be on a first name basis with Christian Dior or Versace.

When she stormed into Aaron's study, she slapped the folder on his desk.

Aaron narrowed his eyes. He recognized an upset female. "Weren't you able to locate him? Did you miss him at the lighthouse?"

"Oh the man was there all right. Papers are taken care of. He has a broken wrist by the way. I got the impression he's looking to hire local people, which is probably the only good thing about the man. After all, he can't very well remodel his lighthouse with a cast. I'll make copies and see that he gets his...*later* when I take them out to the B & B tonight."

"What's he like?"

"A snooty artist type," Kinsey retorted.

"Really? Did he say something inappropriate? He seemed so down to earth on the phone." Aaron scratched his bald head. "Or maybe that was his attorney. See? I'm getting forgetful and confused."

Kinsey gave him a withering stare, put both hands on her hips. "You aren't that absent-minded, Mr. Hartley. No, the only insult was—" She let out a sigh. Out of temper, she dropped down into the wing chair in front of his desk.

"He thought I was your secretary. And his comment upset me."

"Ah." Aaron's look said he didn't understand the slight at all. Not only that, but his face said he thought she might be making too big a deal out of it.

"Oh I suppose I can't blame him. I don't look much like a lawyer. Now do I? But damn it, I passed the Bar! There are four-year college grads out there who couldn't do as well as I did on my very first try."

"That's true. Look, if I gave you the impression that I didn't think you were a real lawyer, I apologize. You don't need to wear a suit to look the part either. There are plenty of shysters out there who wear the three-piece outfit every day and would just as soon skin you for a buck as to look at you. As far as I'm concerned it's okay to wear something comfortable and casual to work. Not shorts or jeans, but those Docker pants are just fine. Just look at me, do I wear a coat and tie in my own house?"

"No but I wanted to look you know professional."

Aaron nodded, knowing she needed a few bumps in confidence. "You did a damn fine job on Murphy's will. I went over it while you were gone, checked your terms and phrasing. Carla's too for that matter. Why those two don't just tie the knot is anyone's guess?"

"Bad marriages." At his stare Kinsey held up a hand. "Don't look at me like that. It wasn't my idea to gossip. But when I got my hair trimmed at the Snip N Curl last Saturday, Janie Pointer told me all about Murphy's divorce twenty years earlier and Carla's cheating husband. Neither one is in a rush to remarry."

Aaron shook his head. "Janie ought to know. She's had two of them. But once Janie got rid of that Sissy Carr for a best friend, Janie seems to have changed…for the better."

"Well, Janie and Flynn McCready certainly seemed to have found each other. They're almost inseparable."

"Odd pair. But then…Flynn's got quite a past."

"Doesn't everyone," Kinsey drawled with complete conviction, wondering why a man like Logan Donnelly acted so pissed off at the world.

And why would a man like that pick Pelican Pointe, of all places, to settle down into small town life?

Following the map Ethan had drawn, Logan drove along a two-lane stretch of highway, past Monterey cypress, bent and twisted by the constant wind. Beach aster swayed in the breeze along with California lilac. He was about to shoot a U and turn the truck around thinking he'd passed the turnoff when he spotted the apple green sign next to the road that read, "Promise Cove Bed and Breakfast, established 2009 by Scott Phillips. Jordan and Nick Harris, Proprietors." He made a left, headed toward the cliffs and the ocean.

The estate was an old, massive Victorian that sat a good hundred yards or so off the road, nestled up against the backdrop of the Pacific Ocean. A grove of willows and magnolias shaded the acres of land in front of the house. It reminded Logan of some of the mansions he'd seen during a visit to The French Quarter in his younger days—only Promise Cove was bigger, grander—and certainly more isolated. It looked a little spooky, which was ridiculous, thought Logan.

He shook off that feeling that wanted to edge up his spine. He decided he must still be suffering from a case of jet lag. What he needed was a couple nights in a row of uninterrupted sleep.

He took a left, followed the long drive until it ended at the side of the house where there were three other cars already parked. Before he'd even had time to crawl out of his pickup, the front door flew open. A dark-haired man filled up the doorway. He strolled outside on the porch to wave before heading for the truck. But then, a little golden-haired girl of about three trotted after him and called out, "Wait, Daddy. Wait for me!"

The man stopped in stride so the toddler could catch up.

"Logan Donnelly, right?" Nick asked a few steps from the vehicle.

"Yep, but you can't be Nick Harris. For some reason I thought you'd be twenty years older. Even your emails sounded…like they were from someone mature."

"We get that a lot," Nick answered easily as he reached down and swung the little girl onto his hip. "This is Hutton, my daughter. What do you say Hutton, we grab our new visitor's luggage and carry it in the house so he can get to his room?"

For a brief moment, Logan had a touch of nostalgia come over him before he came to his senses. His long trip, all the miles he'd covered in such a short amount of time, was obviously catching up to him in a big way. He needed some shuteye.

Even though Hutton bobbed her blonde head up and down, Logan advised, "That's okay. Looks like you have your hands full of pretty girl there. I can get my own bags thanks. Besides, I'll wait until tomorrow to unload all this other stuff."

Nick scanned the packed bed of the pickup. "There's more equipment near the garage. It got here yesterday ahead of you," Nick said matter-of-factly. "We put it around the side of the house for now. That's a lot of stuff for a sculptor."

"More like a contractor for the next few months. Just my tools of the trade," Logan explained.

Nick eyed the man's cast. "How long before that comes off?"

"Unfortunately, another two weeks."

"Well, come on inside then. We'll get you set up in your room. Nothing but the best for the infamous Logan Donnelly," Nick offered with a wink.

About that time a gorgeous female with golden-colored hair stepped onto the porch carrying a baby on her hip.

Nick waved an arm. "And this is my wife, Jordan, with our eleven-month-old son, Scott."

Logan shook his head. "How in the world do you two manage a busy inn with two small kids?"

From the steps, Jordan let out a laugh. "It's never dull, that's for sure. Since Nick's also a member of the town council *and* president of the bank, it makes for a busy, well-rounded life. Welcome to Promise Cove, Logan Donnelly. By the way, I'm a big fan of your work. That piece you did in bronze and steel for the Chicago Zoo was brilliant."

For the first time all day, Logan flashed a genuine smile. "And you, Mrs. Harris, are the innkeeper extraordinaire."

"And you would know that how?"

"Because you have great taste in art," Logan returned with another hundred-watt grin. "Plus, it never hurts a boost to the ego when a beautiful woman admires my work."

When Logan reached one-handed for his garment bag, Jordan spied the broken splint on his wrist. "We'll get your bags."

"Don't be silly. I'll make two trips. You both have your hands full of good-looking babies."

Nick grabbed one of Logan's bags anyway while still carrying Hutton. "Follow me. Your reservation is for one of the best rooms we've got."

Chapter Four

By the time Kinsey reached Promise Cove it was after six. After dropping off Murphy's will for him to review and sign at the store, Kinsey felt like she'd solved one part of the puzzle. Owner Patrick Murphy had gladly taken her application and hired her on the spot. Good thing he needed a cashier on the weekends. Come Saturday, from eight in the morning to four thirty in the afternoon, Kinsey would be back to checking groceries. Sundays, too. He'd gushed over her experience, had delighted in the fact that he wouldn't have to spend days or weeks training her.

Wonder what the town will think of that? Kinsey wondered as she made her way into the B & B via the front door. She hadn't taken two steps inside the wide entryway when Scott David Harris crawled over on all fours and latched onto her legs like a monkey clinging to a vine.

As the baby gripped her skirt in his little fist for balance, he began to try to stand. She watched him teeter, and continue to hold on to the fabric. Kinsey dropped her bag on the hall table so she could bend down to scoop him up in a hug. "Now that's what I call a welcome home. When a great, big handsome man greets me at the door," Kinsey crooned. "I know for sure it's gonna be a super night."

"He moves fast," Nick exclaimed, hustling down the hallway after his son. "I put him down for a sec while I set the table in the dining room, next thing I know he's out here."

"Oh it's okay, more than okay. He'll be walking before you know it. He's adorable."

Nick's lips curved up. "Adorable must mean he takes after his daddy. You let me know when you want to give him back, Kinsey. Dinner's about ready anyway. Chinese stir fry tonight."

Kinsey returned Nick's smile "Yum. You guys are spoiling me. Don't know what I'll do when I leave to get my own place. I feel like a queen every time I walk in here and you guys have supper on the table."

Jordan appeared behind Nick, wiping her hands on a dish towel. "With our newest guest checked in this afternoon, we have a full house, at least over the next few days. Dinner's served in twenty minutes. Have you already found a place in town, Kinsey?"

"Not yet. But it's only a matter of time. I'm looking. Now that they have Nate, Hayden and Ethan might be moving to a bigger house. If they do, they might rent me theirs."

"The Cody's have a cute place," Jordan said. Ever the mother hen when it came to taking care of company, she went on, "We'll hate to lose one of the sweetest people we've had stay here. But we want you to settle into town and that means getting the right place to live. If that's Ethan's place then so be it. But whatever place you find, we'll help you move your stuff down here."

"That is above and beyond necessary," Kinsey told her. "I only have a few things from my apartment I put in storage. It really doesn't amount to all that much."

Jordan tilted her head to study the woman. "You look tired, Kinsey. Are you sleeping? Is everything okay? Did someone in town say something to upset you?"

Kinsey didn't know how Jordan managed to pick up on things so well, but she waved off the question. "I'm fine, just adjusting to the job is all. You know how it is in a new place, starting from scratch. Trying to prove myself takes a toll, but I'm not complaining. I'm up for the challenge." No way did Kinsey plan to share her financial worries with anyone else.

"And it takes time for people to accept you in Pelican Pointe. But remember, Kinsey, both Nick and I used to be outsiders, too. It wasn't all paradise here for us. Don't let anyone in town get to you that includes Hartley, although the man does know his stuff."

"No argument there." Still holding the baby, Kinsey followed Jordan through a swinging door into the state-of-the-art commercial kitchen and bumped smack-dab into Logan Donnelly. It was hard to tell who was more startled, the baby, Kinsey, or Logan. When Scott acted like he wanted to pucker up and cry at the jolt, Kinsey cooed, "It's okay, sweetie. Don't let this…big ol' guy…scare you."

Nibbling on the canapé he'd pilfered from the appetizer tray set out on the counter for munching, Logan sheepishly glanced at Jordan before his eyes zeroed in on Kinsey, who he realized looked perfectly at ease with a baby in her arms. "I…uh…" His brain misfired—visibly. The woman had the most incredible exotic eyes to match the all-American-girl next door vibe she gave off. The pull in his lower belly told him his libido needed a swift punch in its gut to remind him he was done with women.

To get his brain to work right, Logan stuck his hand out and ran a finger along the baby's chubby cheek. "It's okay, big guy. I was trying to hide from your mama so she wouldn't know I stole the finger food."

Scott rewarded him with a toothy grin.

Logan decided it was time to set the record straight. "So you aren't Hartley's secretary but an attorney," he said. When she continued to stare at him, he added, "Troy mentioned it."

Kinsey rolled her eyes. "You do realize that most people these days refer to the support of upper management as an administrative assistant not a secretary, don't you? That is so…old-fashioned."

"Huh?"

"Never mind," Kinsey muttered, clearly annoyed at the man who more than likely had no idea how the other half lived. She knew she was being difficult and didn't care.

Instead she bounced the baby on her hip and said, "I brought your copies of the real estate transaction. They're on the hall table in my bag."

Jordan eyed the tension between man and woman before patting Logan's shoulder. "Don't worry about sneaking an hors d'oeuvres. That's why I put them out, silly. To eat." She picked up another crab puff from the plate and shoved it into Logan's hand. "Here, don't ruin your appetite though, dinner's coming up." She turned to Kinsey. "You want a crab wonton?"

"Maybe later. I need to go change. I've been in this outfit all day. I'm ready for something a lot more comfortable."

But hearing Kinsey decline the food, Logan visibly winced. It brought back memories of Fiona's ridiculous anorexic eating habits.

Jordan held out her hands for her son. "Of course, you do. Here, let me have Scotty. Come here, sweetie, come to mommy." Jordan hefted her son to her shoulder and patted Kinsey's arm. "Now go. I made your favorite tonight for dessert."

"Cherry pie? I think I love you," Kinsey drooled.

A bit confused at her reaction to what he recognized as forbidden carbs, Logan snorted, "Yeah, like you'd really eat that."

"You're right. I'll probably inhale it," Kinsey retorted before heading for the back staircase. "Don't start dinner without me," she ordered, pointing a finger at Jordan. And with that, she dashed up the steps.

"She doesn't really eat pie, does she?" Logan asked.

Jordan's brow creased. "Kinsey? Why wouldn't she eat cherry pie? It's her favorite." Still puzzled, she lifted a shoulder. "Kinsey gave me a terrific recipe for parmesan mac and cheese that Hutton absolutely loves. So, I'd say, she not only eats, but cooks as well."

"It's been my experience women that look like Kinsey usually don't go near sugar."

Jordan gave him a strange look. "Sounds like you need to experience new women." She handed Logan another crab puff. "Did you get settled in okay? All unpacked?"

"I did. The view of the ocean is stunning. In fact, the entire place has my creative juices flowing already and I've been here less than five hours." He held up his injured hand. "Can't wait to get this thing off so I can get back to work, hold a torch again."

"I take it you've been sidelined for quite a while now? Well, I'll respect your artistic side and refrain from asking what your next project is, other than the lighthouse. But I'd be lying if I said I wasn't curious."

He grinned. "You and about a dozen others. My agent's been bugging me for an update. I've known her ten years. If I won't tell her—"

About that time Nick came through the swinging door. "The Isaksons and the Fostwicks are already settled around the table. So are the Whitney sisters. Ben and Sheryl are still MIA." Nick wiggled his eyebrows up and down. "Second honeymoon here for an old married couple."

Jordan giggled. "We get a lot of that here," she told Logan. "Ben and Sheryl Latham are down from San Jose. Ben served in Iraq with Nick. They have the room on the other side of yours through Saturday."

Terrific, thought Logan. He grabbed another canapé, popped it into his mouth. He decided it was time to make his exit. "Guess that's my cue to get out of your way. That stir fry smells tasty and since I'm starving—I better go get a seat."

Logan made his way into the formal dining room, grabbing a chair on one side of the eight-foot-long table covered with an old-fashioned, crocheted tablecloth. The atmosphere immediately put him in mind of all the times he'd sat around his grandmother's table as a kid. The polished antique wood peeking out of the patterned cloth, even the Trilby place settings with the cheerful daisies and silver trim that Noritake hadn't made since 1984 made him feel like he'd taken a step back in time.

He got comfortable next to two older ladies who looked to be in their seventies. The one with silver hair announced, "I'm Kay Whitney and the lady with the punk-pink hair is my sister, Olivia."

"Nice to meet you both," Logan uttered.

An older man in his early sixties turned to extend a hand. "We're Elsa and Henry Isakson over from Sacramento. Took us a vacation to the coast, you know like the young folks do," Henry explained.

"Our spring break," Elsa finished. "Left our store in the capable hands of our son." They went into a detailed account of their jewelry business, while across from Logan, on the other side of the table, a twenty-something man kissed his wife's hand in a purely romantic gesture before exchanging introductions. "We're Cory and Karen Fostwick."

"We're on our honeymoon down from Medford, Oregon," the young bride offered. "If you're the artist, I think we have the room next door to you."

Perfect, thought Logan, just what he needed, a couple of newlyweds along with second honeymooners competing in a humping marathon with him sandwiched in the middle. For about two seconds he considered the all-night-long sound effects he had to look forward to and then mentally checked the contents of what he'd already unpacked. Where had he put those noise-cancelling headphones?

When another couple strolled into the room, arm in arm, Logan felt sure he'd been swept up in a 1980s scene right out of a *Love Boat* rerun.

"You must be the sculptor. They were expecting you yesterday. We're Ben and Sheryl Latham."

About that time, Jordan came in carrying a tray with steaming beef and chicken heaped onto serving dishes. She glanced around the room at her guests. "Even with a full house, we're sometimes crowded but it makes for a cozy setting."

Nick walked in behind her. "Everyone gets to know everybody pretty quick. We thought about setting up several separate tables but most of the guests seemed to really like the atmosphere of sitting around the same table together."

Ben nodded. "Makes it seem more like a home."

Just as Logan was about to dig in to his beef and broccoli, Kinsey sauntered to the table wearing a pair of yoga pants with an off-the-shoulder sexy-as-hell lime green top that showed plenty of appealing skin. Even the newly married Cory took a second look.

"Sorry, I'm late," Kinsey offered.

Logan forced himself to focus on his plate and answered the spattering of curious questions about his lighthouse project, mainly from Ben and Sheryl.

Karen Fostwick and Elsa also seemed interested in how he intended to turn the place into a studio until Nick wanted to know, "When will you get started exactly? What with the hand and all?"

"Hired my first man this afternoon. A young guy by the name of Troy Dayton. His references checked out. Ethan tells me he's a first-rate carpenter despite his young age."

"Troy's a good kid," Kinsey chimed in. "He's had a rough time of it lately finding work and all. I'm glad you saw his potential and hired him."

"Jobs are tough to come by around here. It's a drought when it comes to finding ways to make money. You have to get creative when it comes to employment," Jordan explained.

"Which usually translates into people sometimes having to work two and three jobs," Nick finished.

When the talk died down as people dug into their food, Kinsey took a sip of her iced tea and eyed the newest guest. "Why buy a forgotten lighthouse, Mr. Donnelly, especially one that has no historical designation?" She could tell the question irritated him, which was a bonus for her.

Logan refused to take the bait. He decided to downplay the whole thing. He shrugged and said, "I like restoring old things."

They eyed each other for a few long minutes until Kinsey considered the venue. This was not the time or place to get into a disagreement. So she let the line of questioning drop, even though she was far from satisfied with his casual answer.

After that the chatter turned to the scenic places to visit in the area, including the cove below the cliffs, and some place called Treasure Island that was a must-see before heading back home.

When the talk switched to babies and kids, Logan decided to head back to his room. "I'm making an early night of it. I'm really beat," Logan lamented.

"What, no cherry pie? Does that mean I get his share?" Kinsey asked in a teasing tone. "You don't know what you're missing. Jordan makes pie crust that literally melts in your mouth. I'm pretty sure I've gained five pounds since I first checked in," Kinsey moaned.

Without thinking, Logan uttered, "You certainly wear it well."

Nick recognized the male interest. "You sure you want to pass up homemade cherry cobbler, Logan? It's prepared with the cherries from our own orchard next door served with homemade vanilla ice cream churned with our fresh cream."

"*Organic* fresh fruit, *organic* cream—from their very own farm," Kinsey added as a further selling point. Seeing him think it over, she leaned back in her chair. "Hard to believe our innkeepers here grow their own produce, along with acres and acres of cherry and apple orchards *and* raise dairy cows." She turned to Nick. "I don't know how you guys do it but this place doesn't just feel like home, it's idyllic. With all you do, you two *make* it a home and so much more."

"Thank you," Jordan said with a grin. "At first it was a lot to handle. But after getting Cord Bennett on board and getting help from all our other friends like Hayden, we've managed to make it this far."

That prompted Ben Latham to stop stuffing his mouth with the last remaining crisp vegetables on his plate. "Cord still liking school?" Ben asked. I haven't talked to him since the wedding in December. When exactly does he graduate and go on to vet school?"

"He's almost done with his first year. With advanced placement courses and Keegan's help, he's ready for summer classes. He'll take a full course load both semesters and that will go a long way to getting him prepared for the fall." Nick shook his head. "Don't know how the guy does it and still manages to keep the farm running like a well-oiled machine. But he does."

"I hope he isn't burning himself out," Sheryl added.

"Are you kidding?" Jordan said. "I've never seen a guy turn around his life like he has. He's determined to graduate in record time and get into vet school right along with Keegan."

"That's just it. Do you think he'll burn out?" Sheryl wondered. "With his background all the stress might make him—"

"Go over the edge again?" Nick finished. "I don't think so. He and Keegan stay busy but seem to be happier than I've seen either one of them in a very long time. In between classes, they still have to take care of the rescue center, even though they have hired more help. You and Ben should make a point to visit with him while you're here. That is if you can nail him down for longer than five minutes."

Glancing around the table, Kinsey decided to spice things up a little. Calmly, she picked up her iced tea again, sipped. "So, how is it you guys decided to stay at a haunted B & B?"

At the question, all mouths immediately stopped chewing, all conversation grounded to a halt, including the globetrotter Logan Donnelly.

Henry and Elsa swapped stares and gaped. The sisters, Kay and Olivia, blinked in equal measures of shock while Ben and Sheryl merely exchanged a knowing gaze. But it was Ben who broke the silence. "Is she talking about who I think she's talking about?"

Karen and Cory Fostwick looked intrigued. "Do tell us more," Cory urged. "How cool would it be to go back home with a ghost sighting or two."

For the first time since he'd taken his seat, Logan's lips curved in a smile. "A ghost? Fascinating. Now there's a detail that was left out of the brochure."

Henry finally found his voice. "What kinds of ghosts?"

Kinsey swallowed the last bite of chicken on her plate before she corrected him. "Ghost. Just one. His name is Scott Phillips. The baby's named for him," she pointed casually in the direction of Baby Scott, then threw a grin and a wink at Jordan. Kinsey was delighted when she saw her hostess smiling back.

But Ben Latham almost came up out of his chair. He turned to Nick. "Now wait a minute. What makes her think Scott Phillips is haunting Promise Cove?"

"Doesn't he know?" Kinsey asked. "I thought you guys were guard buddies?"

"I never saw the need to bring it up," Nick explained sheepishly. To Ben he said, "You two haven't been here for a while and when you do come for a visit you deserve to unwind. As I recall, we had a full house the last time you were here, too. Since you never said a word about seeing Scott…I didn't see the need to mention it."

"You're serious?" Ben said. "You honestly believe he's here on the grounds?"

"If you haven't seen him, I wouldn't worry about it," Jordan tried to reassure them all, beginning to realize the talk might result in an unhappy guest or two.

But Kinsey was in a playful mood. "Well, the first time I saw him I almost had a stroke. I'd just checked in, had unpacked and was headed downstairs to the kitchen for dinner via the back staircase. It was the night before my first interview with Hartley. I was a nervous wreck anyway about the job. Plus, I'd just driven three and half nonstop hours from the Bay in traffic. As I walked down the steps, there was this guy walking up, dressed in shorts and a shirt. I thought it was a little chilly to be dressed like that, but I thought he belonged here, another guest heading back to his room—the man seemed so real—until he vanished right in front of me, went poof! That scared the crap out of me though. I was pretty sure I was suffering from travel fatigue…or something."

"And I bet you couldn't sleep a wink that night," Elsa said.

"Not at all. For some reason, when I got back to my room, I slept like a baby that night, woke up refreshed and ready to knock Hartley's socks off."

"Have you seen this ghost since?" Karen wanted to know. "Because I'm with Cory, it would be such a kick to be able to say we saw a ghost on our honeymoon.

Kinsey waved a hand. "Oh lots of times. You have nothing to worry about. Scott is harmless."

But Elsa looked like she wanted to run upstairs, start packing, and hit the road before the sun went down.

Henry put his hand on his wife's arm for reassurance and stared at Nick. "What exactly do you intend to do about a ghost scaring your guests?"

Nick smiled in spite of the question. "Not much I can do, Scott was here first. It's his home, too. He's not a bad sort."

"That's ridiculous," Elsa retorted.

At Elsa's comment, for the first time, Kinsey began to realize she might've caused a firestorm, which hadn't been her intent. "Relax. Like I said, Scott is…more than harmless. In fact, I think he wanted me to get the job, and stay here in Pelican Pointe." Kinsey knew how it sounded.

But feeling slightly guilty for having started the conversation in the first place, she felt like she needed to do a little damage control. "I sometimes feel his presence, even in town. So it isn't like he's inhabiting Promise Cove exclusively. He's all over the area, too."

"Now you're embellishing," Logan accused.

"Actually, I'm not. I've always believed in the paranormal. It's just something my mom and I shared and got a kick out of discussing. That movie *Ghost* for instance is one of our all-time favorite movies. Scott is more like Patrick Swayze, a positive energy force trying to help, unless of course you complain about the accommodations. Then he gets a little testy. Right, Jordan?"

Jordan chuckled as she wiped her son's runny nose and messy mouth about the same time he tried to shovel in more mashed potatoes. "Well, there was that grumpy woman from back East we couldn't make happy about anything. As soon as she got here, she complained because we didn't have a gym on the premises."

"She'd been here for almost a week when I checked in," Kinsey clarified. "Weller was her name. Samantha Weller from Boston, a snooty travel photographer. At least, she seemed that way to me."

Nick nodded as he helped Hutton cut up more of the chicken on her plate. "She was a piece of work all right. We tried to explain to her that she could easily take a walk around the premises for exercise. There are plenty of pathways and trails around here to hike, even the one to get down to the cove. But she didn't seem to be in the mood to appreciate fresh air *or* sunshine or nature— for a travel lover. Anyway, she kept balking at not having a gym, started grumbling about it more and more each day, especially after every one of the meals Jordan fixed for her—which she said was too high in carbs. Then one day…I suppose Scott decided to give her something to be truly unhappy about."

With huge eyes, Elsa leaned forward. "What did he do?"

Nick laughed. "After that, Ms. Weller made a point to tell us about how someone kept messing with her room, rearranging her stuff, going through her things, turning over bottles, that sort of thing. During the entire week she was here there was always something she didn't like about the place. The food Jordan served was either too high in calories, or the bed was too soft, or the stairs creaked too much. Well, you get the idea."

Logan certainly did. To him, it sounded like a carbon copy of Fiona, another high maintenance woman who bitched about every little detail whenever they had traveled together. Even now Logan remembered how she'd embarrassed him with her vocal complaining, nothing was ever good enough for Fiona, not the room, unless it was the penthouse suite, or the room service, or some member of the staff who didn't snap to attention on command.

But Jordan smiled at Nick's description. "Ms. Weller ended up checking out two days early in a huff."

"Nothing to worry about," Nick promised Elsa Isakson and the others. "Scott is not a threat or a danger to anyone here."

"I still wished you'd mentioned it to me," Ben said. "Is that what had you so spooked when you first got here?"

Nick grinned at the memory. Ben had been the electrician who had rewired the old house saving Jordan thousands of dollars in the process. Nick scratched his chin. "I guess it was in the top two. My attraction to Jordan was the other."

Jordan laid her hand on top of her husband's with an unmistakable sigh. The sigh indicated marital bliss in spades. "Thank goodness we got *that* behind us."

As cherry pie was passed to Logan and he took the plate, he announced in the direction of the Isakson's. "They're more than likely just pulling your leg. It's a pretty good marketing strategy when you stop to think about it though. It's a known fact many B & B's all over the country from one coast to the other, advertise they're haunted. And make money catering to the crowd that believes that stuff." He glared in Kinsey's direction. "If I were you I'd take all this talk about a ghost with a grain of salt because I don't believe in apparitions of any kind."

"Really?" Kinsey asked with a wide smile. "If you don't believe in ghosts, you will before you leave Promise Cove. Guaranteed. In fact, I'll tell you what. If you don't see Scott I'll personally help you paint your lighthouse. I'm not a carpenter like Troy or good at construction. But I can wield a paint roller. What do you say?"

Her challenge intrigued him. "I hate to see anyone dangle manual labor as an incentive, especially when they'd lose."

Kinsey shook her head and laughed. "You're in for a helluva jolt when it happens. I'd really enjoy seeing it, too. If you don't care for that wager then we could make it a lot more interesting." Because she felt it was a sure bet—and because she'd started this she would damn well finish it— she raised the ante. "What do you say we bet twenty bucks? I say you'll experience the ghost that is Scott Phillips in a big way." Kinsey looked around the table. "Any other takers?"

"I'd take a part of that bet, but we'll be leaving on Sunday," Ben informed Kinsey.

"Oh it won't take that long. Trust me," Kinsey boasted with pure confidence. "Well, what about it, Donnelly? Are you game? Willing to put your money where your mouth is?"

Logan raised his glass. "Twenty bucks says your ghost is pure fiction."

Nick grinned as he wiped Hutton's chin. "I'm in."

"You talked me into it," Ben nodded, turning to his wife. "Hey, knowing Scott the way I did, I'd say he's just stubborn enough to find a way to stick around."

Olivia Whitney piped in, "A bet? Oh yes, I think I'll wager, too. What about you, Kay?"

Kay sighed, clearly annoyed with her sister. "Of for goodness sakes, we've been here two whole days and haven't seen anything like a ghost. I'm not losing my money." But when Olivia gave her a scowl that clearly said dare, Kay gave in. "Oh why not? She won't leave me alone until I do."

"You're kidding?" Logan said as he looked around the table then zeroed in on Kinsey. "You should know up front, I'm not easily frightened, nor am I some snooty, uptight Boston woman who is easily upset if my stuff is moved around during the day."

"Is that a yes or a no then?" Kinsey challenged, clearly backing the man into a corner.

"Fine," Logan uttered.

Jordan sighed, eyeing the concerned on the faces of the Isaksons and the Whitney sisters. "It'll be fine. Scott's not a malevolent at all. You'll be just fine here, more than fine," Jordan repeated. "Nick and I are determined to see you enjoy your stay." In an attempt to direct the conversation to less divisive topics, Jordan prompted, "Now, Mr. Isakson, why don't you tell us again, what it is you do for a living over in Sacramento?"

Chapter Five

After taking a hot shower, as exhausted as he was from his trip, Logan had decided to settle into his antique-looking, king-sized bed with the hope of finishing John Grisham's latest release, the one he'd picked up two days earlier in the Rome airport to read on the plane.

But surrounded by the color of melon walls a softer shade of ripe cantaloupe, he found himself studying the beach-themed photos that hung on the walls. There were pictures of craggy cliffs amid seashore landscapes. However, the one that caught his attention was a black and white of the Smuggler's Bay Lighthouse in its prime. A group of workers stood around its base looking as if they were proud of the finished product. Logan estimated the date of the photograph to be either 1936 or '37, which would fit with what he knew about its history. He studied the faces of each man, a dozen in all, and the way they were dressed. A sense of pride swelled inside his chest. His grandfather, tall and lean, stood in the center with his arm draped on the shoulders of the men standing on either side of him in obvious camaraderie. And why wouldn't there be a sense of fellowship? The men had built the Smuggler's Bay Lighthouse.

Logan wondered if he could make an offer for the group photo. There were other items placed around the B & B for sale. Paintings done by some woman named Lilly Seybold. Handcrafted necklaces of beads and stones strung together by a Drea Jennings. So why wouldn't the photographs be up for sale as well?

His hostess had referred to his room as the Scallop Suite, mostly because it offered an attractive, hand-stenciled border with a series of calico and lion's paw shells painted along the wall near the ceiling.

He was about to settle back into the pillows when he heard the unmistakable sound of what could only be described as a woman in the throes of passion coming through the walls. It could've been his imagination. But just in case, he slipped on his headphones anyway. This way, if the newlyweds got any louder he'd be able to put the activities going on beyond his room out of his head. It wouldn't take much more of those kinds of sounds though to bring Kinsey Wyatt to mind.

He reminded himself he was done with feisty women. While the conscious mind grew more determined, the subconscious weakened.

His last thought before dropping off to sleep was Kinsey's sexy legs, that off-the-shoulder top she'd worn at dinner. Letting the book fall to his chest, he snored softly with visions of slipping that lime green outfit off Kinsey Wyatt's body and getting her out of those yoga pants.

Thoughts across the hallway from Logan Donnelly veered in a completely different direction. Kinsey got out her calculator. She tallied her monthly expenses, subtracted her income from Hartley and checked the balance in her checkbook. Even with the additional income from Murphy's Market, she'd still be cutting it close each month.

But Kinsey had a plan.

She'd have to find her mettle and overlook what the town would think of her. If she planned to succeed here, she couldn't let things like that matter. After all, hospital and doctor bills didn't wait for the stars to line up. Desperate times required desperate measures.

Tomorrow at lunch, she'd go talk to the owner. For a week now, she'd heard a few rumors about an opening.

Troy had told her as much. She'd have to bite the bullet, she supposed, and forget about nerves.

Unfortunately, Kinsey didn't see any other way around dealing with her staggering debt.

A couple of hours later a noise woke Logan from a deep sleep. Either someone had come into his room or jet lag had caused him to hallucinate. A man stood at the foot of his bed fully dressed in an unbuttoned blue oxford shirt over a yellow Tee with his hands stuffed down in the pockets of khaki shorts. He wore his brown hair short in a military-style cut.

"How the hell did you get into my room?" Logan snarled at the man about the same time he reached for something, anything he could use for a weapon.

All of a once, his cell phone on the nightstand lit up and began to ring. "If you're the fucking press, I'm going to sue your ass this time for harassment! I'm tired of this shit. Leave me the hell alone!"

"Not everything revolves around you," the man said quietly. "You need to stop thinking it does. You might try opening your eyes, see what's real and what isn't."

"What the hell does that even mean? I want you out of here. Now!"

But the man continued to stand where he was. "You need to remember that promise you made. Your grandmother expected more out of you." With that comment, the man vanished into thin air.

Logan didn't have time to bristle at the remark. He barely had time to blink. "How the hell do you know about that?" he roared at no one.

After scrubbing a hand over his face, Logan swung his feet to the floor and stood up. Jet lag aside, it had to have been a dream. Yeah, that had been it. He'd awakened in a strange place, had been confused for a few seconds before he came completely out of sleep.

But just to be on the safe side, he took a walk around his room, checking the bathroom first before bending down to peer underneath the bed.

There was no strange man lurking anywhere. He dragged on his jeans without buttoning them and started for the French doors. He swung one open so that he could step out onto the expansive wooden deck. Stars dotted the night sky. He strode to the railing and looked down into the courtyard.

Logan spotted the man who had just left his bedroom walking along the pathway edged with sunny daffodils and purple pansies. In daylight hours the flowers would burst with yellows and blues. Now they were merely shadows swaying in the night breeze. Logan watched as the infamous Scott he'd heard so much about at dinner, stopped and turned, looked up. Scott glowered at him.

Like an idiot, Logan glared back.

Kinsey's words from dinner taunted him twofold. *"If you don't believe in ghosts, you will before you leave Promise Cove."*

In a span of less than four hours, Logan realized he'd just lost eighty bucks on a sucker's bet. He shook his head. He'd have to dig deep and remember that old adage next time he was tempted to wager against the house.

Didn't he know the odds always favored the home team?

The smell of bacon blended with hazelnut coffee drifted to Logan's nostrils making him sit up in bed. His stomach rumbled in anticipation of breakfast.

Crawling out of bed, one glance at the French doors had him remembering last night's encounter. Scott Phillips had been real or as real as any dream he'd ever had about his past. But Logan knew damn well he hadn't been asleep when Scott had spoken to him.

He'd liked to have blamed the incident on mental strain, maybe nerves at starting the biggest undertaking of his life while the pain of the past hovered over his head like Pigpen's dirt cloud.

But he just couldn't go there. Not yet.

Even though the renovation of a rundown lighthouse would more than likely take the better part of his summer and part of fall, he wouldn't come unglued now over something the home team had tried to warn him about.

If he was lucky he might be able to finish the project by Thanksgiving. That was ambitious thinking he knew. But since taking that first step was at least getting here and settling in, he had to dig deep to regain that momentum. Before he could head in that direction though, there was something he had to do first.

The dining room was still packed by the time he'd showered. He'd even taken the time to shave in hopes he'd given the other guests time to eat and clear out. He wasn't that lucky. Logan wasn't antisocial exactly. But in this town, he intended to keep his guard up. So much so that he simply preferred to grab a meal in relative silence. That was impossible with the Whitney sisters or the noisy newlyweds or the second honeymooners. All of them kept up a steady stream of chatter about what activities they had planned for the day.

When Nick came in carrying a tray laden with pastries, Logan waved a twenty at him. "Nice haunted house you've got here," he muttered to Nick. "When's the next ride kick in?"

Nick grinned back. He lowered his voice. "What time did Scott put in an appearance?"

Logan glanced around the table to see if anyone had picked up on Nick's comment. Luckily the others seemed to be engrossed in forming a day hike to take pictures of wildflowers. "I'd been asleep about two hours, I guess. It wasn't even midnight. Scared the shit out of me though. I thought somebody had broken into my room."

Nick took a seat next to Logan. "Sorry. I really am. I know we were joking around quite a bit last night at your expense, but you didn't seem too interested in the topic. I actually thought Scott might not even bother with you. Kinsey sort of tried to tell you—how active he is around here. And Scott really is innocuous. He likes to help people." Nick had almost said troubled people, but thought better of it. Since Logan's face indicated he'd been shaken by the incident, Nick decided to table the teasing. "I'm sorry," Nick repeated. "It's obvious he's upset you."

Logan wasn't about to mention what Scott had said to him, so he went another direction. "I spent some time in New Orleans about ten years back. There it's hard not to get suckered into a few ghost stories while you sit around listening to the blues in all kinds of historical venues." He spread his arms out wide. "But this is the last place I'd think a ghost would inhabit the rooms."

"It's a long story."

"Why don't you enlighten me over my eggs?"

Nick didn't need much prompting. As the dining room began to clear out, he took Logan through how he'd met Scott in the same National Guard unit and how they had both ended up serving in Iraq. Then Nick explained how Scott had died there.

"A roadside bomb? But the guy looks—"

"All together? Yeah he does. I can't explain it and wouldn't expect anyone to believe it." Nick went on to tell Logan about the promise he'd made to Scott, at some point in the heat of battle, to take care of Jordan and Hutton, unwittingly, in the event anything happened to him in Iraq. "I honestly think Scott had a premonition he wasn't ever going home. But I have no idea when I actually pledged I'd come to Pelican Pointe to check up on his wife and daughter. Whatever karma was out there in the cosmos, I survived and he didn't. After I got back stateside, I was diagnosed with PTSD. At the time, my memories of that day were all screwed up. But after waiting several months, I finally came here to talk to Jordan. At that point in my life, I didn't know for sure what was real and what wasn't."

Logan stared at Nick. That statement hit a little too close to home, a little too eerie. Those were almost Scott's exact words last night. "What's real and what isn't. That's what he said to me along with something personal I'd rather not share."

Nick held up his hands. "No problem. We all have our issues, our secrets. Anyway, here I am, married to Jordan now with two kids."

"Shouldn't that piss him off, the fact that you're with his wife?"

"You'd think. But Scott isn't like that."

"So Hutton is really—"

"Scott's daughter? Yes, but I've adopted her. I think he's fine with that. In fact I still talk to him," Nick admitted quietly. "He's here in spirit almost every single day. And if not here, somewhere in town. There are sightings."

"You're kidding?"

"I know it sounds crazy but I wouldn't have it any other way. It's kind of a joke now, although there was a time when it wasn't, except when it happens to our guests of course."

"And you're okay with that?"

"Like I said last night, this is Scott's home. He grew up here. He lived here long before I ever did or Jordan for that matter. He's part of this place. We occasionally have to refund a guest's money if they are—unhappy or temperamental."

"Like Boston Lady. Look, I don't mean to insult you or anything, but this is all a little much for me to take in. I've got a lot on my mind right now and this is just—well…nuts."

"Trust me, if you're troubled about anything at all, Scott will pull it out of you. It's futile to resist. Okay, that was a joke."

But Logan hadn't yet reached that point where he appreciated the humor.

Later, he thought about Nick's warning as he drove his truck passed two brick columns on either side of the gate and through the entrance to Eternal Gardens. It might've been a dozen years since he'd last been here, but he was fairly sure he could find the Donnelly family plot.

It wasn't a large cemetery by city standards. A line of arroyo willow and valley oak boxed the place in, providing shade if you were in the mood for it. Spangled flannel bush vied with white leaf manzanita along with the bright gold of blazing star wildflowers giving the tree line a burst of color here and there. Spring rain had been good to the clover and the green lawn that spread out for acres. Hearty dandelions dotted the landscape and curved in the breeze as if proud of their stubborn taproots.

Logan walked among the gravestones, some standing no taller than a couple of feet in height while others were grander, more impressive.

Liam and Charlotte Donnelly's headstones were neither impressive nor grand. They'd specifically requested their only grandson stick to something less ornate. At the time, he'd done his best to comply. But now as he walked up to the two granite markers, the first thing he realized was the graves had been woefully neglected.

Another layer of guilt flowed over him.

That melancholy mood he'd fought before getting to this spot, wanted to return. For something to do, he knelt down on the green, began to pull at the stubborn chickweed and foxtail that had taken over. With his one good hand, he tugged on a patch of tenacious hawkweed that refused to budge.

"Looks like you could use a hand with that."

The voice was familiar, eerily so. Logan squinted into the sun from his crouched position on the grass. Once again, he stared into the very real eyes of the man from last night. "It isn't warm enough for heatstroke this early in the morning. You are wide awake and Scott Phillips is *not* standing here," he mumbled to himself.

"That's a nice touch. Talking to yourself like that. But it rarely does any good and often leads to psychosis."

"Fuck you."

"That's the spirit, pun intended. Now, we're communicating."

Logan ground his back teeth in frustration, took the handful of weeds he had clutched in his fist and tossed them in Scott's direction. He watched as the plants sailed through thin air. "What is the point in harassing me? I didn't even know you when you were alive. I'm sorry you died in Iraq, but it doesn't have anything to do with me."

"There are no rules here. You're pissed off at the town. I understand that. But there's no point in taking it out on everybody, especially people who didn't even live here at the same time you did."

"I treat people just fine, thanks," Logan spat out.

"Oh really? How is that possible with that huge chip on your shoulder?"

"What the hell do you know about it anyway?" Logan exploded. "You grew up here. For all I know, you're one of the ones keeping a secret, the one I'm looking for. Or maybe you had the answers once and refused to do anything about it when you were alive."

"Now that just pisses me off. You want to find answers with that attitude? Lots of luck because you're going to need it. Beat your head against a brick wall for all I care. And you know what, Donnelly? When that happens, I'll laugh my ass off."

Logan watched as Scott disappeared right in front of him. A string of profanity spewed out of Logan's mouth until he realized where he was standing. He dropped down on the grass, this time sitting cross-legged. He stared at the marble knowing full well there should have been one other grave in the family plot.

If he had to rip open the town's secrets one layer at a time, he intended to find the answers one way or another. If it caused people to hate him, he didn't give a rat's ass. And that included Scott Phillips, whoever the hell he'd been.

There was one person in town a little more interested in Logan Donnelly's return than everyone else. It hadn't taken twenty-four hours for the news to reach his ears. So the boy had come back to town a man. He intended to keep an eye on the man, a sculptor of all things, an artsy-fartsy, hippie type that people made a big deal about the world over. The first time he'd heard the buzz, he'd driven over to San Sebastian to the library. He'd taken the time to read about Logan Donnelly in slick magazine articles and old newspaper archives. It seems the art world shit themselves every time Donnelly, the artist, created anything with a bunch of metal or a pile of clay, like some damned kindergarten kid might do.

From the wooded area behind the line of trees, he watched the shaggy-haired asshole. Donnelly looked as though he wanted to cry. Something had told him this is where the guy would head to first, the cemetery. His hunch had paid off.

He should take up the game again. In fact, it would be a nice welcome back gift for Mr. Donnelly. And if the fancy-schmancy artist got too close, he'd give the asshole something to remember about old times.

When the long-haired freak finally crawled back into his truck, he wondered why it had taken so long for the man to circle back. Logan Donnelly didn't fit in here, hadn't even when he'd been a boy. Of all the other places in the world an artist could have ended up, there was only one reason to come back to Pelican Pointe.

He was more than willing to pick up where he'd left off. After all, no one here had ever made a big deal out of him the way they had Donnelly. With everything he had done here in this speck of a town, with all that he had accomplished here without ever leaving, maybe the residents needed a little incentive. Maybe they needed motivation to throw him a parade. Hell, didn't they use any excuse to bring the carnival into town?

But no one knew. He'd taken care of that just recently. He had to remind himself everything he did—he did in secret—for years.

All the more reason he wouldn't let the likes of Logan Donnelly intimidate him. He'd show the bastard what true talent was all about.

Chapter Six

As soon as the lunch hour arrived, Kinsey left work and made her way over to The Pointe on Ocean Street with one goal in mind.

The upscale restaurant had once been an old fish hatchery. She could tell that by the faded, but still visible, white lettering on the side of the ancient brick that gave the place its charm. The building had sat empty for more than two decades until the day Perry Altman, a five-star chef from L.A., had made a swing through the area from the interstate on his way to Napa Valley.

To this day, Perry claimed he hadn't gotten lost, but had purposely taken a side trip looking for the perfect spot to open up his own restaurant. What he wanted was a scenic spot along the coast where he could leave his life behind for good in the City of Angels and start fresh.

That one weekend sojourn had changed Perry's life. Not only had he fallen in love with the little town, he'd decided on the spot the old structure would make an excellent eating establishment at a fraction of the cost he'd encounter in Napa or L.A.

Because of that Perry bought the property the next week, started renovations within a month, and never looked back.

The Pointe had been open for four years now. Perry made sure his kitchen offered a different menu entirely from the only other competition in town—the Hilltop Diner. Perry saw to it personally that his customers experienced dining on par with one of Wolfgang Puck's eateries. At The Pointe you got atmosphere, ambiance, a table instead of a booth, tabletops covered with crisp, white linens, matching napkins, place settings using fine bone China, and sterling silver flatware. You could eat under a sun-drenched skylight at lunch or stars glittering above your head at night. You might order lobster bisque while sitting next to a window with a view of the Pacific Ocean. Watch the sun go down over the horizon. Enjoy a glass of chardonnay in front of a roaring fireplace. All the while, a concert pianist entertained diners with tunes from Beethoven to Strauss to Mozart.

The Pointe offered the locals a place to dine out on special occasions like birthdays or anniversaries. Year round, Fridays, Saturdays, and Sundays were Perry's busiest nights. Then in the summer months, tourists with money to blow, ordered bottles of Perry's best wine, his most expensive lobster dishes, and left generous tips for his staff's reputed five-star service.

With nerves jittering in her stomach that made it impossible to actually think about swallowing a bite of food at the moment, Kinsey took a deep breath at the double door and strolled in with all the confidence of a job applicant laden with tons of experience.

When the hostess greeted her, Kinsey recognized Jolene Sanders from her part-time clerk job at Knudsen's Pharmacy. Jolene had a little four-year-old girl and like a lot of other people in town held down two jobs in addition to the two her husband had.

Before Kinsey lost her nerve completely, she forced out the words, "Hi, I'd like to see the owner, Perry Altman, please."

"Sure. Aren't you the new attorney in town?"

"That's me. Kinsey Wyatt." Kinsey stretched out her hand

After Jolene accepted the handshake, she explained, "Perry's in the kitchen—'supervising.' She emphasized supervising with air quotes while rolling her eyes at the same time.

"Is he a tyrant like most chefs?" Kinsey asked, clearly anxious.

Jolene waved a hand at the question. "He's temperamental, all right. Most times he runs this restaurant like a dictator. But the man has a heart of gold. You repeat that, though, and I'll deny each word." With that Jolene disappeared in the direction of the kitchen.

Soon Jolene came back leading a rather short, exotic-looking man who had creamy, toffee skin. Perry Altman greeted Kinsey with the same enthusiasm he might for any other customer he hoped would drop eighty bucks on lunch. He had a quick and easy smile, twinkling brown eyes, and she could tell a love for the business.

"What can I do for you?" Perry asked.

"I hear you need a new piano player. I'm here to apply for the job."

Perry's smile faded. "Can you believe that rat bastard Franco. He left me in a lurch. Decided to traipse off to L.A. to try out for *American Idol* of all things. I gave that rat the best five years of my life and one morning he up and tells me he wants to move to Hollywood. Hollywood," Perry emphasized, rolling his eyes. "Thinks he's going to be the next Billy Joel. I've got news for him. He'll need a lot more than a pretty face in that jungle."

Perry narrowed his eyes as if in recognition. "Wait a minute. Don't I know you? Aren't you Aaron Hartley's new lawyer?"

Kinsey laughed. She'd heard this same thing at least two dozen times already. "I am. But I'm looking for part-time work, Mr. Altman."

"Perry. Everyone calls me Perry. That's one of the great perks about small town living. We all know each other on sight. That's why we're able to spot anyone who looks out of place from across the street."

"You might as well know up front that I also work part-time at Murphy's Market, checking groceries on the weekends. Usually my shift is eight to four-thirty. But that leaves my weekend nights completely free."

"Okay. But you know you'll have to work Friday nights, right? Friday nights through Sundays, six-thirty on the dot to closing, which is usually till eleven p.m. or so. You play until the last customer pays the tab. In addition to those three nights a week, I'd like you available for any special occasions in between that I can book, like birthdays or anniversaries that come up. I don't expect you to play for free. You get the same amount for those gigs as you do for Friday, Saturday, and Sundays. That won't leave you much time for a social life."

"No problem. That's reasonable."

He cocked his head. "Not trying to pry here, but I have to ask. You're an attorney by day. Why three jobs?"

Kinsey sighed. She didn't like revealing personal deets and knew for certain she wasn't required to answer the question. But in this case, it seemed like more conversational than nosy. "I want to rent a house by the end of the month, get settled in here for good. So three's that. But, my mom suffered from cancer for a long time. I lost her last year. Since then I have a stack of her medical bills to pay off. I can't do that without more money coming in. My first love is the law, but—"

Perry's eyes warmed. "I get it. Well, you certainly are a go-getter. I respect that. Are you any good? Do you have any formal training on the piano?"

"My mother's employer gave me lessons starting at the age of six. While my mother cleaned her house, the woman taught me how to play classical tunes. So no, I'm not formally trained but I have been playing for quite some time."

Perry winked at her and tilted his head. "You've certainly piqued my interest. How about an audition? One or two tunes ought to do it."

"Of course. But I'm a little nervous."

"No reason to be. We don't have much of a lunch crowd. Our bread and butter so to speak are the people who come in here for dinner. The place is relatively empty now. You'll just have Jolene and me for judges."

"Lead the way then."

"So you play the classics? I actually prefer that, but just so you know, not everyone shares my musical tastes. I do have a few customers who love a modern tune every now and then. If all you play are the typical standards though, I'll settle for that since I'm in a spot," Perry relayed as he started toward the huge dining area.

"Actually, I play both."

He lifted a brow at that boast, just as the Steinway came into view. Tucked away in one corner of the room sat a massive concert piano opposite the fireplace. Its distinctive wide tail of maple wood gleamed with polished perfection in the sunlight that drifted through the windows.

For Kinsey, the instrument brought back memories of childhood. Good ones.

She put her purse down on the floor and took a seat on the bench. Her fingers hovered over the keyboard a few seconds before she warmed up with *Let it Be*. From there she went into *Songbird* before smoothly transitioning into Ludovico Einaudi's *Divenire*.

Perry's eyes bugged out at what he considered pure perfection. Jolene's did as well.

Kinsey didn't notice. She was into the chords and the music.

A few notes into Sarah McLachlan's *Angel* though was all it took for Perry Altman to make up his mind. "Oh my God, you're hired. You're fabulous. Isn't she, Jolene?"

"Ten times better than Franco."

"I couldn't agree more. You get a hundred dollars a night plus tips and I throw in meals. How's that sound? Will that help with the bills?"

Kinsey let out an enormous breath while tears formed in the corners of her eyes.

"There'll be none of that," Perry warned. "Are you able to start tomorrow night?"

"No problem. I hope I can manage playing in front of actual customers though."

Perry grabbed her arm. "Don't worry about a thing. Get here a little early and Jolene will see to it you get a glass of red wine to settle your nerves. On the house. You'll be fine."

"Thanks, Mr. Altman."

"It's Perry. Are you kidding? Thank *you*. Because you, my dear, are going to increase my business by leaps and bounds. By any chance do you have a little black evening dress?"

Kinsey laughed. "As a matter of fact I do. It's short though."

"Perfect, show plenty of leg. Now let's hear the rest of your repertoire. What else can you play? Entertain me."

On the walk back to work, Kinsey knew she'd have to deal with telling Hartley about her two extra jobs…at some point. But it was a free country last time she checked. Hartley didn't own her. She should be able to do what she wanted in her free time. After all, it wasn't her fault the tightwad hadn't offered her much in the way of salary. Was it too much to ask for enough money to live on?

Logan spent Thursday afternoon familiarizing himself with the town and its residents. Out of curiosity he went into Hidden Moon Bay Books and picked up Ethan Cody's mystery novel. From there, he walked down to Ferguson's Hardware where he got to know Joe Ferguson up close and personal by placing a huge lumber order, not to mention a long list of other materials. Logan wasn't absolutely certain he liked the man. Even though Joe acted as though he appreciated the business it didn't go unnoticed by Logan that the man seemed standoffish almost to the point of brusque. If that kept up he'd take his business elsewhere over to San Sebastian.

When he was done at Ferguson's, Logan decided to have lunch at the Hilltop. As he walked down Main he ran into Troy who was carrying what looked like a small, decorative cedar chest under his arm.

"What do you have there?" Logan asked.

"It's a keepsake box, you know for jewelry, girl stuff."

The artist in Logan stopped to admire the intricate design on top. "If this is an example of your work, I'm impressed."

"I made it for Gina Purvis but she broke up with me last week, almost threw it at my head. She tossed it out her front door and me with it. Broke one of the hinges right off. I was headed into Ferguson's to see if I could find a replacement so it closes again." Troy shook his head in true disgust before he added in a knowing tone, "Women. I'm planning on avoiding the hot-headed ones."

Logan couldn't help it he laughed out loud. "Good luck with that." He slapped the younger man on the back and went on, "Troy, women have been throwing things at us since that first cave woman picked up a rock. If you discover how to avoid their wrath, let me know."

Troy chortled with laughter. "Ain't that the truth?"

"I was just heading into the Diner here, how about joining me." Logan offered, thumbing in the direction of the door. Logan noticed Troy's brow furrow at the invitation and hesitate. He figured he knew why. "Lunch is on me. It's the least I can do for my very first new hire."

Troy broke out in a grin. "I guess I could eat."

As soon as they walked in the door, Dwight Yoakum's *A Thousand Miles From Nowhere* greeted them from the Wurlitzer jukebox at the end of the counter. Logan glanced around the place that hadn't changed much in two decades. The faux black marble-looking counter had been meant to give the diner a retro malt shop feel but instead came off as a tacky knockoff. He noted the black and white checkered linoleum was still stained yellow. The eight padded red stools under the counter were just a little more faded and shabby than he remembered, but that hadn't stopped someone from trying to patch them with a brighter shade of tape. It looked as though the owner couldn't settle on which design of furniture to squeeze in here, so she'd used a little bit of everything. An assortment of chairs was haphazardly shoved under eight mismatched tables.

Logan immediately shook off that nostalgic mood that wanted to creep in.

They took a seat at a booth near the windows. As soon as they sat down a waitress, a cute little blonde about the same age as Troy, came over to drop off menus. "Hi Troy," she drawled. "What can I get y'all to drink?"

"I'll take a Coke."

"Coffee for me, thanks," Logan said before realizing the blonde was staring at him. "Is something the matter?"

"Oh. Sorry. But I just love guys with long hair," she explained and then reached out to touch Troy's white-blond curls. "You have nice hair, too. I'm thinking about going to cosmetology school in the fall. You know, cut hair. Janie Pointer says she'd hire me if I got my license."

"You'd be good at it, Mona. You should do it. Where's Margie today?"

At the compliment, the blonde sent her hundred-watt smile in Troy's direction. "She made an emergency supply run to Costco over in Santa Cruz. She'll be back soon. I'll get your drinks."

When she walked away, Logan lifted a brow. "Friend of yours?"

Troy's grin said it all. "That's Mona Bingham. From Texas. She's Max's daughter, the cook here. She's sort of the reason Gina Purvis broke up with me."

"Sort of?"

"Yeah, Gina accused me of flirting with Mona right in front of her. I didn't think I was."

"Ah," Logan said. In the way of male bonding, he added, "That's another thing women do with extraordinary accuracy. They can hone in on another flirtatious female at a thousand paces and then blame you for it."

"You're pretty funny. Tell me something."

"If I can."

"You mean if you want to?"

"That, too."

"Did breaking your hand have anything to do with a woman?"

"I'll say one thing for you, Troy. You're an observant man."

Troy ordered breakfast and ate enough for two people. Logan got a greasy, artery-clogging cheeseburger. He expected a nasty frozen patty that had one chance to defrost once it hit the griddle. But what he got was the best-tasting burger he'd had in years.

Over their meal, Logan learned a lot about Troy. He had to admit that even if the young man's references hadn't checked out he probably would've hired him anyway. It hadn't taken more than thirty minutes for Logan to peg Troy as a poor kid without much of a family, especially since losing his mother, Susan, to breast cancer right after he'd turned fourteen. Orphaned, Troy had two options. He could either go into the foster care system or move in with one of two uncles, Derek and Dale Stovall. The brothers owned six acres of land south of Pelican Pointe. There were two houses, one belonging to Derek the other to Dale. There was also a trailer they rented out. When the trailer became available, Troy got to leave Derek's house and move to his own place, a godsend to an eighteen-year-old. Since his high school graduation, Troy had picked up odd jobs around town to pay the rent.

"Your uncle charges you rent?" Logan asked.

"Hey I don't expect to live there for free. I pay my own way."

"Completely understand." But hearing Troy's life story, Logan made a decision. "How about you start work for me right now."

His eyes brightened. "Really? Doing what?"

"I just ordered materials that won't be here for another five days. But in the meantime I need help getting my equipment moved from Point A to Point B. And there's more coming any day now."

"I could help with that."

"Then as of this afternoon, you're on the clock."

Around four-thirty, Logan and Troy had made the last trip of the day getting his equipment transported from the cove to the lighthouse. When Logan pulled his truck along the road leading to the B & B, he spotted Nick and Jordan's kids playing on the lawn. For a moment he enjoyed the homey setting just watching a big sister try to roll a ball to her little baby brother. The baby kept trying to eat the round thing rather than roll it back.

Another time, another place, Logan decided, and crawled out of the pickup. Nick and Jordan greeted him from the steps of the front porch.

"You didn't have to move all your stuff today."

"It was taking up a lot of space. Troy and I covered everything with tarps in case of bad weather." He glanced up at the cloudless sky, promising a beautiful spring evening. "But it doesn't look like there's a chance of that yet."

"I wish I could offer you space in the garage, but it's a virtual black hole in there."

"That's okay. My electrical tools have yet to get here. Those I'll keep in a storage space I rented on Ocean Street this morning."

"There's a lot to starting over," Jordan considered.

Logan grinned. "You have no idea." When the kids started to fuss, Logan excused himself and headed to his room to shower and clean up before dinner.

But as soon as he got to the front staircase and started up the steps, he felt an unmistakable change in temperature. The cold air pressed against him like a block of ice. He stopped on the landing, felt the chill on the back of his neck. "Nice try," he muttered to nothing but air. "You've already made your point. And I'm eighty bucks lighter because of it. What more do you want?"

Another wave of ice blasted him. "Pissed off? Join the club. Your temper fits don't scare me as easily as they did some little old lady."

When Logan glanced around the hallway, he fixed a gaze on Olivia and Kay Whitney peeking out at him from behind the doors of their separate rooms.

"Ladies," Logan acknowledged with a nod of his head as he calmly took out his key to unlock his own door.

Over spareribs, mashed potatoes and corn on the cob, no one seemed particularly eager to mention Scott the Ghost, which Logan deemed odd. He'd been prepared to defend his odd behavior on the landing all the while disregarding the episode earlier in the day at the cemetery.

When Kinsey attempted to make small talk, Logan ignored her. In fact, he ignored most everyone except the kids. Since they sat two feet from him, he used his silverware to make up a story about "spoon man."

But once the meal ended and the talk turned to kids and their finicky eating habits, Logan sought out a place to escape. He stepped outside on the front porch for some air. Hoping for a little solitude, his face fell when he spotted Kinsey sitting in the swing. She seemed preoccupied, staring off into the cypress trees.

Even with his brusque attitude firmly locked in place, his eyes landed on her tanned legs. She wasn't dressed like she had been at dinner. She'd changed out of her work clothes and into a pair of low-riding, hip-hugging hiking shorts that were impossible not to notice. A powder blue, button-down sleeveless shirt showed off her toned arms. When she glanced up, their eyes locked.

"Sorry, I didn't mean to intrude," Logan said, beginning to feel like a jerk. Since his contribution to dinner conversation had been nil, he decided to try to make amends. "Believe it or not, I'm not usually this surly."

"Aren't you?" she replied with a tilt of her head to study him.

"I could move on, leave you to your own thoughts."

"Don't be silly. The only place in this house that isn't off limits to everyone is your own room. They call this coziness a big perk at a B & B." She grinned. "So if you're looking for solitude, it's best to either slip away to your own room or go for a walk." She spread her arms wide. "There are acres and acres of things to see here. But don't forget your camera. The lupine's in bloom along the sand dunes. Have you been down to the cove yet?"

When she finally took a breath, he shook his head and admitted, "I've been meaning to walk down there but today was pretty hectic. Which reminds me." With his one good hand, he took a twenty from his pocket, handed it off to Kinsey. "I lost the bet."

She snapped the bill out of his hand before bursting out in a huge belly laugh. When she finally recovered, she asked, "What time? We have our own pool going on the side."

"Figures. That must be why Nick wanted to know the time, too. A few minutes before midnight. I think the odds favored the house. Considerably."

"Damn. Nick won. He probably had inside info. As far as the odds go, they favored Scott." A chuckle escaped her lips. She raised her arms in triumph and did a happy dance where she sat, making the swing bounce. "Woot! I'm glad Scott's on our side though." She patted the wooden slats beside her. "Have a seat. There's plenty of room. Tell me all about your Scott sighting—I promise I don't bite—in spite of the rumors going around town."

As soon as he sat down, his weight made the old porch swing creak even more. "At least the entire town isn't calling you a dirty hippie freak with hair down to your ass. This morning when I went into Ferguson's to order material, I believe his first words to me were, 'hey, they said your hair grew down to your ass. Did you get it cut recently?' I wanted to tell him to eff off. But instead I gave him my best smile and returned the favor."

"What did you say?"

"I told him he wasn't nearly as repulsive as Nick said he was. You should have seen his eyes bug out."

That brought another round of guffaws from Kinsey. "You've got a cruel streak, Donnelly. Maybe the town will nominate you for their Congeniality Contest they hold every year." When she noted the disbelieving look form on his face, she continued, "According to my employer, every spring they have this parade to celebrate spring. Apparently, we must've just missed it. Anyway, they vote on the one resident who's contributed to the community the most. The one that wins is given a hundred-dollar gift certificate to spend around town. But don't get your hopes up. The town's a little slow in welcoming newcomers like us. Besides, it's usually the same people who win again and again. Trust me. It won't be me or you."

"What's their beef with you?"

"Oh my God, haven't you heard? I'm the idiot woman who thinks she can practice law with a degree she earned over the Internet."

Logan's eyes went wide. "The Internet? Why would they think that? Who started that rumor?"

"Oh it's not a rumor. It's true."

"Huh? You mean you got one of those online law degrees and thought you could practice law with it?"

Was the man always so insulting? she wondered. "You bet. In the State of California you can practice law as long as you pass the Bar, which I did. Not to brag." She leaned a bit closer in his direction and whispered, "Don't tell anyone, but I aced that sucker."

"Well then, you should tell the town to—"

"Eff themselves?" She chuckled once again. "I'm afraid I can't do that. Not my style, for one. Then there's the fact that I *do* need a few of them to eventually come around enough to let me draw up their wills and trusts so I'll have actual clients."

"Good luck with that."

"Thanks. Are you going to tell me what happened when you encountered Scott?"

His sigh was more embarrassment than annoyance. "I went to sleep early. I'm still pretty jetlagged. I woke up, couldn't remember where I was other than it was a strange place, not home, or rather not the home I'd had for three years. Anyway, there's this guy standing at the foot of my bed. I honestly thought someone had gotten into my room. It pissed me off. I'm still not sure it wasn't."

She gave him a dismissive stare. "I bet it did under the circumstances. So you're edgy because you've just woken to find a strange man in your room, go on."

"He wasn't there for very long." He didn't intend to repeat the play by play. "So what exactly did you do when you first saw him in your room? It had to scare you."

"First time he talked to me, Scott didn't come to my room. Second, we aren't talking about me...yet. I'll tell you all about it though after I hear what happened to you. So tell me."

He took her through the rest, again holding everything back that Scott had said to him, especially the argument at the cemetery.

"That's it? That's *all* he said? Are you sure you were awake enough to catch everything? Because usually he's a lot more prophetic, like he's talking in riddles or something and you're supposed to figure it out."

"Okay, then why don't you enlighten me about your experience?"

Kinsey sensed Logan putting up the same wall she'd seen yesterday at the lighthouse. "I already told you the first time I saw him, walking up the back staircase as I came down, then poof, he was gone. But the first conversation I had with him was down at the cove the day I got back from my job interview. I wanted a last look around the place before checking out, so I took a walk. Would you like to see it? The cove I mean? The sun's going down soon. If we hurry, it'll be the perfect time."

"Might as well. Lead the way."

"It's not really a walk. It's more like a climb down. But it's worth it. You'll see." She got to her feet, took his left hand in hers. "Come on, I'll show you the sights along the way. It makes up for the way we suckered you into the bet." She popped the crisp twenty dollar bill with both hands for emphasis before shoving it in her shorts pocket.

As they took off around the side of the house and into the back courtyard, Logan noted the woman's gift for gab. He even began to relax a little in the wake of her innate, cheery nature. She admired the quad area, the garden setting where color burst from each budding flower. The early evening air became heavy with the smell of lilies, dianthus, and if Logan knew anything about posies, gardenias.

When the Harris's dog, Quake, bolted onto their path, Kinsey stopped to give the energetic animal what he seemed to expect, a generous belly rub for his trouble. As the dog dropped and rolled at her feet, she tussled with him and said, "You're such a good boy. Aren't you, Quake?"

Right behind the dog, a harried Nick appeared in hot pursuit, toting his son on one shoulder. Kinsey went into what Logan termed "baby mode" as she kept the dog happy all the while cooing at the eleven-month-old boy. "Look at you, what a big handsome guy all ready for bed in your penguin PJs."

"We were taking the dog for a walk before bedtime."

"It's a beautiful night for it," Kinsey reasoned. "How do you keep him from digging up all these gorgeous flower beds?"

"Scott or Quake?" Nick joked. "Both love to dig in the dirt."

"Little boys, dogs and dirt just go together."

"Quake was hard to break from digging. We watched a lot of episodes of *Dog Whisperer* until we felt like we were on a first name basis with Cesar Millan. The key is to tire him out, walk him, exercise him so that he's so tired he won't feel like digging."

"Quake or Scott?" Kinsey quipped back.

"Both," Nick returned with a sly grin.

The homespun scene didn't get past Logan. A big old mutt of a dog, a cute, powdered baby, and one very attractive female who seemed to relish life and appreciate the people who came and went around her. It had been a very long time since Logan had spent any time with a woman like Kinsey Wyatt. Maybe he never had.

After Nick said his goodnights, the two continued on past fragrant magnolias and dogwoods laden with buds and blooms. Fallen leaves and blossoms scattered the ground, providing them with a soft carpet that made a swish-swish sound as they walked. Once they got to a copse of cypress, Logan saw the cliffs up ahead.

The entire time Kinsey chatted about cameras and pictures and photo spreads in magazines. For most of the walk, Logan wasn't able to keep track of her mindset. He wouldn't have described her as scatterbrained or flighty, but she seemed to take in everything at once and comment on it just as fast.

They finally reached a small clearing that opened up to a set of wooden steps built into the bluffs. She took hold of the handy iron-pipe guardrail and led the way down. Logan smelled rosemary and sage along with Monterey pine. Wild blackberries and strawberries lined the trail in addition to patches of ginger, beach grass, and alfalfa.

The last step was a bit of a drop onto a sandy stretch of shoreline that spread out forty yards or so in a half circle. Gentle waves lapped at the beach. Craggy rocks formed a natural tide pool at one end. At the other, Logan spotted an opening that suggested a cavern. A dinghy bobbed up and down, restless in the current.

Kinsey sat down on a jutting boulder to shed her boots and socks. Barefoot now, she stood up and spread her arms out wide, practically dancing to water's edge. She dipped her pink-painted toes into the frigid water of the Pacific.

She turned to look back at him and Logan felt his breath hitch. The breeze tousled her hair. She didn't seem to care. In the light of the setting sun, it shimmered golden brown. It hit Logan then for real. This was no high-strung, insecure model that needed validation every time she passed a mirror.

"Hey, you okay?" she asked. "Is something wrong?"

Something was definitely wrong. With everything else right now, he didn't need a distraction, certainly not one he wanted to undress, just slip those shorts down around her ankles and... "Crap," he mumbled out loud.

"What's wrong?"

"I stubbed my toe."

"But you're wearing shoes."

Nothing got past Kinsey. "Must've gotten a rock in my shoe then on the way down."

"Well then, take off your shoes," Kinsey urged.

He plopped his butt down on a boulder. "Are you ever going to finish telling me about Scott?"

She smiled and drifted back over to him, a stingy sliver of sun at her back. "It was right here, right on this spot that I talked to him the first time. I was sitting where you are. Again, I thought he was one of the guests until he moved closer. Something just flicked on. And then, Scott spoke to me, two words, and I knew."

"What did he say?"

"Sam Wheat?" The puzzled look on Logan's face told her he didn't get the reference. "Sam Wheat, Patrick Swayze's character in *Ghost*. Remember I mentioned it's my favorite movie and was my mom's. She died last year."

"I'm sorry," Logan said, scratching his chin and frowning. "Was Sam Wheat supposed to be some code that you were supposed to recognize?"

She sat down on the rock beside him. "You really don't get it, do you? Scott uttered those two words so I'd *know*. And yeah, it was code for me. My mother was sick a long time, more than eight years. We had plenty of chances to talk about the hereafter. When you're looking death in the face on a regular basis, those kinds of conversations seemed to pop up again and again. Some might handle it differently and not want to talk about it. But Ellie Wyatt faced it head on. I never saw her tackle anything any other way. I'm proud of her for that."

Logan noticed the eyes glisten with tears and felt like a heel. She was obviously still feeling some degree of grief about her mother. But if there were some type of hereafter where ghosts congregated, why then didn't his own—? He caught himself falling into that trap, that line of thinking and refused to go there. When he realized she'd gone on with the story, he was grateful she hadn't expected him to comfort her. "I still don't get—"

"I'm trying to explain it if you'll just listen. My mom and I would often discuss what kind of memorial service she wanted, what she wanted to wear, funeral arrangements, music she was fond of, stuff like that. Ellie Wyatt left nothing to chance, that's for sure. She was too practical. Then every time we watched *Ghost*, we'd laugh and joke that if she could, she'd make her presence known some way, somehow."

Logan listened in fascination. Were people really this gullible? He felt as though he'd stepped into a Pelican Pointe time warp, or maybe an episode of *Outer Limits*. He hoped to hell she wasn't getting ready to confess Scott the Ghost had helped her make a clay pot. "But, you don't *really* believe that this Scott was trying to communicate some message from your mother?"

"Scott's here, isn't he? How do you explain that? You saw him for yourself."

He blew out a pent-up breath because he didn't have a ready answer for that. "I'm still trying to blame it on jet lag."

"Let me know when you've been here for a couple of weeks and the jet lag has come and gone." She looked him in the eye, waited a beat. "You know what I think?"

"I'm sure you'll tell me."

"I think Scott mentioned something personal to you. He pushed a button, and you're reluctant to admit it."

"Great, so now you think you're capable of reading my mind. You know this is loony bin stuff, right?"

"Maybe so. But I've been in a work environment for more than a decade that meets the public every single day. I'm good at reading body language. You've got something troubling you, Donnelly. You'll have to let it go sooner or later."

Chapter Seven

At five o'clock on Friday, the work week done at Hartley's law office, Kinsey had ninety minutes to make it to her first gig. She intended to make a quick trip out to Promise Cove to grab something to eat and change her clothes before heading to The Pointe.

Once she reached the B & B though, the turnaround wasn't quite as fast as she'd hoped. In fact, before she had time to dash upstairs, she got caught the minute she stepped inside the entryway by the Whitney sisters. They wanted to know how exactly she got her hair the same color as Blake Lively's of all things.

"Olivia noticed it right off the bat. She has this thing for hair," Kay explained.

"It isn't colored," Kinsey replied.

"Of course, it's colored," Olivia insisted. "What woman doesn't change her hair?"

Kay urged Kinsey on. "You can tell us. We won't say a word to anyone, we swear it."

Since every minute counted and since she couldn't convince them otherwise, Kinsey made up the first shade that popped into her head. "Sunkissed. Clairol."

Olivia snapped her fingers. "That's it. I knew it. Those Clairol people have the best colors on the market. Told you," Olivia said to Kay.

"Look, I've got to run," Kinsey said as she darted past them into the kitchen to grab a sandwich for the road.

"No doubt a hot date," Kay told Olivia. "Ah, what I wouldn't give to be that age again."

"If only."

But in the kitchen, Kinsey faced another slew of questions from Jordan who wanted to know why she wasn't dining in tonight. "Is it my food?" Jordan asked taking the time to assess her guest. "Wait a minute, do you have a date? Someone in town asked you out?"

"I don't have a date," Kinsey all but chanted it. "I have something I have to do. I'm sorry to ask for food to go, but I'm in kind of a hurry."

Jordan studied the woman's nervous demeanor. "I see that. You're a guest here, Kinsey. You're entitled to make a few demands now and then during your stay. Asking for a meal-to-go falls into that category we innkeepers call 'providing for the whims of our guests.'" Jordan decided to lower the boom. "Murphy tells me he has a new cashier starting tomorrow morning."

"Crap," Kinsey stated flatly, rocking back on her heels. "Okay. Look. I need a second job. My finances are in dire straits. I'm stretched to the limit. As it turns out Hartley's starting salary isn't all that much." Never again would she think she could dash in and dash out without having to provide what seemed like embarrassing tidbits about herself.

"Well, that just is not right," Jordan exclaimed. "You moved all the way down here. He's lucky to get you. Why didn't you say something before now?"

"What was I supposed to say, I'm strapped for cash? What does that sound like to anyone in a new place that doesn't really know you?" When she saw that sympathetic look on Jordan's face, Kinsey almost wanted to come clean about the rest of it. But then what if she bombed tonight and Perry had to let her go? No, it was best to wait to tell anyone about her third job. Even if Jordan had been nice enough about throwing together a turkey wrap, it didn't mean she should divulge anything about the night ahead. But with the next words out of Jordan's mouth, Kinsey started to have second thoughts.

"Then I might have a solution to your housing problem."

"Really? Like what?"

"I need to talk to Nick about it first though. I'm sure he'll be okay with it."

"What? Look, you're already giving me a terrific discount. I couldn't ask for more. I love this place but staying here past the end of the month isn't an option even with a bargain rate. I need to find someplace affordable."

"I understand. But it wouldn't really be *here* exactly."

Kinsey frowned. "I don't understand." She glanced at her watch, noted she needed to get moving. "Okay. Well, I've got to run. Maybe we can talk—tomorrow after you've discussed it with Nick. Thanks, Jordan, for everything."

Kinsey grabbed the food sack Jordan handed her and took off for the stairs.

"Enjoy your evening," Jordan muttered. But she was talking to Kinsey's back as the woman zipped out of the room.

Thinking that she was home free, Kinsey darted up the steps only to get waylaid by Karen Fostwick. Karen wanted to chat about whether or not she could legally find out who was behind a fake social media profile stalking her new husband online. Karen was sure it was Cory's old girlfriend.

It took Kinsey less than a minute to explain that Karen should contact the social media in question with her suspicions and if that didn't work, she should go to the police to file a complaint.

Once Kinsey finally made it to her room, she tossed off her skirt and blouse and pulled out her little black dress. It took her five hurried minutes to put up her hair in a sophisticated twist but another five to dig out the spiky high heels from her crowded closet. Checking her image in the mirror, she added a pair of pearl drop earrings to each ear and stretched a single string of pearls around her neck. Grabbing the sack with her sandwich, she headed to her car.

As if fate had suddenly turned against her, Kinsey turned the key in the ignition and got a grinding noise for her trouble. She counted to thirty, tried again. This time all she got was a dreaded click, click, click. In defeat, she rested her head on the steering wheel.

"Car problems?"

She recognized that voice. Lifting her head, which was beginning to throb at the temple, she saw Logan Donnelly standing beside the Nissan. His brown hair stretched back tight in that familiar ponytail. "I pretty sure it's a dead battery. Maybe you'd be good enough to, you know, give me a jump?"

Logan was pretty sure she didn't mean the same thing he was thinking. "Pop the hood and I'll take a look."

"With one hand?"

"I'll manage. If it's your battery I'm sure Nick's got a pair of jumper cables around here somewhere."

"Great," Kinsey muttered between clenched teeth as she reached down and grabbed the release for the hood. "I don't have time for this."

But Logan responded as if he had radar ears. "Must be some date you've got."

Kinsey let his words go. She didn't have the time or the inkling to set him straight. Instead she crawled out of the car, her open-toed heels clicking on the cement. Impatiently, she sucked in rapid breaths of cool, crisp ocean breeze. If she'd had the time she would've loved a long walk along the beach to calm her nerves. Indulgences like that weren't on her schedule.

The minute she stepped closer, Logan caught her fragrance, some exotic mix of jasmine and vanilla that brought to mind sinking into satin sheets. He had to pull himself back to the situation to remember all the right wires to check. Inexplicably annoyed with her—yet again, Logan spit out, "This isn't the first time you've had trouble starting the car, is it?"

"Well, no. But it usually starts even if it grinds if I'm patient enough and keep trying. Now it just clicks. The other day the dash flickered on and off a bit while I was driving. The lights dim sometimes for no reason. And I heard a whining sound just yesterday." She lifted one silky shoulder. "But it's a fourteen-year-old car. I'm sure it's the battery. If you'll just—"

"I don't think so," Logan interjected. "You'll need it tested though to make sure. Personally, I think your alternator's toast."

"Crap." She looked at her watch again for what seemed like the tenth time in as many minutes. "I've got to be at The Pointe by six-thirty. I hate to ask—"

Logan wiped his good hand on his jeans, dropped the hood back down with a slam. "No problem. Get in the truck. I'll take you."

"Really? Thanks. I'm in kind of a hurry."

"I see that. You're practically jumping out of your skin." Logan couldn't say why but he hated the guy who apparently hadn't thought enough of her to drive out to pick her up. What kind of an asshole would do that?

Once they got on the road, conversation was almost nonexistent. They drove in strained silence bordering awkwardness. It got worse when she took out her sandwich from the sack and started to nibble on it.

Logan gave her a strange look. Finally his curiosity piqued, he asked, "*Why* are you eating a sandwich if you're headed out to dinner? The Pointe's a fancy place with all kinds of delicious food. Oh, wait, don't tell me you're one of those women who won't eat in front a man for fear he'll think less of you?"

Kinsey didn't care for the derision she heard in the man's voice. "Well, if you must know, I'm hungry. Besides, what do you care anyway?"

"I don't," he snapped. "But any woman who can't be herself on a date isn't being honest, fooling everyone around her, including the guy she's dating."

"Relationship advice from a man who just went through his own messy divorce? You're unbelievable, you know that? Plus, you're just a bit full of yourself. You don't even seem to be able to let go of your own baggage." She stuffed half of her uneaten sandwich back in the bag.

Her appetite gone. "You know, I'm a nice person. But every time I get around you, you seem dead set on being an ass."

"Maybe that's because I am an ass."

"You telegraph that, Donnelly. Look, we have ten more minutes of forced time together, maybe more if you get pulled over by Dan Garver for speeding. The speed limit through here is fifty, by the way."

Logan glanced at the speedometer, noted it read sixty-five. He eased off the gas.

"I vote we either not talk to each other the rest of the way, or we think of something civil to discuss."

"Silence is fine by me."

"I'm not surprised. Well, I for one vote civil conversation."

"Miss Bubbly Personality would. Fine, pick a topic."

"After being here a couple of days, how do you like the town so far?"

"Settling in. I'm sure you know how that feels."

"I do. A new place takes some getting used to. It's a little scary starting over. Do you feel that way?"

"It took me a while to make up my mind." He wouldn't admit to all the years he'd resisted coming back here. "But once I did, it's the right move for me. So you like it here?"

"I've always wanted to live in a small town, so yes."

"Small towns aren't perfect. Remember that."

"You act as though you've lived in one before now."

That made him chuckle. "I grew up in Chastain, California. I think last I checked it had maybe a thousand people max."

"But your online bio says San Francisco."

It gave him a little kick to his ego to know she'd taken the time to look him up. "Started out there when I struck out on my own, went to design school there, but I didn't stick around long enough to graduate. After San Fran I tried L.A. for a time."

"What was Chastain like?"

"It had a nut processing plant."

"A what?"

"They shelled walnuts, roasted almonds, that kind of thing. That was the town's claim to fame." He wasn't certain what made him want to talk to her so candidly but the words seemed to roll off his tongue before he could stop them. "But my grandparents lived here."

Kinsey's mouth gaped open. "In Pelican Pointe?"

"Yeah."

"I didn't know that." In fact, not a single other soul in town had mentioned it to her. "So you're a California native who has come back? Did you come here as a boy to visit your grandparents?"

"Oh yeah. Summers mostly. My parents liked to dump my sister and me in Pelican Pointe whenever they could under the guise of working on their marriage, which a miracle worker couldn't have fixed."

So he'd kept that little tidbit to himself, which made Kinsey wonder what else he was holding back. "Ah. So you already know the townspeople here?"

"Not at all. I was a kid last time I was here. Fifteen to be exact. I remember playing sandlot ball with Brent and Ethan Cody though whenever they'd come over from Santa Cruz to visit their grandmother. I think her name was a season. Autumn, that's it. Autumn Lassiter." The tone of his voice indicated it was anything but a rosy walk down memory lane. But just when she thought of a couple of other questions, by that time, Logan pulled the pickup next to the curb in front of the restaurant. "Here you go." He tapped the clock on the dash. "With a few minutes to spare."

She took a deep breath and opened the door. "Thanks. I really appreciate the ride, Donnelly."

The door slammed and she was gone.

He sat there for a couple of minutes, tapping the steering wheel, wondering why the hell he'd turned into such a Chatty Cathy. What was wrong with him? Why did he resent the fact Kinsey Wyatt had a date this evening while he...?

In a huff, he shoved the gear shift into Drive, stepped on the accelerator to turn the truck into a U-turn in the middle of Ocean Street and headed back to a Friday night alone.

With two minutes to spare, Kinsey walked through the front door of The Pointe. That glass of red wine to calm her nerves would have to wait until she took her break.

Perry spotted her immediately. "I wasn't sure you were going to show."

"Sorry, I got hung up. But I'm here and ready to go."

He tilted his head, looked her up and down wearing the little black dress with its scoop neckline and flare skirt. "If I were straight I'd hit on you in heartbeat. As it is, you'll get plenty of tips. Now move your butt to the bar." He pointed a finger. "Do not pass Go. Grab that glass of wine, take it with you. You look like you could use it because you're on in two minutes."

Unlike Kinsey, surrounded by noise and chatter, Logan spent his evening in relative solitude. That is once he finished sharing pot roast with the Harrises, the Fostwicks, the Lathams, and the Whitney sisters.

He had to admit Hutton was a kick to be around. The miniature chatter box sort of reminded Logan of what Kinsey Wyatt must have been like at that age. Baby Scott was just as entertaining with his attempts at imitating his older sister.

Logan listened, until once again, just as it had the night before, the talk around the table turned to children. It didn't take a genius to figure out Ben and Sheryl Latham missed their own three kids back in San Jose. While Nick and Jordan had their hands full making sure the newlyweds and Kay and Olivia got everything they needed, the Lathams doted on Hutton and Scott.

Amid all the racket, Logan found himself missing the one person who had tried to befriend him, the one person he'd been pushing away ever since he'd first laid eyes on her.

When the meal was done, Logan quietly excused himself to head outside. He needed a walk along the cliffs to clear his head. But ultimately where he ended up was the same spot he'd spent with Kinsey back on the sandy stretch of beach down at the cove.

The waves, gentle and constant, both soothed and troubled him. Just that afternoon Nick had offered him the use of a longboard. Maybe he'd take him up on it. How long had it been since he'd slapped a board in the water anyway? Wasn't surfing for carefree kids on lazy summer days with too much time on their hands and a lifetime ahead of them?

Those days had long since slipped away. Didn't he know for certain there were some kids that would never grow old or have the luxury of a future?

Surfing brought back painful memories, memories of happier times, memories he didn't need right now clouding his head.

He would be wise to remember that pain, because he couldn't very well let his guard down now.

Later that night Logan dreamed he had his arms curled around Kinsey as they lay in bed, tangled in rumpled sheets. Her hair smelled like rain and spring. He could feel her warm breath make his skin tingle. He touched a silky shoulder and felt her body snuggle further into his. Her long legs locked around him…

Something roused him from sleep.

Feeling like a junior high kid who'd just experienced his first wet dream, Logan saw the man standing at the foot of his bed again. As if he'd been caught in some carnal act, Logan snapped, "What the hell do you want from me?"

"Megan wants you to find her. Are you ready to accept help?"

"Don't say her name! You have no right to say her name."

"Then you let me know when you're ready to listen."

Before Logan could react, the man was no longer there. Running a shaky hand through his hair, Logan mumbled, "This place is nuts."

Chapter Eight

Kinsey's alarm went off way too early. She rolled over to shut off the annoying bleep, bleep, bleep coming from the clock radio on the nightstand. Six-thirty.

She'd fallen into bed less than six hours earlier when Perry had dropped her off around midnight. Now, she crawled out of the sheets to grab a much-needed wake-up shower. As the water did its job to wake her up, she decided she needed to clear her head before putting back on a uniform.

A brisk walk around the grounds was just the ticket.

She put on sweat pants and a top, grabbed a bottle of water from the stash she kept in her room, and slipped down the back staircase.

Once outside she made her way through the quad, following the fragrant pathway past flowers and shrubs heavy with the blossoms of May. For a city girl, who had lived her entire life in cramped apartments with narrow hallways and smelly streets, the setting at the B & B provided a scene she'd only dreamed about. Promise Cove was like a snapshot come to life from the pages of *Country Living* magazine. Or maybe a picture postcard one might pick up on the rack inside Murphy's Market.

When the footpath opened up to the wide space of trees and shrubs, she headed out along the cliffs as the sun barely inched its way on the horizon to the east. The brilliant orange sky had her looking upward and the minute she glanced back down, Scott Phillips met her pace stride for stride.

"You're out and about early today."

"I'll be cooped up for eight hours inside. Now's my only chance to take advantage of this." She swung her arms out wide. "It's so beautiful here, so peaceful. I can understand why you don't like the idea of ever leaving it."

Scott smiled in that way of his as if he knew a secret no one else knew. "So you won't let anyone run you off?"

"No! It might be different from what I'm used to, but I'm determined to make a go of it here. If I wasn't I wouldn't be looking at places to live."

"About that, Jordan and Nick think they have a solution."

"She mentioned that last night. I haven't had time to ask her about it."

"I'm glad to see you aren't letting Aaron's low salary put a ding in your determination. It'll work out, Kinsey. It all will. You'll see. You've got what it takes to make it as a lawyer here. Don't let anyone tell you different."

"How do you know that? I could be the worst one on record."

"Nah, you have too much heart for that, Kinsey. And there are certain people here that will need your energy and your expertise. Wait and see."

She automatically checked the time on her watch, afraid she'd be late. "I gotta get to work soon though."

"There's still time. You did good last night, Kinsey. As a matter of fact, you play piano beautifully. People all over town are talking about the smart and savvy attorney that's also a fine musician."

"Oh Scott. They are not. After they see me check groceries and pound on a piano, I'll be lucky if they trust me enough to make *copies* of their will let alone *write* one."

"Overall, this town is a good little place to live. But even I know that sometimes the people in it need a good swift kick in their backside to accept newcomers. Be patient with some of them. They resist a changing of the guard. But there's a new girl in town."

She gave him a quick smile. "Thanks. I guess I needed to hear that right about now. My confidence is a little on the low side lately." She glanced at her watch again. "But right now I need to grab something to eat and then beg a ride from Jordan to take me into town."

"Jordan's happy to get you there. Nick can take care of the kids."

When she started walking back, she turned, saw him still standing in the same spot. Kinsey stopped as if she'd just thought of something else. "You were there, weren't you? At The Pointe last night, looking out for me? I felt— a presence. You should've moved a glass or something. Sam Wheat would have."

"Maybe I'll work on that. Did Donnelly renege on his bet?"

She shook her head. "He paid up the next day. Nice job by the way."

Grinning widely, Scott gloated, "It's one of the perks I never tire of getting to use."

"Do you think he'll ever come around? He dropped me off at work last night and seemed troubled, even sulky."

"That pretty much nails the guy's attitude."

"He's keeping something back, isn't he?"

"Patience, Kinsey. The man needs a ton of it from the people around him."

Kinsey walked through the back door to see Jordan busy at the kitchen counter. The same spot where she'd left her the night before.

"The Isaksens checked out last night," Jordan announced as she filled a sippy cup with milk for her son. Baby Scott sat in his high chair gleefully pounding a spoon against the plastic tray. With each smack Scott seemed to get a kick out of the clamor.

"It was just a matter of time before they left. They were still grumbling about asking for a refund yesterday at breakfast," Kinsey revealed, taking a seat on one of the bar stools.

"Which they got," Nick offered. "It was worth it to stop the complaints."

"I'm sorry. It's my fault. If I hadn't brought the whole thing up they would be none the wiser. Who knew they would be so upset they'd want their money back?"

"I got the impression they wanted an excuse for a free stay," Jordan disclosed. "I overheard them talking outside at one of the tables where they took their lunch yesterday. It happens in this business." Jordan turned to Nick. "Do you want me to tell her about the apartment?"

"Go ahead," Nick said.

"What apartment? There are no apartments in Pelican Pointe."

Nick grinned. "Oh I don't know there's at least one. As it happens it's vacant."

"Really? Where?"

"Studio living at its finest," Jordan teased. "The apartment over the garage. We affectionately call it Studio 45. You know, the reverse of 54."

"Private joke," Nick declared. "I lived there when I first came to Pelican Pointe. As a matter of fact, so did Hayden."

"Scott said…" Kinsey stopped short.

Nick exchanged glances with Jordan.

"Doesn't matter, I'll take it," Kinsey said flatly.

"Don't you want to check it out first?" Jordan asked.

"If it's good enough for Hayden, it's good enough for me. I am curious about it though. When can I look at it?"

"It's across the courtyard. It won't take but five minutes. Run over there and check it out. The door's unlocked."

Kinsey hopped down off the stool, danced in place. "I'm sorry to have to ask but I need a ride—"

"I'll take you into work," Jordan offered. "Logan mentioned to Nick your car wouldn't start. Now go check out your new digs. On the drive into town, maybe we can come up with a new décor. Pick a color and we'll slap some paint on the walls."

"Really? That sounds fantastic. What *is* the rent though?" Kinsey asked, prepared to negotiate a deal.

Nick threw out an incredibly low number.

"That's…unbelievable. Are you doing this because my car conked out?"

"We're doing this because we don't want you getting frustrated and heading back to the Bay area."

Kinsey's eyes got bleary as she dashed over to hug Jordan. "How can I ever thank you both for helping me?"

"You haven't seen the place yet," Nick said.

"It doesn't matter. I love it already."

Once Kinsey walked through those double doors at Murphy's Market, she wore her store uniform with an air of pride. Whether or not it was Scott's influence, she didn't know. Or it might've been Jordan's pep talk on the drive into town. Her hostess had almost echoed Scott's words verbatim. Give the town time. Give the people a chance to accept her. Things would work out.

She'd known when she'd packed up her stuff back in San Francisco that it wouldn't be easy establishing herself in a new place. But she'd hoped and she'd dreamed of starting over. While she certainly didn't plan on failure here, she had to believe that they were all correct. Scott and Jordan and Nick, even Hartley, all seemed to agree it just took time.

Kinsey Wyatt was more than willing to give the town the time it needed. After all, she had a place to live now. With her extra income, she would have more money coming in. She didn't want to head back to the Bay. She wanted to be a part of bringing the town back from the dead. Oddly, she wanted to see her new little town thrive.

But who was she kidding? Those dreams of making it as lawyer might have been a little too fancy for someone who didn't really have a conventional law degree. With some resignation Kinsey realized she might've been deluding herself. At some point, she might have to consider that maybe checking groceries is all she was ever meant to do. Maybe all this time she'd been trying to reach too high. Maybe her expectations were just a little too grandiose.

If all she had to offer Pelican Pointe was a cashier at the store, she'd have to be happy with that.

After all, there wasn't a thing wrong with working hard to earn a living, or wearing a uniform to do it.

This one was pretty simple in its design. Murphy had issued her a green apron with the store logo to be worn over a white pocket shirt embroidered with the logo on the left side. Murphy also provided a pair of khaki pants. She looked like a mannequin on display right out of the Gap store.

One thing she learned within the first hour though. The townspeople were curious about her. Working at the only grocery store in town she got to meet the residents, one by one. In Kinsey's lane alone it soon became apparent the line stretched out longer and longer. They pretty much all wanted to know the same thing. By ten o'clock she'd answered the same question more than two dozen times. Why had the newly hired lawyer already given up on her job with Aaron Hartley to run the checkout stand at Murphy's Market?

At this rate it was only a matter of hours before one of them ran back to Aaron, in Paul Revere mode carrying the news about her extracurricular weekend activity. At least one of them.

"Maybe with the next round of curiosity seekers, I should make an announcement," Murphy suggested, once the store had cleared out from the first wave. He stood in front of the bank of windows facing Main Street and scratched his chin in amazement. "I can't believe everyone in town ran out of milk at the same time this morning."

"How on earth did they know I was here?"

A sheepish look crossed Murphy's face. "I guess I might've mentioned to a few people I'd snagged an experienced cashier. Look, you stepped into this without me having to train you. That's a big deal for this old grocer. Next batch of nosy busybodies, and I'll set them straight."

"Do you think it will do any good?"

"It might. It couldn't hurt," Murphy said with a shrug.

About that time another group walked through the double doors. All seemed to gawk in the direction of Kinsey.

She sighed and glanced over at Murphy. "I think you should. This is fairly ridiculous."

Murphy walked to the little customer service counter in front of the store. He picked up a microphone. Over the intercom, Kinsey heard the words, "Now listen up, people. All of you damn well know I'm short-handed here since Alma Parker high-tailed it out of town with Clive Chester leaving me high and dry for a second cashier. For the time being, Kinsey has graciously agreed to help me out. Kinsey Wyatt is still very much employed as an attorney at Aaron Hartley's law office. Now, if you don't want to have to stand in a long line to check out at one check stand every time you come into shop, I suggest you refrain from asking her a bunch of stupid questions and start treating Kinsey with a little more respect. Try acting a whole lot nicer than you have been. Capiche?"

There was some grumbling at first. Some muttered how Murphy was a damn fool for taking it upon himself to make a big deal out of their natural curiosity. But not long afterward, the questions slowly ground to a halt as people went about their shopping or left the store without purchasing a single item.

By the time Logan came down for breakfast, it was almost nine. He had the dining room to himself, which he knew was a rarity with so many guests for the weekend. Jordan brought him a cheesy, bacon-filled omelet with a mug of vanilla bean coffee.

"I guess I slept late. Everyone seems to be gone already."

"Ben and Sheryl went on a hike since this is their last day. The honeymooners are down at the cove sunbathing. And the Whitney sisters seemed to have a thing for the area's flora and fauna. They've gone wild with their camera phone." She snickered before going on, "There's no time schedule here, Logan. If you wanted to sleep till eleven, I'd still fix you something to eat when you got up. That's the beauty of running and staying at a B & B. Personal service."

"I guess after her date, Kinsey is sleeping in, too."

Jordan eyed Logan, studied his face. "Kinsey was up at first light. She's in town. Working."

"On a Saturday? She's a dedicated lawyer, I'll give her that. How'd she get into town anyway? Her car needs an alternator."

"I dropped her off at Murphy's Market. She has a weekend job there checking groceries. Today's her first day."

Logan stopped chewing and stared at Jordan. "Checking groceries? Why?"

Jordan stared at the renowned artist. Were there really people who lived in an alternate universe, who didn't realize the real world sometimes involved making ends meet anyway they could? It hadn't been that long since Jordan had been a member of the club. Did Logan simply not understand how money problems could wedge into real life, cripple your self-confidence and leave you depressed? "Why does anyone get a job? I assume Kinsey needs the extra income to fatten her bank account. I do know her mother had a lengthy bout with cancer, died last year from it. I think Kinsey has medical bills to pay off.

And it seems Hartley didn't crack open his wallet very far when he offered her the job here."

"She mentioned her mother died. If she's having money problems, it's a damn shame about her car."

"It's never a good time to have expensive car repairs pop up." Jordan sighed. She and Nick may have solved Kinsey's housing problem, but the car thing was another matter entirely. She'd have to talk to Wally and see if he'd consider working a discount for her. Jordan didn't want to see Kinsey unhappy after only three weeks in town.

"Well, all I know is she had a hot date last night. I dropped her off at The Pointe at six-thirty to meet up with some guy. Least he could've done was come out here to pick her up. Why are women always attracted to that kind of rat?"

Jordan hadn't known Kinsey's destination. But since she didn't know why Kinsey had spent her Friday night at The Pointe, Jordan wasn't going to elaborate. It wasn't like Kinsey to evade, but last night the woman had done just that. Of course, Kinsey was entitled to her privacy. "What makes you think she had a date?" Jordan finally asked.

"Are you kidding? She was dressed to the nines when she left out of here. Perfume, heels, the hair up on her head twisted in some sophisticated knot. And that little black dress said first date to me."

"Hmm. The Pointe? Logan, did she actually say she had a date?"

Logan frowned. Had she? "Not in so many words but she acted like she did. Why else would a woman dress like that?"

"Maybe she had dinner with a new client."

"Some client. I think I should switch lawyers. My attorney sure never went to the trouble to look like that for a meeting. Mine's short, balding, and pushing fifty."

"I'm sure Kinsey would consider taking you on as a new client," Jordan joked.

"Something to think about," Logan muttered as he began to replay the trip last night into town. If she'd been going to dinner, why then, had she eaten on the trip there? She couldn't be waitressing in that black dress. Or could she?

"Have you ever eaten at The Pointe?" He asked Jordan.

"Sure."

"What does the wait staff wear?"

"Black pants and a white shirt with a black apron. Why?"

"Then it had to be a date because she damned sure wasn't going there to wait tables in that get-up."

Chapter Nine

That afternoon when four-thirty rolled around, Kinsey punched out with two hours to kill. Since she didn't have a car to make it back to the B & B, she decided it was just as well after what had happened last night when she'd tried to make a quick turnaround only to get caught answering a dozen questions.

That's why she'd brought a change of clothes with her, an emerald green dress with a V neck and three-quarter sleeves, heels to match, a leftover from her mother's eighties wardrobe. The outfit was a tad retro but then she thought it might work for the older dinner crowd. At least she wouldn't risk running late again. Murphy knew about her third job and had agreed to let her come back as time got closer to use the ladies room to change clothes. Kinsey just had to find something to do to fill two hours.

But first she had to talk to Wally Pierce at the gas station about her Nissan. She started walking—and thinking.

Last night, once she'd started playing the nerves had vanished. She was almost as surprised as most of Perry Altman's diners had been. Some she had recognized. Like the veterinarian, Bran Sullivan, and his wife, Joy. They had been having dinner with their daughter, Donna, and her husband Ricky Oden. Ricky played guitar and mandolin in his own bluegrass band, *Blue Skies*. As if in a show of support, the fellow musician had made a point to give her a thumbs-up right before dropping what looked like a twenty dollar bill into her tip jar.

Marabelle Crawford and her sister, Ina, who had to both be nearing the sunny side of eighty, had done the same, albeit in a much smaller denomination. But it was the gesture that touched Kinsey the most.

After her first number ended, it had embarrassed Kinsey that Wade Hawkins, the retired history professor with a wild head of white hair, had put down his fork to applaud and kept doing so until others had followed his lead.

Reverend Whitcomb and his wife, Dottie, had made a point to slip her a note that she'd be welcome at the Community Church anytime to play backup piano for Etta Mae Searcy, who'd had the job for at least a quarter of a century.

Now that she thought about it, as the evening had progressed, the diners seemed to linger longer. Whether it was her playing or simply kicking back to celebrate the end of the week, they had ordered second bottles of wine, stayed to indulge in dessert, and linger over their conversation.

As she went back over everything from last night, she decided Scott had been right. So had Jordan. Kinsey just had to give people time to get to know her.

By the time she reached Wally's her attitude was so much better, she sailed into the little office where Lilly, Wally's wife of almost a year, sat behind the counter. The previous June, Lilly had married Wally Pierce, the service station owner and the best mechanic around. Wally had even adopted Lilly's kids, Kyra and Joey.

"Hi," Lilly said in greeting. "How's it going, Kinsey? How was your first day at Murphy's?"

"Hi, Lilly." Kinsey went into a detailed account of her first hour on the job and the curious townspeople. When she got to the part where Murphy had used the intercom for his announcement, Lilly cracked up.

"Yay, Murphy!" Lilly exclaimed. "But if you're here about your car, Wally hasn't had a chance to get to it yet. He's been swamped."

"What are you talking about? I need Wally to tow it into town. My car wouldn't start up last night. It probably just needs a new battery or wires or something. Even though, Donnelly the great sculptor, thinks it's the carburetor." Kinsey rolled her eyes.

"Logan's the one who called Wally out to Promise Cove. Wally towed it here this morning around ten. Logan said it was the alternator. Wally seems to think he's right."

"My car's here? Donnelly already called Wally?"

"Yep. Couldn't have fixed it anyway though, Kinsey. We had to order parts from Santa Cruz. Should be delivered first thing Monday. Your car's on the lift now though, will stay there over the weekend. But like I said, Wally got sidetracked with one of the farm trucks for Cord Bennett's crew. They need it for deliveries ASAP."

Kinsey did several quick calculations in her head before asking, "How much does an alternator run?"

Lilly tossed out an amount.

"Phew! With my new jobs, I can handle that. I'm still trying to understand why Donnelly took it upon himself to call Wally though." She wasn't sure if she should be grateful or pissed. "That man's only been here four days and is already *so* infuriating to deal with, especially getting past that superior attitude he has. Have you noticed his habit of talking down to people?"

"Hmm, sounds like to me he's trying to do a nice thing maybe to make up for it."

Was it just that simple, Kinsey wondered? She sighed. "I guess I'm showing my bitchy side because I didn't get much sleep last night. But who knew the man even possessed a nice side? Did you know he barely says a word at dinner? He just sits there scowling at everyone."

"I thought you said he talks down to everybody? If he just sits there and doesn't say anything how does he do that?"

"Whose side are you on anyway?" Kinsey snapped in a huff. She blew out a breath. "I am being bitchy, aren't I? Logan Donnelly did a nice thing and I'm giving him a hard time."

Lilly snickered. "The only thing I noticed about the man is that he's fairly gorgeous."

"Just because he's gorgeous doesn't mean he should get a pass when he's a jerk."

"Of course not but…those green eyes of his and that sexy hair would be enough if it was just those two things. But the guy looks like he's been working out." Lilly fanned her face. "He's better looking in person than the photo on his website."

"Tell me, does hubby of less than a year know you routinely ogle sexy men with long hair?"

"I'm married, not dead," Lilly said by way of explanation. "Besides, who doesn't look at a hunk like Logan? Because I happen to be one of those women who adore long hair on men, I look. Sue me. And Logan Donnelly has a mane of hair to die for. Can I help it if I snagged the only other man in town with long, sexy hair?"

Kinsey harrumphed. "Wally *is* hot. I noticed that right off. He has that whole surfer look going for him, too." She sighed again just thinking how long it had been since she'd last had sex. She thought it was right after her mother died. "So Logan came into town? You saw him earlier?"

"He came in about two-thirty, talked to Wally for a bit about your car. They had their heads buried under the hood. I remember because it was the same time Donna Oden stopped in for gas. Donna took her sweet time watching Logan mill around your car. Anyway, Donna let me know you wowed everyone at The Pointe last night."

"I don't know about that but Perry was very pleased because he got a booking for Abby's wedding in June, Abby Pointer not Abby Anderson. Right now, Perry's walking on air pretty much as high as Abby is at the prospect of such a huge event. He's sure the entire town will turn out for it. Anyway, it seems when Paul Bonner got back from Afghanistan he finally popped the question to Abby."

"Oh that is so sweet. Abby and Paul should make their own little red-haired Colleen a flower girl," Lilly suggested.

"I think that's the plan."

"See, things are already looking up for you, Kinsey. There will be other special events, too, an opportunity to make extra cash. Many of us around town have taken the pledge to look out for our own, help each other out more."

"Jordan said the same thing. She and Nick, Murphy, too, are committed." But as she thought about that statement, Kinsey wondered about Logan. Would the man ever allow anyone to look out for *him*?

Saturday night Logan was due to meet with the Lighthouse Preservation Commission for dinner at The Pointe. The representatives intended to bring him up to speed on what exactly he needed to do to bring the lighthouse back to the way it had looked in the beginning.

Even though Logan had pored through massive amounts of old documents, including photographs, spent hours researching everything he could on the Smuggler's Bay project, he had a pretty good idea what he needed to do. But it wouldn't hurt to keep an open mind. Besides, he thought it best to form a partnership of sorts with the Commission. Their expertise on historical matters would be invaluable. Staying in their good graces, so to speak, would get him closer to his goal to accomplish what he wanted.

That's why he'd agreed to sit down over dinner, meet with them, and discuss his plans in detail.

Once Logan walked inside the lobby at the restaurant, he spotted two men, both holding fat briefcases. Logan knew John Norris and Dan Sullivan on site by their descriptions they'd given him in the emails they'd exchanged over the past three months. John, the older of the two, had thinning black hair graying at the temples and looked to be in his late fifties, while Dan was a good twenty years younger. That might be why Dan came across as glib, always quick with a joke and not nearly as staid as his counterpart. Logan had been able to tell that much about both men from their back and forth online banter.

"Logan Donnelly, I'd know that face from the Internet," John said, offering his hand in greeting.

"And you're John Norris. Good of you to drive all this way. I appreciate it. You, too, Dan."

"No problem. We've both been here several times before on trips to check out the lighthouse. We were ecstatic to learn someone had finally recognized its potential and finally snapped it up. Plus, it gave us an excuse to head here. Perry Altman runs a quality establishment," John added. "I always stuff myself."

"Don't know about you guys but I've been craving the lobster for a hundred miles," Dan said about the same time Jolene picked up menus to direct them to their table.

Behind the Steinway, Kinsey spotted Logan sit down with two men in the dining room, watched as Perry personally came over to fuss over the trio. From three tables away she could hear Perry pandering to Logan by telling him what a big fan he was of the man's work.

Typical, she thought, as she went into her renditions of Chopin's *Nocturnes*. About that time, the music must have caught Logan's attention because he looked over in the direction of the piano—and did a double-take.

Kinsey saw his jaw drop open, stay that way until one of the men he was sitting with said something to him. When he leaned to his right to reply, she noted his eyes were still on her.

Logan couldn't stop staring at Kinsey, or the green dress she wore with the simple matching velvet choker wrapped around her sexy throat. She'd twisted up her caramel hair again in a knot similar to the way it had been last night, but this time soft wisps curled around her face and neck. He found himself itching to remove those pins holding it all up. He purposely had to focus on the lilting notes coming from the piano and not on her long legs which ended in matching opened-toed pumps. This time, her toenails glittered green. No woman's feet had ever looked so inviting.

Logan scrubbed his good hand over his face. Jesus, he needed to muzzle on his libido. After several long seconds, his two dinner companions followed Logan's eyes to the woman.

"Wow, she plays really well. She wasn't here the last time I dined at The Pointe. I'd remember," John commented.

"Hey Perry," Dan said, motioning for the owner to come back over. "Who's the good-looking piano player?"

But Logan didn't wait for Perry to answer. "That's Kinsey Wyatt. And she's supposedly an attorney by day." He was beginning to wonder if that were true. The woman looked perfectly at ease letting loose her passion for Chopin's weeping tempo.

"Really? I think I might need the services of a lawyer before I leave town," Dan cracked as he patted his own chest.

Out of the corner of his eye, Logan continued to watch the way Kinsey's long slim fingers gracefully moved over the keys. Resentment built in him. She could have simply shared this with him last night but for some reason had chosen not to. But it wasn't just that. Logan had prepared for this meeting with John and Dan for months. Now in the span of a few minutes, all his effort had been for nothing because he struggled to get his attention *off* Kinsey Wyatt. Why did the woman pull at him so? And why did he keep letting her?

When their food arrived, Logan forced Kinsey into the background and did his best to focus on the list of recommendations from John and Dan, things about the lighthouse he hadn't even considered. The Commission already had a team in place that specialized in the type of masonry work the lighthouse required. If he wanted the best, Logan should consider bringing them onboard. The crew had finished a similar project in Oregon two weeks earlier and was available for immediate assignment.

It sounded good to Logan. After the three men spent another hour going over all the details that would work best on the outside of the lighthouse, the ironwork, the craftsmanship it would take, after comparing notes on the history they had painstakingly dug up online, Logan watched John and Dan pack up their notes to leave.

Logan headed to the bar, ordered a beer and sat there waiting for Kinsey to take her break. But to his surprise for the next several hours, the woman didn't so much as budge to go to the bathroom. Stubbornly, he decided if he had to, he'd wait for the restaurant to close. Because he intended to stick until Kinsey got off work.

He told himself he wanted to make sure she had a way back to Promise Cove. But it wasn't the truth. While he might not want to leave her without a ride—even though she had certainly found her own way back to the B & B the previous night without him—they needed to clear the air.

Around eleven-fifteen the place started to empty out. Busboys began to clear and stack dishes, wipe down tables. The wait staff began to tally their tips. Kinsey stood up and stretched her back. One glance at her tip jar and she knew it had been another good night. As she counted out her money, minus the cut she gave the wait staff, she made a mad dash to the restroom. To get there she had to go through the bar area. Since only the die-hards lingered, it wasn't difficult to spot Logan sitting by himself at a pub table nursing what looked like a soft drink. She quickly slipped into the bathroom and was back in ten minutes, fresh lipstick in place. It was time to deal with Mr. Donnelly.

"So you had my car towed, did you?" Kinsey declared, hands on her hips.

He'd wondered if Kinsey meant to avoid him since he'd watched her duck into the ladies' room. But here she was looking bright as a California poppy, standing right in front of him as if ready to do battle. That was fine by him. "Why did you let me think you had a date last night? Why didn't you just tell me you played piano here?"

Kinsey pulled out a chair and sat down. "You seemed to have it all figured out so—I thought—" She lifted a shoulder. "Why burst your bubble? By the way, thanks for taking the initiative to call Wally. I didn't get to the car thing until after I got off work late afternoonish." She grinned. "Which meant Wally probably wouldn't have ordered the parts until Monday. This way, I get to pick it up sometime late morning. Thank you."

Even though he wondered if she had the cash to pay for the repairs, he said nothing. "I thought you might be mad."

"I was—for about five minutes—then it occurred to me you did something nice. Besides, Lilly sort of reminded me that it's one of the perks of small towns. We should do nice things for each other more often."

About that time Perry came over. "I hate to break up this cozy little scene and shoo you two out of here, but we're closed. Everyone's ready to go home. We're all just exhausted. It's been a busy night." He pointed a finger at Logan. "Don't forget what you promised me. But if you do anything to hurt my piano player, I know people that will hunt you down and stalk you at art shows, even leave bad reviews for your work under all manner of unknown socks you'll never be able to trace. Never mess with my restaurant or my piano player. Now scoot, both of you. Unless of course this handsome guy doesn't intend to offer you a ride back to Promise Cove?" Perry lifted a brow in question.

"I'll see she gets home," Logan replied.

"Thanks," Kinsey piped up. "I appreciate it."

"Hear that. Now get out of here and go someplace dark and romantic to do whatever it is young people do on such a beautiful moonlit night. Just don't do anything I wouldn't do." He winked as he led them out to the lobby and the double front doors.

The minute they stepped outside, Logan pointed to his truck. "I'm parked over here." He watched as Kinsey slipped off her shoes.

After being cooped up for hours, she drew in deep breaths of the cool night air, and said, "Perry's right, it *is* a gorgeous evening."

When she looked up at him, once again Logan had to fight that urge to run his fingers through all that hair.

"Wait! Do you hear that? You can hear the surf from this spot."

Just as she'd done when they'd walked down to the cove a couple of days earlier, Kinsey all but skipped across the dark lot. He knew she'd gotten up very early that morning. She'd stood on her feet at Murphy's Market for eight hours only to clock out there and put in another five more hours at the restaurant. Granted, she'd been sitting on her butt, but it still took a lot of energy to keep up the oomph enough to play like she did. And yet, to Logan she didn't seem ready to fade. Kinsey, the livewire, reminded him of a Barbie version of the Energizer Bunny.

Once they got on the road, Logan muted the ear-splitting Wasting Arrows CD he'd been listening to on the drive into town so they could have a conversation.

"What did Perry mean back there when he said you promised him something?"

"As soon as I'm out of this." Logan held up his cast. "As soon as I'm able to start to work again, Perry wants to put on a show of my latest work in the gallery he owns in Santa Cruz."

"I didn't even know Perry owned a gallery in Santa Cruz. That's fantastic."

"I'll have to contact my agent, make sure Valerie sees to all the details."

"You don't seem…too excited about it. You know, Perry Altman didn't live here when you were a boy, Logan," she pointed out.

"I'm aware of that," he uttered. "But since I only have a few pieces on hand, that isn't enough for a show. There's a fair amount of pressure in getting work done and ready to exhibit. And I've got a lot on my plate right now. It could be next spring or beyond before I get to work again."

"For an artist that must...I don't know, cause you a certain amount of heartache when you can't create."

That surprised him. Not many people understood that the creative process could be long and arduous but when it was taken away it left an emptiness inside that couldn't be filled or replaced with anything else but that specific outlet.

"How did you hurt it, your hand?"

"It's a long story. Could we talk about something else?"

"Sure. I've read about temperamental artists and their moods. Never met one though until you, although I did know a guy in high school who went on to be a screenwriter."

"Maybe you should enlighten me about moods."

"I'm sorry you're so unhappy here, Logan. I read on the Internet about your recent divorce. You must miss her," Kinsey said softly.

Logan took his eyes off the road long enough to give her a long hard look. "Who? My ex-wife? Are you nuts? I almost allowed that succubus to drain my creativity. I almost lost my heart and soul to that witch."

"Wow! Bitter much? But Fiona Perez is so...beautiful. All those photos online of the both of you—"

"Showed a very troubled couple," Logan finished. "And those were the good days. What Fiona Perez excelled at was lying and manipulation. She could teach a course in how both are done to perfection."

"I see."

"And?"

"It explains why you spend much of your time putting up a wall so that the outside world doesn't see how unhappy you are about things or how much you're hurting."

"I've got news for you, I'm over Fiona Perez."

"I wasn't talking about Fiona."

"Psychoanalyzing me after four days is a little presumptive on your part, don't you think? We've had what, three conversations? You know nothing about me except what a million other people have read on some professional website."

"Right. That's my point. People know what you want them to know but nothing substantive or true."

"What's that supposed to mean?"

"I didn't know you once lived in Pelican Pointe. I don't think anyone knows that. You keep things close to the vest, hoping no one gets to the real Logan Donnelly."

"Look, we all didn't grow up cheery and bubbly like Kinsey Wyatt."

"Boy, are you way off. You're entitled to your privacy. Everyone is. But you do not have to yell at me to get your point across. It's unnecessary. There's not a thing wrong with my ears."

He puffed out a breath. "You're right. For a long time it seemed like I was on the receiving end of shouting matches so often that yelling and screaming in public—fighting over the least little thing—has become a bad habit. It takes a while to leave that behavior in the dust, to remember normal people don't usually act like that. But then normal wasn't in Fiona's vocabulary. I admit to picking up some other bad habits along the way. Self-preservation, I guess. It will take some time to get back to myself."

"Was it really that bad?"

"Worse. I'm trying to put a pretty spin on it here. Weren't you ever in love with someone or thought you were and then realized too late you'd hooked up with a very nasty person?"

"Not really. Unless you count tenth grade when I thought I'd fallen in love with Jimmy Trammell only to find out he was sneaking around with Beth Thurman every chance he got behind my back."

"Are you always so happy?"

"What's wrong with happy? Just because I don't snap at everyone around me doesn't mean I don't have my fair share of problems."

He recalled the conversation at breakfast with Jordan. "You're right," he muttered as he took the turn into Promise Cove.

"What was that?" She cupped her ear. "Say that a little louder."

"Kinsey Wyatt, smartass extraordinaire, who knew?"

"I'm a woman with many talents."

"I've noticed. And secretive."

"Says the man who refuses to talk about his past."

After bringing the pickup to a full stop, Logan shut off the engine. They sat there for a couple of minutes in the quiet. Finally he turned to her and said, "I've been combative with a lot of people lately. You shouldn't take it personally. The breakup with Fiona was fairly public. It played out in the press and took its toll. Needless to say, I was glad to board that plane back in Rome and leave Fiona's influence behind. I'm determined the past is over and done with, a past I'll never repeat. I'll never make the mistake of marrying again. Ever."

"Why did you come back to Pelican Pointe, Logan? Does it have anything to do with Liam Donnelly?" When his jaw dropped, she was fairly certain she was onto something. "I found the name of the architect who designed the lighthouse online. Is that why you came back?" Her question was met with silence. "Maybe if you trusted someone enough to talk about it—"

"Do I look like I want to—?"

Without letting him finish, she slid her feet back into her shoes. She opened the door and climbed out of the truck without a word. Resisting the urge to slam it shut, because the lateness of the hour and the noise would most likely wake up a few of the guests sleeping inside, she gave the door a light shove to close it.

Behind the wheel, Logan scrubbed a hand over his face. This had to stop. Even he was getting fed up with his defensive demeanor. He crawled out of the truck. As Kinsey rounded the front of the vehicle to head inside, he grabbed her arm. "Wait. I'm sorry."

She wrenched out of his grasp. "You spend a lot of time saying that. Or haven't you noticed?"

He looked down at the ground, rubbed his forehead. When he glanced back up, he found her staring. And why wouldn't she be? Her penetrating eyes, her sensuous mouth…it hit him then. "I just realized why you drive me nuts?"

"I drive you nuts? Since when?"

"Since I've wanted to do this." Logan reached out, ran his hands through those thick wisps of hair that hung free. He removed one clip holding those long tresses in place, then another. All that golden brown tumbled into his hand. It fell around her shoulders like a veil. He took a good hold, bunched the strands up in the fingers of his one good hand. He tugged her into him. His mouth crushed hers. He felt her jangle of nerves blend with raw lust. He also felt the moment those nerves settled, and she yielded.

For Kinsey his lips and tongue were like chocolate silk. She took greedy bites. She'd known the lure of attraction. But this was like hot flame rising up inside an inferno. Because his hands were everywhere, gripping her hair, behind her neck, exploring her back, feeling her rear, the inferno ratcheted up quick as a fire bolt. Gnawing hunger grew between them. It whipped and pulled until the craving brought overwhelming need. It was that need that snapped them back to reality. They broke apart.

Lips wet, she looked up into his eyes. "For a guy with only one good hand, you still have some decent moves." But she found herself being studied like a specimen under a microscope. "What's the matter?"

Her lips were swollen from his roughness. He took hold of her chin. "I'd love to sketch this face, that pouty mouth of yours, capture those cheekbones then sculpt you in clay." His eyes changed when he noticed hers were wide with surprise. "Don't pretend you don't know how beautiful you are."

"I haven't thought about it one way or the other."

He almost wanted to believe her. "I get this cast off, will you pose for me?"

"You're serious? Sketch? I thought you were a sculptor?"

He sent her a withering stare. "I sketch a subject first before I create an armature." When he saw her blank look, he added, "A framework, especially if I'm using clay. And you would be exceptional, graceful in clay, like you were tonight at the piano."

Was this a pick-up line he used often? she wondered. She glanced at the front door of the B & B, and lowered her voice. "Look, we can't stand out here like this without waking up all the guests inside. There are kids in there. Since this morning I've got a place to live, an apartment."

He frowned. "There are no apartments in Pelican Pointe."

"That's what I said. But apparently there's a studio over the garage. I'm renting it. It's actually more like a little loft. The furniture's a bit dated." She laughed. "Well, dated as in the 70s, but I can work with it. You should see the old urn top maple bed." When she realized what she'd said, she stammered, "I...I...didn't mean you should see it. I meant you should, you know, check it out."

Logan grinned and it transformed his face. Those eyes of his went from cool green to warm, exotic jade. "If that's an invitation, I accept."

"You mean right now?"

"Why not? Like you said, we go in there we're bound to wake somebody up. Lead the way."

"You know, you aren't bad looking—when you take the time to smile."

"That's okay. You smile enough for twenty people."

They walked around the side of the house following a trail of moonlight. Mounting the stairs beside the garage, Kinsey tiptoed up the stairs trying to prevent her heels from clicking on the old wood. She found the door still unlocked. She flicked on the lights as they stepped inside. She twirled around and said, "Well, what do you think?"

With the eye of an artist, Logan surveyed the space. He noticed the bank of windows first at the back of the room on the ocean side that in daylight would let in plenty of western sun in the afternoon.

The scuffed hardwood floor had seen better days, but it shined with polish and effort. A 70ish pale green sofa sagged with the weight from the past. That piece of furniture divided the living area from the bedroom, which was really just an antique urn top Maplewood that stood sturdy and strong in the corner. Storage was scarce. A blanket box at the foot of the bed would help out, but it was the 1920's era armoire in the corner that would have to double as closet space.

An old box TV sat at an angle on a squatty two-drawer table in the opposite corner, a DVD player underneath.

There was no kitchen. One wall had a two-burner stovetop, a microwave situated on a square table top, a stingy counter with a slice of overhead cabinets, and a compact refrigerator.

A white wrought iron table and two matching chairs with Kelly green cushions were tucked under the windows, providing a place to eat as well as a view of the ocean beyond.

Logan took the time to stick his head into the bathroom. There was no tub, just a shower stall. But it had all the necessary comforts. "I like it."

"So do I. I'm going to paint the walls. I think a soothing mint green. What do you think?"

He shook his head. "You want more light, open it up some?"

"More light would be nice."

"Then go with the ripe cantaloupe color like they used in my room, a shade lighter. Have you seen it?"

"I have. It reminds me of a melting Dreamsicle." She tilted her head to study the walls again. "You're right. The softer color will brighten up the place. I want to cover that old sofa with slipcovers maybe in a dark brown."

He nodded. "Good choice. Use contrasting colors, accessorize with pillows in lighter tones."

"You're really good at this. Most men don't have a flair for decorating."

"I'd be a poor excuse for an artist if I didn't." Logan went over to the little refrigerator, stuck his nose into the box. "Hey, there's one of those miniature bottles of red wine in here and some cheese sticks. Did you even bother to eat dinner?"

"Now that you mention it, I am starving. Maybe we can find some stale crackers." She opened the cabinet and hit the mother lode. "Would you look at this?"

Logan watched as she started pulling out a small box of crackers, a mini-loaf of bread, along with peanut butter.

"There are grapes and apples in here and a jar of blackberry jam. Ever had peanut butter and jam sandwiches at midnight?"

"Are you kidding? What's a late-night meal without PB&J?"

He traced a finger around her mouth, warning her of what he planned to do before actually lowering his head to her lips. This time their tongues danced while he slowly drew out the kiss. The urge to devour was there at the fringes, that age-old desire to mate.

It felt glorious to be up against a hard male, sinking deeper with every sensation, every taste.

As if having second thoughts, he released her chin. "Kinsey?"

"What?"

"Let's chow down."

It took her a full minute to come out from the daze where his mouth had worked its magic and realized he'd switched gears. He was talking about the food.

They took their bounty, not to the table, but spread the food out like a picnic on the tapestry rectangular rug that decorated the area in front of the couch. She went back to the cabinet to dig out two jelly jars for glasses.

"Do you plan to sleep here tonight?" He asked as he poured the wine in equal amounts.

"No, my clothes are still in my room. I didn't have time to move stuff in yet. I had to be at work at eight. And I want to paint the room before moving in."

He checked his watch. "It's been a long day for you."

"I know, but it's hard to come down from the adrenaline of getting through two very different jobs in the span of twelve hours. Logan, will you do me a favor?"

"Sure."

"Will you tell me about Rome? I've always wanted to go there, see the monuments and museums, the Colosseum."

For a split second, he didn't want to go there in his head. But eyeing the look on her face that told him she was genuinely interested, he changed his mind. "Instead of Rome, how about if I tell you about the southern coast of Crete? There's this fishing village called Elounda with a little harbor nestled in between rolling hills…"

Chapter Ten

Sunday morning, Kinsey punched her time card with five minutes to spare at exactly seven-fifty-five, bleary-eyed from burning the candles from so many ends. The next time she decided to stay up until three in the morning with a globe-trotting artist who could hold his own while discussing decorating ideas, along with travel and art and politics, she needed her head examined.

Okay, so maybe they'd done more than just talk. What female could resist a guy with a clever tongue, one that could take her breath away? He also had a knack for recounting the places where he'd lived, all those exotic far off locales she'd longed to see.

It seemed Logan Donnelly had been everywhere.

Kinsey had just enough time to count out her day's cash and load the till before she started a pot of coffee brewing. Once she finished those chores, she dashed to the front door to turn the lock and let in her lone customer, waiting outside. Troy Dayton looked like he was just as groggy as she was, and still trying to wake up.

"You working on Sunday, too, Troy?"

He nodded. "It's more like a team meeting in preparation for Monday though. We're organizing the site. We start gutting the keeper's house, pulling out all the rotting wood in the morning. He's ordered supplies. He's paying me time and a half because it's a Sunday. Can you believe that?"

Kinsey's heart warmed a bit. "Anything over forty hours a week or eight hours a day is the law in California."

"But I just started working for him Thursday, only worked eighteen hours so far over the three days."

"I guess he's being generous then. What else does the job entail?"

"Well, today I'm helping him plan out what he wants done, a time schedule we stick to. He wants to go over everything before it begins for real tomorrow. A lot of his tools got here yesterday. Saturday delivery if you can believe that. We've already moved most everything to the site. It's gonna be a huge project, Kinsey. It's the biggest one I've ever worked on, that's for sure. And it'll be a job for at least the next six months." He sniffed the air. "That coffee about done?"

"I'll arm-wrestle you for the first cup," Kinsey teased as she got down to-go cups and lids.

"You look like you didn't get any sleep."

"Right backatcha. Your new boss talked my ear off last night. It was like he finally let his guard down for five minutes and opened up enough that the floodgates poured. I have to say, he isn't nearly as big of a jerk as I first thought. That was my initial impression of him. But after last night…"

"Let me be the first to start the rumor mill then. Kinsey Wyatt and Logan Donnelly." Troy wiggled his eyebrows as he picked up the pot of coffee and poured the liquid into the Styrofoam.

"Are you kidding? Me with Logan Donnelly?" Kinsey snorted and rolled her eyes. "Yeah. Right. Troy, that guy was married to one of the top models in the world— beautiful face, skinny body. Look at me. Do I look like I could compete with his memory of *that*?" Kinsey pointed out as she stirred cream into her coffee.

Kinsey was no fool. Despite their shared string of lip-locks last night, despite the way Logan had described his ex-wife only hours earlier, she'd already decided to discount all of it. She tossed all that pent-up resentment about Fiona Perez into that same bargain bin where markdowns ended up. For one thing, didn't most men fantasize about famous models? And Logan Donnelly had married one, which meant he couldn't be all that much different from the average male lusting after a hot body and a beautiful face. Just because he'd railed on his ex-wife didn't mean that if Fiona Perez showed up in Pelican Pointe today, the man wouldn't jump at the chance at getting back together with a woman like that.

No, the two of them might have stayed up and talked. They might have necked like high-schoolers. But it didn't mean a thing. After all, Logan had made sure she got the message in no uncertain terms that he wasn't looking for anything long-term. And that was the deal breaker for Kinsey Wyatt.

"I think you're selling yourself short, Kinsey. You're as hot as Fiona Perez."

"Hmm, maybe you need glasses, Troy," she shot back as she went around to her check stand to open the register for the day.

"Well, if you ask me Donnelly doesn't seem too happy about having been married to this Fiona. I think she broke his arm somehow."

"What? He said that?"

"He hinted at it. That's why I think he's relieved he isn't around her anymore."

"That could be, I suppose. But right now the man's bogged down in his own self-avowed 'sworn-off-women phase.' We just don't mesh that way, Troy."

"I don't know. On some level the guy seems like he's had a rough time with women."

"That comes through loud and clear. He doesn't even have to advertise it or wear a sign."

"You know what, Kinsey?"

"What?"

"You're funny."

She bumped his shoulder. "Yeah? If you were eight years older I'd fight Gina Purvis for your hand." Troy and Gina had been seeing each other for more than three months. Gina worked for Doc Prescott as his receptionist. But eyeing the look on Troy's face, Kinsey tilted her head.

At the moment Troy looked none too happy about the relationship.

"See, that's what I mean. I've never known a woman, except maybe my mom, with such a cool sense of humor," Troy told her before he added, "And Gina and I broke up."

"Aw, since when? I'm sorry." But Troy seemed to have something else on his mind. Since he was now employed full-time and seemed to be excited about his job, she didn't think it was work related. She decided to change the subject. "You should know, Troy. Since you were my very first real friend in town, I'm fond of you, too. But you knew that. Did I say thanks for telling me about the opening at The Pointe? I got the job, by the way, played Friday night and last night to a packed house." Kinsey laughed. "I thought I wouldn't be able to do it, play in front of people. But my car wouldn't start so I was running late. Donnelly brought me into town and we sort of had words. With all that going on, once I got there, I just jumped right in without overthinking it too much."

Troy grinned. "If I had the money I'd come see you play. But the only thing I could afford on that menu is a soft drink. If I were twenty-one I could sit at the bar though. I'd like to hear you play sometime. I bet you wowed them. You had to be nervous though. Friday nights at The Pointe are always crowded. I've seen the parking lot. It's usually packed."

"Scared witless. It's probably a good thing I didn't know that beforehand. About the crowd I mean. I might never have gotten out of Logan's truck. But once I started playing, I was okay." She tilted her head to study the younger man again. "Okay, spill it. You look worried or troubled like something else is bothering you. What is it?"

"I'm thinking about asking Mona Bingham out. Every time I go into the Diner she's nice to me, gives me refills even when I'm just there to read the classifieds for jobs. And I found out Mona's birthday's coming up next month. Any idea what I could get her? Something nice, you know.

Although I don't have a lot of money for anything too expensive. Could you help me think of something nice?"

"Sure. Why don't you make her something, Troy? You're an excellent carpenter. According to Keegan Bennett, the rescue center still features the miniature aquatic replica you built for the kids to play with during their visits."

Troy scrunched up his nose. "Women like store-bought stuff, Kinsey."

"Not every time. Not always. Why don't you make her a nice jewelry box? The kind you showed me you wanted to start selling."

"Aw, Kinsey, no one really likes those."

"I do. If I had the money, I'd buy one in a heartbeat. Listen to us. We're both so strapped for cash we can't see straight. Look, here's an idea. Why don't you approach Jordan Harris and ask her about displaying several of your jewelry boxes out at the B & B?"

"I don't know, Kinsey. Gina threw the one I made for her out the door and onto the front porch about the same time she told me she never wanted to see me again."

"Then Gina isn't worth your time, Troy. Be glad you saw the real Gina now and not later."

"That's what Logan said, too. You think Jordan might go for that? Putting several of them out on display?"

"I don't see why not. Lilly Pierce's drawings are hanging in every guest room. And Jordan displays Drea's line of jewelry there. Why not your artistic endeavors?"

"You know what, Kinsey?"

"What?"

"I was pretty down when I came in here. But you made me feel better."

Kinsey grinned, bumped his shoulder again. "Anytime."

Troy checked his watch. "I better get moving. Don't want to be late on my fourth day."

When he started to put a dollar down on the counter for his coffee, Kinsey shook her head. "My treat, Troy. Now get out of here."

"Thanks again, Kinsey. You have a good Sunday."

Because the curious had thinned out since yesterday, Kinsey's second day was much quieter. Murphy had let her open up so that he could sleep late, a rare occurrence for him.

But once church let out, a little past noon, customers began to trickle in to pick up milk and other staples for Sunday dinner or dessert.

One of those was Janie Pointer, who was there to pick up the makings for chocolate sundaes. The other, was Myrtle Pettibone, who loaded up her cart with cat food. As Kinsey scanned the items in Janie's cart, she looked up, spotted Aaron Hartley standing in line behind Myrtle. His arms were folded across his chest. There was no ignoring his defiant gesture. The man had no cart, no basket, and no groceries, which told Kinsey she'd been busted.

Aaron didn't wait for her to finish with Janie's groceries. Instead he blurted out, "Girl, what in the hell are you doing here?"

"You watch your language, Aaron Hartley," Myrtle warned. "And on a Sunday, too. Is that why you weren't in church this morning, couldn't wait to come here to yell at your new girl. What does it look like she's doing, you fool?"

"I'm yelling at her because I put her to work as an attorney in this town, not to check groceries again in Murphy's Market or pound on a piano for Perry Altman."

"Looks to me like she can do lawyering, you old fart," Myrtle harrumphed before slapping cans, one by one, onto the conveyor belt.

Through his rant, Kinsey noted Aaron's face color kept inching up from pink to red. The fact that he looked as though his blood pressure had risen twenty points in a span of a few minutes had Kinsey concerned for the man's health. Not only that, she suddenly realized he looked as though he might seizure. And his hands were shaking.

"Aaron, please don't make a scene here. Let's talk about this. Calmly," Kinsey pleaded.

"Why didn't you tell me to my face what you were planning to do? You've known since Thursday and didn't say a word."

"This is exactly why. I knew you'd be upset," Kinsey snapped back.

About that time Murphy came out of the back to see what the commotion was all about. "Okay, okay, everyone just take a deep breath. Aaron, surely you don't begrudge me hiring a stellar employee that I didn't even have to train."

"I thought she'd put this behind her. I thought Kinsey Wyatt wanted a chance at becoming this town's lawyer, to dedicate herself to a profession she claimed to have a knack for." Aaron pointed an accusing finger at Kinsey and demanded, "You decide what it is you want, to check groceries or practice law. You...can't...do both," he wheezed out. With that, the old man stormed past all of them and sailed out the automatic door.

Murphy waved his hand. "Go," he told Kinsey. "Go explain things to him now, else he'll just stew about it the rest of the day until you get to work tomorrow."

Kinsey scooted out the door and down the street to catch Aaron.

She found him slumped against the bank building next door. With a shaky hand, he was desperately trying to dab at blood running from his nose with a wadded up handkerchief. All the while he gripped his own shirt in a fist so tight his knuckles were a pasty white.

Kinsey saw him clutch at his chest. She looked around, started waving her arms to get the attention of a passing motorist driving a champagne-colored pickup truck. The driver screeched to a halt. When Kinsey saw who sat behind the wheel, she shouted, "Logan, call 9-1-1! Hurry! I think he's having a heart attack."

Logan ran up, holding his cell phone to his ear, explaining the situation, detailing where they were. "Main Street, First Bank Pelican Pointe. You can't miss us."

By this time, Kinsey had eased Aaron onto the ground. "It's okay, help's coming. Stay with me, Aaron."

"I...don't...want to...go...alone," Aaron gasped.

"You won't be alone. I'll go with you. What's taking them so long?"

"It takes time. You want to get him in my truck?"

About that time, Murphy came jogging up. "Let's get him over to Doc Prescott's. It's closer."

Logan and Murphy started to lift him when sirens blared in the distance. "We'll let the paramedics decide where to take him," Logan reasoned. "I don't think the office is open today anyway. It's Sunday."

About that time the red emergency vehicle with the gold and white lettering pulled up at the curb in a screech. Two men got out, grabbing their gear. Murphy seemed to know them, but then Murphy knew everyone.

"Deacon, Brian," Murphy acknowledged with a nod.

A man with caramel skin, nodded back. "Murph, what've we got here? What happened to him?"

"We think he's having a heart attack."

"He got upset in the store," Kinsey started to explain with her hands still clasped in one of Aaron's. "He ran outside. I found him standing right here, clutching his chest. We got him to lie down. That's what he's doing on the ground." Kinsey had to let go and take a step back as soon as the man Murphy had called Deacon started to work on Aaron taking his blood pressure and other vitals.

"It's...not...my...heart," Aaron choked out.

"Have you taken any meds?" Deacon wanted to know while Brian started an IV drip to stabilize the elderly man.

"I...I...take...cytarabine...among...other things."

"I see." Deacon and Brian exchanged looks. "We need to transport him to the hospital in Santa Cruz."

"No," Aaron rasped out. "Murph...get me over to...Doc's. He'll know...what to do."

"It's a Sunday, Aaron," Logan pointed out. "Doc's office is closed."

Murphy looked none too happy about the decision of where Aaron should be transported falling on his shoulders. "If he needs medical attention now wouldn't it make more sense for you guys to take him two streets over though instead of all the way to Santa Cruz? What's wrong with him anyway?" Murphy asked Deacon.

Deacon shook his head. "That's not for me to say. If he wants Doc Prescott to look at him, I don't have a problem with taking him there. I've got Doc's number on speed dial. I'll give him a call right now, ask him to meet us at his office."

Kinsey watched as the two EMTs transferred Aaron to a stretcher, rolled him to the back of the vehicle and loaded him inside. The entire scene was so reminiscent of what she'd seen happen to her mother more than once that Kinsey didn't realize she was crying until Logan thumbed away a tear rolling down her cheek. Automatically she stepped into his chest.

Logan suspected she was thinking about her mother. He did his best to make her feel better. "Kinsey, I'm sure he'll be fine."

But Kinsey shook her head, unable to say anything. She might not be a nurse, might not have a regular college degree, but years of taking care of a cancer patient that routinely underwent treatment, Kinsey knew exactly the reason Aaron had been prescribed cytarabine. She thought back over the last three weeks. Aaron had been frail and weak from the get-go. He often left the office in the middle of the day for a nap. But now Kinsey suspected it wasn't his age making him so tired. Once a week, he disappeared for two or three hours, ostensibly to "stretch his legs." More than likely, he'd been going over to see Doc.

When Brian came back to pick up his gear, he looked at Kinsey and said, "He wants you to make the ride with him."

Kinsey glanced up at Logan, then at Murphy, who bobbed his head in the direction of the ambulance. Kinsey took off and crawled into the back with Aaron.

At his coastal ranch north of town, Jack Prescott, or rather "Doc" as he was affectionately known around town, was just sitting down to leftover stuffed pork chops for lunch when his phone rang. He gave his wife a knowing glance and answered the phone.

He'd recently celebrated his fifty-ninth birthday. After spending twenty years as chief resident of emergency medicine in one of San Francisco's busiest ERs, Jack had burned out early. Needing an escape, he'd decided to retire. He'd packed up almost eight years earlier and moved to Pelican Pointe on ten acres of coastal ranchland to ride his horses, go fishing and spend his retirement years in relative peace.

But in a little town where the sick and injured had to traipse over to San Sebastian or Santa Cruz for medical care, it didn't take long for word to get out that they had a physician, a noted surgeon, living among them. Once that happened, people started showing up at his house at all hours of the day and night for medical treatment or advice about everything from the stomach flu to needing broken bones fixed or gashes stitched up.

It didn't go over well with his wife, Belle. When Belle grew tired of the constant traffic and people coming and going at all hours, she put her foot down. She encouraged her husband to come out of retirement to open a clinic with regular hours.

Turns out, Doc found he enjoyed his little practice much more than he'd ever enjoyed the aura of emergency surgery.

It didn't take Deacon five minutes to make the trip to Doc's clinic. Kinsey didn't even have a chance to apologize to Aaron before the ambulance pulled up in the driveway of a renovated Mission-style house, two blocks off Main Street. All Kinsey knew was that Aaron looked pale and weak. Sick. She'd seen sick too many times to be put off by it.

Before she knew what was happening, Deacon and Brian hopped out when a Jeep Laredo came to a stop and parked beside them. As the EMTs unloaded the stretcher, Doc unlocked the front door.

Kinsey followed them into a front room designated as the waiting area. It pretty much looked like any other typical doctor's office. There were a dozen uncomfortable banquet chairs to sit in, tables littered with magazines, and the obligatory reception counter. Deacon and Brian wheeled Aaron down the hall and into one of three professionally furnished exam rooms.

Kinsey knew because she'd been curious and peeked in. She'd been surprised to see it contained the same state-of-the-art medical equipment as in much larger doctor's offices.

Doc spotted her and said, "Go grab yourself a soft drink out of the kitchen. I need to talk to our patient here." And with that he closed the door in her face.

By the time she found the small kitchen in the back, Deacon and Brian were already digging out their own cans of soda from the refrigerator.

"You're the new lawyer," Deacon declared as he popped the top on his can of Pepsi.

"Yes. How'd you know?"

"Word gets around. Besides, I'd remember you. Your eyes, they look like Heidi Klum's."

Kinsey smiled, recognizing the come-on. "And what do Heidi Klum's eyes look like?"

"Hazel with less green, more brown. Deacon's right, just like yours," Brian reiterated moving closer to check them out.

"We're having a raffle next month for charity. Can I put you down for a couple of tickets? Bring a friend."

"What's the prize?" Kinsey wanted to know.

"Us," Brian said with a smile.

"Well, one of us. You bid on a date, Brian or me," Deacon said.

"So this is your pitch?" Kinsey surmised.

But about that time Doc motioned from the doorway. "Kinsey Wyatt, you can come in now." She followed him down the hallway. All the while he gave her an update. "I've started him on another IV. He's weak but he wants to talk."

The minute she walked into Aaron's exam room, she knew for certain what was wrong. There was no doubt he was very ill. "You scared the life out of me," she blurted out. "I'm sorry I didn't tell you about my other jobs. But…knowing my mother had cancer for years, that the disease took her life, you should have said something about how sick you were."

"I…know…we both…need to make a better…effort at talking. I admit…I over…reacted. I should've paid you more…to start. It was a probationary period. I wanted to see what you could do." Each word was an effort for him.

Because of that, because Doc Prescott still stood to the side, Kinsey turned to the doctor for answers. "What does he have? Exactly. What type of cancer?"

"Acute Myeloid Leukemia. The disease affects the bone marrow. When the bone marrow doesn't work correctly there's an increased risk of infections and bleeding, the healthy blood cells diminish and the cancer progresses."

"And the prognosis?"

"His lymph nodes are swollen, so are his liver and spleen. He's anemic. He's on a cocktail of chemo and antibiotics." Doc shot a look Aaron. "If he takes a lot better care of himself than he did today, he's got about six months."

"What about a bone marrow transplant?"

"He had one, about a year ago."

Kinsey bit her lip, crossed her arms over her chest. She turned back to the patient, prepared to still do battle. "My mother's hospital bills are killing me financially. If you weren't so cheap I wouldn't have had to commit to these extra jobs in the first place. Now that I have, I won't disappoint Murphy and Perry. They're counting on me, Aaron, just like you are. I think I can pull it off, do all three jobs without a hitch. But if you give me an ultimatum like you did just now at the store in front of everyone in town, then I'll have to start sending out resumes and looking for another job."

Aaron met Doc's eyes. "I told…you…the girl…had spunk."

Doc nodded in approval, slapped Kinsey on the shoulder. "Sometimes he needs a good, swift kick in the ass. Something tells me you're just the one who can do it, too."

Chapter Eleven

Kinsey didn't get back to the market until after two o'clock. When she did walk through the doors, Murphy was full of questions she couldn't answer truthfully. She evaded because she had no intentions of letting on that Aaron Hartley had stage 4 cancer. That was something for Aaron to divulge when he was ready for people to know.

Although it did seem odd to her that no one around town seemed to realize that Hartley looked gaunt and ill. How long before she got here had he been fighting the disease on his own. How was it possible in such a little town that they hadn't recognized how he'd changed? Kinsey looked back over the last three weeks. Hell, hadn't Aaron changed in the short time she'd been in town? Were folks so used to what Aaron looked like that no one had taken the time to really "see" him? Surely people realized he'd dropped weight.

When her shift at Murphy's ended the last thing Kinsey felt like doing was sitting around playing in front of a room full of people. But she couldn't very well call in sick.

She changed into a flowing, tea and candle skirt in bright blue. It wasn't as elegant or as a dressy as her previous two outfits, more like festive. But if she had to sit and play piano tonight after what she'd learned about her employer, then she wanted to do it wearing bold colors.

In spite of her determination, once she got to work, she found she couldn't shake her mood. Her tastes in selections ran from melancholy to broody. As she began to play James Horner's *One Last Wish,* Perry came over to prod her into livening things up a bit.

She switched to Bach.

About seven-thirty she looked up to see Jolene leading Logan to a table to the left of the piano under the bank of windows with a view of the ocean.

For some stupid reason just one look at him had her heart racing. That pull in the belly every time she was around him was getting to be a habit, a bad one and had to stop. Damn it, what was he doing here anyway? The meals at Promise Cove were included. Why the hell didn't he eat there like all the other guests?

Logan ordered a glass of red wine and noticed Kinsey staring at him. When her lips curved, he was glad to see it. She hadn't been the same since Hartley's heart attack earlier. But here she was, sitting at the piano just as she had been the night before.

He ordered grilled salmon and felt guilty nibbling on it while Kinsey worked. So after taking several bites, he had the waiter box it up.

By around ten-thirty the crowd in the dining room had thinned out with only a few stragglers lingering over dessert. The people left in the bar had dwindled down to only Logan and Wade Hawkins, who sat two stools apart, nursing their glasses of wine.

"You settling in?" Wade asked Logan as he hopped from one bar chair to be closer to sit next to Logan. "There's a lot to bringing back that old lighthouse. Glad to see someone taking the time to do it right though, lot of history there. You're doing a good thing."

Logan looked at the man with the wild head of white hair. "Settling in okay. Been busy getting things ready to kick off for real come Monday."

"So you like it out at Promise Cove?"

"Sure. It's one of the best B & Bs I've ever had the pleasure of staying at. Nick and Jordan run a first-rate inn."

Wade nodded in agreement and peered at the sculptor over his wine glass. "So...no unusual sightings of any kind yet?"

Chills bumped along Logan's spine. He wasn't sure if it was the subject matter or annoyance that Kinsey must have opened her big mouth about something he wanted to keep private. In spite of that, Logan tried for a casual tone. "Sightings? Like what?"

"I guess not. It's just that I'm writing a book about the paranormal, specifically right here in Pelican Pointe. I was hoping to get your take about all the ghostly activity out at the B & B."

Logan stared at Wade. "Despite what anyone's said to you, I have no firsthand knowledge of any paranormal activity. And if Kinsey's told you any different—"

"No one's said a word to me. I just wondered if you'd experienced anything out of the ordinary so far, that's all. You've been there less than a week so maybe it's a little soon for that to take shape."

But Logan wasn't sure *what* the guy's angle was.

Wade, however, took Logan's silence for an opening to go into a detailed account about how he'd taken his sensors out to the old Victorian on two separate occasions and how both times his electronic gadgets had tripped out. "I have firsthand experience myself dealing with earthbound ghosts."

Fascinating, thought Logan that intelligent people could believe in such nonsense. And some people labeled *him* eccentric. "I'm sure you do. So you've seen Scott?"

Wade found Logan's question intriguing since he hadn't mentioned Scott by name. "Oh yes, many times. Most people in town report sightings off and on. Scott Phillips, for reasons of his own, roams the streets of Pelican Pointe and definitely patrols the grounds of his childhood home. I believe he's here to guard those he loves to keep any harm from coming to them."

Logan considered that. It was a shame the ghostly Scott couldn't take that one step further to protect everyone in the town, like innocent, defenseless, young girls. "Gotten a whole lot of miles out of that story, have you? Ghost stories usually sell well. I wish you luck with it."

Used to a degree of skepticism, Wade simply went on unruffled, "Most ghosts hang around because they have unfinished business on earth. In Scott's case I'd say Scott's world is right here." He spread his arms out wide, then adjusted his glasses. "Knowing that doesn't need to upset you. But if you should see Scott, I'd be interested in hearing your story. Ethan's seen him, you know. So has Hayden Cody."

Not surprising that's something the former deputy had held back in his emails. But in a complete about face, Logan heard Wade ask, "You fish, Mr. Donnelly?"

"Not in a long time. Why?"

"You look stressed out. Fishing relaxes a person. Several of us, Murphy, Bran Sullivan, Doc Prescott, Wally Pierce, Carl Knudsen, even Joe Ferguson, we get together sometimes to fish and play poker. You play poker?"

"I've been known to."

"Next time we get together, I'll make it a point to let you know where."

About that time, Kinsey had finished with her set and walked up to the bar. "Hey Wade. How's it going?"

"It's going fine, Kinsey." Wade picked up her hand, gave it a kiss. "You play that piano beautifully. If I were twenty years younger I'd take you away from all this." When he saw her smile, he added, "You take requests?"

She put a hand on his shoulder. "For you, Wade, absolutely. I liked it when you stood up to applaud the other night. *That*...made my night and I had just gotten started. What would you like me to play?"

"I wouldn't mind a little Bill Withers every now and again. You play that, you'll make this crowd a lot happier. That's my first request. But you ever heard of a guy named Johan Blohm?"

Kinsey knitted her brow in thought before her lips curved. "The Swedish band, The Refreshments? Sure. You surprise me, Wade. I had you pegged for a classical fan all the way. Shows you what I know."

"I drag on my dancing shoes now and again. I want you to play something special for Abby Pointer's reception. Johan does a mean Boogie Woogie. Since I heard you were doing the wedding, I want you to let your hair down 'cause I think you can play that piano, girl. But you need to liven things up," Wade prompted as he studied the man beside him.

Kinsey chuckled. "Boogie Woogie, huh? I played it a time or two, just not sure I play that as well as Johan. But for you, I'll give it my best shot. How's that sound?" Kinsey eyed Logan who sat there looking tense, brooding into his Coke.

"Couldn't ask for more." With that, Wade drained his wine glass and stood up. "Well, it's time for me to head to the house. Looks like you guys are closing up anyway." To Logan he said, "Let me know if you want that poker game. We'd love to take your money sometime."

"See ya, Wade," Kinsey said all the while eyeing Logan's demeanor. She noted the scowl on his face that said he couldn't wait to get something off his chest. "What's wrong?"

"You off the clock?" Logan asked as he tossed some bills on the bar. He picked up his to-go box with the food left over from dinner. As soon as he saw her head nod, he added, "Then let's take a walk. Outside." He took her by the arm, yanking her through the front door and out into the parking lot.

Kinsey puffed out a breath, beginning to get pissed off. "You *are* upset. Look, it's been a long day for me. I'm tired. I want out of these shoes. I really don't feel like a lot of drama right this minute. So if you don't mind—"

"Too bad," Logan muttered. Still holding her arm, he tugged her along to his truck. Once they settled inside the cab, the two still said nothing.

All the while resentment built in Kinsey. The curtain of silence might as well have been a brick wall. If she had her own transportation she would have already been headed home by now, instead of dealing with this sullen man. This is exactly why she didn't like having to rely on anyone but herself. *Ellie Wyatt, wherever you are, Kinsey thought now, I love you for teaching me the importance of being my own person.*

Kinsey folded her arms across her chest. Annoyed, she spoke in defiant, clipped terms, emphasizing each word. "If you ask me, you and your artistic temperament can go suck an egg. Am I at least allowed to ask where we're going?"

"You'll see." He headed up Ocean Street, veering toward the lighthouse. The truck bumped along the narrow road, taking the hairpin turn in the dark with careful deliberation. Just before they reached the uneven dunes, he brought the truck to a stop and cut the engine.

He immediately picked up the to-go box with the cold, grilled salmon inside and shoved it in her direction. "Here. Eat."

She looked down at the box. It took her several seconds before she realized what he was offering. When he impatiently flipped open the lid and she saw the tasty fish, the green beans, and the baby red potatoes inside, her heart tripped. How could this man be so gruff one minute, and then so thoughtful the next? "You brought me dinner?"

"I don't think you had much time to do more than grab a snack in between jobs. You're bound to be hungry after sitting for several hours without eating. It's like a model who poses for hours sitting in one spot. I know something about that. Doesn't Perry let you take a break? He should let you take a break," Logan grumbled.

She dug into the food with the plastic knife and fork he'd also thought to include. "I get fifteen minutes, but I usually end up in the ladies' room just relishing the quiet." She looked through the windshield and out into the darkness. "It's a little spooky out here this time of night," Kinsey announced as she watched clouds drift over a fat, low-hanging full moon. Beach grass swayed in the breeze that whipped in right off the ocean. She could hear the distant sound of the surf pounding the rocks below the cliff.

"Believe me, this place will liven up plenty tomorrow for real. Did you know they used to call this spot Make Out Pointe?"

"It's a great place for it. Did you ever bring a date here when you were fifteen?"

Shit, he thought, he'd opened himself up for that one. "No." But he wondered now if maybe Megan had ever come out here to these cliffs to neck with one of the locals. An interesting idea to mull over, he decided as he looked around at the wooded area to the north. The thicket of Monterrey pine and cypress would be a perfect place to bury a body when you were done with it. He shut his eyes to shake off that image.

"Wonder if Scott ever brought his dates out here?" Even in the dark, she noticed that one question brought another disgruntled look to his face. "What did Wade say to upset you back at the restaurant, Logan?"

"Not a thing. Why do you ask?"

She finished nibbling on the food and closed the lid. "Oh come on. You think that irritation goes unnoticed. It doesn't. Why are we out here?"

All of a sudden Logan unsnapped his seatbelt, turning to her in the dark cab of the truck. He roughly took her chin, crushed his mouth to hers.

Heat bubbled in degrees, hot as August sun on blacktop. The kiss drew out, waking every sensation from the top of Kinsey's head to the tips of her toes. Her brain lost focus. Longing, rich and thick, spread slowly through her bones like molasses through a sieve.

Logan felt her yield, felt his own hunger for her take over inside him. As the sound of waves crashed in the distance, he slid her onto his lap. "I've wanted to do that all night, ever since I walked into the restaurant, ever since I had to sit there and watch you caress those piano keys. I want you, Kinsey. Honest to God, I've spent days trying to get you out of my head. But no matter what I do, nothing works."

For an answer, she grabbed his long hair just as he had hers the night before. She tugged him closer, ran her hands up his arms and around his muscular shoulders. She trailed kisses down his jaw line. "Do you always get what you want?" she asked, a bit breathless. She took a bite out of that little dimple in his chin.

"Not always. But in this case I'm fairly confident I will."

"Cocky, aren't you?"

In response, he moved her hand to the front of his jeans. "Feel that? What do you think?"

"Hmm."

His long, lean fingers skimmed over her breast. A thumb flicked at her nipple. He inched her top aside, so he could chew at her shoulder. Just as he started to bend his head to take advantage of the angle and go lower, Logan caught a shadow out of the corner of his eye. He stopped, looked out at the cliffs. The man crept along the waist high beach grass near the dunes. "Someone's out there," Logan declared in a whisper.

"Where? I don't see anyone. It's probably just an animal of some sort."

"No doubt of the two-legged variety," Logan muttered, uneasily. "I know what I saw. Let's get out here. I should have my head examined for bringing you out here in the damned dark in the first place like we were two horny teenagers who had nowhere else to go."

Automatically taking the time to smooth her hair back, she adjusted her top. "I don't know about you but right now I'm pretty horny."

He grinned as he started up the truck and turned the vehicle around. They took off bumping over the same ragged stretch of rutted landscape as before. "That was the idea. But I'd feel better if we got back to the B & B where we have no less than three beds available to us."

"Three?" She did a quick addition in her head. "Ah, I get it. Your room, my room, or the bed in my new apartment. What time exactly do you have to be at work tomorrow?"

He sighed. "The first day, around seven to kick the whole thing off. Make sure everyone knows what to do. Troy and I spent a lot of time scheduling the entire week out so there should be no disagreements about assigned jobs. But with a bunch of guys I don't know, there's bound to be grumbling. And I've got the crew coming in from Oregon. The Preservation Commission arranged it."

"But it's almost one o'clock now."

"Exactly. Which means when we get back to the B & B we head to our separate corners." When he saw the disappointment edge along her face, nothing could have pleased him more. "We're going to get there, Kinsey. If I didn't need to get a few hours of sleep, I'd take you to bed tonight."

He reached over and took her chin. "Look at me." When her eyes met his, he added, "The first time, I want no distractions between us. I'm amping up for tomorrow already. You're winding down and tired from your two-day, work-a-thon weekend."

"Right," Kinsey sighed, more than a little unwilling to admit her lust bubble had deflated and she wasn't exactly happy about it. She wasn't sure she understood his abrupt departure completely either. But then so much about him remained a mystery. "I still don't understand what spooked you so much. This is Pelican Pointe, Logan, where nothing *ever* happens."

"You'd be surprised at that," Logan returned, knowingly as he headed the truck due north to Promise Cove.

Chapter Twelve

Three days later, the cliffs near the lighthouse hummed with the sound of electrical saws, sanders, and construction workers wielding hammers. It was backbreaking work while rock music blasted from the portable boom box Logan had set up for his crews and vied with all the clatter and noise.

Logan watched as the scaffolding went up around the base of the tower. He found himself grateful to John Norris and Dan Sullivan. Thanks to both men, they'd found and Federal Expressed him blueprints of both the keeper's house and the lighthouse. Something Logan had been unable to put his hands on until three days ago.

Things were coming together even though Logan had hired the Oregon crew sight unseen. He'd been more than apprehensive about the decision. But for the past few days, the men had shown a remarkable dedication that impressed him. Since the crew's arrival, he'd watch them fall into an easy rhythm that spoke volumes about how long they'd been together as a team. He knew firsthand a construction site could be loud and bawdy, but if the people didn't mesh it caused problems down the road. So far, the men from Oregon had had no awkward adjustment period. In fact, they'd hit the ground running with an expertise he admired. It told him they knew what they were doing. Besides, he needed as much help as he could get. He wasn't ashamed to admit John and Dan knew far more about the restoration process than he did. That much he'd gleaned from their meeting on Saturday night. Plus, his "tower" crew was some of the best stonemasons in the business, go-to guys who routinely traveled from Canada to Mexico caring for and maintaining lighthouses up and down the Pacific coast. They'd assured him the original masonry on both structures could be brought back to life.

The Commission had also put him in contact with experts that specialized in getting the lantern room at the top functional again. Logan would save that for last though. But he'd be lying if he didn't admit that the best thing about owning a lighthouse was making it operational after so many years of non-use. To do that, the old drum lens would have to be removed and replaced with a state-of-the-art aero beacon that when installed would flash a white beam every ten seconds out to sea.

But for now, the lantern room was put on the backburner where it belonged. Logan had other more pressing issues to deal with.

Getting his studio finished at the top was a priority. He hoped to get that room ready so he could get back to the creative process he'd missed. Maybe that was at the core of his sour mood these past months.

He looked over at his "keeper" crew. He'd started with five local men. Troy Dayton and his uncle, Derek Stovall, were a package deal. Logan had hired Sam Turley because he was a big man who worked like two. The ex-soldier, Paul Bonner, had gotten the job because he excelled at electric work even though so far Paul hadn't been put to the test. Drake Boedecker was the last man he'd hired. Drake was a bit clumsy but had shown Logan he was willing to show up and work hard. All in all, seventy-two hours into the project, Logan was pleased with the way things were going.

The "keeper" team had spent their first few days gutting and tearing out the rotted walls of the one-thousand-square-foot keeper's cottage. This had to be done before they even thought about beginning the remodeling. When they were ready, the crew would shove out a wall to enlarge the space and double the size of the interior.

Before Logan could even begin to consider this place his home, he had to put his own stamp on the job. He'd started that first week having to make some tough decisions. Even though Derek was a little rough around the edges, the man seemed to know the most about construction. So Logan had designated Derek Stovall his foreman. Because Logan considered Troy the go-to guy for the staging area and materials, the kid's job included keeping track of supplies in addition to all his other duties. Logan felt sure Troy could handle it. It hadn't taken but a couple of days for Logan to peg Troy and Derek as the two hardest workers, although Paul Bonner and Drake Boedecker were no slackers. Logan wasn't so sure about Sam Turley.

Logan had discovered through rumor and rumblings that the Turley brothers had a long and troubled history. He found out Sam was known around Santa Cruz County as a hothead, much like his brother Salvatore. Born ten months apart in San Sebastian to a couple of teachers, Sal and Sam were almost twins. Both brothers had long rap sheets for drunk and disorderly, disturbing the peace, and driving while under the influence. If Logan hadn't been desperate for workers he might've passed on a guy reported to enjoy nothing more than looking for a fight in any dive that would let him drink.

But since everyone within a hundred miles said Sal was the more aggressive brother, he decided to give Sam a chance. Because even now, Sal was incarcerated in the maximum security Kern Valley State Correctional Facility after pleading guilty last fall to assaulting a police officer, namely Ethan Cody. But no one Logan had talked to had made the mistake of thinking Sam Turley was a choirboy.

Sam had already given Logan grief about what was sure to be a hot, sweaty job of reinforcing the spiral staircase up to the lantern room. And they weren't even ready to start there yet for probably another three months. After Logan spent twenty minutes arguing with Sam about the placement of rebar, Logan was already having second thoughts about his decision to hire Turley.

As the outside crew started the sandblasting for the day, taking off the years and years of old paint, rusty metal and corrosion from the tower, the keeper crew started ripping out old clapboard.

Logan stood back watching all the activity. A degree of pride moved over him. He realized then he'd come a long, long way, not just in miles and distance but in getting to this very spot in his life.

Now if only he could find the answers he needed, maybe he could stop imagining shadows and ghosts in the dark.

Aaron had gone back to work Monday morning without a hitch in his routine, although in a limited capacity. Despite the fact that he and Kinsey had squared off on Sunday both acted like the air had cleared. They seemed to be back on even footing.

For Kinsey, it was a relief to know Aaron didn't hold a grudge. But then she didn't either.

Their first client of the day turned out to be Ethan Cody who brought Hayden along pushing Nate in his stroller.

Kinsey immediately began to coo over the baby, who had a thick mane of raven hair and cinnamon skin like his daddy. "Wow, he's gotten even bigger just since I've been in town."

Hayden beamed. "He has, hasn't he?"

"Kid's growing like a weed," Ethan added.

"Don't you miss law enforcement, Ethan?" Aaron asked in a wheezy voice.

"I miss a few things about it. But overall, the job itself? Not really, especially not the hours, certainly not having to be on call twenty-four-seven. I'll leave that to Garver. That gets old pretty quick," Ethan answered. All the while Ethan stared at Aaron who looked as though the man had aged ten years overnight. Ethan sent a knowing gaze in Kinsey's direction. When Ethan saw her nod, he knew. Ethan had picked up on the vibe that said Aaron didn't have long to live and Kinsey had just confirmed it. "My agent sent me over the latest contract from my publisher. I need someone to look it over. The thing is ten pages long and reads like *War and Peace*. I want to make sure I'm not getting ripped off."

Aaron nodded. "I think we'll be able to decipher the ins and outs for you, Ethan."

Kinsey opened a drawer and took out her own copy of Ethan's debut novel, *Silent Death*. She held it out to him with a pen. "Might as well get this out of the way, how about autographing this for me? I haven't finished reading it yet, but I'm about halfway done and it's…disturbing while keeping me turning the pages."

Ethan grinned widely. "No problem. That's what I like to hear. It's weird getting used to people asking me to sign it."

"After you've done it a few thousand times, it'll get easier I'm sure," Kinsey speculated. As soon as he finished though, Kinsey got down to work. Perusing the contract line by line, Kinsey did most of the explaining and the revising with Aaron offering only a comment or two from the sidelines. Aaron willingly sat back and let her take the lead.

Kinsey took out a red pen and began to mark up the changes. "Let's clarify the language here so there's no ambiguity," she suggested, pointing to a paragraph under subsidiary rights. "And let's better define the exact work described here so neither side is surprised when you deliver your next manuscript. I'm removing the words 'upon execution' so there's no confusion in what either party expects If the book is ever made into a movie." She grinned. "Or should I say when? Plus, you need more specific language that covers your royalties here, here, and here. And we'll remove this catchphrase altogether. It's a loophole that favors the publisher."

Ethan raised his eyebrows. "Wow. She's pretty good," Ethan said to Aaron.

Aaron nodded. "She's a smart girl. But I should get some credit for my brilliance at finding her and bringing her here."

Ethan gently slapped Aaron on the back with a wink. After all, it looked as if one good strong wind would topple him over. "You always were a visionary, Aaron."

"Once upon a time, I guess. But then so was Edmund Taggert, starting that organic farm like he did. Everyone thought he was crazy. Remember that, Ethan? All my friends are either confined to nursing homes, ready to die, or they've already gone to meet their maker."

Hayden laid a hand on his shoulder. "You aren't there yet, Aaron. Would you like to hold Nate?"

A smile curved on Aaron's lips. "Remember holding his daddy here when his mama, Lindeen, brought him by a few times. Ethan couldn't have been more than ten months old. Brings back memories." They listened as Aaron went on about when Ethan had been a baby, watching him grow into an active toddler, then into a teenager.

But as soon as Kinsey had finished going over the document, Ethan bobbed his head behind Aaron's back in the direction of the door. Kinsey got the message. After explaining to Aaron that she needed to talk to Hayden about getting one of Ethan's books mailed to a friend, Kinsey sailed outside behind the Codys for a quiet chat.

"How sick is he?" Hayden asked once they got to the end of the driveway. "He's dropped a lot of weight."

"If I answer that, I'll need your assurance that you'll keep it confidential. You two are actually the first people that seem to have picked up on his gaunt look. And after Sunday…"

"We heard," Ethan said. "When an ambulance shows up on Main Street, stuff like that moves through town faster than a Santa Ana wind. But people are saying he had a heart attack, which of course I see for myself it wasn't his heart. You don't recover like that in three short days."

"We won't say a word to anyone, Kinsey," Hayden promised as she tucked the baby back into his stroller.

Kinsey hesitated. "Look it isn't that I wouldn't like to share. In fact, it would be great if I could. But I'm very new here not just to the town but to its various dynamics. And as an attorney I'm very cognizant of the legal ramifications if I disclose a private matter that gets out to the public. If that happens, my credibility is shot with less than a month in. So let me just say this. Aaron Hartley is in his late seventies. I think the whole town needs to realize the man won't live forever."

"That's a very polite way of saying that we should all make a concerted effort to take the time to pay Aaron a visit over the next few weeks. In a totally inconspicuous sneaky kind of way, of course," Hayden determined with a sly smile.

Kinsey nodded. "You heard him in there. I think that's an excellent idea. Not only that, but after living his entire life in this town, he would love the chance to go back and recall the things and the people that meant the most to him."

"I hear your moving into my old digs," Hayden said. "And fixing it up."

"I'm starting the paint job tonight."

The two women chatted about colors and accessories until Nate started to get hungry. As Hayden and Ethan turned to go, Hayden said, "You take care of Aaron, Kinsey. The man has no family that I know of."

"That's true," Kinsey agreed. "But then I don't either."

Around noon, Kinsey headed over to Wally's to see if her car was finally ready. Despite Wally's promise to have the Nissan ready on Monday, he'd discovered a few other pressing problems that had to be fixed right away before he'd let it out of his garage. The man was nothing if not a perfectionist. It seemed her little hatchback had decided to fall apart and Wally was determined to put it back together with more than chewing gum and string.

Bottom line was the Altima was all she had. And there was nothing like having your own transportation no matter how ancient it was after not being able to drive for five straight days. Having to depend on other people to get you where you needed to go sucked. She loved the idea of getting it back, even with its peeling paint job, its persnickety dashboard clock that never kept the right time, and the radio knob that refused to stay on no matter how many times she put it back. She wanted to get behind the wheel again. If that meant having to put the repair bill on her one and only credit card, then so be it.

Lilly greeted her behind the counter, where it seemed to Kinsey the woman stayed and never took a break. "Your car's done, Kinsey. Wally finished it about thirty minutes ago."

"I'm so glad to get it back, Lilly. I'm tired of Nick and Jordan having to run me back and forth into town."

"That's Nick and Jordan though. They're used to hauling guests around. And now with that Oregon crew staying out there, things are hopping."

"That's just it, they both have better things to do than cart me around. Anyway, I'm glad I'm moving out. The B & B is getting crowded and according to Jordan next month kicks in their busy season."

Lilly stuck her head into the garage and yelled, "Wally, Kinsey's here to pick up her car."

Wally came through the door wiping his hands on a red rag. His long brown hair tied back in his proverbial ponytail. Lilly was right. He and Logan were two of a kind when it came to thumbing their noses at traditional haircuts.

"Hey Kinsey. I fixed the oil leak around your head gasket. Put in the new water pump. That's one of the reasons it kept running hot. The other is your radiator. Flushed it because it was starting to clog up."

"I guess that's what happens with an older car."

"The car's aging, Kinsey, no doubt about that. Parts are gonna start wearing out every time you turn around, but it runs a lot better than it did when you brought it in. You've got a new alternator and that should stop the dash problems flicking on and off. You let me know if it doesn't, I'll make it right. The work I did should get you around town without any problems. But you keep an eye on the temperature gauge, and I'll see if I can get my hands on a used radiator. In the meantime if it runs in the red, you bring it in. I'm giving you a discount today because I did so much work. How's that sound?"

"That sounds great, Wally. I appreciate it." When Lilly handed her the bill, Kinsey dug out her trusty Visa, and calculated in her head how much the amount would increase her payment next month.

Once she'd crawled behind the wheel again, in her head, she went over all the bills still yet to be paid. She decided she needed a distraction. From the Pump N Go she headed to the lighthouse to see how Logan's day was going compared to hers.

As soon as she parked and got out, she realized Logan had been right. The place was jumping with activity. There were men with masks standing on a scaffold working high on the tower at the top. Dust and powder feathered down like soft drops of fine misting rain. The keeper's house was just as busy while another group of men hauled out trash and rotten wood. She knew Troy was in there somewhere busy scraping out debris and pulling out fixtures.

She spotted Logan beside his truck, his back to her. It wasn't until she got closer that she realized he held a cell phone up to his ear. The tone of his voice and his mannerisms indicated he was enjoying himself far more than she'd ever seen him. He was almost animated as he kept up a lively chatter with the person on the other end of the phone. "I don't know, sweetheart. I'm up to my ass in remodeling right now and will be for months to come. How about you? You staying out of trouble?"

Kinsey knew it was wrong to eavesdrop. But she couldn't help it. Whatever the woman said on the other end, she made Logan laugh. And it was that laugh, that strange sound coming from the man that had her staggering to a stop. This didn't seem like the same moody man whom she'd seen so often since he'd arrived in town. This side to him was upbeat, even buoyant. And since he was obviously flirting with the person on the other end of the phone, Kinsey deduced the caller was female.

Her temper spiked. And Logan had had the nerve to make fun of *her* cheery disposition. Because she recognized he seemed downright cheerful and she'd never seen him like that, she decided to make her exit quick before he noticed her.

She spun on her heels and fled back to her car.

By the time Logan caught a movement out of the corner of his eye, Kinsey was more than halfway back to her Nissan. "Valerie, could you hold on a minute?" He held the phone up to his shirt and lifted his voice to yell after Kinsey. "Hey! Where are you going?" But Kinsey never even bothered to glance back at him. Speaking into the phone again, Logan told his agent, "Sorry, Valerie. I'm back. No, you don't need to worry about me. I know exactly what I'm doing here."

As Kinsey's car bumped along the uneven ground, she couldn't help the disillusionment from seeping through her. She'd known it all along. But hearing it, having it verified in such a way that he'd been chatting up another woman on the other end of that phone, made her a little ill. She couldn't help it. What if she'd given in and slept with him? A man like Logan probably didn't know what it was to be faithful for longer than a week at a time anyway. That's probably what had prompted his divorce.

She had to stop making leaps in logic, let alone unproven accusations. It wasn't like her. But hadn't Logan put the moves on her and then backed off? Hadn't he suggested they would end up in bed? And they would have. Now that she had time to think about it, maybe the woman on the other end of the phone had done Kinsey a huge favor.

With time still left on her lunch hour, she decided to shake off Logan Donnelly. She headed to Ferguson's Hardware to pick up the paint she needed. If she wanted to move into her new digs, she would do it with new walls. As she walked through the doors, she reminded herself she didn't need a man to feel good about herself.

Ellie Wyatt had taught her that much.

From nine in the morning until six in the evening five days a week, Gerald Colter's domain was the paint department at Ferguson's Hardware. In his off time, Gerald played fiddle in Ricky Oden's bluegrass band. He did it well enough that the group had cut a CD. It sold like hotcakes in places like San Sebastian as well as the Central Valley and up and down the coast. The notoriety had given Gerald a glimpse into experiencing a snippet of local Celebrity Ville.

He enjoyed the limelight such as it was because it had given him an inroad of sorts with women. While thirty-six-year-old Gerald wasn't drop dead gorgeous by any means, he wasn't homely either. He was reed thin with a ready smile and a quick wit that showed up in the twinkle of his blue eyes whenever he told a joke or recited a funny story.

Gerald zeroed in on Kinsey Wyatt's approach like a heat-seeking missile closing in on its target. "Hey there, you're the new lawyer. We haven't met yet," Gerald stuck out his hand, introduced himself. "What can I help you with today?"

Kinsey perused the paint samples, looking for just the right color. "I'm looking for a ripe cantaloupe, only lighter. You sold that shade to Jordan Harris some time back. But I need a lighter version of it, something in the same palette, but not nearly as orangey."

"Okay." Ever prudent, Gerald began to draw out Kinsey's specifics. Used to the demands of his customers, their unusual tastes and frequent changes of mindset,

Gerald suggested a few different hues, soliciting Kinsey's feedback.

"No, too pink," Kinsey said.

Gerald tried again.

"No, too dark."

Gerald held out a different sample, waited patient as Job for Kinsey's decision. When he saw another shake of her head, he tried again.

This time she scrunched up her nose and said, "No, way too pumpkiny."

After more prompting, a trio of back and forth shakes of the head, no one was more pleased than Gerald when Kinsey finally settled on a soft, pale apricot. "That's it. Perfect."

That's what he liked to hear. He mixed her paint, all the while the attractive woman went on and on about her new apartment. "How many gallons do you think it will take?" Gerald asked.

Kinsey thought for a minute. "Oh at least two gallons."

"How many square feet are we talking about?"

"Hmm, I'd say no more than five hundred and fifty," Kinsey decided.

"Do you need brushes and rollers?"

"Nope. Jordan and Nick are providing all that. But Jordan mentioned you had a catalogue I could browse through to look at fabric for slipcovers."

"We do. Upholstery fabrics. Some of them are pricey though," Gerald warned. Because it hadn't taken long for it to get around town that the new attorney was having financial problems, Gerald added, "But if you're on a budget, I'd like to make a suggestion."

Cautious, Kinsey chewed her lip and said, "Go ahead."

"My mother sews. She's good. You ask anyone in town and they'll tell you that Emma Colter is a fine seamstress. Abby Pointer asked my mom to make her wedding gown. She has an entire selection of slipcovers she's already finished. They're a lot more reasonably priced than anything you'll find in that catalogue."

"Where can I see her work?"

Gerald smiled. "She's two streets over on Cape May. I'll call her to let her know you'll be stopping by."

Kinsey left Ferguson's with two gallons of paint and directions to get to Emma Colter's house. Excited about decorating her new place, she didn't give Logan Donnelly another thought.

Chapter Thirteen

That night Logan didn't reach the B & B until well after seven. It had been a productive few days so far but an exhausting time of getting organized, and getting the project off the ground.

As soon as he climbed out of the truck, he heard what sounded like a radio in the distance blaring rock music. Curious, he followed the beat, surprised to find Eddie Vedder's voice drifting from the windows above the garage.

He found the door wide open to the apartment. Peering inside, he saw Kinsey standing on a ladder, gripping a paint roller in her hand like a soldier on a mission. Sheets of plastic covered the furniture and tarps covered the floor. Good thing too because she'd left a trail of splattered paint drops here and there and everywhere. She was a messy painter, he noted and grinned in spite of the grueling day he'd had. He took a minute to admire her legs in the low-riding shorts she wore and to watch her butt move in rhythm to the song as she made another up and down pass over one section of the wall. The soft shade of cantaloupe she'd slapped over the old paint so far seemed to energize the room. Or maybe it was the woman.

When the tune changed to Red Hot Chili Peppers, he didn't try to yell over the song. There was no point. Instead he went over and turned the volume down on the CD player. "Don't you ever take a day off?" he said.

At the sound of his voice, she dropped the roller. "See what you made me do! You scared the life out of me!" She immediately hopped down to retrieve it. "You should let a body know when you're lurking about. What are you doing here?"

"The door was open. The rock was so loud you couldn't have heard me anyway," he pointed out. "You didn't answer me. Don't you ever take a day off?"

She lifted one shoulder, still annoyed with him over what she'd heard at lunch. "I want to paint before I move in. Nick and Jordan don't mind if I check out of my room this weekend. In fact, with all the out-of-state workers, they could use my room. And I'm ecstatic to get settled."

"How come you didn't hang around today at lunch? I saw you at the site. Why didn't you stick around?"

"You were on the phone."

"So? You could've waited until I finished my conversation, said hello. I could've shown you around."

"I don't think so. I don't usually make a habit of listening to men's conversations, especially when they're in the middle of flirting with women so openly over the phone."

For a moment his temper wanted to flare at the allegation. That is, until he caught the spurt of jealousy he saw in her hazel eyes. Logan's own twinkled with amusement. "You overheard my conversation with Valerie?"

"I have no idea who it was," she said as frost gathered in her voice.

"Valerie," he concluded. He couldn't say why picking up on the green-eyed monster thrilled him so much, only that it did. "Kinsey, Valerie Trace is my agent. I've known the woman for more than a dozen years."

"What do I care? How you talk to other women is none of my business." She'd almost added that he'd never talked to her like that with such warmth in his voice, but managed to hold her tongue from making the comparison.

"Even if the woman's old enough to be my mother, has been happily married for thirty-five years to the same man, and has a couple of cute little grandkids to show for it?"

"Humph," Kinsey muttered. "I know what I heard."

He stepped closer, smeared the drop of paint spatter stuck to her cheek. "You heard me sweet-talking my first and only agent who happens to love my work and shows it by making galleries pay through the nose for it."

Her eyes lifted to his. He saw the flush on her cheeks and heard the grudging admission, "I'm sorry then."

"Don't be. It's a definite boon to my ego." And how sick was that? he wondered.

"You certainly don't need more of an advantage."

"I have an advantage?"

"Oh be quiet." She needed a change of subject. Putting her hands on her hips, she asked, "What do you think so far? This is such a cute little place I can't wait to get moved in. By the way, good call on the color. It has enough orange in it to pop yet not enough to make it look pumpkin, which is not the look I'm going for. Gerald at Ferguson's had to mix it five times to get the perfect shade. I think he got exasperated with me a couple of times."

He let her go on as she scoffed at the mediocre hues Gerald had come up with. As soon as she bothered taking a breath he asked, "Want some help?"

"What? Of course not, you look beat. It's been a grueling three days for you at the site. I've got this."

He admired her sense of independence, the fact that she didn't seem to expect him to pick up a brush just because she was elbow-deep in paint. Maybe that was why he wanted to be a part of finishing the job. Maybe that was why he wanted to see her moved in and her new place take shape. He wasn't exactly sure the reason. But something about her pulled at him and had since the first time she'd walked up to his lighthouse. It could've been that he wanted to get her flat on her back in that urn top maple bed. Whatever it was had him offering, "Do you have an extra brush?"

She eyed him for at least half a minute. "Have you eaten dinner, Logan?"

"Not yet."

"Jordan brought over chicken and pasta salad for me when she found out I intended to start this tonight. It's in that basket on the counter. There's plenty. Go sit over by the window and eat. That way you'll get a bit of fresh air and not breathe in so many paint fumes."

"I'm used to the smell of paint and chemicals," Logan pointed out.

She tilted her head and smiled. "I'm pretty sure that's in your bio somewhere. But it isn't necessary to help me. I've painted walls before. In fact." She turned back to her work. "One wall and I'm almost done."

"I'll eat on one condition."

She grinned. "I guess I could eat another drumstick. That is what you were going to say, right?" She went over to the fridge, took out two Newcastle Ales, handed one off to Logan.

"Maybe." He opened the basket and sniffed the food. "This looks fantastic."

"Jordan's a good cook. She makes fancy dishes though that I've never tried. Now me, I know how to fancy up tuna, make meatless spaghetti, fix a meal out of potatoes, and do wonders with ramen noodles."

Logan stared at her. "I hear you on the noodles. I didn't have much money when I first got to San Francisco. Those were lean times. My parents didn't support the idea of their son becoming a 'sissy artist.' I believe those were the exact words my father used as I packed my bags to walk out of his house at eighteen. Anyway, once I got to the big city, my first job was a carpenter by day. Troy sort of reminds me of myself at that age. Raw talent. No one around to support your efforts knowing you're on your own no matter what happens. That first year, I'm not sure how I made ends meet. But I'd buy ramen noodles and eat those until I couldn't stand the sight of them. Where did you and your mother live in the Bay, Kinsey?"

"We called it the Tendernob. My mom worked for a Nob Hill family about twenty blocks from our house. For years she rode the bus back and forth. You wouldn't believe the difference a couple of blocks can make though."

"Oh yeah, I would. I used to live in a rundown two-hundred square-foot studio apartment half the size of this one near Sixth and Market."

"You're kidding? I lived off Golden Gate Avenue."

"Neighbors and didn't know it. We could have picked up our dry cleaning and rubbed elbows with each other."

"Well, you have a few years on me," she said with a glimmer in her eye. "It's interesting we had to come to a tiny town like Pelican Pointe though to run into each other."

While they finished the chicken he told her about his time at the arts institute. They reminisced about the Tenderloin National Forest, where Logan had helped paint one of the murals and Kinsey had volunteered in high school to plant some of the vegetation.

"That was back before my mother's diagnosis. It's still one of my favorite places in the neighborhood. That and Boeddeker Park. My mother used to take me there as a kid."

"Love the mural there."

"Oh yeah. That area, my area, is one of the best."

"I'm surprised you left it."

She moved a shoulder. "Too many memories maybe, time for a change of scenery to start fresh."

"I felt like that. But after moving to L.A. it just didn't seem to have the same ambiance as the Bay did."

By the time they got down to cleaning up, he was tugging her out the door. "The smell of paint is overwhelming in here. Let's take a walk down to the cove. I could use the fresh air."

"But…I wanted to finish this tonight."

"Take a walk with me and I'll help you when we get back. Like you said, you're almost done. One wall, two rollers, won't take us all that long."

If only she could resist those sharp green eyes, the little dimple on his chin, and all that long hair. How sad was it that she couldn't or didn't even want to try?

The full moon seemed so close they had only to reach up and give it one good yank for it to fall into their hands. Stars glittered and twinkled as she followed Logan along the trail to the familiar steps.

"Give me your hand," Logan offered, reaching to take hers to guide her down the steep stairs.

Once they reached the sand, Kinsey had held her curiosity in check for too long. She hadn't even known who his agent was. And she'd considered sleeping with the guy. She might have given him the benefit of the doubt with the conversation she'd overheard *if* he ever bothered to open up about himself. Why couldn't he talk to her like he did this Valerie person? Not knowing that much about him just led to misunderstandings. Even though his mood seemed lighter, she had to dig. She considered now as good a time as any. "Why did you come back here, Logan? To Pelican Pointe?"

He stalked off a few feet and she watched as he stomped back over to her as if judging whether or not he could trust her. He must have deemed her worthy because he said, "I need to know what happened to my sister, Megan. She died in this town. I want to find the person who killed her."

Kinsey's mouth gaped open. That was the last thing she expected him to say. All kinds of questions bombarded her brain. "When did this happen? Exactly? You're certain the killer is still here in town? That's why you were spooked at the cliffs the other night?"

"I'm convinced the killer is still here. Someone here, some everyday-looking guy walks around with a secret, walks among all of us every day without a backward glance or a thought of what he did to Megan." All of a sudden he wanted to tell her all of it because there was so much more. But before he could, she was asking for details.

"Wait a minute. Back up. First tell me what happened to your sister?"

"I was fifteen at the time. It was August, nearing the end of our time here. My grandfather and I decided we'd go camping out to Yosemite to cap the summer. We did stuff like that together all the time. But Megan was two years older. She'd gotten to that age, a teenage girl, where she wanted to be around her friends, not her little brother and grandfather. Megan stayed behind. I wanted her to go. I begged her. Like any good kid brother, I made a nuisance and nagged on her about it for a week before we left. And like any older sister, Megan dug in her heels and said she was too old to go camp out in the woods like some little kid. The last words we said to each other were bitter, yelling, typical brother and sister stuff."

"Logan, you had no way of knowing that would be the last time you'd speak to her. When did you learn that she'd died?"

He shook his head, stormed off again, came back. "She went missing, Kinsey. Megan disappeared, vanished into thin air. That June and July she'd been dating someone, sneaking around. I know because she came back home a couple of times late, way after curfew. I don't even remember his name. My grandmother didn't know who it was either. If we did, I'd hunt him down, get some answers from him. But when it happened, I was too overcome with grief to think clearly when she didn't come back."

"Of course you were. So wait…let me understand. During the summers you and Megan came here to stay in Pelican Pointe with your grandparents. Every summer?" There was a story there, Kinsey suspected.

"Pretty much every summer up until that last one. After Megan went missing, I didn't come back at least not until it was too late." When he saw her questioning look, he added, "My grandmother's funeral. Up till then though, when I was a kid I spent all school year waiting for summer vacation. At one time, coming here was something to look forward to. But I was a kid then. I loved it here because I learned to swim here, learned to surf in the water off Smuggler's Bay. So did Megan. We were inseparable back then. After she disappeared, it wasn't the same. But at the same time I missed coming here, spending time with my grandparents. Does that make sense?"

"Sure. This place held good memories and then bad."

"My grandparents were never the same after that either. I think they blamed themselves. I know my father blamed them. Maybe I just outgrew the place. I don't know." He ran a hand through his hair. "All I remember when it happened was that I hated the town. Someone here knows something. I can feel it. It may have been twenty years ago—"

"But you want answers. That's completely understandable considering the circumstances."

"Damn right I do. But you don't understand, Kinsey. Pelican Pointe wasn't exactly a big tourist destination, even back then. There was no hotel for tourists to book. Hell, the only hotel in the area had gone out of business and the Fannings had purchased the property so they could turn it into a marine rescue center. Most of the time the tourists bypassed Pelican Pointe altogether. If they wanted to stay in the area for any length of time they headed to Santa Cruz to do it. We didn't get a lot of strangers in town. Get it? And if we did they stuck out like a sore thumb. That's why I think whatever happened to Megan, happened at the hands of a local."

"Sounds reasonable. So you look at everyone as a suspect."

"Sounds pathetic I know. But I look at anyone over a certain age. Megan was seventeen. Anyone say around the same age as me up to five or ten years older. That's a general range of thirty-five to forty-five and up now."

"What was the town like back then?"

"Not much has changed. But back then kids pretty much had the beach all to themselves. The grownups did their thing. We had all day to do ours. All we had to do was hike down the cliff, carry our surfboards, hit the waves, spend the lazy days of June, July, and August on the beach. It was an idyllic place for two active kids to spend the summer. Back then Megan and I were close, two years apart and she was a bit of a tomboy. We did everything together. We had to be. Our parents weren't that—visible, I guess you'd say. Our grandparents made it easy on us to just…be kids. They didn't fight like Mom and Dad did. They had rules. We had chores. You went to church. You were at home by a certain time. That sort of thing."

Her mind was on overload considering the options. "If it's a local they had to own some type of business to stick around for so long."

"Why do you say that? I've thought the same thing but I'd like to hear why you think so."

"Well, for one, look around this town. It's difficult to make a living here unless you have some type of stable income. Why stay around a place for twenty years if you don't? Who has the most stable incomes in town? Business owners, especially ones that have been in the area over decades. That is, if your killer is still here."

"Wow, that's remarkably astute. Why is it you didn't ask if I thought she just picked up and left?"

"Logan, I see it on your face. You wouldn't have taken this huge step to come here if you didn't think something bad happened to her. What do *you* think happened to Megan? Surely you have a theory?"

"That's just it, Kinsey. I have no idea. The minute we got back from the camping trip, my grandmother told us Megan had gone out that Friday night on a date and never came home. We didn't have cell phones back then. And even if we had, I doubt my grandmother could have gotten through to us."

"How is it your grandmother didn't know who Megan was dating?"

He shook his head. "I don't even know that. But that summer was different than any other in a lot of ways. Megan and I had grown apart. Maybe it's just one growing up faster than the other. And frankly, I didn't pay much attention at the time. I didn't know that nugget of info would ever come up."

"I'm really sorry, Logan. But didn't your grandparents file a missing persons report?"

He nodded. "Of course they did. They had to wait forty-eight hours though. Things were different back then. That was the rule. Anybody went missing you waited for an eternity before doing anything about it. I never thought she ran off, Kinsey. Megan didn't pack any of her clothes. She didn't take a single, goddamn thing with her. What teenage girl takes off without the money she'd been saving, or her makeup, or her best pair of jeans? If I tell you something you have to promise me you won't tell another living soul."

"Give me a dollar."

"Huh?"

"Give me a dollar. It's my retainer fee. You're retaining me as your lawyer. That way what you tell me is in strict confidence, client to lawyer privilege." When he gave her a strange look, she added, "It's the law, Logan. I'm sworn to keep whatever you tell me confidential."

He looked so relieved to hear that, he withdrew a dollar from his wallet, handed it off.

"That makes it official. Now, what is it you want me to promise I won't tell anyone?"

"There have been at least ten young women, teens, girls really, who have vanished from this area without a trace."

Again, Kinsey's mouth dropped open. "Ten? That just vanished? Are you sure about that? From Pelican Pointe? Come on, Logan. That would make the papers. It would be on the Internet."

He shook his head. "I don't think anyone's bothered connecting the dots. But I've discovered a lot."

"The disappearances…they're not a coincidence." She found chills running up her arms. "Why have I never heard of this before? What does law enforcement say? What about Ethan?"

"Not much. They take reports, file them away, and they tell the families they'll keep an eye out for their kids. That's exactly what they did with Megan. I want to know what happened to her, Kinsey. I *have* to know. At this stage in my life, after all these years, I have to find the answers. I promised my grandmother I'd find out. My sister deserved better. She deserved a better brother than I turned out to be."

"You were fifteen, Logan. What could you do?"

"I haven't been fifteen forever, Kinsey. I haven't been a very good brother or a grandson for that matter. Instead I did everything I could to put this town behind me and that means I put Megan out of my head."

"Logan if you hadn't concentrated on your work this might've made you go crazy with doubts." And now so much more about his moods clicked into place.

"I got as far away from here as I could get so I wouldn't think about Megan. Only to make a promise to my grandmother that I never had any intentions of keeping—I walked away from it—until now. It's past time I kept that promise and looked into what really happened to Megan. I'm here to do that twenty years late."

Kinsey thought of the lighthouse. "And more, I'd say."

"Yeah and more." He ran his hands through his long hair. "My grandfather, Liam Donnelly, designed the lighthouse and helped build the tower six decades ago."

"Liam Donnelly? So I was right? I knew the two names were connected."

"Yes, you were right. You're the only one who made the link. While spending time in this little backwater town on a project he'd taken, he met my grandmother. At thirty years old, a self-avowed bachelor, he fell in love with a nineteen-year-old girl. Times were different back then."

"Oh I don't know, these days you have fifty year old movie stars dating twenty-year-olds. On both sides of the aisle, not so different at all."

"True. But this was in 1936. I'm convinced they truly loved each other. The only times they were ever apart was when he traveled to do his job. And then, of course, the day he died. I'm not sure he ever got over Megan's disappearing like she did. Then there was my grandmother's anguish over losing them both. Losing both of them broke her heart, her spirit."

"What about your parents, Logan?"

"Good question. They seemed to go on like nothing had happened. Except now my dad used Megan's disappearance for one more reason to hate his father. After all, Megan hadn't disappeared on his watch. I think they blamed my grandmother for it the most. I had a fractured family, Kinsey. It wasn't Ozzie and Harriet."

"I've got news for you, Logan. No one has an Ozzie and Harriet kind of family. No one."

"Tell me about yours."

"I had my mother. That's it. Short and sweet. I'm what happens when a very, wealthy married man has an affair with the help, gets her pregnant. Of course, my mother was fired on the spot when the whole sordid thing came to light. My sperm donor father died shortly after I was born, head-on collision on the 101. Drunk driving. His fault. He also killed someone in the other car. His wife survived. But according to my mom, his family had to pay out a substantial amount in damages to the family of the woman he killed. Apparently they could afford it. In spades."

"What was his name?"

"Addison Kinsey." She waited a beat to see if he recognized the affluent name. "My mother's own little joke, a form of revenge, I suppose. Although I do wish she'd thought of something more original than Kinsey Addison Wyatt."

"*The* Addison Kinsey? Kinsey Industries?"

"Ah, I see you've heard of the sperm donor's family."

"Who hasn't? *You're* Addison Kinsey's daughter?"

She laughed at the look on his face. "So my mother said. I wouldn't actually know with absolute certainty without causing an uprising of some sort. I doubt Addison

Kinsey's heirs would welcome me with open arms at the family reunion."

"I don't see that ever happening either, not with what I know about the storied Kinsey family. Their wealth goes all the way back to the late nineteenth century. They made their money in the Central Pacific Railroad, along with a few gold and silver mines thrown in. Haven't you ever been curious?"

"Not really. At this stage in my life, I don't need the Kinseys or their money. The sad thing about all of it is my mother still loved the guy until the day he drove his car into someone else's. In Ellie Wyatt's short life, and believe me her life was way too short, I don't ever remember her dating. She might have before I turned four or so, but in my memory she never even bothered with it. She was one woman who seemed truly happy without having a man in her life. I once tried to set her up with my seventh-grade science teacher, who I had a major crush on at the time. I sat around dreaming the two of them might actually be a couple. But my mother wanted no part of it."

"Wonder why?"

Kinsey lifted a shoulder. "I managed to work that into the conversation once before she died. She said something romantic like 'once you find *the one*, no one else will ever do.' But…I never really bought the idea there's only one person out there for you."

"It's a myth."

"For once, I think we've found something we agree on."

He reached out, took hold of her chin, brought her lips up to meet his.

About that time the high tide surged around their feet, danced in and out in playful tag. They both stood there wet, caught up in want and need, drowning, not in the pounding surf, but locked in heavy combat, fighting their emotions. Neither was quite prepared to take that next step.

From high above the cliffs, he watched the couple on the stretch of beach below. So Kinsey Wyatt was Logan's woman. That might make things more interesting down the road. It would certainly make his own reconnaissance more thrilling. His life was settling into a rut anyway. He'd have to pick up the pace.

He hadn't been able to understand what they'd said to each other. All he knew was the conversation had been intense before the make out session had kicked in.

If he knew Donnelly, and he thought he did, he wanted to keep his options open. After all, the man would never find his sister. But that didn't mean he couldn't play head games with the asshole. All part of the fun, he decided as he started back to his car. He'd take a drive out to his special place. It was past time he paid his girls a visit.

Chapter Fourteen

As soon as the paint dried on the walls, Kinsey started the move over to her apartment. Even though she didn't have all that much stuff, mostly clothes, it had taken a half a dozen trips back and forth from her room and up the steps to the studio to get everything tucked into its rightful place. Kinsey knew from experience, living in a small space, it was best if you found a place for everything and kept it there right up front.

She remade the bed with crisp white sheets, plumped the pillows, and once again, spread out the goose down comforter over the top. She'd polished every surface, every stick of furniture the night before with lemon oil. In fact, she'd defy anyone to try to find a speck of dust anywhere.

Around eight o'clock she looked around and declared the move-in complete. Her clothes were put away, hung up in the armoire or arranged in the drawers. Her toiletries were laid out in the bathroom. She'd even stopped at Emma Colter's on the way home and picked up the slipcover for the sofa, which was now a rich, deep brown that contrasted with the apricot walls.

First chance she got, she would pick up some decorative pillows at the thrift store. And as soon as Wally pronounced her car able to make it back to the Bay, she'd take the trip there to pick up the rest of her stuff. It wasn't much, mostly keepsakes and photographs, some of her books and treasures that wouldn't fit in the car. But all of it would make the place seem more like a home. Her home.

She'd even taken that first step to wean herself off Jordan's cooking. Using her employee discount at Murphy's, she'd packed her fridge to the gills with the necessary staples like milk and eggs, added cold cuts and cheese. Her cabinets were full, too. There was no chance she'd starve without Jordan's cuisine.

"How do you like it?"

She jumped a little at the sound of Scott's voice. But she tried to recover quickly. "I love it! It's so much larger than my little room. How does it look?"

"It looks like it's had a makeover from one of those do-it-yourself home channels. Donnelly really nailed the color for the walls."

"He did, didn't he?" She turned to face Scott. "You know why he's here, don't you?"

"I've always known he'd eventually come back here to look for Megan."

"Scott?"

"What?"

"Do you know who killed Megan?"

His blue eyes searched her hazel. "Yes." Before she could say anything, he held up a steady hand. "Don't go there, Kinsey. Let's say I did tell you. Let's say I gave you a name. What good would it do? What could you do with that information? You'd still need evidence, you'd still need proof. You start accusing someone and people in town will think you're on a witch hunt. You're just now settling in, trying to establish yourself. That's the last thing you need here. If I gave you or Logan a name, you'd never convince anyone in town of anything without solid proof."

"Is there solid proof, Scott?"

"Yes. But again, there are some things I don't see, some things I don't know. Believe it or not, I don't have all the answers to every question in the damn universe. You and Logan will need to work together to solve this thing. If you don't, if you allow it to skate by, it will remain a mystery forever. You and Logan get one shot at this, Kinsey. And that would be a shame if you two blow it now because the families of those girls deserve to know what happened to them after all these years. Do you understand?"

"I think so. But you can't even get Logan to talk to you. He doesn't even want to acknowledge that he sees you, Scott."

"You think I don't know that. I've never seen a more stubborn man. You'd think an artist would be able to think outside the box, have an open mind about things. Who knew the guy couldn't get his head out of his ass long enough to consider new possibilities?"

"He's so…angry…so pissed off. Do you think that's the reason he's so unwilling to accept you?"

"Probably. But that's why it's up to you. I want you to promise me something though."

"Sure."

"Be very careful, Kinsey. You're an intelligent woman. Don't be fooled into trusting anyone that gives off a vibe. Trust your gut instincts. You'll need them."

"What are you still doing hanging around here this time of night?" Logan asked Troy when he spotted him standing outside the construction trailer.

"Just making certain everything's ready when they deliver the lumber tomorrow morning. Should be here around eight a.m. It'll take up a lot of room when it does get here."

"That's why we'll store most of it in the tower until we're ready to use it in the keeper's house. Keeps it out of the weather."

Troy cleared his throat. "I wanted to thank you for teaching me to use the computer like you did. I never had nobody take the time like that to walk me through the software program so I could do the ordering."

Logan had thought as much but it was nice to know Troy appreciated learning something new. "You get this down and you can go anywhere to get a job. That's the truth. Construction sites always need good supply people that can track orders online and keep track of inventory."

"How do you know that? You sound like you've worked construction even though I know better. Artists don't do stuff like that."

Logan smiled. "I wasn't always an artist, Troy. I had to earn a living just like everyone else before someone spotted a single piece of my sculpture they wanted to buy. Until that happened, I worked as a carpenter."

"Get out. Really?" He cleared his throat again before Logan could answer. "I was upset when you gave Derek the foreman's job instead of me."

Logan nodded. He'd known that, too. "Your uncle has more construction experience. It wasn't a slight to you."

"I know that now. But I was your first hire. I thought, you know, you'd make me your foreman because of that. But now, I'm glad you didn't. I wouldn't like it very much to have to ride roughshod over Turley."

"Derek seems to have his number in that regard." He locked up the trailer and said, "It's getting late. Something else on your mind?"

"I wanted a man's take on something."

"Okay, shoot."

"Kinsey says I should make Mona a jewelry box for her birthday. But it won't be a store bought present. And I know women like fancier stuff they see in stores. Do you think I'd be wasting my time if I made her one special?"

"Troy, if Mona doesn't appreciate your artistic talents, you gotta keep looking, son. If she isn't right for you, keep looking."

"That's what Kinsey said."

"Yeah, well, Kinsey's a smart woman."

The Friday before Memorial Day, Logan got his cast off. The orthopedist, a Dr. Allen Jax in Santa Cruz, seemed to think his range of motion was within normal, even though the wrist and part of the hand looked pale and scaly—and itched like hell. Sitting on the exam table, Logan felt like he was ten years old again.

"You'll have some weakness in the tendons and muscle. That, too, is normal and will pass," Dr. Jax confirmed.

"This is the third cast I've had sawed off in the last year, I know the drill."

"Good, then you know not to go out and pick a fight."

"It wasn't on my agenda." But one thing he knew for certain was, before the weekend was out, he intended to put an end to the tension that had built up between himself and Kinsey Wyatt.

"You know about the exercises then?"

"Never got to that point before."

"Well, the x-rays show everything's healed but I'll give you a list of exercises to do to take it slow, build up over time to gain the strength back."

"Will I get my full dexterity back?"

"I can't answer that. If you do the strengthening exercises religiously, those should get you where you want to go—eventually. If you experience pain, take four to six ibuprofen, use ice locally to take the swelling down. Take it nice and slow and I think you should get the dexterity to around ninety percent."

"Then I guess I'll have to settle for that."

Memorial Day weekend always kicked off summer. That was the rule.

It might've been a three-day-holiday for some but not for Kinsey. The only day she got off would be Monday. She had her schedule to keep at Murphy's and the weekend crowd of tourists that would surely find their way into The Pointe for fine dining or cocktails. She knew

Perry Altman expected big crowds as people who lived inland would invariably pile in their cars for a day trip to the beach. While here, they'd spend their dollars up and down Main Street, or in the shops along the pier on Ocean Street. They'd come to Pelican Pointe to visit the Fanning Marine Rescue Center, or to participate in the Memorial Day parade. If they were trying to get away for the weekend, they'd make reservations at least overnight at Promise Cove.

Kinsey knew from Jordan that the inn was booked solid for the entire three-day weekend. She was thrilled to have her own place. No more bumping into people on the staircase. Even if that place was a stone's throw from the main house, it was to her, separate from all the other "guests."

There was a certain amount of freedom in Aaron knowing that after she finished up work today, she'd be able to change into her little black dress right there in the bathroom down the hall at his house. No more sneaking around.

She'd only seen Logan in passing, a couple of times at breakfast, a couple of dinner conversations. Either he seemed preoccupied with his project or he'd been avoiding another conversation about his sister, as if he'd been regretting his decision to share Megan with anyone else. It had occurred to Kinsey more than once that it was almost like a test, to see if she'd rat him out. It was almost as if he expected her to give away his secret at the first opportunity.

His evasion was starting to piss her off.

Oh there had been a few daytime phone calls, a few text messages, but for the most part Logan Donnelly had kept to himself. That was either on purpose or he'd been caught up in his project and didn't or wouldn't make time to see her.

For God's sake they had slept right across the hall from each other until she'd moved out. If she'd thought the guy might knock on her door in the middle of the night for a quickie, she'd been greatly disappointed. He hadn't even walked across the courtyard to see if she got moved in okay. Not that she needed his help.

But she would admit to no one that she'd spent her last three nights across the hall from him edgy and tense. She'd been tempted to slip into a sexy teddy, slink out of her room and just tiptoe across the hall, knock on his door, and seduce him by simply crawling into his bed. To hell with a long-term commitment. To hell with a serious relationship. All she'd been able to think about since that first Saturday night they'd kissed and necked was having that mouth of his all over her body.

It was just sex, wasn't it?

She'd had uncomplicated sex before, she could damn sure do it again. Another woman might have done just that. But Kinsey Wyatt refused to throw herself at a man, especially one as cocky and arrogant as Logan Donnelly. No, he'd have to make the first move. She wouldn't go begging to get his attention. In fact, she got the distinct impression he was used to women falling at his feet.

But the temptation was there. That's why she'd be wise to keep him at a distance.

And one huge reason, she was glad she no longer stayed at the main house. She couldn't very well sneak across the courtyard in a trench coat to tap on the man's bedroom door at two in the morning.

But God, how pathetic was it that she'd already consider doing that?

With the holiday weekend, the B & B was all but bursting at the seams. By seven that Friday evening, Logan felt the walls closing in. He watched during meal time as parents did their best to wrangle rowdy, over-stimulated children to sit down to eat their suppers. If that wasn't enough, they had to catch them to get them ready for bedtime. After one little boy of about three, spilled his chocolate milk all over Logan, he decided it was time to escape. But when he went to his room, he found he couldn't settle.

All week his mind had been on Kinsey. He'd tried to avoid her though after their walk on the beach. He shouldn't have confided in her about Megan. He'd known better. But it really was a simple matter. It had been a burden he'd never shared with another living soul. He'd opened up that festering wound by coming back here. And now, if Kinsey decided to tell any number of people he'd just have to live with the consequences.

Truth be told though, it had felt damn good to tell someone, to finally get the secret he'd been holding back out in the open.

Restless, he decided to take a walk and watch the sun go down over the water.

He stayed at the cove until well past dark until a couple from Fresno looking for their own little chunk of solitude intruded on his turf. He should have gone into town for a drink at The Pointe or a beer at McCready's. But after putting in another tough week supervising two crews, he'd needed to clear his head. He especially needed to decide what he wanted to do about Kinsey Wyatt, other than getting her horizontal.

On the walk back up to the house, he made his decision.

Around quarter to twelve, Logan sat on the steps leading up to Kinsey's apartment waiting for her to come home. He heard her old car chug up the long driveway as if on its last leg. He knew for a fact Wally had done what he could to keep the heap running. But when he heard the squeal of her brakes near the side of the garage, alerting everyone to her arrival, the sound reminded him the

Nissan needed to be replaced with a newer car. The stretch of road between the city limits and Promise Cove was unlit and remote. He didn't like the idea that she made the trip late at night alone three times a week in a car that could easily break down if you happened to so much as look at it the wrong way.

The sound of her heels tapping on the pavement as she made her way to the stairs allowed him to know the minute she spotted him. He saw her eyes go wide.

"You weren't at the restaurant tonight."

"No." He held up his wrist.

Her jaw dropped open. "You didn't say a word about getting your cast off."

"That's because I've been there twice already and both times they had to recast it. I wasn't sure this time either so I kept it to myself. Kinsey?"

"What?"

"Come sit down. Get off your feet."

"Logan, I've been sitting for hours. I thought I'd put my stuff up and take a much-needed walk on the beach to relax."

He moved his legs aside and said, "Then run up and do that. I'll wait here." He watched as she dashed upstairs as energetic as she'd been at breakfast two days before.

When she came back, without sitting down, she reached out to touch his hand, the one that had been covered up ever since she'd met him. She felt along the jagged skin. "I love your hands." She kissed the palm brought it to her cheek.

"I love your eyes. They're so trusting, so honest."

"Logan?"

"Yeah?"

"I'm all moved in. My bed even has fresh sheets on it." So much for not throwing herself at him. But she could only curb her hunger for so long.

He pushed off the step and was in front of her in long strides, tugging her back up the stairs. He pulled her through the open studio door, shoved it closed. Reaching out, he ran one long, lean finger down her cheek. "I've wanted to get you out of this dress ever since I first saw you wearing it."

"So who's stopping you?"

With that, he whirled her around, ran the zipper down, stretched the fabric back and off her shoulders. Kinsey wiggled free until it fell around her feet. She turned to face him, standing before him in a black bra and thong.

He yanked her up against his chest, heard her sharp intake of breath as anticipation stretched out between them. He backed her up toward that old urn top Maplewood.

Running her hands under his Tee shirt, she pulled it off over his head. She raked her nails through all that hair while her mouth sucked along his throat. Her fingers wandered down to the top of his jeans. She heard the low growl hum in his throat.

"Not yet. Just looking at you right now, I'm about to pop out of these as it is. We're going to take this as slow as I can manage it, which means…we're taking care of you first." He moved in, covered her mouth at the same time his hands gripped her rear end, lifted her up off the floor.

She wrapped long legs around his waist, threw her arms around his shoulders.

The first assault was all teasing and tasting. They ate at each other, taking ravenous bites until his fingers roamed back, unhooked the bra. He used one hand to travel downward to the silky stretch of fabric that was left, tearing at the flimsy lace, ripping it off in one strong snap.

They fell back on the bed.

His thumb found a pebble-hard nipple. He lowered his mouth to it, took a slow turn at feasting on one breast, then the other. He slicked his tongue along her belly, grazed on a satiny thigh. But nibbling only made him hungry for more. There was tender flesh to sample, gentle brushstrokes meant to explore every curve and fold. Nips lingered and had her hips rising off the mattress. The little quivers whipped along until pleasure flooded her.

Even as the tremors played out, she reached for him. In the whole of her life, she couldn't ever remember wanting anyone more.

He toed off his shoes, unsnapped his jeans to twist out of them.

"Hurry," Kinsey urged, breathless and impatient. She wanted to feel him on her, in her.

He inched back up her body, kissed flat belly, and used his lips to caress soft skin. He covered her mouth again.

At the same time, she reached down to stroke, wanting to give back a measure of what he'd given her. But her touch brought out a guttural growl from his throat again. She saw his eyes darken, saw the yearning to mate snap and bend. She brought him into her in a frenzied rush, the joining, hot and tight. When his hair draped down in a curtain around her face, she smoothed it back so she could see his eyes.

"Kinsey."

"Logan."

He brought her arms up and over her head. They locked hands. Her legs went around his waist. They took each other as fast, hot flares rose up between them. Damp skin to damp skin, need raced along like whitecaps rushing to shore.

They let the current take them on a fast ride in a slick froth of fiery gold and deep blues. They soared up together, first into, and through the curl. Release simmered on the edge until the wave finally crashed and allowed that complete slide into the drowning bliss.

He wasn't sure he could move. Not since high school had he been quite so desperate. He needed his breath back so he could say something, anything. It didn't surprise him she was the first to speak. "That was—"

"Quick?" he finished with a wide grin.

She let go a rolling laugh from deep in the belly. "That too. But I was going to say…worth the wait."

"Ah. Yeah. I'm having trouble moving just now." He touched her cheek, placed a tender kiss on her mouth before moving off her.

They lay side by side until he reached for her and she snuggled into his chest. "I'm exhausted, Logan. If I don't get some sleep…"

He stroked her hair, brought her further into him. "Then sleep. Morning will come too soon."

Logan was right. It seemed like she'd no more than closed her eyes than the alarm buzzed at six-thirty. Beside her, the man lifted his head without even opening his eyes and then let it fall back down into the pillows.

She patted his chest, wishing she had time to nibble and taste along those pecs. "Stay in bed. If I could I would. But I've got to take a shower before heading to Murphy's." Rolling from underneath the warm comforter, she made a mad dash to the bathroom to pee and turn on the water.

Kinsey had the drill down to a fine art. She knew exactly how many minutes she could spend in the shower without running late, exactly how long it would take her to get into town, barring any problems or interruptions to the norm.

When Logan yanked back the curtain, she let out a shriek that she was sure could be heard all the way to the main house. Without saying a word, he stepped under the stream of water, nipped her around the waist to assault her mouth, all in one deft motion. She inched up his body until he picked her up, cupped her rear end.

Eyeing that look on his face, Kinsey knew the norm as she'd known it had blessedly just come to an end.

When he backed her up against the tile for leverage, when his hard body made use of hers, she decided for this kind of interruption to her routine, she'd gladly show up a little late to work.

To hell with everyone else.

Chapter Fifteen

Main Street was packed with tourists who'd gotten an early start to the weekend. The slotted spaces had all been taken. Even at this early hour, pedestrians filled the sidewalks. Some poured out of the Diner where they'd probably just eaten breakfast, or streamed out of the drugstore where they'd more than likely loaded up on their day's supply of suntan lotion.

Kinsey noticed another group on foot walking toward Ocean Street either heading for the old wooden pier or the beach. Since most of them carried coolers, umbrellas, lawn chairs, and towels, her bet was they planned on scoring the perfect spot of sand early on with no plans of moving any time soon.

By the time Kinsey found a place to park, she clocked in at Murphy's with a scant two minutes to spare. The look Murphy gave her seemed to say he knew why she was late and what she'd been doing just thirty minutes prior to showing up.

It was possible she wore some kind of sign indicating she'd gotten laid after a year-long drought. She certainly felt looser…more relaxed than she had in a long time. So it probably showed on her face that she'd had two bouts of sex within a span of eight hours, a record for her.

As she counted out the money for her cash drawer, Kinsey's mind wandered. She couldn't help it. Had she ever had sex like that before? Had she ever been tempted to tell a man she loved him? The answer to both those questions was a resounding no. It was ridiculous to even entertain that kind of thinking since most of the time she didn't even understand the man's moods. But who could think with reason and logic when he knew how to do all manner of things with that skillful mouth of his. When a few beachgoers streamed through the door, she wished she'd remembered to ask Logan how he'd planned to spend his day off without her.

As she rang up a woman buying a six pack of beer along with bottles of water and juice, Kinsey wondered how soon it would be before she got a repeat performance from Logan.

Logan hadn't gone far. He'd driven to the site to take a third set of measurements on the non-bearing wall they intended to knock down to make certain he'd ordered enough materials. It wouldn't do to run short. But he needn't have bothered. He spotted young Troy doing the same thing. Was the kid just dedicated or was something else going on?

"I know payday was yesterday. I know because I signed the checks. I'm pretty sure I'm not old enough to get absent-minded yet. But I don't remember agreeing to pay you double time to show up on Saturday," Logan quipped from ten feet away.

"Oh. Sorry. But I know you want this wall down. I've been studying the blueprints every day at lunch. I just wanted to see if I could figure out how you intended to get it done."

Logan had to give it to the kid. Troy wasn't just curious, he was motivated. Logan could relate. He'd been much the same way once upon a time.

"Here," Logan offered, handing him the blueprints to roll out. "How about we go over it together? It wouldn't hurt to walk it through one more time just to be sure of the dimensions."

As they worked, Troy chatted. "You got plans tonight?"

"Hope so. How about you?"

"I'm getting together with Mona. And Sunday we plan to spend the day together at the beach."

"Oh yeah? I see you made your move."

Troy grinned. "Well, yeah. Tonight we're watching a movie at her house with Margie and Max. I'm hoping after that, I can talk her into taking a walk with me." Troy cleared his throat like he had something else to say. "Jason Healey is a waiter at The Pointe."

"And?" Logan asked, cocking a brow.

"Jason's a buddy of mine. He says you've been hanging around the restaurant every night that Kinsey plays." Troy wiggled his eyebrows up and down. "What do you say?"

"I say Jason should mind his own damn business or that maybe the CIA could use his superb power of observation."

Troy hooted with laughter. "I think you might be the best boss I ever had, Mr. Donnelly."

"Logan, it's just Logan. And blowing smoke up my ass like that just might get you a nice fat raise in record time, kid."

That Saturday night Troy and Mona walked hand in hand as they made their way through the crowd along Ocean Street, eating the hotdogs they'd bought from a portable vendor. As the couple passed McCready's, Ricky Oden's voice in rare form singing about *Poor Ellen Smith* drifted from inside.

"I don't know why we can't go into the bar to order a Coke and listen to the music just because we aren't twenty-one yet. It's a dumb rule," Troy groused.

"I know, but it's okay, Troy. I like it out here under the stars. In fact, why don't we head down to the beach?"

"Sounds good to me." Troy noticed her shivering a little. "Are you cold, Mona? Here," Troy offered without waiting for an answer. He pulled off his blue jean jacket, wrapped it around her shoulders.

"Thanks. I am a little cold. Who knew it got this chilly in California? It's certainly cooler than Texas right about now."

"You miss Texas?" Troy wanted to know.

"Nah, not any more. I did when I first got here. But I like working at the Diner. I like Pelican Pointe. At first I thought it was boring and there wasn't anything much to do here, but then I've been studying for my GED over at the library in San Sebastian. Did you graduate high school, Troy?"

"Yeah, my mom sort of made me promise I would before she died. I figured if I let her down, she'd know it and wouldn't be too happy about it. Plus, my uncles sort of stayed after me about homework and stuff."

"That's good. I wish my mom had done that since my dad, Max, just up and left us."

"Were you mad at him about that, about Max, I mean?"

"For a long time I was. But coming out here we sort of reconnected and I guess he's straightened his life out now. He and Margie go to AA meetings at the church every Sunday afternoon regularly."

"My uncle Dale tried that. But it didn't work for him. He ended up dying in a motorcycle accident. I think he was drunk at the time."

"I'm sorry," Mona said.

"Yeah, he was a strange dude all right, but I still miss him every now and then. Not like I do my mom or anything but when people die they leave a big void in your life."

"It's sweet the way you still remember your mom. I saw you out at the cemetery once, putting a bunch of wildflowers you'd picked on her grave. When I asked Margie about it, she told me all about your mom and how she died of breast cancer."

"Margie sort of looked out for me after that. She and my mom were friends for a long time."

"I know. Margie still talks about her sometimes. You can, you know, talk about your mom anytime you want. I don't mind. It won't bother me, Troy, if you do."

"Really? You know what, Mona?"

"What?"

"You're sure a whole lot different than Gina."

Six streets over from the beach, Gina Purvis spent her Saturday night fuming. The twenty-one-year-old had worked as Doc Prescott's receptionist since the week after graduating from high school. She'd walked into his office with spunk and confidence desperate for a summer job and never left. She liked answering the phones, making Doc's appointments, and enjoyed every step of the process in learning the software so she could keep Doc's books.

Even though, she still lived with her parents, she'd come a long way in three years. And she intended to go a lot farther. She had her sights set on becoming Doc's office manager one day—at least until she met the right man and settled down.

Determined to make something of herself in a town where jobs were hard to come by, Gina had it all planned out. That's one of the reasons she'd broken up with Troy Dayton. He didn't seem to have any luck at finding work and keeping it. Not only that, she got fed up with listening to his lame excuses and his stupid ideas about wanting to make a business out of selling crap that he'd made—out of wood—specifically those stupid jewelry boxes. Who in their right mind would buy stuff like that when they could just go online and order nicer things from a warehouse? And it wouldn't look clunky and stupid like Troy's did.

It wasn't her fault Troy wouldn't listen enough to take her advice. The guy never listened. That's why she was boxing up all the stuff he'd ever given her, like stuffed animals she'd never asked for, the ring he'd made her out of copper, and all his stupid CDs. She hadn't even wanted the stupid things in the first place. Troy had a habit of making his own music CDs, a mix of songs they had liked when they'd first started dating instead of just going over to San Sebastian and opening up his wallet to buy them like everybody else did. Troy was just too darn cheap. That was another reason she'd ended things with him. A girl deserved store-bought things and a man that could afford them without grumbling about it. Gina wanted a guy who would take her out to dinner to fancy places like The Pointe on a regular basis or buy her flowers from the florist instead of picking them out of a stupid field next to the road.

For two weeks Gina had been pestering Troy to come by and pick up all his junk that she'd boxed up. But so far he hadn't done it. She was getting sick and tired of the box sitting there taking up space. Every time she looked at it, she remembered the three months she'd wasted on Troy Dayton. She wanted the box gone…for good.

That's why, tonight, she'd show him. She'd take it by his old rundown trailer and dump the box of stuff on his front lawn if she had to. That would teach him not to ignore her and to answer her damn text messages and phone calls.

After telling her parents where she was going, Gina grabbed up the box and headed to her little red Mazda RX-7, determined to show Troy Dayton once and for all that Gina Purvis was not a woman to be dissed.

He'd had his eye on Gina for quite some time. Ever since he had walked into Doc's office for a back sprain and saw her sitting behind the counter. He'd been drawn to her big brown eyes, her slim figure, her youthful spirit. When it had been his turn to see Doc, Gina had even helped him into the exam room. All the while Gina had her arms wrapped around his shoulders, he had known it would be her…eventually. At twenty-one Gina was a little older than the others. But sometimes the hunter had to settle for what he could get. It wasn't a perfect world. And Gina wasn't a perfect solution. After all, he didn't like to dip his toe into what the locals had to offer too often, too often might raise a red flag. That's the last thing he needed.

After all, he'd perfected his method quite a bit over the years.

But as he stared out the front windshield into the night, he noticed Gina's car up ahead begin to sputter and cough right on schedule. And now, here she was, ripe for the picking. It was only a matter of time before he had the twenty-one-year-old right where he wanted her. Then all he had to do was play the scene out he'd cleverly created and offer her a ride home.

Piece of cake, he decided as he crawled out of his own vehicle. He walked to the Mazda, tapped on the driver's side glass. When he saw her jump, when he saw her roll the window down in response, his lips curved up. "Looks like you need some help. Good thing I spotted you when I did. I was about to turn off the road up ahead."

Recognizing the man, she breathed a sigh of relief. "Thank goodness, it's you. You scared me half to death. My car just…started smoking and then died. I was going along fine but then it just quit running." She spotted the gloves he wore, thought it strange because it didn't seem cold enough for leather.

"Let me take a look. Pop the hood for me."

"Would you? That'd be great." Dutifully, Gina reached under the dash, pulled the lever for the hood release.

While he had his head down he pretended to jiggle wires, inspect belts and hoses to make the ruse look real. Finally, he approached the window again. "Sorry but it looks like Wally's going to have to tow you in. These little Japanese models are a mystery to me. Why don't you jump in my car there and I'll take you home?"

"Good idea. I wished I'd stayed put tonight," Gina grumbled, never once thinking twice about the offer. She grabbed her purse which had a perfectly good cell phone tucked inside she could've used to call her dad. Instead of being afraid, Gina hopped out of the car, walked unconcerned to a white SUV and hopped inside.

Gina's parents, Clint and Eileen Purvis, didn't discover their daughter hadn't come home Saturday night until seven o'clock the next morning. That prompted Eileen to start phoning all of Gina's friends only to learn no one had heard from her.

By noon, Clint decided he'd waited long enough. Out of habit, he put in a distraught call to Ethan Cody. A parent now himself, Ethan, had in turn, phoned the sheriff's department who in turn notified Deputy Dan Garver. Since Dan still hadn't yet made the move to Pelican Pointe though and because it was a busy Memorial weekend in Santa Cruz, Dan didn't respond to the call to the Purvis home until close to six o'clock Sunday evening.

There was a reason Deputy Dan Garver hadn't yet made the move to Pelican Pointe. The twenty-five year old deputy didn't like the town at all. He preferred living in Santa Cruz and wasn't the least shy about sharing that fact when pressed. He'd spent all his life in Santa Cruz and considered a tiny dot of a town like Pelican Pointe a demotion.

But when he got a call like now, Dan couldn't very well ignore it any more than he could the town.

Once he got to the Purvis place though, even then, Dan had been reluctant to file a missing persons report on the girl. After all, it wasn't illegal for a young woman to spend a Saturday night on the town partying and then come home sometime late the next day. "Maybe she's out with some guy that you two don't even know anything about, had herself a little too much to drink, lost track of the time, and stayed over at a friend's house. It is a holiday weekend and young people do tend to party."

"Dan Garver, you do not have to stand there and remind me it's a damn holiday. I know that. I also know Gina and she would never do anything like that. Hasn't done that in all the years she's dated. She'd call home first if she decided to stay overnight somewhere. She didn't. And Eileen's spent the entire morning calling everyone she knew," Clint Purvis pointed out.

"Besides, Gina specifically went to see Troy Dayton. They recently broke up. That's where you should start looking, with Troy," Eileen tossed in.

"That's just it," Dan reasoned. "She and Troy may have hooked back up again for the evening. Did you think of that? Did you call him?"

"Of course, we called him. Troy says he never saw Gina last night and that he hung out with Mona Bingham. The boy's either a liar or something's happened to our Gina," Eileen said, her voice starting to show signs of breaking from worrying over her baby girl all day.

"Never did like that boy," Clint mumbled. "Fought too much with my Gina, if you ask me. If he's done something with my Gina—"

But even with their unwavering declarations from two worried parents, Dan believed they were overreacting. It had taken the threat of calling Brent or Ethan Cody at home for Dan to take down Gina's information and file an official report.

Because of the delay in getting the word out, people drove right by Gina's red Mazda sitting on the busy Coast Highway all day Sunday without knowing she'd disappeared. It wasn't until Betty Brinker and Pete Alden were coming back from Santa Cruz around midnight Sunday night that they spotted Gina's abandoned car and thought it odd it was still in the same place as it had been earlier when they'd left town. Then and there from the side of the road, Betty used Pete's cell phone to call Gina's parents. That's when they learned the woman hadn't been seen for more than twenty-four hours.

The location was less than a mile from Troy Dayton's trailer.

Playing piano at The Pointe three nights a week got Kinsey a front row seat to the crazy antics of some of its finest citizens. By observing without letting on you were, she knew, for example, what kind of wine Thelma Thompkins ordered every time she came in. Thelma was fond of crab cakes and washing them down at one sitting with an entire bottle of merlot from the Alexander Valley.

Kinsey knew that Doc Prescott and Murphy were the most generous tippers while Frank Martin, the bank vice-president, was tightfisted when it came to leaving a gratuity.

On a routine basis, Kinsey saw who ate too much, who drank too much, and had to have someone drive them home. Because of that she had come to believe Carl Knudsen, the pharmacist, obviously had a problem with alcohol. So did his wife, Elaine. The Knudsens came in at least once every weekend like clockwork and ordered the same thing. The couple started with martinis, drank four apiece, and then dined on lobster. Sometimes they wobbled to the front door with a little help from Jolene. Other times Kinsey was told the couple simply strolled out the restaurant to walk the six blocks home. It made her wonder how carefully Knudsen, the sole pharmacist in town, filled prescriptions. Was Carl able to stay sober all the while he did his job?

When she mentioned it to Perry Altman, they laughed about it until Kinsey said, "It sort of reminds me of that character in *It's a Wonderful Life*, you know, Mr. Gower, the druggist who drinks and if not for George Bailey dispenses the wrong medication to a customer. What if that happened here? It could be a serious situation one of these days."

"Wow, you're right. To tell you the truth, I've thought the same thing. It's one of the reasons I get all my drugs in Santa Cruz," Perry said with a wink.

"Thanks for the tip," Kinsey said, only half-joking. "But that doesn't really make me feel any better. Not everyone can go to Santa Cruz every time Doc writes them a prescription."

"I'll tell you what I heard about Carl. He's had a chip on his shoulder for most of his life about this town. It seems he wanted to leave Pelican Pointe behind for good many times, even told his parents he wanted no part of sticking around to run the family drugstore. Carl couldn't wait to get out long before he ever graduated high school. Apparently, Carl's family had plenty of money to send him to UC Berkeley. In high school, he was supposedly a smart guy. Anyway, he was all set to go when his father died suddenly, which messed up his plans. His mother made him stay home to commute back and forth to UC Santa Cruz, mainly so Carl could keep the family drugstore going. At the time, Carl had a younger brother, Mark, and he was hoping Mark would eventually graduate college and take over the pharmacy so that would free up Carl to get out of here and do whatever it is he wanted to do with his life."

"Why didn't he then?"

"Good question. I heard Mark died from some kind of heart ailment. No one really talks about it. His death sent Carl into a depression and I guess a struggle with the bottle. He's been drinking heavily ever since. At least he's been that way for as long as I've been in town."

"What about Elaine?"

"Carl met Elaine in Santa Cruz in college. You know Elaine's Kent Springer's sister, right?"

"You're joking. I didn't know that. Elaine Knudsen is Kent Springer's sister, the developer guy who killed Sissy Carr and tried to start a fire at Promise Cove?"

"One and the same."

"I would never have guessed this town held so much drama when I first set eyes on this place."

Perry shook his head. "Small towns, honey. Besides, none of us picked up on the drama thing."

The drama thing, as Perry had called it, bugged Kinsey, especially knowing what she did about all the missing girls Logan had mentioned. Of course no one else had that knowledge.

Later when she glanced up from the piano to see Jolene leading Logan into the dining room, Kinsey had the urge to stand up and pump her fist in the air. Instead she transitioned into Christine McVie's *Songbird* just because she could.

Their eyes met from across the room.

Jesus, Logan thought, the woman had the most gorgeous eyes. Logan hadn't even heard the waiter ask what he wanted to drink. In fact, he turned a blind eye to everything and everyone else in the room except the woman at the piano. He needed to sketch her just as she looked tonight. The way the light made her hair shine, the perfect posture, the way she moved with each note, the way her fingers glided over the instrument. He felt certain he could capture that flowing form. While his hand had healed he'd gotten out of the habit of carrying paper wherever he went like he had in his younger days. Another by-product of his time spent with Fiona. Out of desperation to catch the moment, without pencil or paper, he took out his cell phone to snap her picture.

Kinsey had to smile when she saw him bring out his phone to use as a camera. She knew then, ever the artist, what was going on in that head of his. Good thing he didn't have a clue what was spinning around in hers.

Never one to watch the clock, she did now. She had approximately ninety minutes to entertain the remaining diners. Because when she got done here, she knew one thing. She intended to give Logan a private showing, one he wouldn't soon forget.

Chapter Sixteen

Come Monday, Pelican Pointe's annual Memorial Day parade came and went without its two newest citizens. Logan and Kinsey spent their day off, lazing in bed, making love, eating the omelets Kinsey had whipped up and munching on fresh wild strawberries she'd picked near the cliffs.

As a cool ocean breeze drifted in through the open windows, they lay naked between the sheets, getting to know each other in the way lovers do when they have all the time in the world.

He skimmed kisses down her thigh all the way to her knees and back up again. "You have such velvety skin."

She crooked her finger at him and said, "Come back up here and I'll show you velvety."

"Yeah?" He licked his way back up to her nipple. "I like your tattoo." With his finger, he traced the small, two-inch outline of a dream catcher over the curve of her left breast.

"I got it after my mom died." She ran a finger along the tat on his right bicep and the heavy triangle inked there. Inside were the words, "Never forgotten."

Along his other bicep was a date. When he saw her eyes track there, he said, "The date Megan went missing."

From that point Logan was determined to lighten the mood though. He didn't want her spending the first day off she'd had in months thinking about such serious topics as murder. So he told her all the silly jokes he knew in a string of rapid fire nonsense. "What do cats eat for breakfast?" Logan asked.

"I don't know."

"Mice Krispies."

"Eww."

"Don't be such a girl. What did the sea say to the sand?"

"You're going to tell me."

"Nothing, it just waved."

She giggled like a teenager. "You must feel like you're slumming every time you come in here."

He frowned. "What did you say? Why would you think that?"

She spread her arms out wide. "Look around you, Logan. This is hardly a villa outside Rome. You couldn't find a place more contrasting than what you're used to if you tried. In case you haven't noticed, I'm living over a garage."

"What the hell difference does that make? It's eclectic. Have you forgotten I grew up less than two hundred miles from here in a blue-collar, speck of a town that's only claim to fame was a nut factory. I'm not Fiona Perez with a stick up my ass for chrissakes."

Realizing she'd pissed him off, she backtracked. "Okay, okay. I just meant we're very different, you and I, that's all. You've seen the world, lived an artist's life. You've been married. Me? I check groceries on the weekend, play piano to make ends meet and have never had a serious relationship that lasted longer than three months."

He took her chin firmly in his hand. "There's no shame in checking groceries or playing piano. I've done things to make ends meet I'm not exactly proud of."

"Yeah? Like what?"

"In my Los Angeles days, I modeled to pay the rent."

She wiggled her eyebrows up and down. "So if I Google those particular phrase there's a chance I might come up with nude photos of you on some website?"

"Sketches," he corrected with a grin. "No digital cameras were used in the making of my limited contribution to the art world as a model." When he saw her eyes go big, he went on, "Nude yes, porn no. And my time doing so was very brief before I gave up on the L.A. scene entirely. You and I both know that if there were videos out there the press would have uncovered them by now. But I'm not proud of those days." He picked up a strand of her hair. "Why no long-term boyfriends, Kinsey? What's wrong with the men in your neighborhood?"

"Simple. No man wanted to get hooked up with a woman dealing with all my problems. My mother's cancer took both time and money. I put everything on the back-burner, except my mom's illness, to focus on job and school. Guys want attention. They don't want a woman distracted by her menial jobs, term papers, and her mother's chemo treatments." When he gave her one of his piercing looks, she shrugged. "It's a fact."

"I guess it is."

Because neither of them had any inclination to join the throngs of people that bunched along the beaches in town, lazing on towels, baking in the sun, they didn't care to mingle today with anyone. That included the guests they could hear, laughing and playing down at the cove. The din drifted from the open windows as they stayed burrowed in their own little, self-imposed, inner sanctum.

Intent on taking advantage of their time alone, they played half a dozen hands of gin rummy and hearts. When card games grew old, they turned on the television, only to get nothing but snowy reception.

Kinsey sat on the floor to go through the stack of movie DVDs under the little table. When Logan joined her, he groaned at the choices. "There's nothing here but chick flicks. I'm not watching *Mamma Mia, Dirty Dancing,* or *Beaches,* anything but those three."

Kinsey snickered and shook her head. "The selections are rather limited. What about either *Party Girl* with Parker Posey or *Jerry Maguire*?"

Logan sighed. "Looks like it's Tom Cruise then." He was about to slide in the disc when he spotted another DVD in the stack. "Wait a minute, what's wrong with *Princess Bride*? 'Hello, I'm Inigo Montoya. You killed my father. Prepare to die,'" he mimicked in his best Spanish accent. "Funniest movie made in the eighties."

"Looks like we have a winner," Kinsey declared. "You start the DVD, I'll pop the popcorn."

For the next couple of hours, they laughed at all the memorable lines, sometimes repeating them before the actors could actually recite them.

Afterward, they nibbled on cold cuts and cheese and opened a bottle of pinot noir they found hiding in the back of the cabinet.

"I have no idea where this came from. I didn't buy it."

"Obviously left behind by the last occupant. Don't look a gift horse in the mouth."

"I think that gift horse had to be Hayden."

"Cody? Really? There's a story there."

"I'm sure there is. Let's take our supper outside where it's cooler."

They spread out a blanket high above the ridge to watch the fireworks until the talk inevitably turned to Logan's past.

There'd been something she'd wanted to know ever since she'd discovered he lived here. "Tell me about your early years in Pelican Pointe? Where did your grandparents live?"

"Do you know where the rescue center is?"

"Sure, it's in the older section of town."

"There's a little side street, Athena Circle, behind the old newspaper office, a cul-de-sac really with about fifteen homes or so, mostly little Spanish bungalows. These days a lot of them need work. But my grandparent's house is no longer there. The house mysteriously caught fire and burned to the ground about two months after my grandmother died. I'd flown in for her funeral, flown out again. That was twelve years ago, the last time I was in this town to be exact, until now. Since my grandmother left me the house, I got this phone call in the middle of the night from some sheriff's deputy that it was gone, toast. For me, it was like another strike against Pelican Pointe."

"And another reason you wanted nothing to do with the town."

Finally someone got it. "I dragged my feet enough times, told myself there was no reason to ever come back here. After all, there were no family ties for me here anymore. But…about six months ago I was on the Internet one night, came across the lighthouse for sale. It was like a sign or something."

"You were checking out the town, looking for any updated news on Megan's case." It wasn't a question.

"You have it pegged pretty well. That's when I got in touch with Ethan Cody. He hadn't given up wearing a badge then. We got to emailing each other back and forth regularly, one thing led to another."

"When did you learn about the other missing girls?"

"I found articles here and there doing random searches on the Internet, but nothing ever definitive. Then I came across a website listing the names of people gone missing. On that list was another seventeen-year-old, who had left Washington State for Hollywood some twenty-five years ago and was never seen or heard from again. The blog post mentioned she'd last been seen on the Coast Highway near Pelican Pointe. Her name was Carly Radigan. I tracked down her brother, Ian Radigan. From there, Ian and I started digging. Before that though, I'd never found anyone I could relate to. We still email each other off and on."

All of a sudden realization hit her. "Logan, twenty-five years ago you would have been around ten years old at the time Carly Radigan went missing."

"Exactly, which means there's one mean-ass son of a bitch out there who's been killing girls a helluva long time. And I want him stopped."

Chapter Seventeen

Because Kinsey and Logan had locked themselves away from the world all day Monday in their own little cocoon, they had no idea Gina Purvis had gone missing. When Logan got to the job site on Tuesday morning though, it was all both crews had on their minds. No one had seen or heard from the young woman since she had left home Saturday night around eight-thirty to return a box of items belonging to Troy Dayton. Gina had never made it back home.

While Logan was still trying to wrap his mind around the fact that another woman had disappeared, he learned Troy had spent the better part of Memorial Day answering questions from Dan Garver about the last time Troy had seen Gina.

"Garver acted like he thought I did something to her," Troy groaned.

"Did you?" Sam Turley asked. "I always thought she was a little hottie. You were stupid for breaking it off with her."

"I never even saw her Saturday night. I haven't seen her in weeks. And I didn't break it off. She's the one who broke up with me. She always seemed pissed off at me about something because she said I never had any money. She always wanted to go out and do stuff, stuff I couldn't afford to do."

"That's women for you, Troy," Drake Boedekker added. "Always wanting to spend a man's cash."

"What exactly did Garver say to you?" Logan asked, as a nagging feeling started to crawl up his neck.

"He wanted to know where I was Saturday night, stuff like that."

"You were with Mona, right?" Logan wanted to know.

"Well, not all night," Troy admitted sheepishly. "It was our first date for chrissakes. But I was with her until around midnight when I walked her home. You know they found Gina's car near my trailer. I told Garver that Gina had been bugging me, texting me for the better part of a damn week to come by and pick up a box of my stuff she said was in the way. That's the last time I even heard from her."

That left Logan to wonder if Troy's interrogation meant the cops had already jumped to a swift conclusion.

About that time, Derek slapped his nephew on the back and said, "Don't worry, son, I'm sure she'll turn up and when she does she'll probably be all pissed off about something else."

As the morning wore on Troy took some light-hearted ribbing from the rest of the crew about what he'd done to the difficult Gina. But Logan found it no more amusing than Troy did.

They'd just finished lunch when Logan looked up and saw a patrol car making its way down the bumpy road toward the work site. As soon as Dan Garver stepped out of his patrol car, Logan somehow knew what was about to happen.

"Troy," Dan said. "I have a warrant for your arrest."

"For what? Why?"

"The first degree murder of Gina Purvis."

"But I didn't do nothing, I swear it, Mr. Donnelly."

Logan listened as Dan proceeded to read Troy his Miranda rights and then put the kid in handcuffs. Logan pointed at Troy and cautioned him, "Don't say a word, Troy. I'll get you a lawyer."

Dan shook his head. "You'll be wasting your money, Mr. Donnelly. But then I guess you have enough of it to toss around on crazy shit like this." Dan threw his arms out wide. "No one in town cares about this lighthouse coming back. It's an eyesore and as such ought to be torn down, if you ask me."

"I don't think anyone asked you, Deputy. But I'd like to know why you think I'd be wasting my money on a lawyer for Troy?" Logan demanded.

"Because a couple of hours ago we found the body of Gina Purvis dumped not fifty yards from Troy Dayton's trailer."

"So? What does that prove exactly? Do you even have a cause of death yet?" Logan asked.

"Well, I don't exactly need the coroner to tell me Gina was raped and strangled."

Logan watched the sickening look form on Troy's face at hearing those words. He knew then with absolute certainly that Troy hadn't killed Gina Purvis.

"What do I do now, Mr. Donnelly?" Troy yelled, almost in tears from the backseat of the police car. "What's gonna happen to me now?"

Dan glanced back at Logan and sent him a look. "He'll be arraigned some time tomorrow morning. No sooner than that because it's too late in the day to take place before then."

And with that, Logan watched as the car bounced along the jagged landscape with Troy on his way to jail.

Logan turned to Derek. "Do you have the money for an attorney?"

Derek shook his head. "I've been barely scraping by for six months or more. So has Troy."

"Okay, that's all I needed to know. Somebody give me directions how to get to Aaron Hartley's place. Then all of you get back to work. Now! I'll be back as soon as I can."

"Logan? Thanks," Derek muttered. "The boy's a good kid. I don't think he killed anyone."

"I know that. And I know someone else who'll think the same thing."

When Logan got to the house on Landings Bay he wasn't sure whether it was an office or a home, wasn't sure he should knock or walk right in. He rang the bell. It was Kinsey who answered the door.

"Well, hello. To what do I owe this visit? Need a lawyer?" Kinsey cracked. But when she noticed the serious look on Logan's face, she added, "What's wrong?" She motioned her head for him to come inside.

"Garver just arrested Troy."

"For what?"

"For killing Gina Purvis. A couple of hours ago they found her body near Troy's trailer. I don't have any more details than that."

"What? I don't believe that. Troy doesn't have it in him to kill."

About that time Aaron appeared in the entryway. "Are we representing Troy Dayton? Because if we are, I may have to recuse myself and let you handle whatever needs doing."

"Why?" Kinsey asked.

"For one, I'm in no shape to take on anything as serious as murder. And two, I've known Clint and Eileen Purvis for years, was at Gina's christening three weeks after she was born." When he saw the letdown on Kinsey's face, he lifted one thin shoulder. "I have to pick my battles, Kinsey. The ways of a small town."

"I may have known Troy for only a matter of weeks, but I'm not letting him go through this by himself. He's my friend, Aaron. My first friend in Pelican Pointe. And I believe in him."

Logan nodded. "Same here. As of right now, I'm retaining Kinsey as Troy's lawyer."

Kinsey sighed. "Now wait a minute, slow down. I don't have the legal chops to handle something like this. I won't risk Troy's freedom depending on me."

"I'm afraid for now you're it, Kinsey," Aaron said. "Unless you want to turn Troy over to a public defender to handle his arraignment, you'd best find him a good defense attorney and fast."

"He's right," Logan agreed.

"How serious are you about going to bat for Troy," Aaron asked, narrowing his eyes at Logan. "In other words how deep do your pockets go for a guy you've known for such a short amount of time?"

"I believe in the kid," Logan stated flatly. He wasn't sure why exactly he felt so adamant only that he did. He glanced over at Kinsey, waited for an indication from her.

"Ditto."

"Then I'd get Collier Davis out of San Francisco. He's the best. And something tells me, you're going to need the very best."

Logan and Kinsey soon discovered that getting a high-powered defense attorney to rearrange his schedule to travel from the Bay down to Pelican Pointe overnight was no easy task. In fact, it was turning out to be impossible. So far they had yet to even get Collier Davis to return Logan's phone call.

Because of that, Logan and Kinsey stood inside the criminal court building in Santa Cruz the next morning. By nine o' clock it became clear they had two choices. They could postpone Troy's arraignment, which would only prolong his confinement. Or it would be up to Kinsey to get through what Aaron had assured her was a very brief process.

Dressed in her Donna Karan suit, Kinsey paced up and down behind the defense table. She sucked in a breath and looked around the room. Who would believe Kinsey Wyatt stood in an actual courtroom about to speak to a judge as an attorney? She was so nervous her underarms felt like she hadn't taken a shower in two days. "Uh, Logan, how many times do I have to remind you that I haven't actually appeared before a judge before? As in ever. Well, except for that time I fought a traffic ticket. But that was traffic court, Logan. This is completely different. I don't think I'm doing Troy any favors here."

"Kinsey, there's no one else. Aaron took you through all the steps last night—twice—now's your chance to show 'em what you're made of. Besides..." He didn't even have time to finish his sentence before a deputy appeared at a side door. Wearing the typical orange jumpsuit, Troy shuffled along in ankle chains and handcuffs.

"Kinsey!" Troy uttered in disbelief, brightening almost immediately. "I can't believe you actually came. And Mr. Donnelly." He reached out to shake Logan's hand with both of his handcuffed ones.

"Troy, I need to know..."

But he didn't let her finish. "No...no...Kinsey, I didn't do this. I never laid a hand on Gina."

But there was no more time to talk as Judge Driscoll Leonard strolled to the bench carrying a manila folder. A steely-eyed man in his late fifties, Leonard sat down, immediately tapped his gavel once and began to go over the file. "Is the accused Troy Dayton represented by counsel?"

A nervous Kinsey cleared her throat. "Yes, your honor. Kinsey Wyatt, attorney-at-law, Pelican Pointe."

"Ms. Wyatt, have you read the indictment?"

"Yes, Judge Leonard, I have."

"Then you know your client, Troy Dayton, is charged with the first degree murder of one," Judge Leonard looked down, referred to the paperwork again. "Gina Purvis, twenty-one years of age. How does your client plead?"

"Mr. Dayton is rendering a plea of not guilty, your honor."

"Let the court records show the accused pleads not guilty." Judge Leonard stared at Kinsey straight on and asked, "Are you aware, Ms. Wyatt, the district attorney has filed a motion to deny bond?"

"Yes sir. But the accused has a steady job. He's never been in trouble before with the law in any way. And we assert that he is not a flight risk. He doesn't even have a passport."

The judge looked over at George Stein, the prosecuting attorney, a short man twice as old as Kinsey. "Mr. Stein, let's hear your argument to oppose bail?"

"Judge Leonard, the state doesn't believe Mr. Dayton should be released back into the community due to the violent nature of the crime. Your honor, Miss Purvis was strangled with some force. Her hyoid bone wasn't just fractured, it was shattered. She was also sexually violated. Because of that, we respectfully ask the court to keep Troy Dayton in custody."

The minute Kinsey saw Judge Leonard nod his head, she knew without his words what the ruling would be. Troy wasn't going anywhere.

But then the judge made it official. "The court agrees. Bond denied."

Kinsey spoke up, stuttering slightly. "Your...honor... we would like to schedule...a bail hearing as soon as it's convenient to the court."

Judge Leonard turned to a laptop computer bought up his calendar. "Counselor, how does a week from today sound?"

"A week from today will be fine," Kinsey nodded.

Judge Leonard tapped his gavel and with that, Troy's arraignment came to an abrupt end.

Kinsey turned to Troy. "I'm sorry. Look, don't panic. I'll—"

"It isn't your fault, Kinsey. But I didn't do this. I swear I never laid a hand on Gina, let alone kill her. Last time I seen her, was when she broke up with me, standing right there on her front porch. That's the last time. I swear it on my mom's grave, Kinsey. You of all people know what she meant to me."

Kinsey put a hand on his. "I believe you, Troy. If I thought otherwise, I wouldn't be standing here. But it's apparent you need a really good defense attorney. Logan and I will work on that before the bail hearing next week. Just...hang in there."

"We both believe in you, Troy," Logan told the younger man. Beside Logan, Derek Stovall spoke up, "Troy, I know you didn't do this."

"Thanks," Troy muttered as the deputy began to lead him back through the side door. "But I want you to represent me, Kinsey. I trust you. I don't want no stranger."

In spite of the deputy's sneer, Kinsey leaned over as far as she could so that Troy could hear her. "Troy, I'd love nothing more, but this is over my head, *way* over. You need a seasoned attorney, not some novice like me. Don't worry though, Logan and I will find you the best one we can get. We've already made some calls."

As two deputies led Troy through the door, Logan raised his voice. "We know you didn't do this, Troy. Kinsey and I both believe in you."

After Troy was gone, Logan took Kinsey's hand from behind the railing where he stood. "Relax, you did fine."

"Not really. Troy's still in jail." Still on wobbly knees, she scooted back her hair from her face. "I can't believe this is happening," Kinsey lamented as she picked up her bag. But then something hit her. "Oh my God!"

"What's wrong?"

"It just occurred to me. Gina Purvis was raped. They must have DNA. If they have DNA, *that* has to exonerate Troy."

Hours later back in Pelican Pointe, Kinsey sat at her desk with that nugget of hope still fresh on her mind. While Aaron rested in his room upstairs, Kinsey had taken off her suit jacket to pore over the stack of law books he'd left piled on her desk. Little sticky notes adorned the pages indicating how to handle discovery and subpoenas. She had her nose stuck in a book when Logan walked in, sweaty from manual labor.

"Has anyone ever told you how sexy you look in lawyer mode? Just like in court this morning."

"I'm pretty sure I've never been in lawyer mode until this morning. What you saw was sheer panic along with a good dose of fear."

He scooted textbooks aside to prop a hip on the corner of her desk. Tucking a strand of long caramel hair behind her ear, he told her, "What I saw was a lawyer who cared. Troy saw it, too. You here all by yourself?"

She saw that flicker of desire she'd taken advantage of for most of yesterday cloud his green eyes. "Aaron's upstairs. Asleep. Afternoon nap. He usually takes one about now."

Logan cocked a brow. "He does need his rest."

"Why are you here?"

"Why do you think?" He ran his finger from ear to throat. "You have a sexy neck. Especially this little spot right here." He nibbled along her jaw to her mouth. "What's your attitude toward sex in the workplace?" He grinned when he saw her mouth gape open. "I can see I've interrupted your train of thought. Chalk it up to my bohemian lifestyle."

She chuckled. "I heard that about you. The long hair, the gold hoop earring, throw in your mysterious past, and it all makes you a little too avant-garde for Pelican Pointe."

"Who me? I'm an old-fashioned romantic, a traditionalist when it comes to the classics, a lover of black and white movies—and my stock portfolio is packed with nothing but conservative investments."

"But a risk taker when it comes to your art, like the bronze sculpture outside the symphony hall in Seattle or the spectacular piece you did for the science center in Santa Fe."

He smiled. "You know my work rather well. But you never answered my question."

She waved a hand toward the doorframe. "As you can see there's no door to close and lock."

"Hmm, small problem but nothing we can't deal with. What about the copy room? I'm thinking you need desk sex to spice up your afternoon."

She snickered. "The copier is in Aaron's office."

He raised a brow. "And does his office have a door?"

"Logan, we can't—"

"Oh but we can. Let me show you what I had in mind," he said as he tugged her up and across the hall and into Aaron's office.

Chapter Eighteen

The next day Troy Dayton's supporters gathered inside the living room at Promise Cove for a strategy session. It wasn't just Kinsey and Logan in Troy's corner anymore. Since Troy's court appearance, Kinsey and Logan had met with their friends only to discover everyone seemed to be in agreement on one thing. Troy didn't kill Gina Purvis. Now they just had to convince a stubborn Ethan Cody of it. Hayden crowded in next to Nick and Jordan sitting on the sofa while Cord and Keegan Bennett spread out on the floor beside Wally and Lilly Pierce.

Ethan walked back and forth with a fussy Nate on his shoulder. Ethan was the only one in the room that wasn't yet convinced of Troy's innocence.

Kinsey acted as hostess so Jordan could get off her feet for a few minutes. She passed around coffee to anyone wanting it, offering the sandwiches Jordan and Hayden had fixed. But no one seemed hungry enough to eat.

Logan didn't have a baby to walk but that didn't keep him from pacing. He wanted to make a point so he said, "Ethan, just because they found Gina's body at Troy's trailer doesn't mean he killed her. Garver jumped the gun and you know it."

Ethan handed the baby to Hayden and scrubbed the palms of both hands down his face. "If you're talking about any other missing persons cases, Logan, of course, I know Troy had nothing to do with those. When the first one disappeared Troy hadn't even been born yet. And he was still in diapers when Megan vanished."

"Who's Megan?" Nick wanted to know.

Ethan and Logan exchanged glares.

It was Logan who told them. "My sister. She went missing here in Pelican Pointe twenty years ago."

The stunned look on the faces around the room said it all. No one had known that until now.

"While Ethan might not think Gina's death has anything to do with the other missing persons cases, I do. It's just that simple. The fact Troy has been accused of something so horrific, has escalated things for me. Considerably."

"It isn't personal," Ethan snapped then let out a sigh. "Look, according to the info Dan got from Gina's parents, she went out that night specifically to see Troy at his trailer. The box of stuff was still in her car. Troy may possibly be the last person to see Gina alive and doesn't want to admit it."

"I don't believe that. The guy readily admits Gina had been bugging him for a week about coming by to pick up that stuff she'd boxed up. She got upset when he didn't jump Saturday night."

"Not only that, there are text messages and several phone calls to prove it," Kinsey stated.

"I'm aware of that. But it looks bad for Troy that they found Gina's body right fifty yards from his trailer. You can't connect Gina's death to the others because the others are—"

"Still missing," Logan finished. "Yeah, not finding a body means nothing much gets done. I get that." Logan looked around the room before focusing on Ethan again. "Why don't you tell them, Ethan? Tell them the rest of it. Now that they know about Megan, tell them what kind of history there is in Santa Cruz County?"

"Not relevant here, Logan. Not at all, there's no point in bringing up ancient history."

"Says you." Logan took the time to study each face staring back at him. "Are any of you aware that at one time there were three serial killers operating at the same time in Santa Cruz County? So many that the district attorney at the time dubbed this county as the murder capital of the world."

"Ancient history," Ethan repeated. "Just because you found a bunch of crap on the Internet about what happened decades earlier doesn't mean squat now. Investigative legwork—"

"Was non-existent in Megan's case," Logan broke in. "And I'd bet the others were just as poorly dealt with. Because basically law enforcement decided a seventeen-year-old teenage girl took off despite having no history of doing so in the past, and she left without taking any of her clothes, or makeup, or money with her."

But Kinsey held up her hands in peace, eyes bugged out as if just understanding the implication of what Logan said. "Wait a minute. You didn't say anything about three serial killers working in the same county at virtually the same time. That certainly didn't come up in my interview with Hartley. I'll be honest, if I'd known that I doubt I would've taken the job. And that's coming from a life-long inner city girl. I mean this looked like the quintessential little town. A single woman leaves San Francisco thinking she's found a safe haven in a quiet, peaceful town, only to discover the county had a serial killer problem." Kinsey shook her head. "That's more than a little off-putting."

"I'm glad I didn't know that either when I lived out at the Cove all by myself for such a long period of time," Jordan exclaimed. "I'd have gone nuts knowing that."

Ethan sighed. "See what you started? For chrissakes that was three decades ago. And they were all caught, tried and convicted, locked up?"

"Were they? How can you be so certain? You've got missing women cases going back as far as twenty-five years ago…unsolved. That's a fact, Ethan. Look, I'm not blaming your brother Brent for the lack of action, if that's what you're thinking. Some of these cases happened when we were all in our teens. But what if it were your sister, Ethan? What would you do?"

"Probably the same as you. I know you're upset, Logan. You have a right to be. And whether you believe it or not, I do wonder about Troy's guilt. You met him a month ago. I've known the kid his entire life. Susan Dayton, his mother, might have had her share of problems. But she took good care of that boy up to the day breast cancer claimed her life."

"You know, that's one of the things Troy and I have in common," Kinsey noted. "I met him the very first day I interviewed with Hartley. I was walking around town looking in windows on Ocean Street, wandering around, daydreaming about what it would be like to live in this idyllic little town. This white-haired teen bumped into me as he was coming out of the bait shop. He could've done what thousands of other people do every day and brush past me to go on his way. But he didn't. Troy apologized, stopped to talk to me. When he found out I was in town to interview for a job, we got to talking even more. I asked him about an inexpensive place to eat. We walked down to the Diner. We split the cheapest sandwich on the menu, a grilled cheese. And we spent two hours there during which time we discussed how both of us had lost our mothers to breast cancer, how painful it had been. Troy was easy to talk to. Or maybe I just needed a shoulder. I don't know. At the time, Troy was it. I told him about my piecemeal education. He told me how difficult it was for him to find work. I felt his pain about his predicament and he felt mine. Because I've been there, wondering how to stretch my pennies to pay the light bill or the rent. That kid was the first person in town, besides Hartley, who was nice to me. That's why I'd bet every cent I have in the bank, which I grant you isn't much, but I'd bet my last dollar that Troy Dayton did not kill Gina with everything I own."

Logan jingled the change in his pocket. "That about sums it up for me, too. Troy is the first guy to get to the job site every day. He'll do any job I give him and won't bitch about it for two hours afterward. He's shown me character, determination. So yeah, I've only known the guy a month or so, Kinsey a few weeks longer than that, but I know Troy's a good person. Not only that, Troy's got heart. I think the guy is in love with Mona, or at least as in love as someone thinks they are at that young age. He showed me the jewelry box he was making Mona for her birthday next month. That to me says he'd already gotten past the breakup with Gina, which means there was no motive for him to kill her over a bunch of crap in a box."

"He showed me one of his jewelry boxes, too. Troy has talent there. I'd planned to display them in the rooms. I told him I thought they'd sell," Jordan added and shook her head. "Troy just doesn't have it in him, Ethan. Surely you can see that."

"Troy helped me out last June when Scott was born," Nick added. "Jordan and I had our hands full with a newborn and a toddler. Not only a new baby, but we had a houseful of guests at the time. Our timing was more than a little off, for sure. Then, an unusual summer storm hit us, lightning, wind, the whole bit. Blew brand new shingles off the roof. Troy was the first guy to come out to help. He patched the roof, sawed trees, worked like a fiend for three days straight to help us. When he was done, I sent him over to the farm to see if Cord could use a hand there. My vote is the same as the rest. Sorry, Ethan. But Troy didn't do this."

"He picked apples for two weeks, and according to Silas, was his best worker," Cord explained. "He didn't miss a day of work, even offered to stay late. Troy still makes himself available to do the milking in a pinch if something comes up for me, which lately is a lot. Like if I need to help Keegan with a rescue or assist in a surgery. I've used Troy several times now that the Miller boy joined the military. I even referred Troy to the center because Keegan can always use an extra pair of hands there."

Keegan nodded. "Troy's worked there off and on since Christmas. Pete said he did everything he asked him. But the poor guy doesn't have a strong enough stomach to work around animals for very long, especially if they're sick. But that's nothing against Troy. A person needs a strong constitution to clean cages and deal with the puke and poop on a regular basis. It isn't for everyone. The first time Troy had to clean out the cages and work around a sick animal, he had a rough time of it. I felt sorry for him. He tried, he really did. But he's a terrific carpenter. Last year during the street fair, Troy volunteered to build us our aquatic model, a replica of marine life under glass. It's so sturdy the kids sit on it, play on it, even pretend they're living in the sea. It's one of our most popular features."

Lilly let Keegan finish and then stated, "Troy stopped by the service station a couple of weeks ago. That old truck of his was acting up."

"I showed him how to change out his spark plugs," Wally added. "Took me maybe twenty minutes. Didn't charge him because he brought Lilly one of those jewelry boxes in exchange for the labor and parts. I couldn't turn him down when he needed his truck running so he could look for work."

"You should see it. The wood is gorgeous, all handmade from an old cedar tree he found not far from where I used to live in that trailer with the kids," Lilly said. "How could a man work with his hands like that and then strangle and rape his ex-girlfriend just because they broke up?" Lilly shook her head. "I don't think he could. And I don't think Troy cared one way or another whether he got that stuff back from Gina either."

"Troy came by the bookstore looking for work," Hayden tossed in.

"Not you, too," Ethan groaned. "My own wife?"

"It was hectic that day. Nate was fussy, too. That was the afternoon you said you desperately needed to work on your new manuscript to get your ideas down before you lost them. Troy catalogued six boxes of used books for me that day, Ethan. Saved me hours and hours of having to do it myself. He was polite, worked hard. In fact, now that I've listened to everyone else, I've never seen Troy any other way. I gave him a full day's pay, a sandwich, and a bottle of juice. It's all I had. The juice, that is. I didn't have a soft drink to offer him."

"That had to be a month ago," Ethan stated.

"That's about right. If you're saying you think a month went by before he suddenly decided to turn mean then direct that rage toward Gina over a breakup, I'm not buying it." When Nate started to kick up a fuss from his baby carrier, Hayden went over to pick up the baby. "Troy held your son that day, Ethan, rocked him to sleep right there in the store. I'm sorry, but the man I saw that day who handled our son with kid gloves wouldn't kill or hurt anyone."

Ethan ran his hands through his long, black hair. "So everyone in this room considers Troy a candidate for sainthood, an innocent man, incapable of strangling the life out of his ex-girlfriend, someone he supposedly loved at one point?" He checked each pair of eyes, and watched each head bob in agreement.

"No one's saying the guy's a saint. Innocent of murder, yes, that's the point, isn't it?" Logan snapped. "But Troy damned sure didn't cause ten other young women to vanish into thin air within the city limits of Pelican Pointe. I happened to think Gina's murder and the ten missing women are related."

"I agree," Kinsey said.

When each one of the others said the same, Ethan twisted up his mouth and said to Logan, "You just won't let this drop, will you?" When Logan just kept up the stubborn stare, Ethan added, "Okay, okay, let's suppose for a minute, there's a stone-cold serial killer walking among us."

"An indiscriminate, opportunistic killer, you mean, living in or near the area for years. One that would need to control every aspect of his crimes, which is making young women disappear. He subdues his victim, controls the environment from the get-go which is the abduction right down to the killing itself," Logan determined.

"All the while showing another face to the outside world, which is us, we're the outside world. Then he works hard at convincing everyone around him he's just a normal, everyday kind of guy," Kinsey surmised.

"You do realize you've just described Troy?" Ethan pointed out.

"No. For this discussion I'm taking Troy out of our hypothetical serial killer equation," Logan stated. "For one, he isn't the right age. You said so yourself. No, we're looking for someone who is approximately twenty-five years older than Troy. Try to stay with me here, Ethan."

"He'd have no discernible pattern either." When everyone turned their heads to stare at Lilly, she added, "Well, after all, so far he's left no clues. There are no crime scenes. Ethan would've known about them. No one's found a body—until…Gina."

"Yeah, what about that, Logan? How come this hypothetical serial killer leaves Gina's body out in the open when he's never even given us a body before now? They don't change their patterns."

"Sure they do."

"What makes you an expert? Just because—"

"My sister became a victim to one? That's right, Ethan. I've had years to research this type of killer. And I know this much, they learn from their mistakes. They change MOs all the time to keep their crimes from getting linked. They're hoping to fly under law enforcement's radar. And look, twenty-five years goes by and you guys still haven't connected his crimes."

"Okay, okay," Ethan uttered. "I suppose that was out of line for me to say."

"Let's go to neutral corners for a minute," Kinsey suggested. "What if maybe this time the guy made a mistake? Or something interrupted him, got him out of his rhythm," Kinsey offered. "Or, for whatever reason, the killer purposely wanted Troy to get the blame for this. Someone Troy knows, someone close to him, someone that has it in for him, I just don't know. But this time, the killer didn't have time to get rid of the body for a reason, but left it near the trailer for someone to find."

"It didn't take long for that to happen," Jordan said.

"No, it didn't take long at all," Logan agreed, rubbing a hand down his face. "Okay maybe my imagination is getting the better of me here but I think someone wanted Gina's body to be found right away. The killer wouldn't have left it there otherwise. Either that or someone came along and, like Kinsey said, got him out of his usual pattern. He didn't have time to dispose of the body."

"Knowing Troy would get the blame," Nick surmised. "What time did Troy get home that night?"

"He said around midnight. I went to the jail yesterday to sit down with him at length, found out more of the specifics, which aren't really that helpful. He dropped Mona off at her house on foot. Then got back in his truck where he'd been parked all evening, went home, went to bed. He didn't hear or see anything out of the ordinary."

"But her car was sitting right there at the side of the road," Ethan pointed out. "Troy had to drive right past it."

"I don't have all the answers, Ethan," Kinsey admitted.

"Okay, we need a list of suspects. Anybody in town fit the mold? Who are the bad asses around here?" Logan wanted to know.

"The Turley brothers," Nick and Ethan both announced at the same time.

"Sal and Sam Turley," Ethan stated flatly. "Troublemakers extraordinaire of the hard-ass variety. They have a long history within a fifty-mile radius of starting fights, usually just to make a point."

"I know all about the Turley brothers," Logan acknowledged. "His references checked out but each one made a point to mention the guy's a hothead. After a month on the job, I've seen his temper for myself. Sam will go off over the least little thing. Maybe we're on to something here. He bitches a lot, but other than that, he isn't what I would've termed an indiscriminate killer."

"And you know so much about character," Ethan quipped before adding, "Anyone who hires Sam Turley gets what he deserves."

Logan sighed. "Okay, I see your point. But it just means Sam's good at putting on one face to the outside world while he hides a much darker side, which means from now on, I keep my eye on Sam Turley at the work site."

"That probably won't do a bit of good, although I would watch him. Sam's not too bad if you get him alone, away from Sal. When he's with his brother, beware. He'll do anything Sal says. Anything. Sam's a follower. Plus those two will turn a bar upside down in nothing flat," Nick explained.

"Sal's serving time, so Sam's been a little lost for more than a year now without his brother telling him what to do," Ethan detailed.

"Where would a serial killer put his victims though? That would be a lot of bodies to bury. He'd have to have someplace convenient," Wally pointed out.

"Are you kidding? That's easy. We live right next door to the perfect dumping ground," Logan returned.

"The ocean," Kinsey offered.

"Exactly." Logan noted the stares from his friends, noted the sympathy on their faces. He wasn't sure how he felt about that, so he added, "I've already spent a considerable amount of time thinking about that distinct possibility."

"After all, look what happened to Sissy Carr," Keegan put in.

"You think Gina's death could have something to do with Sissy's?" Nick wanted to know.

"But Kent killed Sissy. Didn't he?" Jordan asked.

Ethan shook his head. "Brent and I thought he did. But law enforcement hasn't found hide nor hair of Kent Springer in more than two years," Ethan said. "His credit cards haven't been used, nor has his social security number. And in this age of technology, it's difficult to completely disappear."

"But not impossible," Logan stated.

"Kent did have a half million dollars in his possession at the time he and Sissy went missing," Nick offered. "That money could have bought him a new ID and then some."

"True," Ethan agreed. "But we have no proof of that. All we know for sure is when Harold and Drake Boedecker came across Sissy Carr's body, she was a floating corpse."

"We should do something for poor Eileen and Clint Purvis," Lilly suggested. "They're in my Sunday school class at church. We should find out when the funeral is."

"It's Thursday," Kinsey offered. "Clint came to the office yesterday to see Aaron. He needed help locating Gina's brother to let him know about her death. Apparently, the brother took off when he turned eighteen. His parents haven't heard from him in six or seven years now."

"I don't see how anyone will be able to find him then before his sister's funeral," Cord reasoned.

"What do Clint and Eileen say about all of this? Are they thinking Troy's responsible?" Keegan asked.

Cord nodded, sent a look toward Logan. "Unfortunately, they do. I think it's a given in this town. We, the people in this room, are the exceptions. Well, except for maybe Ethan."

"Then we'll just have to show the good residents of Pelican Pointe that Troy Dayton is no killer," Logan vowed.

Chapter Nineteen

Word had finally leaked out that the renowned sculptor, Logan Donnelly, had bought the Smuggler's Bay Lighthouse. Logan couldn't help but wonder why it had taken so long for them to get around to him. When the San Sebastian Chronicle contacted him wanting a quote, instead of hanging up on the reporter, Logan had recognized an opportunity.

Usually he eluded the press like a kid avoided eating green veggies. But now that one of his employees had been accused of murder, going public might be a chance to tout Troy's innocence in a sanctioned capacity. An interview might be just the thing to let the entire area know Troy had people in his corner. Even if it was a newspaper as small as the neighboring town, it would bring attention to Troy's case.

Sure enough, two days after the article hit the streets, Troy's ten supporters ramped up their campaign. Now that it was public knowledge Troy had supporters, Logan and Kinsey had posters printed up offering a reward for information leading to the arrest of Gina's real killer.

It wasn't exactly the most popular move they could've made since most the town considered Troy Dayton a cold-hearted murderer.

But that didn't deter the members of the group from taking turns going door to door contacting the local business owners around town asking if they could put up the posters.

Ferguson's Hardware didn't dare refuse Logan since he was spending a crap load of money there on lumber and other materials.

Kinsey likewise convinced Perry Altman to put one up in the lobby of The Pointe. The same was true at Murphy's Market where two decorated each glass side panel by the front doors—one you could see going in—the other you couldn't miss on the way out.

Wally plastered the front windows of the Pump N Go with several. And since Nick was the bank president, Jordan tacked her poster up inside the lobby without any real problems. As it turned out, with a change at the top, the financial institution all but oozed friendly assistance these days.

Finishing up at the bank, Jordan's next stop was the Hilltop Diner. Max and Margie gladly agreed to put up two, one for the front windows and one to put behind the register. From there Jordan headed to the row of businesses along Ocean Street where she met up with Keegan.

Keegan had put up posters at the Fanning Marine Rescue Center and Cord had followed suit out at Taggert Farms. Cord's drivers had even taped a few signs to the inside back windows of their delivery trucks. Together Keegan and Cord had talked Bran Sullivan, the town vet, into putting up one at his house which also doubled as the vet's office.

No one offered too much in the way of resistance. At least not until Keegan and Jordan ventured back down to Main Street and into Knudsen's Pharmacy. Keegan had no sooner gotten her pitch started, than Carl Knudsen shook his head, his cordial demeanor went south. The pharmacist held up a hand. "Stop right there, Keegan. You're not putting that up in here."

"But why?" Keegan wanted to know. "Troy didn't kill Gina Purvis."

"He wouldn't have been arrested if he hadn't done it," Carl stated emphatically. And after five minutes of trying to dissuade him of that belief, Keegan and Jordan gave up and left.

It was about that same time that Kinsey and Lilly encountered their first pocket of resistance at both the Snip N Curl, then again at McCready's. When Wally found out, he stubbornly took the posters from the women and stormed back inside to have a discussion with Janie Pointer himself. After that, he went into the bar to confront Flynn McCready. Five minutes later, Wally came back empty-handed.

"What did you say to make them change their minds?" Kinsey wanted to know.

Wally grinned. "I told both Janie and Flynn if they ever wanted their cars worked on any time in the future, they might better take the posters."

"Good idea. But do you think the signs will stay up?"

"If they don't, they'll have to get their oil changed in San Sebastian or Santa Cruz from now on. And I'd personally love to be the one to tell them what they can do if their cars need work."

By two-thirty that afternoon, they all met back up at the big booth in The Hilltop Diner for lunch and coffee, except for Keegan and Cord who both had to dash off to make afternoon classes they couldn't miss.

As Nick nibbled on his turkey sandwich and fries, he decided there was something he needed to get off his chest. "It's hard to believe the serial killer bit. I mean, the more I think about it, the more I want to believe those girls just ran off, that they're out there somewhere and all this is a bad dream." Nick met Logan's eyes. "But as much as I'd like to believe it, as much as I'd like to go on thinking this is a great place for my kids to grow up, I don't think it's possible that ten girls could go missing like that. What I can't understand is why this isn't all over the local news? The whole thing is bugging me."

Logan waited for Nick to get to the point. "But you love this place."

"Now I do. But when I first got to town, I hated it. The people did everything they could to make Jordan's life miserable which made me resent them for it. Turns out, part of the problem was Sissy Carr. She'd been spreading gossip about Jordan ever since Scott moved back here."

"And?" Logan prompted.

"And now I'm beginning to look at every face that comes into the bank and wonder is this the guy?"

Jordan sighed. "I thought it was just me. Glad to know I'm not the only one doing that. You have to remember, Scott thought this was such a great little town. For a while there I couldn't figure out why. Now, Nick and I are almost right back where we were wondering. We've had several late night discussions about who in town might be doing this," Jordan said in way of explanation. "Now we're dealing with something so evil, it's difficult to imagine that someone living here is...doing this and we have no idea who it might be."

Kinsey chewed the inside of her jaw. Should she mention that Scott had admitted to her that he knew who had killed Megan? She stared over at Logan, saw the stubborn set of his mouth, and decided this was not a good time to bring it up. After all, the man didn't like acknowledging he'd ever seen Scott, let alone have a conversation about him.

But later, Kinsey couldn't let the subject go. It kept nagging at her. So when they got back to her place, she turned to Logan. Before she could say anything, he surprised her. "Okay, what's bothering you? You hardly said a word during lunch, then barely talked during the ride back here. You're too quiet."

She knew no other way than to blurt it out. For ten minutes she went over everything Scott had said to her verbatim.

"Scott said what? That's...ridiculous. Wait a minute. You had one of your infamous conversations with this guy and he actually admitted to you he knew who killed Megan but refused to tell you? What the hell kind of game is that? So this ghost knows whose killing young girls and has been for years, but won't name him? What kind of benevolent spirit is that, Kinsey? Think about it."

She pushed her hair off her face, began to pace. "I knew you'd react this way. I hesitated telling you because I knew you wouldn't get it."

"What's there to get? I think I've got a handle on this guy now. I won't take the bait, so he works on you."

"Why do you say that? Unless…Scott tried to talk to you about this very thing, didn't he? And you blew up at him just like you're doing right now. You know what, Logan? No one can talk to you. I thought, hey, this is your sister we're talking about. You might want to think outside the box on this, reach out to any resource you could get. The way Scott explained it to me was this. Let's say he gave me a name. What good would it do? We'd still have to find proof."

"That's just it. This is too important to have Scott Phillips playing games with you or me."

"Well, he said we needed to figure this out on our own, that no one would ever believe us without proof. He has a point, Logan."

"To hell he does. Give me a name. I'll go after the son of a bitch. You want evidence. I'll get proof."

"Oh my God, you would do it, too. You want to go after the guy and maybe you're the one who'll end up in jail? You think about that. Is that what you want? Because that isn't how it works."

"How the fuck do you know how it works? This is my sister we're talking about. There are nine, now ten, other lives destroyed by this bastard and you want me to play by the rules. I don't think so."

And with that Logan stormed out of the studio, slamming the door hard enough to shake the panes in the windows.

Logan felt weird seeking advice from Wade Hawkins. But he didn't know where else to go. He'd called Ethan to get directions to a rambling, western-style ranch house, located two miles north of town. The place reminded Logan of a rustic ski lodge complete with wooden front porch and railing. It brought to mind the Ponderosa, that house where the Cartwright brothers called home on the old television reruns he'd seen of *Bonanza*.

Wade greeted Logan with the same cheery disposition he'd shown in the bar that night when the old guy had wanted to talk about ghosts. After following Wade into a massive living room with log-paneled walls, vaulted, timber plank ceilings, and a stone fireplace that took up an entire wall, Logan settled into one of the wing chairs.

"What can I do for you?" Wade asked.

"You should have told me that Sunday night in the bar you were the local expert on paranormal activity."

"I thought you knew that when I told you I was writing a book. It's clear you were skeptical that night of anything paranormal." Wade steepled his fingers, tucked them under his chin as if thinking. "Have you had a change of heart?"

"No. I'm here because both times I saw Scott Phillips I was still jet-lagged. He obviously was a hallucination or something. Before that incident occurred Kinsey had mentioned him at dinner. In fact, the entire conversation pretty much centered around Scott in his ghostly form. Power of suggestion."

Wade smiled. "Then why are you here?"

"Because Kinsey believes she sees him, talks to him. And it's significant."

"And this upsets you. You're looking to have her committed for some reason," Wade said with a twinkle in his eye.

Logan finally allowed a smile to form on his lips. "I wouldn't even want to try. Kinsey is…her own person, a little quirky. She believes this ghost stuff is real."

"And you don't."

"Of course not."

"So your own sightings you've chalked up to nothing more than jet lag and ignored Scott for the most part? What do you want from me, Logan?"

He felt fairly ridiculous asking the question. So he hesitated, a little too long.

Wade took the opening to suggest, "So Scott said something specific to you that only you and no one else would know?"

"How do you know that?"

"Honestly? Hayden reported a similar encounter. So did Nick, Keegan and Cord Bennett for that matter. And Kinsey showed up on my doorstep two days ago."

Logan blew out a frustrated breath. "Nick mentioned it. But I didn't know about the rest. It's just that…Kinsey seems to think that in her first actual conversation with Scott, he used some code word that only she would get."

Wade noticed he didn't include himself. "That's fairly typical to establish trust, so that he's assured of putting you at ease. But that didn't work with you."

Logan got up to pace. "It pissed me off."

An opening, thought Wade. He wanted to keep Logan talking. "Scott does that...frequently."

"Why? I thought he was supposed to be this benevolent, helpful entity and here I find out he's anything but."

"Really? Scott's brought harm to Kinsey? In what way?"

He'd backed himself into a corner with that. "How do you think?" Logan snarled. "He's playing with Kinsey's head. And I don't like it. He dabbles in the truth, can't seem to commit to an honest dialogue."

"Interesting," Wade muttered. "From everything I've heard Scott's always been a pretty straight shooter with everyone. He throws in a few riddles now and again to make you think. I've heard he can be a major pain in the ass when he gets in a mood. But for the most part Scott's fairly candid. Are you certain you aren't looking at him with blinders, putting up a barrier of some sort to protect yourself from whatever it is he's trying to convey to you?"

"That's…absurd. Why would I block something I don't even consider possible? If he isn't playing games why doesn't he just speak his mind?"

"You tell me. Look, let me make a suggestion. Seek Scott out, try having a reasonable discussion about something innocuous for starters?"

"And that would be…what?"

"I'd say that's up to you."

After leaving the Ponderosa Logan headed to Eternal Gardens to test out Wade's idea. He wasn't sure what he expected to happen. All he knew was he wanted Scott to show up and talk to him again.

Logan got out of his truck, made his way to the Donnelly family plot. This time he'd stopped at the florist in town to buy flowers. He arranged the pink roses in the urn and sat back to wait. After five minutes or so, Logan grumbled. "You didn't have any trouble appearing before you son of a bitch?" Silence. "Not man enough to face me now, huh? What is it with you?" Still nothing.

"You're pretty good at giving people the cold shoulder." Still silence. "I could've sworn you said I should let you know when I'm ready to accept help."

"Are you?"

Logan whirled around to see Scott standing five feet from him. "What do you know about Megan? Did you really tell Kinsey you know who killed her?"

"First of all, what I say to Kinsey is none of your business." Scott pointed an accusing finger at Logan. "You browbeat her for believing she sees me then you come out here expecting me to open up to you. I don't think so."

"Now you're playing games."

"I'm trying to get you to understand that I can't just give you a name. It doesn't work like that."

"Then suppose you educate me because I'm not familiar with the rules according to Scott."

"I went out with Megan a couple of times that summer, actually a lot more than a couple of times."

"You're making that up to piss me off. It's working."

"I can't win with you. You argue when I try to tell you anything. You don't want to listen." Scott threw up his hands in frustration. But as Scott started to fade away, Logan spoke up, begging, pleading. "Don't go. I'm sorry. I'll do anything to find out what happened to Megan. Please. Tell me what you can about what happened to her. Anything at all. Your terms."

Scott's voice said, "She was supposed to meet me that night under the pier."

Chills ran along Logan's arm and the evening was too warm for it. "That Friday night she went missing? You were the date, the guy she was meeting? All this time, you were the one I couldn't remember."

"It was me. But that night, Megan never showed up, Logan. I waited underneath the pier most of the night until well after four a.m. She often snuck out of the house to meet me late at night. That place was our spot. We'd make out there sometimes. Either there or I'd pick her up in my old Chevy and bring her out to the cove." As if that memory held on a little too long, Scott stopped talking to gather his thoughts. When he finally spoke again, he said, "The cove was the best place. We'd spend hours there swimming or just lying on the beach. Megan was happy, Logan. We were both happy. In love."

Logan sensed there was more. The chills were gone now. But sweat streamed down his back. "What are you not telling me?" He watched now as Scott began to pace back and forth in full form. Whatever it was, Logan had a feeling he wasn't going to like hearing it.

"Until this moment I've never told another living soul what I'm about to tell you. I don't want you judging Megan. Promise me you won't do that."

"I'd never do that."

"Don't use the word never!" Scott snapped. "It's one of those words that has a habit of coming back to bite you in the ass when you least expect it."

"All right." Logan swallowed hard and took a step closer to Scott. "Tell me. Now."

"Megan was pregnant. I was the father. We were just kids, Logan. She found out the first week of August, a couple of days before she went missing. From the first time I saw her that June we couldn't keep our hands off each other. We made out practically every time we were together, every time we touched each other. I guess it was inevitable."

Logan's fists bunched at his sides. "If you're about to tell me you killed her because of that, so help me God, I'll dig up what's left of you, here and now, and drive a stake through your fucking—"

"Are you nuts? I was in love with Megan! I'd have married her in two heartbeats even as young as I was. Hell, it wouldn't have taken that much. I'm trying to fucking tell you I didn't just lose Megan that night she didn't show, I lost the child she was carrying. I was in love with your sister, Logan. All the way in love and she just— disappeared. One day she was here. In one night she was gone. I was frantic, worried sick. That first week after she went missing, I thought maybe she'd gone to San Francisco. We used to talk about going there. So I got in the car like an idiot just to see if I could find her. For two days I drove around the city, going to all the places we'd talked about seeing together. I don't know what I'd hoped to accomplish. But I had to do something. After I got back, I went to see your grandparents. They told me Megan didn't even bother to take a single item of her clothes or her money with her. I knew then something bad had happened. I just didn't know what."

Logan watched as the man choked up, got tears in his eyes. How was that even possible? he wondered. But Logan was convinced what he saw was heartfelt anguish on Scott's face. He had to force out the words. "But you know what happened to her, don't you?"

"I spent years not knowing. Even when I moved Jordan back here I had this tiny little corner of my heart that hoped, prayed Megan had made it back to Pelican Pointe in the years since I'd been gone. That she was living right here with my child, alive, happy, even if she was with another man, I didn't care at that point. I'd fallen in love with Jordan. But if Megan was here, living happily ever after, at least I'd know she was okay. But—"

"Is Megan dead?"

Scott swallowed hard and nodded. "I know it now—with certainty. And something inside you has always known it, too."

"Tell me. Give me a name, goddamn it! Stop this fucking bullshit game of yours, once and for all, and give me his name."

"Do you think I don't want to? Do you think I don't want the son of a bitch who killed her to pay? Of course, I do. I want it more than you could possibly imagine. I've waited for you to come. I've waited years for justice, to see the bastard get what's coming to him, for you to finally find the balls to walk back into this town and do something about it other than bitch and moan and feel sorry for yourself."

Deflated, Logan muttered, "Then I don't understand." It was Logan's turn to pace. "Screw your rules. What can you tell me about the bastard? At least give me something concrete."

"Everything that's happened here is connected. Everything. Find the pattern. Kinsey is here to help you. Let her." With those simple words, Scott faded away.

This time Logan held his tongue. Something during the confrontation had moved inside him. Whether it was steely determination, or just plain, old-fashioned Donnelly stubbornness, he couldn't say. But whatever it was he couldn't wait to rush back to Kinsey, to tell her what he'd learned.

Almost an hour later, he stood in front of the studio door and knocked. When Kinsey opened it she took his breath away in a thin pale blue robe, a pink tank top and pink-plaid pajama shorts. He wanted to eat her up. A wash of candlelight flickered behind her. Dolores O'Riordan's voice in the background reminded him dreams were impossible to ignore. Logan cocked his head to one side. For a minute he simply stared at Kinsey's face, her eyes. For lack of anything else, he held out the two dozen yellow roses in his hand. "You might not want to answer the door like that."

She rolled her eyes and took the flowers, stuck her nose into the huge blooms, deeply inhaled the fragrant buds. "Nick installed a peephole two weeks ago. Where have you been, Logan?"

"I went out…to see Wade Hawkins. Do I get to come in?"

She brought the door back wider. "Why?"

"So I can tell you I'm sorry."

She studied him. "No, I mean why did you go see Wade?"

"To get his take on Scott. Look, I owe you an apology. Kinsey."

"It's okay. I realize you don't have to believe the same things I do. It isn't a prerequisite in order to sustain a relationship."

"No, it isn't. But I was wrong. I had a long talk with him."

"Wade does like to talk…"

"No, not with Wade with Scott."

"What?"

Logan told her everything Scott had said, almost word for word. When he was done she had to sit down on the sofa.

"Oh my God, Logan. Why didn't we consider that?" When she saw the look of confusion on his face, she added, "No, really. Listen. In order to solve this we have to think back to Megan's life at the time. What was happening here in this town back then? Who was here? We need to make a list."

He grinned at that. "Scott said you were here to help me and that I should let you."

"Let me? Well, he's right about one thing. We need to find the pattern. And to do that we need Ethan's help. We need those files on the ten women, Logan. Do you think you could stop arguing with him long enough to work on that?"

"I'll do my best."

"Hmm, why do you suppose Megan and Scott didn't meet at the lighthouse? Didn't you say the town considered that place Make Out Point?"

"If you don't mind I'd rather not think about my sister like that—"

Frustrated with him, she blew out a breath. "That isn't what I'm getting at here, Logan. Even teenagers in love appreciate their privacy. They'd look for a spot where if someone approached they wouldn't be caught in the act, so to speak, someplace out-of-the-way. There was a reason Scott and Megan didn't meet at the lighthouse."

"Maybe they'd been caught there before."

"Or maybe they suspected someone might be watching them there."

Logan sucked in a breath, ran a hand through his hair. "I've been underneath the pier. There's no way anyone could sneak up on a couple in the throes of passion there without making a lot of noise from all the rocks you have to deal with."

"Exactly, and if two people suspected a voyeur lurking about, the pier would provide a better degree of privacy where they'd have time to cover up, fix their clothes if they heard feet crunching on those rocks."

Logan shook his head. "You're brilliant, you know that? That's amazing."

"That's more like two teens getting creative. Tell me something. Why the change of heart? Scott must've indicated to you he was trying to help that first night you were here."

"I don't know exactly, other than the fact I'd spent a couple of years trying to piece together all the girls that had gone missing here, years consumed with hunting down facts. I was steeped in reality, dealing with details, not a bunch of paranormal crap. I even created a spreadsheet about it."

She frowned. "And when were you planning to share that?"

A sheepish look crossed his face. "Until about an hour ago, I was determined to do this alone."

"And now?"

His eyes had changed. She recognized that look as he took a slow perusal down her body. "That robe, I want you out of it." The music drifted to Rufus Wainwright's piano chords and *Hallelujah* as he tugged her toward the bed.

The tenderness she saw in his green eyes drew her in. Her breath backed up as his arms came around her. Nothing prepared her for the tender kiss he placed on each corner of her mouth or the way his long, lean fingers stroked her flesh.

They swayed in place until his hands made quick work of the robe. It dropped to the floor as he yanked her top up over her head. His hands slid into her shorts, cupped her rear end. All the while he feasted along the curve of a breast, tugged on a ripe nipple.

He eased her back on the mattress.

His tongue tasted, flicked over her belly button, licked at skin sweet as honey. He skimmed downward, brushing along her inner thigh. The warmth drew him in.

Kinsey gripped the sheets as sensations built, as blinding pleasure shattered through her.

When he moved above her, she leveraged up, shoved him back on the pillows, and straddled his body. "My turn now," she whispered, her voice husky with the urge to give back. Taking the lead, she leaned over him, made sure the peaks of her breasts brushed along his chest. She took long, slow sucks on his neck, ate at his mouth before gliding down his lean torso. She used her teeth to nip, her tongue to arouse. Feathering his hard abs, she licked along his belly until she guided him into her.

Locked as one, her hips began to pump. Tempo began to layer slowly, ever so gently. Then the blood spiked for real. Gentle waves began to snap and break with want. Arching her back, she rode in sweet and fiery measures with one purpose. Need spiraled up then sprinted along in a burst of blinding light. The brilliant orange and red shimmered just before the colors merged, splashed hotter, brighter. As Kinsey took them both through the flash fire, Logan finally let go. Every barrier he'd ever created dropped away.

And with it, found the peace that had so eluded him.

By the time she collapsed on top of him the music had changed to Springsteen. While the drumbeat kept time and Bruce warned about a brilliant disguise, Logan reached up, toyed with a few strands of her hair. "That was intense."

"Maybe we should yell at each other more often."

"Until this minute I would've said that was a bad idea. But…I can't argue with the results."

"Were things really that bad with Fiona, Logan?"

"I'm not bringing that woman into this bed, not now, not ever," he stated flatly.

Kinsey blew out a sigh. "I'm not…but you're so…furious. Is she why you've closed yourself off, become so guarded?"

Logan sat up, smoothed his hair back. "Kinsey, she damn near broke my spirit. If that wasn't bad enough, I almost let her."

Kinsey swallowed hard, needing to know all of it. "You loved her that much?"

"At the time I thought what I felt for her was love. It wasn't. I'd never before been in that kind of all-consuming relationship. Believe me, it burned out quick. Maybe I'm just not wired to make that kind of connection with anyone. Some people aren't meant to."

"Ever?"

"I'm not walking that path again, Kinsey. Not for anyone."

"Well, that's blunt enough."

"You need to know where I'm coming from."

"Oh believe me, you're coming through loud and clear."

Chapter Twenty

A week later Troy's supporters needed to regroup.

Inside Ethan's living room, they met to go over what they knew in the hopes they could come up with something, anything that might shed light on Gina's real killer.

Standing in front of the bookcase, Kinsey looked around the room. After thirty minutes of hashing things over, it was more like grasping at straws, thought Kinsey as she noted the mood of the team was much more somber. As if the longer Troy remained in jail, the more reality took hold Troy Dayton was truly up against a wall. And it was up to the people in this room to do something about it.

"The prosecution has DNA. And I'm convinced when they announce the results it'll come back exonerating Troy," Kinsey ventured.

"So, what are we supposed to do, let Troy rot in jail without helping him out? Most of the town is convinced he's guilty. I'm not even sure how he'll get a fair trial," Jordan pointed out.

"The trial will be held in Santa Cruz," Ethan stated. "The jury pool will probably be residents from there. And it will likely take months to get to trial."

"Whoever did this to Gina had to be watching her when she left to give Troy back his stuff," Logan considered. "The killer followed her."

"Rumor has it Gina's vehicle was tampered with," Wally added. "I don't know what they did to it because the cops towed it into Santa Cruz. But there are several age-old methods to disable a car. If that rumor turns out to be true, let's say the car sputters and stops leaving Gina alone sitting at the side of the road in the dark. Someone stops to help her."

"Only he isn't there to help," Jordan added, chills forming on her arms.

"Do you think Gina knew him?" Hayden asked.

"It's possible because if she screamed, no one in that area reported hearing a thing."

"It's a very remote, dark area of town," Lilly added. "I wouldn't even go out at night with the kids when I lived out there."

"Exactly," Logan said. "For us to believe a stranger did this, we'd have to buy the fact that someone unfamiliar to the area, exits off the interstate, veers onto the 101, follows the Coast Highway, happens to see a young woman experiencing car trouble and then decides to pull over to kill her then and there."

"And conveniently the victim has just broken up with her boyfriend, who lives less than a mile down the road where the body is ultimately found," Hayden added.

Kinsey paced the length of the bookcase. "If your point is that a stranger couldn't have done all that, I agree. But it also doesn't do a whole lot to help Troy either. Having had a brief discussion with the prosecutor this week, his theory is that Troy left Mona at her house, after dropping her off, he then headed home to his trailer, that he encountered Gina along that dark road. The two of them argued, and in a fit of rage, Troy dragged her out of the car, took her to his trailer where he strangled her and dumped her body five hundred feet from his front door," Kinsey concluded. "The problem with all of that bunk is it doesn't jive with the evidence."

"You'd think with all that activity Troy's fingerprints would be all over her car," Nick surmised.

Kinsey shook her head. "Forensics turned that car upside down. Troy's prints were nowhere on that Mazda. The D.A. shared that much but little else."

"That should be enough to tell them he wasn't there," Logan retorted.

"You'd think. But their theory is he must have gone back, wiped his prints off the vehicle. Troy was her boyfriend up until a few weeks ago. Their reasoning is his prints should have been there…somewhere." When others shot her weird looks, she added, "I'm serious. That's what the D.A. said."

"You're kidding?" Hayden said flatly. "It sounds like we might be fighting an uphill battle we can't win."

"Where are we on the DNA?" Cord asked.

"Still waiting on the results. You want my two cents? My guess is they're dragging their feet on releasing the results because Troy's DNA wasn't found on Gina."

Logan wanted them back on track. "Okay, people, what exactly *do* we have that points to someone else other than Troy? At this point, we need a suspect list to give Troy's defense attorney, which brings me to Collier Davis. Davis finally got back in touch with me. He's agreed to make the trip down from the Bay to talk to Troy, doesn't mean he'll represent him, just meet with him, decide if he wants to take Troy's case or not."

"I'll help with the legal fees," Nick offered.

"Okay, thanks for that. As soon as Davis agrees to represent Troy I'd like to be able to provide him with a list of people we think needs to be checked out, which means hiring a private investigator."

"A private investigator might be the way to go. Because unless we find someone who has a history of abusing women, what chances do we have of finding Gina's killer?" Nick asked.

"It's like finding a needle in a haystack," Cord said. "It could be anyone."

"The only guy I can think of with a history like that was Kent Springer and he's been dead for almost two years now," Nick offered.

Lilly fidgeted in her seat. She cleared her throat. "Do you really think it might be someone like Kent? Someone with a history of making sexual advances or having problems dealing with women?"

"We all know Kent was suspected of doing away with that woman over in Santa Cruz. Those were the rumors. But Nick's right, we can't blame this on Kent Springer," Wally pointed out.

Logan made a mental note to background this Kent person. The guy may not have killed Gina but he damned sure could be the man who had taken Megan.

Lilly toyed with the zipper on her purse, clearly hesitant about the topic. "This may not mean anything, but I've wanted someone to know about this for quite some time. Maybe now's the right moment," Lilly finally blurted out, still nervous. "I probably should've mentioned it to you before now, Ethan, but at the time, I was brand new in town with two little kids and I didn't really think anyone would believe me anyway. Besides, I was afraid."

Ethan noticed the look of panic form on Wally's face.

"You're starting to scare me, Lilly. You'd better tell me what you're talking about," Wally stated.

Lilly swallowed her mouth suddenly very thirsty. "It's about Derek Stovall, my stepfather. It's probably nothing."

"That look on your face sure doesn't make me think it's nothing," Wally replied with tension layered in his voice.

"Just don't overreact, okay?"

"Again, not making me feel better here, Lilly."

"Fine," Lilly said through gritted teeth. "When my mom married Derek we moved down to Pelican Pointe. I spent some of my teen years here. I met Kyle on a trip back to Monterey and married him." She looked around at the faces in the room, landing on Jordan.

"I remember unburdening my soul to Jordan the first time. Not sure I ever thanked you for pulling me out of that hopeless feeling I had without friends. I'm convinced meeting you that day at Murphy's Market was what turned my life around."

Jordan reached over and took her hand. "I feel the same way. You were my first friend here, Lilly. Tell us what happened with Derek."

"Remember my mom died while married to Derek. But things had been rough for me and the kids back in Monterey. Since Kyle got locked up after I pressed charges against him, I couldn't afford the rent there anymore though. When Derek found out he offered me a place to stay. He said he had a trailer that me and the kids could live in. I jumped at getting out of Monterey to make a new start without Kyle. I thought it was the perfect solution to my problem."

"Sounds like it should've been," Wally offered, all the while he jingled the keys in his pocket anxiously waiting for her to get to the point.

Lilly shook her head. "When we got here Kyra was barely three and little Joey had just started walking real good. I didn't have the money to pay for a babysitter while I hunted down a job in town. It was Christmastime and I was just settling in when I went on county assistance." She looked for understanding in Wally's eyes but all she got was a confused line of worry on his face. "Derek started hanging around a little too much after I got here. He got drunk one night and said some things about my mom dying."

"What sort of things?" Ethan asked. "I remember when she died. The coroner ruled she took an accidental overdose of sleeping pills and that was the end of it."

"Yeah, but I heard Derek Stovall told the coroner she'd been depressed for some time," Wally countered.

"At the time, I thought that was true. That she was depressed because I was in an abusive marriage with Kyle and her grandchildren were in that situation, living it every day. That was my fault."

"But you don't think that now?"

"I don't know. But Derek made it sound like he wasn't surprised my mom took sleeping pills."

Wally was still staring at Lilly. "But there's more to this than your mother, isn't there?" Apprehensive to hear the rest, he watched as Lilly took a deep breath before going on.

"After I moved into the trailer Derek started coming around...uninvited. Dale would, too, sometimes."

"Why didn't you tell me this before now?" Wally blurted out.

"Because look at you. I knew you'd want to go out there and punch Derek's face in, maybe Dale's, too. Do you think I want another husband locked up in jail? Do you?"

"She's got a point there," Nick said with a grin. "But if it's any consolation that's what I would've wanted to do."

"A punch in the face is the way I would've gone," Cord agreed. But when Cord looked over at Keegan, she wasn't laughing at the joke.

"I think we need to hear what Lilly has to say. Without any more interruptions," Keegan suggested. "Go on, Lilly."

"Before he died in that accident, Dale hung around, too, just not nearly as much as Derek did. Derek tried getting real friendly the longest. It got so I wouldn't answer the door when he knocked. But he had a key, of course. He owned the place. One night I got out of the shower and found him standing in the living room. He had his shirt already off."

Hearing that, Wally all but exploded in fury. "Damn it! What happened? Please tell me you got out of there."

"If you'll settle down, I'll tell you. I started screaming the house down that night, so loud I'm surprised the whole town didn't hear me. I was scared, which was no act. My yelling woke up the kids. They both started crying. It was chaos for a few minutes before Derek made like he was there to fix the sink and left. There wasn't anything wrong with the faucet or the drain. Those two things were probably the only stuff in that old place that worked just fine." Lilly swallowed hard. "Derek kept coming back though. He'd try to hug me, get me to hug him back. Dale did it too a couple of times before he died. They were both creepy."

"So the entire time you lived out there, that son of a bitch and his brother, made sexual advances toward you and you never said a word about it to anyone," Wally accused.

Ethan stood up and got in Wally's face. "And your yelling at Lilly is making it so much easier for her to tell us about it now."

Immediately contrite, Wally went over to Lilly, wrapped his arms around her. "Ethan's right. I'm sorry. But I really wish you would've said something to me."

"On that we agree," Ethan said. But about that time he glanced over at Keegan who looked like she was about to cry. "Keegan? What's the matter with you?"

Cord turned his head just in time to hear Keegan admit, "It was Dale who did the same thing to me."

"Shit," Cord said. He took a deep breath of his own and reached for her hand. "Recently?"

"Oh no, Cord. Dale died the same year my grandmother died, two years back I guess. You remember, Ethan? That motorcycle accident south of here, out on the 101?"

"I do. It looked like Dale got drunk one night and veered into the path of an oncoming eighteen-wheeler—on purpose."

"Committed suicide?" Cord said with raised eyebrows. "What the hell? So the guy's no longer in the picture? Good, because I'm fairly sure I'd hunt him down just to beat him senseless." He turned back to his wife. "How old were you when this happened?"

"The last time was a couple of years ago, I guess."

"The last time? How many times did he do this?"

Keegan sighed. "The first time I was about sixteen. Back then Dale used to volunteer at the center sometimes. He'd stop by the house to check on me, or so he said. It seemed to happen every time my grandparents went off to save an animal. A couple of times he tried to hug me like he did Lilly. Once he tried to lure me into his truck. Then when I wouldn't get in, he got out and tried to kiss me. I pushed him away though and took off. Another time I got lucky when Pete showed up before Dale had gone too far. Lilly's right, Derek and Dale were both creepy."

"What can we do about this Derek Stovall guy, Ethan?" Cord asked.

Before he could answer Hayden cleared her throat from the hallway. So far during the meeting she'd been absent because she'd had to nurse Nate, but now, she stood there wringing her hands in the doorway.

Ethan instantly picked up on the vibe and body language. "Not you, too? Why the hell—" He stopped, realized he sounded and acted exactly like Wally had. He took a breath before he asked, "Tell me what happened?"

"Derek Stovall came into the bookstore right after I opened. We weren't even married yet."

"And?"

"He asked about several books. I led him over to where they were—" She chewed on her bottom lip. "Before I knew what was happening, Derek had me cornered there. He tried to put his arm around me. Like Keegan said Dale did to her, I pushed him away from me and told him to get out. He never came back."

Ethan walked over, wrapped his arms around her, and whispered something in her ear before turning back to the others. "I'll talk to Brent about Stovall. You guys do realize I'm no longer wearing a badge."

"We realize that, Ethan. But you've got Brent's ear. He'll listen to you," Wally pointed out.

"We certainly can't leave it up to Garver," Logan added. "He has an innocent man locked up and isn't about to admit it, especially since we can't even convince Ethan here that Troy had nothing to do with Gina's murder."

"I'm starting to see a pattern here. What's the likelihood that three out of four women in this room encountered Derek and Dale Stovall and they made blatant sexual overtones toward all of them?"

This time, Nick noticed Jordan's hand shaking. "He never did that to you, did he?"

"Not Derek, no."

Chills formed along Nick's spine at the answer. His arms went numb. The words wanted to catch in his throat. "Who then?"

"Kent Springer."

Nick remembered how Kent had almost set fire to the B & B before it had ever opened. Kent Springer, the sleazy developer had wanted the land. "When? You never said a word."

Jordan lifted a shoulder. "It was long before you showed up. One day I was outside digging in the front flower bed. Hutton was about six months old, I guess. She was sitting in her baby carrier when Kent drove up. He got out of his car, strolled up to me like he owned the place, started chatting about what a great location I had and asked if I'd consider selling."

"He put his hands on you." It wasn't a question.

"He tried. I pushed him back a full step, told him I wasn't interested, and ordered him to get off my property. He threw out a slew of insults, warned me he'd more than likely own the cove one day because I'd never be able to make the mortgage."

"When was this?" Nick asked.

Jordan chewed her lip, thinking. "Scott had been dead about two months. Even then I knew the man was fooling around with Sissy Carr. Everyone did. That was long before you came to Pelican Pointe, Nick."

And one more reason he should have listened to that little voice inside his head a lot sooner than he had. "You still should have mentioned it before now."

Jordan squeezed his hand. "Why? You took Kent down…right there in our driveway." She smiled recalling the middle of the night when Nick had spotted Kent with the gas cans at the corner of the house and took off after him. Nick had caught up with Kent right before he'd reached his car. Brent and Ethan had arrested him on the spot for attempted arson. Those charges were one of the reasons Kent had gone on the run.

"Yeah…well…if I'd known he tried something with you, I'd have given him more than a damned concussion when I tackled the bastard."

"Okay, so where does that leave us? I've got two names that top the suspect list. Sam Turley, the hot head, and now Derek Stovall who can't keep his hands to himself," Logan said.

"Hey, ten missing women, and two, no, three local residents, who seem to have a thing for making untoward sexual advances at women, I think that means something," Kinsey replied. "Which makes me wonder, how many other women in town kept this kind of thing to themselves without saying a word to anyone about Derek, Dale, or this Kent person?"

"Good point. Maybe we should casually, you know, find out," Wally suggested.

"What about adding people Gina knew?" Nick suggested.

"Everyone knew Gina. High profile job at Doc's office, meeting and greeting patients, where she came in contact daily with just about anyone in town that needed a doctor," Cord said. "Could Gina have had another boyfriend no one knew about?"

"Oh God, I hope not," Kinsey uttered. "That would just point to Troy as being a jealous lover."

Logan nodded. "Thinking like a good defense lawyer, I like it."

"But I'm with Kinsey and Wally on this. Maybe we should talk to a few women around town, find out if Derek made advances toward them," Cord suggested.

"Isn't it strange this Derek happens to be the only one of the three still alive—" Nick said.

Ethan shook his head and didn't let Nick finish. "I won't stand here and sanction amateurs going out asking questions, nosing around, compromising a murder investigation."

"Well, someone needs to," Logan pointed out. "It wasn't much of an investigation already since law enforcement made an arrest so quickly." Then he narrowed his eyes at Kinsey. "Derek Stovall hasn't come on to you, has he?"

She shook her head. "I wouldn't even know what he looks like. I mean if I saw him at the remodeling site, I didn't pay any attention to him. Obviously, he isn't interested in messing with a lawyer. Or, maybe I just haven't been in town long enough. But if his track record is any indication, he'll get around to me…eventually. Maybe I could entice him in some way and we'd have him…you know, on record, or video?"

"Don't even think about it," Ethan cautioned.

"About that I'd have to agree with Ethan," Logan said.

Hayden piped up, "No, Kinsey, you really don't want to do that. I think Derek's got cold eyes. When he had me up against those bookshelves, he scared the crap out of me that day."

"Hayden's right," Lilly concurred. "He met my mother over the Internet. I remember cautioning her about his cold blue eyes in the picture he used for his online profile. Do you think Derek might've…you know, done something to my mother, Ethan?"

Wally glared at Ethan. "If you don't take that up with the coroner, maybe Lilly and I should. If the next of kin raises a big enough stink…" He looked over at Kinsey for confirmation. "Maybe Lilly and I should retain a lawyer."

Kinsey nodded. "I could file a petition to have the case looked at again."

"That won't be necessary. I'll take all of this to Brent. We'll check out Derek for prior sexual offenses. I'll also ask about getting copies of the files on the missing women."

Logan stared in wonder at Ethan. "Since when? Brent wouldn't even let me look at Megan's file that day when I met with him."

"I know. But I think there's no better time than the present to crack open these cold case files and go over them one by one."

"Thanks for that. When?"

"I'll let you know, maybe over the next couple of days. That's why I'm serious, guys. I do not want any of you going out that door confronting Stovall or Turley or anyone else for that matter. I'm as angry at what Stovall did to Hayden as any other man in this room. And I intend to bring Stovall to Brent's attention. But I'm going through proper channels. Now, I suggest strongly that you wait this out for an investigation to run its course. If you don't, all bets are off." He pointed a finger at Logan. "Because if just one person tells me that any of you have been nosing around on your own, I'll file a complaint and have whoever it is thrown in jail. Are we clear on that?"

There were grumbles from every man in the room. But in the end, one by one—Logan, Nick, Cord, and Wally—all agreed to adhere to Ethan's edict.

At least. For now.

Chapter Twenty-One

The next day, Ethan Cody slapped a thin stack of file folders on his own kitchen table and said, "Brent and I made copies of the ten cases. What you're looking at, in the order in which they went missing, are the files for Carly Radigan, Angela Fetterman, Janie Shively, Rebecca Linseed, Megan Donnelly, Aurella Gonzales, Penny Hargrove, Kimmie Pederson, Belinda Truitt, and Sandra Flowers, ages fifteen to nineteen. These are the ones reported missing. Who knows if there are more that might have happened in other jurisdictions? But these are ours. A few were labeled runaways. But the end of the line for these files might've happened right here in Pelican Pointe. I don't even want to think about the ones no one bothered calling in to make an official report."

"No offense, Ethan, but even when someone bothered with it, the cops didn't do much."

"I won't argue with that assessment."

"Then why are you doing this?" Logan wanted to know.

"I'll tell you why. The minute Kinsey called me last night to tell me they didn't find Troy's DNA on Gina, Brent and I had a serious discussion about it. We went through all the scenarios. Come to find out what was bothering Brent is the same thing bugging me."

"Let me guess. You want to know why Troy didn't see Gina's Mazda parked on the side of the road that night?" Kinsey surmised.

"You got it. Even though that could be construed as trivial, it demands explanation. And I think I've got it. "

"Really."

"Brent read over Troy's police interrogation and something popped out. At least to him it did. Troy said he was so jazzed about how his date with Mona had gone he wore his earbuds all the way back home. The radio in his truck doesn't work, hasn't since he was in high school. But he has an old iPod his mom gave him for his fourteenth birthday before she died. He takes it everywhere and listens to it in lieu of a radio. Anyway, during Troy's polygraph he was asked if he saw Gina's car that night. His answer was a resounding no. The polygraph examiner said he was telling the truth. Troy never saw that Mazda sitting there because he simply wasn't paying attention to detail."

"He was high on the successful date with Mona."

Ethan nodded. "I know it seems minor, but believe it or not, those kinds of inconsistencies bother seasoned investigators," Ethan explained.

"So what are you saying? Are you saying you believe in Troy's innocence now?"

Ethan grinned. "You wouldn't have all these files if I didn't."

Kinsey slid out the folder on the bottom of the stack. "So Sandra Flowers was the last one to go missing. When was that exactly?"

Ethan looked uncomfortable. "Last August. She was sixteen. That happened on my watch."

Logan sorted through the stack until he came to Megan's file. He spread it out on the counter, began scanning the words. When his eyes landed on Scott's name in the file as someone a Detective Augustine had talked to, Logan was able to confirm what Scott had told him. According to what was in the police log, Scott had admitted to Augustine Megan hadn't shown up at their meeting place that night. For some reason, Logan felt relieved it validated Scott's story. But in a span of minutes, Logan had finished reading the entire case file. There wasn't that much inside the barebones folder.

Kinsey started to read the one marked Janie Shively and shook her head. "This is it? It consists of two single sheets of paper, one of which is the missing persons report filed by Janie's mother in Spokane, Washington. The detective assigned to the case made a couple of phone calls along with a few notations about the results, and that seems to be the extent of his investigation."

"Same here," Logan said after closing Megan's file. He looked over at Ethan. "Megan's case is as lacking as the others. There's the missing persons report filed by my grandparents. Attached to what amounts to three pages of notes from a Detective Augustine that lists who he interviewed at the time. There are about twenty people here. And that's it."

"That sounds about right. Not much was done about these cases back then, Logan. I told you that the first time we traded emails. Not one member of law enforcement thought these cases were even connected. No one put it together."

"Well, that much hasn't changed. Has it?" Logan grumbled. "They still don't."

Kinsey grabbed another file. This one was a little thicker. She thumbed through it telling Logan, "This one belongs to Ian Radigan's sister, Carly, the one who went missing twenty-five years ago on a chilly March evening as she hitchhiked down to Hollywood from Portland, Oregon. Hollywood? My God, don't these girls realize that's not a good idea. There are a lot of dangerous miles to travel from Oregon to Los Angeles on foot. The detective on her case was someone named Don Figueroa, who writes that witnesses reported seeing a young blonde matching Carly's description on the shoulder of the 101 the evening of March 20th at approximately seven-thirty. Many remembered the time because they said a rain shower moved through the area. There were at least a dozen other motorists that said they saw a maroon pickup stop and offer her a ride. Well, this is a first. Figueroa considered Carly abducted and believed the girl was likely taken right there from the side of the road when she crawled into that vehicle."

Kinsey put down the file. "Whatever and wherever it happened, we certainly know Carly accepted a ride from the wrong man. And it occurred only five miles outside of Pelican Pointe, Ethan."

"There's a definite pattern. I don't think ten girls go missing within a fifteen-square-mile radius of Pelican Pointe and it's a coincidence." Ethan took out a map from the kitchen drawer, unfolded it and spread it out on the table. "Last night Brent and I sat right here and came up with this. The red Xs indicate where five were last seen. That's north and south of Pelican Pointe, up and down the 101 and west to the Coast Highway."

"The sad thing is there are no bodies, no crime scene photos. Essentially we have nothing," Logan lamented. He studied the chart before he said, "How do you find a serial killer when we have no DNA, no fingerprints, basically nothing?"

"You start digging with what you *do* have. I'd say it has to start at ground zero at the beginning," Kinsey said matter-of-factly indicating the files on the table. She began to pick up one folder and then another jotting down notes on a legal pad as she went. "We comb over these witness reports, go through the lists of people the various detectives interviewed. We compare our findings. Maybe something here, any little tidbit we can glean, will click and jump out at us. First up, we determine if the people that top our suspect list, like the Turley brothers or the Stovall brothers, are mentioned in these reports. If they aren't, fine, we move on. Doesn't mean we exclude them, far from it. But we don't waste our time on supposition. Right now, we need facts. And like it or not, these police reports are all we have at the moment."

"She's right," Logan said as he took a seat at the table. "If we split up the files, it'll go faster."

Two and a half hours later, each of them had made a lengthy list, which they compared to each other's. "Three of the girls were hitchhiking the 101. One was headed north, the other two going south, presumably to Los Angeles. Three of them were driving their own cars through Pelican Pointe when they experienced car trouble. The cops found their cars disabled on the highway. They had reportedly stopped for gas earlier at Pierce's Service Station, which is now Wally's Pump N Go."

"Which means they came in contact with the owner, Wally's father, Jimmy. Jimmy Pierce is added to the suspect list," Ethan said.

"Exactly," Kinsey agreed. "But I'm glad Wally isn't here to witness this."

"But if we're thorough, we can't be influenced by outside feedback. From here on out, we include everyone mentioned in the reports regardless of status. And at this point it could be anyone," Logan pointed out.

Kinsey gnawed her lip before reluctantly nodding in agreement. "Reading the reports, of those three girls who had vehicles, the cops at the time thought their cars had been tampered with, disabled by putting sand in the oil systems."

"Because when the families came to claim the vehicles the cars wouldn't run. The nearest place to tow them to would've been Pierce's service station. The engines were toast," Ethan added. "And see right here. These initials and dates were added later to the files after the reports were taken. They indicate the detectives updated the info."

"And even though the D.A. in Santa Cruz refuses to confirm, we suspect this was the method used to disable Gina's Mazda." Kinsey made a note of that on her sheet of paper. "Three of the girls were locals. We'll include Megan Donnelly on that list even though she was visiting for the summer. She'd spent plenty of time here since she was a little girl. So we'll consider her familiar enough with the town, the area, and the people so that whoever took her, she quite possibly knew him. That leaves the one girl who was labeled a runaway right from the get-go by a

Detective Wayne Hanson, which may or may not be correct."

"Rebecca Linseed," Ethan finished. "You can put her in the local category. The Linseed family lives over in Scotts Valley. In the report, the patrol officer noted Rebecca didn't get along with her stepfather. For that reason, he tagged her as a runaway. Her mother says she didn't have a car and set out on foot. So local *and* hitchhiking."

"Whichever she happened to be, she probably didn't make it very far," Kinsey stated flatly.

"Okay so we move Rebecca into the local pile and assume she was on foot, a runaway. Inventory time. We've got one runaway, three hitchhikers, three who were driving their own cars, traveling through Pelican Pointe whether going north or south, but never made it to the other side, and three local girls who simply vanished into the night," Logan uttered in disgust. "So the locals are Megan, Belinda Truitt, and Penny Hargrove."

"That coincides with Logan's spreadsheet he came up with," Kinsey noted.

Ethan rolled his eyes at Logan before he said, "Don't forget Gina. We might as well include her especially if her car was tampered with. But yeah, that about sums it up. We're at eleven victims and only one body."

"In the Carly Radigan case, one of the locals on the witness list that Detective Figueroa talked to on four different occasions was Kent Springer. Whose name, by the way, seems to keep popping up wherever we go which means we stop ignoring it just because he's dead," Logan stated. "Our man could be deceased."

"I agree. Interviewed four times tells me Figueroa wasn't satisfied with Kent's answers the first three times," Ethan pointed out.

"Exactly, so for now we have thirty names on our suspect list. In addition to Derek and Dale Stovall, Sal and Sam Turley, we've been able to add Jimmy Pierce, Flynn McCready, Carl and Mark Knudsen, Kent Springer, Joe Ferguson, and just about every other business owner in

Pelican Pointe because apparently the detectives made the rounds."

"Maybe we're going about this all wrong," Kinsey grumbled, clearly getting frustrated. But then, all of a sudden, she grabbed Logan's arm. "Wait a minute, why didn't I see this before now?"

"What?"

"Ethan, can you determine who in the area owned a maroon pickup twenty-five years ago? Maybe go through registration records?"

"The one seen picking up Carly Radigan? Good catch."

"Bingo."

"I'll see what I can do. Maybe jog someone's memory."

"In the meantime, Kinsey mentioned something to me weeks ago that resonated," Logan asserted. "The person we're looking for has to have a sustainable income here in town; otherwise, he would've struck out for greener pastures a long time ago. I mean even Stovall and Turley are decent enough construction workers they continue to earn a living in the area. Times might be tough, but neither one moves on. Something keeps them here. If the guy we're looking for is a business owner, he has a comfortable enough lifestyle that keeps him grounded here, same as Stovall and Turley."

"I said that?" Kinsey asked.

Logan chuckled. "Yes, you did, and it's a good theory."

"But what do we do with it?"

"We keep digging until we hit pay dirt."

Chapter Twenty-Two

As June came to a close, Logan couldn't quite get a handle on his relationship with Kinsey. Somehow over the past two months, they had slid gracefully into their own couple's routine. Even while she managed to hold down three jobs, seven days a week, they spent most nights cozied up in her little loft. On weekends, he would often hang out at the restaurant or at Murphy's until she got off work. It wasn't uncommon for him to drive her back and forth because they were usually both headed in the same direction anyway. Nor was it strange for him to persuade Jordan into making sandwiches or some type of box supper for them to eat at midnight when Kinsey got off work.

He knew Nick and Jordan, like the rest of the town, kept tabs on their comings and goings, mainly because he rarely slept in his bed at the B & B anymore.

But frankly, Logan didn't give a hang what the town or anyone else thought. And apparently neither did Kinsey. Since Troy's arrest, his supporters had made some enemies in town. In fact, it had split the town down the middle. Some were just as entrenched in their belief that Troy was guilty as hell and should spend the rest of his life locked up. Those were far too many and impossible to dissuade.

So far their own "investigation" had yielded them squat and life had gone on. Troy was still in county awaiting trial and that hadn't changed because the judge had refused to grant him bond.

During the June gloom, he and his crew had made great strides on the inside guts of the keeper's cottage. Even without Troy on board, the rest of his crew, Paul, Drake, Derek, and insolent Sam had already run brand new electrical conduit throughout the house, installed new windows, removed countless piles of rotted wood planks and were in the process of replacing them with new cherry hardwood flooring.

Within two weeks they would have the new staircase completed. The work on the tower had progressed as well. That team had sandblasted the lighthouse, resurfaced and repainted it, all the while removing corroded ironworks and replacing it with retooled metal they'd salvaged from other lighthouses.

At nine-forty-seven a.m. Logan was standing at the base of the tower dealing with their first official county inspection out of Santa Cruz when the ground began to tremor beneath his feet. He heard someone from the tower crew standing above him yell, "earthquake."

The men on the keeper crew inside the bungalow dropped their tools and Logan saw them pour outside on the run to head for the open spaces.

For almost fifty-two seconds, the earth rumbled and shook. Contrary to popular belief, crevices did not crack open, and swallow up a member of his crew. But it did create havoc and caused the tower crew teetering on the scaffolding above Logan to grab for the support ropes to keep from falling off.

As quickly as the vibration began though, it was over. Paul Bonner was the first worker back inside the house. As soon as Logan heard Paul's shout, he told the inspector, "It usually isn't like this." And took off in a run to see what was going on in the keeper's cottage. What he saw had him yelling for everyone to stay back.

The earthquake had split open one of the interior walls from floor to ceiling near what had once been the kitchen. As Logan approached the sizeable crack in the plaster, he noted it was a good twelve inches wide. On first glance, the gap exposed what looked like an anteroom no larger than a small closet. Logan did his best to peer into the opening without touching the now damaged support beam. "We need to clear away this debris and brace the rest of the wall before it collapses completely," Logan said to Derek who had come up behind him to lean in over his shoulder.

"That's gonna put us way behind schedule. Way behind," Derek grumbled. "What is that smell? Is that methane? Should I clear everyone out of here, Logan?"

The odor hit Logan's nose about the same time it did Derek's. "Good idea. Keep everyone back until we know what we're dealing with. Give me that pry bar over there," Logan directed.

"You sure that's a good idea. What if the whole thing comes crashing down?"

"I've done this before, Derek. I don't plan on yanking it hard, just enough so I can see inside and locate the source of that smell. Get me a flashlight."

"Maybe something crawled back in there and died," Derek reasoned as Paul Bonner handed him a flashlight to pass to Logan.

"We're about to find out," Logan said as he gently increased pressure on the pry bar so he could get his head and left shoulder through what was now the entrance to another room. With the light, he scanned the black hole from wall-to-wall, squinting into the dark. Spiders had taken over the area and weaved an intricate pattern of gray, stringy cobwebs.

About three feet from the opening, Logan saw a squared, wooden door that had been left propped open. It looked as though it led down to what Logan assumed was a root cellar. He managed to inch further in by leaning against the stronger side of the wall for support. Dust filtered down ending up in his hair and on his face. He squeezed the rest of his body through the opening until he stood inside the room. The air in this spot had an overpowering stench that took his breath away. He quickly pulled out a painter's mask from his jacket pocket, covered his nose and mouth.

The wooden floor creaked under his weight because it was as rotted as the rest of the place had been the first time

Logan had laid eyes on it. Careful not to put his foot through a weak plank, he stepped to the open door, peered down. Once again, he relied on the beam from the flashlight to see. But this time he noted the four walls were made of dirt in a space that was no more than six feet in diameter. His eyes tracked the light and landed on an unmistakable object in the corner. Logan sucked in a breath of fetid air. The urge to throw up hit him right before the urge to run. But there was nowhere to go. He backed up this time, putting his heavy foot through the flooring. He jerked it out, wedged his shoulder through the opening and couldn't get out of there fast enough. The moment he was free, he reached into his back pocket, fumbling for his iPhone.

Derek saw his hands shake. "What's wrong? What's in there?"

For the first time Logan noticed Paul Bonner standing next to Derek. Logan jerked his head toward the door. "Leave. Get out. All of you. Now! Go wait outside."

With his hands still shaking, Logan thumbed through his contact list until he found the number he wanted. Holding the phone up to his ear, he waited for an answer. "Brent, you need to get over to the lighthouse. We found a body in what looks like a root cellar. You heard me right. And you better bring a forensics team with you."

If the earthquake created chaos at Logan's work site, the discovery of mummified remains brought pandemonium.

Brent Cody arrived on the scene bringing what seemed like half of Santa Cruz County with him. By the time Logan had finished giving his statement it was almost five o' clock. He had done his best over the course of that time to describe what he'd seen, what he'd done, what he'd touched inside that dark cubby hole. He could tell them with some certainty he knew the remains had been female, either that, or a man with long blond hair. The only saving grace for him is it hadn't been Megan's hair color.

The one thing Logan hadn't mentioned is that he'd probably never get the image out of his brain.

When he looked up and spotted Kinsey, his heart felt like it flipped over in his chest. She had a tendency to do that to him. She came running up, peppy as ever.

"I heard what happened. Are you okay?"

"I'll never be okay after seeing that. You want the gritty details?" He thumbed a hand over his shoulder. "I just finished the story for them."

She laid a hand on his arm. "Not necessary. When you're ready to talk, I'll listen though. I just got back from a visit with Troy."

"How is the kid?"

"Holding up, I guess. What else is he gonna do?"

"I hate to say this, Kinsey. But I think finding this body just might be the turning point."

"Okay, now you've piqued my interest. Let's hear it."

"Come on. We'll go someplace we can talk. Trust me, they're going to be here a while. They'll have to tear that root cellar apart, even if they have to do it brick by brick, layer by layer of dirt."

As they crawled into Logan's truck, the forensic criminalists had barely gotten started. Logan had already been told that the site would remain shut down until they had completed gathering all their evidence, an event that might possibly take as long as a week or more depending on what they found.

That corpse had a story to tell. And Logan hoped like hell it would make things pop in Megan's favor.

Chapter Twenty-Three

At Sheriff Brent Cody's urging the district attorney dropped the charges against Troy Dayton two days before the Fourth of July. It took another twenty-four hours after that before Santa Cruz County released Troy from custody the day before the holiday.

Logan and Kinsey, along with Mona Bingham and Derek Stovall, lined up outside the jail in the loading and unloading zone waiting for him to emerge. By the time the outer door finally swung open and Troy appeared, four people began to applaud. And applaud they did.

As soon as Troy spotted them, he started waving his arms, hands free of cuffs. Then all at once, Kinsey watched him break into a run, down the ramp and into Kinsey's arms. "Man, am I ever glad to see you guys. How'd you get me out of there anyway? You know what, I don't even care. I'm so glad to be outta that place and outside." He whirled around and gave Logan a hug as enthusiastic as he had Kinsey. He did the same with Mona, who was waiting to give him a chaste peck on the cheek. But Troy was having none of that. He grabbed her around the waist and brought her into his chest. With Derek, Troy simply held out his hand, but his uncle surprised him. Derek threw his arms around Troy's shoulders. "Man, you're a sight for sore eyes."

Kinsey turned Troy around to face her, took hold of his chin, which had a purple bruise on it to go with the shiner under his left eye. "What happened? Did you get into a fight?"

"I got beat on some. But I held my own. Most of the time, anyway," Troy said with a grin.

Logan slapped him on the back. "I got locked up once during Mardi Gras. Got into a fight with a man dressed up like a clown."

Troy laughed but there was something about the kid that had changed. The merriment didn't exactly jive with his eyes. "Well, I don't ever want to be locked up again. That sucked."

On impulse, Kinsey grabbed Troy and hugged him again. "I'm so glad you're out of that place. Listen, there's a party out at Promise Cove. All you have to do is put in an appearance for a short while and then you can go on your own way. But there'll be food and cake—along with a lot of people who were in your corner from the start without much prompting from us—those people want to wish you well, Troy."

"Sounds good to me. I just want to get as far away from this place as I can get."

Not everyone was thrilled that Troy Dayton had spent only five short weeks locked up.

He intended to make a fuss about that the only way he knew how. He also planned to hold the one person he felt responsible for Troy's release accountable. Kinsey Wyatt had no business practicing law in the first place. If she had a regular degree, that might be one thing. But she didn't. Women should never be allowed to compete in a man's world anyway. They were inferior, emotional beings that were basically good for one thing only, a man's release. Men needed their bodies. What men didn't need was a mouthy, demanding, nagging woman at home.

He wasn't sure yet what to do about the "find." He didn't like the idea of sharing his work with the world in such a public way. Everywhere he went in town people were talking about the "body." It had turned into a spectacle he didn't appreciate.

From the minute he'd found out Logan Donnelly bought the lighthouse, he'd been afraid the man would eventually stumble upon his secret. He'd have to figure out a way to make him pay for that.

After watching the tender scene unfold outside the jail, he walked to his Cadillac Escalade and slid behind the wheel. He had a party to go to and he didn't want to be late getting there.

Not only was Promise Cove packed for the Fourth, the place had been decorated especially to welcome Troy back to Pelican Pointe. When Logan made the turn into the long driveway and Troy set his eyes on the red, white, and blue banner, he got tears in his eyes. From the back-seat, sitting between Mona and Derek, Troy struggled for words. "This is all for me? Get out. You guys didn't have to go to all this trouble for me."

Kinsey turned in the front seat to look at Troy. She reached out to take his hand in hers. "Oh but we did, Troy. We most definitely did."

At the sound of Logan's truck pulling up to the side of the house, people began to pour out the front door to crowd onto the porch. They waited for Troy to crawl out of the backseat of Logan's truck. When he did, they all noted the tears streaming down his cheeks for real. Troy spotted Margie and Max, Nick and Jordan, Lilly and Wally, Cord and Keegan, Hayden and Ethan Cody, even Ethan's brother, Brent.

Logan raised his voice as he climbed from behind the wheel. "Troy doesn't believe this is all for him."

With that, everyone started clapping their hands together. Nick and Jordan were the first to walk down the steps and Troy met them halfway. But then everyone surrounded him at once. "Why all this for me?"

"We all think you're pretty special, Troy," Nick said, slapping him on the back. "You need to start believing that, too."

For the rest of the evening, people from town came and went. Most of them lined up and waited their turn to speak to Troy and give him a hug. Murphy and Carla Vargas did. Pete Alden and Betty Brinker did. So did Perry Altman, Drea Jennings, Carl and Elaine Knudsen, Frank Martin, Bran and Joy Sullivan, Ricky and Donna Oden, along with most of Cord's crew from the farm. Troy's co-workers were all there, including Paul Bonner and his girlfriend, Abby Pointer. Wade Hawkins put in an appearance. Even Aaron came, although his physical strength seemed to lessen a little each day.

Of course, not everyone accepted the invitation. Janie Pointer, Abby's sister, stayed away using the excuse that she'd been doing Eileen Purvis' hair far too long to be disloyal to a customer now. Janie also added for Wally's benefit, that he shouldn't try to guilt her into coming to a party she didn't want to attend. Flynn McCready failed to show, as did Joe Ferguson and Doc Prescott.

But the no-shows couldn't put a damper on Troy's welcome home celebration.

For three hours children squealed and made noise as kids tend to do. Adults huddled in conversation, some whispered in the corner, while Troy mingled with some of the town's leading citizens.

As Logan and Kinsey made the rounds, Logan happened to look down at Kinsey and see her almost stumble. "You look exhausted. How much alcohol have you had?"

"I took the one glass of champagne that was offered but never got to drink it. I do feel tired though. Maybe I'm coming down with a summer cold."

"Kinsey, you're holding down three jobs. Tomorrow is your first day off since Memorial Day." He automatically reached out, felt her forehead. "No fever. In all the excitement did you remember to eat?"

"I nibbled on some of Jordan's canapés."

"Come on. Let's get some decent food in you, something besides finger sandwiches," Logan suggested as he elbowed Carl Knudsen, the pharmacist, from in front of the wine and cheese tray to get to the buffet. Logan eyed the offerings. "What'll it be? Baked ham or roast beef with some nice green beans or those little corn-on-the-cob things?"

Kinsey scanned the choices. Once again, Jordan had outdone her last event, which had been Scott's first birthday party, a couple of days earlier. But for some reason she didn't feel very much like eating. Since she needed to put something in her stomach, she decided on the least offensive thing. "I'll take a little of that ham and the green beans."

For the rest of the evening they kept an eagle eye on Troy just to make sure he was dealing with the crowd okay and vice versa. They didn't want anyone making a scene, at least not tonight. Kinsey and Logan were well aware Troy still had his detractors, people who believed that even with DNA, it had been Troy who had ended Gina's life. While they understood that, they kept up a steady stream of chatter with most of the guests in an attempt to feel out any that might be hiding a grudge. After all, Gina's killer was still out there.

But after Margie and Max made an early exit and took Mona with them, Troy's energy seemed to wane. Ethan and Hayden also had to leave because a fussy Nate refused to settle down.

After that, the revelry began to taper off. Guests began to dwindle to a few stragglers until even those eventually said their goodbyes. Once everyone had gone, Troy tapped Logan on the shoulder and wanted to know, "Derek and Paul told me they found a body in the keeper's cottage. They said the site was closed. Is that true or were they just pulling my leg? Do I get to come back to work?"

Logan flinched at the question. Troy caught the look and said, "Please don't tell me you've already replaced me."

Logan looked around the room at the die-hards. Most of Troy's supporters had hung back, knowing they would need to fill in the gaps at some point. But the core of it would fall on Logan's shoulders. There was no better time than now to do it. "There are some things you need to know, things that happened over the last five weeks."

Kinsey came over and put her arm through Troy's. "It's true the site is shut down, will be for probably another three days."

"I don't understand. Don't they just take the body out of there to the morgue so we can get things back to normal?"

"It doesn't work that way, Troy." Logan took him through a detailed account of what had transpired, how the discovery of mummified remains played a pivotal role in getting him released from jail. It was especially significant since Brent had gone to the district attorney to lay out the details about a serial killer.

Kinsey picked it up from there, presenting the serial killer theory first and foremost and how that had brought Logan back to Pelican Pointe.

"Your sister disappeared? You lived here before? I wish I'd known you then. I did miss a lot," Troy admitted.

"I was just a kid myself, younger than you are now. But not everyone knows that or why I'm back here, Troy. For now, I'd like to keep it that way. The people in this room know but I don't want it becoming common knowledge yet."

"So you don't want me saying anything to Mona? Is that it?"

"I'd rather you didn't. I saw your face when Mona left. Are you disappointed she didn't hang around longer?"

He shrugged. "Some. Okay a lot. But I guess she was tired. I realize she may not want to have anything to do with me now."

Jordan went over to him. "I don't think that's the case at all. But you'll have to give her some time if it turns out you're right." She patted him on the shoulder. "I've got to put the kids to bed. You look drained, too, Troy. Would you like to stay here tonight?" Jordan glanced at Logan and smiled wickedly. "I believe Logan's room is available."

"Really? I mean, y'all aren't scared of me? I don't have my truck either. In fact, it's still impounded as far as I know."

Nick shook his head. "If I thought you were a danger, I'd never let you anywhere near my kids. Do you remember when Scott was born, Troy?"

"Sure. We had that big storm. I helped you patch the roof."

"No, that isn't quite right. *You* patched the roof for me. We had a houseful of guests with a newborn baby and a toddler. Jordan had just given birth. You were the only one who showed up to help me. At the time, I'd never been so glad to see anyone pull up in the driveway than I was to see you that day."

Troy looked embarrassed. "I was out of work, Nick. That day I made the rounds to everybody in town. You were the only one that put me to work."

"But if it hadn't been for you, the roof would've leaked, which means we might have lost guests, probably would've checked out of here never to come back. So if you want to spend the night instead of going back to your place, you're welcome in this house anytime."

Troy grinned and looked at Logan. "I guess I won't ask how come it is you don't need your room."

Logan picked up Kinsey's hand, kissed it. "I'm pretty sure the whole town's aware of that."

"By the way, if anyone's interested, I went to school with Belinda Truitt. We were in tenth grade together. I remember she went missing around the time she turned fifteen."

"One of the local girls," Kinsey finished. "Please don't tell us you were dating her."

Troy shook his head. "No, Belinda and I never went out. We had a couple of classes together though. But her disappearance was a puzzler."

Slightly relieved at that and annoyed with herself for thinking the same way the district attorney might, Kinsey asked, "Troy, do you remember anything else about Belinda's case at all."

He scratched his blond head. "Just that they found her car at the side of the road like they did Gina's, but out on the 101. Rumors at school said someone had messed with her car."

"Wait a minute. That had to be five years ago," Wally spoke up. "Belinda drove an older model Nissan hatchback as I recall, similar to what you drive, Kinsey. I remember that car. I towed that Altima into my shop. Someone had indeed messed with it by removing her oil cap and adding sand."

For the first time in five weeks, Kinsey's heart soared. "If we can connect those two incidents, we might be onto something that I could hand the D.A. Tomorrow we need to go through those police reports again at Ethan's."

"Tomorrow's the Fourth of July, Kinsey. I think Ethan mentioned he and Hayden will be in Santa Cruz the whole day at a barbeque," Nick said.

"Then I guess we'll have to wait until the day after." Kinsey turned back to Troy. "By the way, did either one of your uncles ever own a maroon pickup truck?"

"Not that I know of. Dale rode a motorcycle most of his life. And Derek's drove his white Tacoma ever since I was a kid." Troy gestured to Wally. "But this is the guy that pretty much knows what everybody in town drives."

Wally nodded. "I might be able to make you a list at that. Give me a couple of days. You're sure it's maroon?"

"That's the color the witnesses reported. Not red, maroon."

"Maroon trucks aren't all that common around here. If I can't come up with a fairly accurate record though, I'm sure Lilly and I can go through my dad's old accounts and come up with who owned what even as far back as twenty-five years ago. Even back then, his shop was the only one around for miles."

Kinsey and Logan exchanged grins before Logan said, "You know what? We might just figure this thing out after all."

Chapter Twenty-Four

There were reasons Kinsey thought something didn't feel right when she woke up the next morning. For one, as Logan had mentioned it was their first day off together since Memorial Day. They'd talked about doing something fun, like motoring over to check out Scott's Treasure Island, a little speck of land across from the cove. But after getting out of bed, after whipping up pancake batter that had sounded like the perfect start to the day, she'd gotten sick at her stomach and thrown up.

While they both waited for the nausea to pass so they could get on with their outing, there was a knock on the door. When Logan answered it, Troy stood there looking uncomfortable, shifting from one foot to the other. "I'm sorry to bother you guys but I don't have a way back home. I waited as long as I could for y'all to come down but when you didn't…I called Derek but he's not home. I didn't want to ask Nick and Jordan because let me tell you it's crazy over there at the main house."

Logan chuckled. "That's okay. I felt like that a couple of times. Kinsey's not feeling well though, that's why we stayed in. Come on inside and I'll grab my keys. I'll take you home."

When Troy spotted Kinsey still in bed, he whispered, "Thanks. What's wrong with her?"

"Stomach flu. She mentioned not feeling well last night and it's hit her hard this morning." Logan turned back to Kinsey and asked, "Is there anything you want me to pick up while I'm out?"

"No, I think I'll just curl up here in bed and take a nap."

Logan leaned over to give her a kiss and muttered, "This is what holding down three jobs, seven days a week will get you. Sick."

"Stop that and go take Troy home."

As Logan closed and locked the door behind him, he walked down the steps with Troy. When they got to his truck, he shook his head. "Stubborn woman, she will not give up one of those damn jobs no matter how sick she gets. Watch and see. She'll get up and go to work tomorrow no matter what she feels like."

"Leave me out of this 'cause I don't understand women any better than you do."

"And you never will. You know why? Because there's no getting them ever."

"Does that mean Kinsey is a lot like Fiona Perez?"

"Oh hell no. Fiona Perez is a manipulative viper with a right hook that makes Joe Frazier look like an amateur."

"Wow. Really? Then she *is* the one that broke your hand."

"She took a damn statuette and cracked my skull open with it. Took sixteen stitches to close. When that wasn't enough she started hitting me anywhere she could reach."

"Why'd you marry her?"

Logan sent him a contemptuous glare. "We're all allowed stupid mistakes, some of us more than others. It's how we get past them that counts."

"I'm sorry about the lighthouse. I know you wanted to stick to the schedule. First, my getting arrested made you one man short. And now this body's discovered in a closet and has you shut down. You know I don't remember that closet being on the blueprints we looked at. Either that or I don't know how to read them like I thought I did or what I was looking at."

Logan took his eyes off the road long enough to stare at Troy. "With everything that was happening that day I never thought one way or the other about it. You're right though. I've got the blueprints in the back. We'll take a look at them as soon as we get to your place."

"Why's that important?"

"Because. Either the Restoration Commission gave me the wrong plans which I doubt or someone went into that keeper's cottage at some point and purposely walled up that room so no one would ever know it existed."

It didn't take long to reach Derek Stovall's land less than a mile southeast of town. Troy's home was an old rundown aluminum trailer about fifty yards off the road, well past the main house where Derek lived. Logan noted a few rickety boards acted as a slab of porch.

"It's not much I know," Troy said as if embarrassed. "That's why I need a good steady job to get out of this place."

"Let me ask you something. I've heard some bad things about Derek. I want to know if they're true."

"Like what?"

Logan explained what the women had told Ethan about Derek.

Troy listened and nodded. "Abby Pointer and Abby Anderson told me the same thing. They wanted me to talk to Derek, see if I could get him to stop coming around so much at the rescue center and the Diner whenever Abby worked her shift. I did try, but I don't think he understands how creepy he comes across. Is he in trouble?"

"I don't know how it'll end up. Did he ever come visit you while you were in county?"

"Nah, I didn't expect him to. He's not very, you know, warm and fuzzy like that. When he hugged me yesterday, it kind of surprised me. Never has been like that. But he did step up when my mom died and kept me from going into a foster home. I gotta be grateful for that, Logan."

Logan slapped him on the back. "I know. Just don't be surprised if one day a woman presses charges against Derek for sexual assault. His luck won't hold forever, Troy. Now let's take a look at those plans."

Logan wasn't sure what he was expecting but he wasn't prepared for how small or hot the inside of the trailer was. He had to duck his head to keep from bumping it on the low ceiling. It wasn't just that the cops had ransacked the place, the odor inside was horrific. "Is something rotting in here?"

"Oh God, look at this place?" Troy ran a hand through his curly hair. He flicked the light switch on and off only to discover he had no electricity. "Damn, they cut off my lights." He sniffed the air, went over to open the refrigerator and waved a hand in front of his face. "Whew! All my food's gone bad."

"You can't stay here, Troy."

"I don't have any place else to go, Logan."

"It's hotter than hell in here. Let's go back outside. We'll spread the plans out on the tailgate of my truck."

When they reached the back of the pickup and began to go over the blueprints, Logan saw what he hadn't remembered. The room had been there on the original 1936 floor plan. It had been used as a pantry with a door in the floor that led down to an old-fashioned root cellar.

"So the killer dumped that body in the dirt cellar and walled up that room so no one would find it," Troy reasoned with his arms folded across his chest. "He had to have some know-how to get that done, right? Or he paid to have it done?"

Logan nodded. His mind whirled with possibilities, landing on his top two suspects who were both laborers, Derek and Sam Turley. But Derek had been right there beside him the day they'd discovered the structural damage to the house. If Derek had known what was waiting behind the walls, wouldn't he have tried to do more to prevent anyone from getting inside that room? Instead he'd acted as surprised as Logan. "You're right. It took a certain skillset to work with drywall and plaster."

"I guess whoever did it could've watched one of those do-it-yourself shows to find out what to do. Did they have those on TV twenty-five years ago? Once you bought that place did you ever bother to thoroughly inspect the lighthouse, check it out? I mean go over it from top to bottom? Is there a basement in the tower?"

"Of course, I checked the place out. Sure there's a basement there that they used for storing all kinds of supplies. But—" Logan suddenly had a sinking feeling in the pit of his stomach. "I wasn't looking for bodies— behind walls that had been bricked up—why didn't I look for bodies? Could it be that simple?" Logan scratched his chin. There was something else he needed to bring up though. "Look Troy, I can't just drop you here and leave you, not without electricity. You have to be straight with me. When you say you have nowhere else to go, what about staying at the main house with your uncle?"

Troy shook his head. "I'd rather not have to do that."

"And you won't say why?"

Troy itched at a red welt on his neck as if stalling or weighing whether or not to trust Logan completely. After a few long seconds of strained silence he said, "I was fourteen when my mom died. After the funeral I was scared what would happen next. I don't know maybe I should've taken my chances with one of those foster homes. Because Derek started hitting me shortly after I moved in with him especially when he drank or got real mad about something. So when this place became available, I jumped at getting out of his house. It might be within walking distance but at least I'm not living under his roof anymore. I'm not going back. I'll rough it out here without the basics before I move back in with Derek."

Logan's mind raced with options. "You don't have to rough it, Troy. I know a place you can stay. And a place where you can earn some money while you're there until the cops let us back on the work site. Now go pack up your stuff." Logan eyed the astonished look on Troy's face before adding, "And don't argue. I'm still your boss."

While Troy went inside to get his things, Logan placed a call to Nick. Logan briefly explained Troy's living conditions and then asked, "You mentioned there's a vacant little house at the farm where the former manager used to live. I'll pay you to let Troy stay there for a couple of weeks. He's willing to work. In fact, I think he needs something to do to get his mind off of everything that's happened. The farm would do that."

"The little Foley house? Sure. It's been vacant since Will and Fran moved to Tulare. And I'm sure Cord can put him to work, even if it's harvesting the vegetables. There's always something that needs doing. I won't take your money. The house is empty. Troy needs a place. It's as simple as that."

"Thanks, Nick. Troy isn't picky about what the job is. And this way he doesn't need a car to earn a little spending money. Kinsey got the runaround when she tried to get Troy's truck out of impound."

"The cops are holding onto it. That doesn't sound like Troy's completely out of hot water."

"That's why the farm will get him away from this place and a change of scenery, for now anyway. It's a temporary fix until things smooth out."

Once Logan got Troy settled, he was tempted to breach the police tape that now stretched across his land to reach the lighthouse so that he could go through the tower foot by foot. Technically the body hadn't been discovered in the tower anyway so he was breaking no laws. And the place did belong to him.

Briefly, he considered heading out to Eternal Gardens to put flowers on the graves of his grandparents but then remembered the florist shop was closed up tight for the Fourth. That pretty much made his decision for him.

Logan circled back toward the lighthouse. When he got close, he parked his pickup on a narrow dirt road near the tree line. He walked through the copse of trees along the side until he reached the sandy dunes covered in knee-high beach grass.

"Don't you think this might be a bad idea?" The now familiar voice of Scott asked.

Logan rolled his eyes. "I'm too impatient to wait for the police to tidy up here. I want to inspect that tower, look around in the basement."

"Wouldn't you rather be spending time with Kinsey on her day off?"

Logan sighed. "Is that your way of hinting I'm on the wrong track?"

"If you're determined there isn't a lot I can do to discourage you. But if I were you I'd be with Kinsey right about now."

"I see why Wade considers you a pain in the ass."

"Wade said that? Old coot," Scott mumbled. "Thinks he's an expert in paranormal. I ought to go pay him a visit."

"You do that," Logan said as he took out his key to unlock the door to the lighthouse. "You coming inside?"

But Logan didn't wait for Scott's answer. Instead the door closed in Scott's face. He shook his head, muttering, "You are one stubborn ass, you know that? Look in the woods, Logan. You're ice cold here and wasting your time. Follow your instincts, Logan. Go back home to Kinsey."

Kinsey had celebrated better Fourth of Julys. She still didn't feel any better. In fact, she was feeling zapped, even a little sorry for herself. Maybe Logan was right about the three jobs starting to take their toll. Not only that but the least he could do was spend time with her today. Tomorrow they'd go right back to their busy schedules.

When the door finally opened around five o'clock, Logan stepped back in carrying a plastic container in one hand and a bunch of long-stemmed wildflowers in the other.

"Jordan says her chicken soup will fix you right up."

But Kinsey zeroed in on the brightly colored buds. "You picked me Indian Paintbrush? They're beautiful," she exclaimed with a sigh.

"The florist was closed. I had to improvise. Troy isn't the only one who can pick flowers."

"Did you get him settled?"

"That trailer is a disaster—no electricity, no food, no running water—I couldn't leave him there, Kinsey."

"Of course not. Where is he?"

Logan told her how he'd dropped Troy at the farm and the plan.

"So he'll get to earn a little money. He needs to get his mind off all of this for a few days anyway. Maybe you could take him fishing. Isn't that what guys do to bond?"

"No. We watch Raider games on satellite and drink beer and eat pizza."

"Why would you watch the Raiders when you could root for a real team like the 49ers?"

Logan frowned. "Because the 49ers are for elitists, the champagne and caviar crowd, while the Raiders have the infamous Black Hole. Don't tell me you're a 49er fan."

"Okay I won't tell you. But I thought you lived in San Francisco. How could anyone cheer for a team with so many losing seasons like the Raiders? I mean they're basically the Cubs of the NFL who wear all that silver and black like they're mean and tough, but can't back it up."

"Just because I lived there doesn't mean I went over to the other side. And the Raider Nation is all about good times and bad times, staying together through thick and thin."

"Wow, that's all you've got? I don't know, that's pretty weak. Who knew you were a Raider fan. I just assumed—"

"You know what they say about assuming. You must be feeling better?"

She smiled at the way the man could warm her heart. "Better now. All I needed was for you to get back to torment me."

It wasn't until later that night while brushing her teeth before bed—she stared at her pale image in the bathroom mirror—that it hit her. Kinsey did a quick calculation in her head. She counted on her fingers. If she thought it would've changed the outcome, she might've dug out her calculator. But there wasn't much doubt the numbers didn't add up.

Oh God. That couldn't be why she felt so sick, could it?

In a daze, she flicked off the bathroom light and headed to bed. As she crawled under the covers Logan was already stretched out. Her head hadn't hit the pillow when he brought her into him. They snuggled, her hand resting on his heart. When he turned his head to place a kiss on her hair, a sigh escaped from her lips. How tenuous was their relationship? she wondered. Could it withstand more stress? They were just getting started.

"Okay, what's wrong?" He asked, sensing a mood.

She decided to table the glum outlook until she was sure. "Nothing, I'm just sorry we didn't get to see Treasure Island today. I was looking forward to spending some time on the water."

"It'll still be there. Besides I don't think you were in any condition to deal with choppy surf."

"Hmm, you're probably right." With that, she slid onto him, lowered her mouth to his. "And all this time I've been sleeping with a Raider fan, who knew?" She shook her hair back as anticipation warmed and thrilled her. Or was it the way his fingers caressed and touched her body? Or maybe the way his tongue slicked along the curve of her breasts?

"And all this time I've been seduced by a woman who doesn't fully value my silver and black." Arousal bloomed. Trailing kisses, he used his fingers to cleverly tweak and tantalize. When she took him inside her, they instantly found their easy pulse and flow. The rapture speared up and up. Together they soared over craggy cliffs and stormy sea until finally they plunged over the crest as one.

Chapter Twenty-Five

The next day just as Logan had predicted, Kinsey dragged herself out of bed to go to work. It didn't take long for Aaron to notice her pale, tired look as soon as she sat down at her desk.

Aaron tilted his head to study his employee. "What's with you? Too much partying yesterday, young lady?"

"Oh please. I picked up some kind of stomach flu at the party and it's still hanging on today. That's all," Kinsey insisted. No one could accuse her of not being able to propagate a lie.

"If you're contagious you should go home. I don't want to catch whatever it is you've got."

"There's no chance of that," Kinsey muttered as she started working on Myrtle Pettibone's will and the list of the woman's dispensations to relatives.

Aaron took Kinsey through Myrtle's estate, line by line. "Myrtle's appointing her middle son, Edgar as executor which will likely piss off the eldest one, Cyrus. Can't say I blame Cyrus much. So when you deliver the will for Myrtle's signature try to persuade her to reconsider going with Cyrus."

"How do I do that?"

"You have a way with people, Kinsey. I noticed it right off when you walked in that door. Sometimes being a good lawyer in a small town like this means guiding the client through a minefield. They may think they know what they want but it's up to a good attorney to make the right choices."

"And the right choice for executor of their mother's estate is Cyrus Pettibone?"

Aaron nodded his bald head. "You charm her into naming Cyrus instead of Edgar and you'll avoid a huge can of worms down the road. You mark my word and see."

"Okay, got it. You think of everything, Aaron. Plus, you know this town like no one else does and the people in it."

"If only that were true," Aaron decided. "I'm not sure you ever really know people, Kinsey. You remember that, too."

An hour later, Marabelle Crawford and her sister, Ina stopped by to see Aaron. Kinsey didn't think either woman was there for legal help. But the visit kept Kinsey from stewing over her predicament. While Aaron's housekeeper, Alice, served tea and cookies, Kinsey picked up on a definite vibe. After the women left, Kinsey turned to Aaron and said, "How come you didn't marry Ina? She obviously has a thing for you."

Aaron rolled his eyes. "We were sweet on each other back in high school, took her to the dance three years running."

Kinsey noted his eyes glistened at the memory.

"Thought she was my girl. But after I headed off to college, Ina ran off with a Fuller Brush salesman. Must have been 1962. I went on to law school and she had three kids by the guy. Man never did marry her either. They lived together common-law for years before he died in 1990."

"You're kidding? Why not?"

"Said he didn't believe in marriage. But he sure did believe in having kids."

"It's not too late, Aaron."

"Oh, honey, I'm afraid it is. I don't have the energy or the inclination for anything more than being friends with anyone these days."

When noon finally got there, Kinsey took her lunch break to drive forty miles into San Sebastian to pick up three different home pregnancy tests at the first drugstore she located. From there she drove down each of the streets until she spotted a Burger Barn. Taking the box inside the ladies' room, she ripped it open and prepared to face the music. Five anxious minutes went by as she stood waiting in the smelly stall only to see the indicator turn pink.

Tears welled up in her eyes. Stunned, she wiped off her face, splashed cold water on her cheeks, and somehow managed to make her way back to the Nissan. For God's sake, what now? she wondered as she rested her head on the steering wheel. She had to think, to clear her head.

Glancing at her watch, she knew she'd be running late. But all of a sudden it really didn't matter much. With some resignation, she turned the key in the ignition and headed back to Pelican Pointe.

At the office, her afternoon didn't get any better. Carl Knudsen came in without an appointment in a snit wanting to know his best recourse for dealing with a teenage shoplifter he suspected of pilfering an eight-pack of batteries. Knudsen felt the best method was to point a gun at the boy's head to put the fear of God into him.

After forty-five minutes of trying to explain to the pharmacist why that wasn't a good idea, Kinsey had to play hostess to Dottie Whitcomb who had stopped by to chat with Aaron. Kinsey could tell the man was visibly tiring. She hoped Dottie noticed it, too. Any other time, Kinsey would have been grateful for Dottie's visit but circumstance had her mind floating elsewhere.

Later she tried to put the finishing touches on Ricky and Donna Oden's will—after giving up she smuggled the second box into the hall bathroom—and waited. Once again, she watched as a great big fat plus sign formed in the little round window. Two for two made her stomach queasy. She promptly threw up.

For the third test, she waited until she got home. Good thing, too. This time the stick clearly spelled it out for her as if mocking her attempts to change the result. The word PREGNANT showed up in the oval window clear as day. Fighting nausea again, she took down a box of crackers from the cabinet and began to munch, hoping the feeling would pass. After a few minutes, she put on the kettle for some chamomile tea. After downing the tea, she crawled into bed and for the first time all day, indulged in a good pity party. She cried her eyes out.

Over the next few days, she managed to dodge Logan's questions about her health using an age-old summertime excuse. The heat of July was getting to everyone. It was a fairly ridiculous notion to think that she could continue to keep her secret. But how did you tell a man he was going to become a father when he had vowed to never make a long-term commitment to anyone ever again? Did that include a child? she wondered. It seemed history had played another cruel joke on one of the Wyatt women. First, Ellie Wyatt had fallen for a guy who couldn't or wouldn't pledge his undying love no matter the reason— and now it seemed—so had Ellie's daughter.

Three days later, both crews went back to work on the keeper's cottage and the lighthouse. The site wasn't exactly back to normal yet, but it was slowly getting there. The men mentioned the remains at least ten times a day in passing while pulling down beams or carting out debris.

Repairing the earthquake damage would take time and meant they would work in close proximity every day to the little pantry where a life had mostly likely been taken. Derek Stovall didn't seem affected by the location any more than he did the banter about it. Logan wasn't sure what to do about the man. The guy seemed cool as a cucumber sandwich. The same could be said for Sam Turley. But Troy seemed a little distracted. On the other hand, he'd picked up his hammer and tool belt without a hitch in his friendly demeanor and seemed to be making the best of things as if he hadn't just spent weeks locked up at county expense.

Given their history, it amazed Logan that Troy could work side by side with his uncle without rancor or spite. It showed him, once again, the kid's resilience along with a tough shell.

At the sound of a car Logan spotted Ethan's approach. At first, he didn't think too much about it until he saw the man's set jaw. This wasn't a friendly social call.

"You've made some progress here, Logan."

"I know. The place is really taking shape. Once we get back on track, it'll be even better."

"I thought I'd stop in, give you an update. Wally and Lilly are poring through boxes of his dad's old records. Wally feels sure he'll eventually find invoices documenting work on the cars we're interested in."

He couldn't say how he knew, he just did. "But that isn't why you're here."

"No, it's not. Because this town has ten missing women, Brent contacted most of their families for dental records to send to the lab. Even Rebecca Linseed's mother came through. This morning the lab got a match. What you found in that root cellar were the remains of Carly Radigan, seventeen years old."

"The first girl, the hitchhiker who went missing?" Logan stomped off, turned back. "Brent's notified Ian Radigan?"

"The brother? Yeah, he has. I thought you'd want to know."

Logan would have to give Ian a call later when he could form a thought. "I appreciate it. At least Ian knows where his sister ended up. Would be nice to give him the how and the why and come up with the son of a bitch who did this to his sister. Please tell me you got something on Stovall? He's starting to bug me."

"In what way?"

"In every way," Logan hissed. "I'm starting to mistrust him. And he's given me no reason to do that other than beating the shit out of Troy when he was younger." Logan narrowed his eyes when he saw the expression form on Ethan's face. "But you already knew that, didn't you?"

"School nurse reported bruises on the boy when he was about fourteen. I arrested Derek for it, even got him to plead guilty. He spent six months in jail. That's what got his DNA entered into CODIS and his prints in IAFIS. But the lab couldn't match him to Gina's Mazda, her body, or those prints on the root cellar door."

"Not Derek then. It doesn't take that long to check fingerprints. You already got a match, didn't you?"

Ethan looked away. When he glanced back over at Logan, he told him, "Brent got three hits this morning. But don't ask me anymore than that because I can't tell you. They're working on an arrest warrant even as we speak."

"Three hits but only one warrant? That's odd."

Ethan shook his head, stuck his hands in his pockets. "That's all I can tell you until LE is ready with the warrant." To change the topic, Ethan asked, "How's Kinsey doing? I saw her yesterday and she looked flat worn out. Those three jobs are catching up with her."

Logan frowned. Hadn't he been nagging her about that same exact thing? "She's had the stomach flu since the Fourth, been throwing up off and on for almost a week now."

Ethan squinted into the sun. He tried to overlook the little nugget that he should keep his mouth shut. But he decided to help out another male. Ethan slapped him on the back. "Last time Hayden stayed sick for that long, she was pregnant. But I'm sure what Kinsey has is the flu."

Logan started to laugh, but instead swallowed down the mirth. It caught in his throat about the same time he went over the last week in his head. He finally found his voice. "How did you know it wasn't a bug?"

Ethan grinned. "Hayden took one of those home pregnancy tests. They're pretty reliable. What we had was knocked up in spades and I guess that test was right. Eight months later Nate showed up."

It was after six when Logan reached the studio. It was warm inside the four walls, even with the windows open and the stingy ocean breeze blowing in. He found Kinsey curled up on the comforter sound asleep.

He laid his hand on her forehead, checked for a fever. Her skin felt cool to the touch. When he sat down on the bed, she rolled over. Her eyes full of sleep and exhaustion, he stroked a finger down her cheek. "Kinsey?"

"Hmm?"

"What's wrong with you?"

"I'm just tired that's all." Her stomach jittered and fluttered, and felt like it wanted to toss what she'd had for lunch. She sat up, head spinning and said, "What time is it?"

"A little after six."

"I didn't make anything for dinner."

"That's okay. Can you keep food down, maybe some soup?"

Soup sounded like the last thing she wanted to eat or smell. She shook her head.

"Okay, that's it. I think you need to see a doctor. If you don't want to see the guy here, fine. Tomorrow I'll take you into Santa Cruz. There's a group of doctors who office in the same building as Dr. Jax. We'll go there."

Her stomach lurched. "Logan, I'd have to make an appointment probably weeks in advance for that. I can't just show up and expect a doctor to work me into his busy schedule. Besides..." She took a deep breath and blurted out, "I'm pregnant."

Logan blinked. A part of him had already known that was true the minute Ethan had mentioned it. Logan had to remember to inhale air. His green eyes flashed accusingly. "How long have you known?"

"Four days."

"And in all that time you never said a word to me!"

"I was trying to figure out how to tell you without you exploding at me just like you're doing now. I knew you would."

He ran a hand through his hair, which he'd taken out of its rubber band and let hang loose. "You've already taken that home pregnancy thing?"

"Yes. Three times."

"Three? I guess there's no room for error then?"

"There's always a chance, I suppose, it could be wrong, but I did the math. I wouldn't bet money on it going the other way."

He was going to be a father. How in the hell could he ever be a father? And did he want it to go the other way? Logan reached out, took her chin, tilted her face up to meet his eyes. "Were you ever going to tell me, Kinsey? Am I that unreasonable?"

She placed a shaky hand on her stomach. "Of course. Eventually. Sometimes."

He noticed her hand shaking and felt like the biggest jerk. He picked it up, kissed the palm. "There's no need for that."

Kinsey frowned. "You don't seem furious."

God, did she think that little of him? "I'm stunned. I'm in shock. But I'm not angry. Why would I be? You didn't get pregnant by yourself." He touched his lips to hers briefly, then narrowed his eyes. "You thought I'd be furious?"

She nodded. "I know how you feel about relationships. You've made that clear enough times. And we've known each other for what amounts to the speed of light. I don't expect long-term here, Logan."

She wasn't crying. She wasn't playing any trump cards or making demands. She wasn't having a drama-queen moment. No, Kinsey Wyatt was too grounded for that. She remained perfectly calm while he could admit to being more than a little rattled. But then she'd had five days to get used to the idea while he'd known for ten minutes or less. He finally realized what she'd said. "Why? Why don't you expect long-term, Kinsey. Are you telling me you don't want it?"

"I want the baby, Logan. I'm not getting rid of it."

Relief circled through his heart. He brought her into him to spread kisses along her jaw until he got to her mouth. Fire and heat ramped up. His hand moved to her flat belly. "This is exactly how you got knocked up," he mused as he thought of Scott's identical words that day they'd confronted each other at the cemetery. He ran his hands through her hair. "We'll figure this out together, Kinsey. Do me a favor though."

"What?

"I want you to consider giving up one of your extra jobs. I don't care which one it is, your choice."

"I'll think about it. How's that? There's something I should probably mention though. Logan, Aaron's in the final stages of leukemia. He's deteriorating little by little. I don't think he has much longer."

"Leukemia? Not his heart?"

She shook her head. "I'm not sure exactly how this town feels about having a new lawyer here. So I need to keep my other jobs just in case, my options open."

"You're a good lawyer, Kinsey. If the people in this town don't accept that, then screw 'em. You'll open up your own practice."

"Logan...that isn't practical. I have my mother's hospital bills—"

"Shhh. Don't worry about that. We'll deal with that together, too."

"No, we won't." Steel formed along her spine and she dug in. "My mother's bills are my responsibility and mine alone. I have no intention of letting you take that on."

Logan sighed. "And I won't stand around watching you work yourself into exhaustion. Not while you're carrying my baby."

She rested her head on his chest. "Like you said, I guess we'll work it out."

"Good. Because I'm pretty sure we're going to need a lot more than five-hundred-square feet of space."

Chapter Twenty-Six

A couple of hours later, Logan's cell phone chimed just before they crawled back into bed. "It's Nick," he informed Kinsey as he held it up to this ear. "Hey, what's up?"

"Sorry, it's so late, but you might want to head over to the main house. Wally and Lilly have just gotten here. There's something Wally wants to share and it can't wait until tomorrow."

"Okay, we'll be right over." He turned to Kinsey. "Wally's found something. Do you feel like hearing what it is?"

"Are you kidding? I couldn't fall asleep now if I wanted to. I'll throw my jeans back on."

Fifteen minutes later, Jordan let them into the kitchen where Wally and Lilly already sat at the table, mugs of coffee already steaming in front of them.

"It took Lilly and me two days but we eventually got through more than six boxes of my dad's old stuff. Because Kinsey told us the names to look for, we found Belinda Truitt's Nissan Altima, Penny Hargrove's Honda, and Charlotte Donnelly's Chrysler. All three cars were brought into the shop with identical problems. Sand had somehow gotten into the oil system. All three had severe engine damage because of it. My dad even made notes on the repair jobs. I brought them with me." Wally unfolded several old, dated invoices and several pieces of paper where Jimmy Pierce had written out the diagnosis for each car. "It's almost like someone had taken a funnel and added enough sand to clog up the oil filters, thereby basically, burning up the engines. All three engines had to be completely overhauled. I might point out that in a town this size it's uncommon to see sand poured into the oil tube with a funnel once let alone have it happen three times."

Logan turned to stare at Wally. "I remember my grandmother's Chrysler. She'd just bought that thing the previous spring. That car had less than twenty thousand miles on it. When did your dad do the repairs?"

"The repair date on the invoice for Charlotte's was September twelfth, twenty years ago."

Logan shook his head. "My God, by that time, I was back in Chastain, starting my sophomore year of high school, wearing a backpack, sitting in geometry class going about my stupid life. I never even knew my grandmother allowed Megan to take the car out that night."

"Maybe she didn't have permission," Kinsey pointed out.

"You're right. Scott mentioned that Megan often snuck out of the house to meet him."

At that declaration, Nick cocked a brow, stared at Jordan. The stunned look on her face told him this was the first she'd heard of Megan and Scott as an item.

"This happened what, when they were both seventeen?" Jordan wanted to know.

Logan nodded. There was no way he intended to tell Jordan about Megan getting pregnant. In his mind, there was no need to travel anywhere near that path. "It seems Scott and Megan dated that summer." And he left it at that.

Kinsey couldn't have been more proud of him for that. To get everyone off that tantalizing tidbit, she brought them back to the topic at hand. "So Wally, your father, Jimmy Pierce, had to put a new engine in all three cars? Tell me, did you find anything in your dad's stuff that might tell us who owned a maroon pickup twenty-five years ago? Could your dad have owned a truck like that?"

At the question it finally dawned on Wally why she wanted to know, why she'd asked Troy the same question. "You think my father did this to these women? That's nuts. He had a heart attack several years back. I'd suggest paying him a visit and asking him directly but it might push him to the brink and he'd likely have another one. I won't risk that."

"I don't blame you," Logan quickly answered. "I don't believe your father is our guy. But I won't lie to you we added him to our suspect list two weeks back."

Wally bristled at that until Kinsey explained, "Wally, try to understand. The police reports indicated three of the missing girls had their own cars. They were on the road, just passing through Pelican Pointe when they stopped here to gas up. The only service station here is owned by your dad."

"So add to that list, Belinda Truitt, Penny Hargrove and the fact Megan probably drove Charlotte Donnelly's Chrysler the night she went missing, and that's six that leads right back to my dad's service station. Jesus. Was someone trying to set him up for this?"

"That's a possibility."

"Geez, I'm beginning to know how Troy felt. But he didn't do it. I know my father."

"So did you turn anything up about a maroon truck?"

Wally pulled out another piece of paper. "As a matter of fact, I did. Here are the people in town who brought in that color pickup for repairs."

"Five names," Logan said just as Ethan came through the back door.

"By any chance is Carl Knudsen's name on that list?"

"Yeah. He's number five."

"You'd better move him up to number one. When Carl turned sixteen his father threw him the keys to a brand new maroon Chevy Silverado. Tonight I can confirm the fingerprints forensics found on that cellar door." Ethan ticked off the numbers on his hand. "One thumb print matched Kent Springer's. His prints are on file from the time he was arrested right here at Promise Cove for felony arson. Four fingers from Carl Knudsen's right hand were a match to the ones the state has on file from Carl's pharmacist license. And the third match was from Carl's little brother, Mark, who as a sixteen year old, left behind numerous prints all over that door. They all matched the prints from Mark's pharmacy license."

"Thank God for that," Wally said. "I was starting to worry for my dad."

"So three of Pelican Pointe's most upstanding citizens were involved in killing Carly Radigan?" Logan assessed.

"They weren't so upstanding when they committed the murder. Twenty-five years ago Carl would've been about eighteen, Mark sixteen, and Kent twenty-one. They were all just punks."

"They weren't punks when they kept up the killing. Now were they? You lost out on putting Kent Springer away two years ago." Logan spared Ethan a glower. "I kept hearing the name come up so often that I surfed the Internet for anything I could find on the guy. Springer was a nasty man."

"You don't know the half of it," Nick stated. "He tried to set fire to this house one morning. The bastard cracked his skull open on his own Cadillac Seville. If I'd known I had a serial killer sitting in my kitchen that morning, I might've been tempted to take care of him myself."

"If it hadn't been for Nick catching him in the act, Hutton and I might not be sitting here tonight," Jordan tossed in as she reached for Nick's hand.

"But for a while there, Kent's name kept coming up every time other women went missing. Until now, no one connected the dots."

"Until now Brent never had anything concrete. Now he does," Ethan snapped.

"But Kent's dead," Lilly reminded them all.

"We don't know that for certain," Ethan corrected.

"But we know for certain Mark Knudsen is. I went to the man's funeral five years ago. He had some kind of heart ailment."

"You're sure Derek and Sam aren't part of this little killing club?" Logan asked.

"The only thing I'm sure of is that the fingerprints on that root cellar door link three men to the death of Carly Radigan. Carl and Mark Knudsen and Springer."

"How did Carly Radigan die exactly? Do they know yet?" Kinsey managed to ask.

"The coroner says likely strangulation. Her hyoid bone was broken."

"Just like Gina's," Kinsey said, feeling bile start to inch up her throat.

"Have they picked up Carl?" Logan wanted to know.

"He left. His wife Elaine says he threw some things into a bag, headed for his Cadillac Escalade, and took off. Brent put out an APB."

Logan shook his head. "Tell me about this Knudsen guy. Any major quirks that would indicate where he put the other victims? Hunting lodges? Favorite fishing holes? That sort of thing."

"I went fishing with him once. Carl's a scary dude at times. He has a temper you don't want to mess with. He's fishing buddies with Wade though. Wade might know more. A man tends to share when they're out fishing in a quiet spot," Wally offered. "But I thought the theory was he dumped them in the ocean." When Wally noticed Logan flinch, he added, "Sorry. But I thought that was the prevailing consensus."

"I don't think so," Logan advised. "My two cents is he'd want a place where he could keep revisiting his victims.. It's just an idea that keeps rolling over and over again in my head."

"I saw Knudsen's temper flare firsthand today. He wanted to take out a gun to a thirteen year old who he suspected had stolen a pack of AAA batteries," Kinsey reported.

"He'd already started to crack from the pressure. From the moment we discovered Carly Radigan, he knew it was a matter of time before the cops came knocking," Logan theorized. "With this guy still out there I won't rest easy until the cops pick him up."

"That's a given," Nick said. "We should all be extra vigilant."

Carl Knudsen hadn't gone far. At least not until he'd finished his business, not until he'd paid that bastard Donnelly back for ruining the perfect life he'd made. Why hadn't Donnelly and Wyatt stayed out of his business? If everyone in town had simply fallen in line and believed that no-good Troy Dayton had killed Gina, he'd still be in his own house, watching television with his wife right about now, getting ready to sleep in his own bed.

But no, they'd both been instrumental in that damn campaign to find Gina's real killer. What a joke. What did they know about it anyway?

His own wife certainly never understood him. Elaine. Some help she had been over the years. She'd always sided with her brother, Kent, anyway, and today, when he'd needed her the most, had been no exception. Carl took another pull on his bottle of vodka, hoping the liquid could settle him down some.

Tonight he would stay at his special place, the place no one knew about. Tomorrow he would seize the opportunity. Opportunity always presented itself if you knew how to bring it around. Carl knew how to bring it around. Hadn't he been doing that very thing for over two decades now? No one would be laughing at his quarter century success rate. There was no doubt he'd achieved immortality. No matter what happened over the next few days, for now and all time, people would know his name. The name Carl Knudsen would mean something in this shitwater of a town. He'd probably even have followers. Isn't that why he'd gone down this path in the first place, to make a name for himself, to stand out from everyone else?

No, no, that wasn't quite right. His mother had caused this. It was all her fault. He'd never wanted to stay and waste his life running a goddamn drugstore. His brother, Mark, was supposed to step in and fill his shoes in that regard. But no, even when Mark had done exactly what she wanted, she still wasn't satisfied. His mother had insisted it be Carl, her eldest, year after long year. He'd sacrificed his own happiness to please JoAnne Knudsen. At one time he'd wanted to see the world, experience something beyond the city limits or county line. He'd had plans to get out of this town for good. But because of his mother he'd gotten pulled into living a life he'd never wanted. It was her constant nagging that had made him so angry. Even now, he could still hear her sharp tongue, over and over again in his head.

Carl took another long drink to stop the rage from completely taking over. He sometimes blacked out when that happened. And he couldn't afford to do that now.

No, he had to focus on paying Donnelly back and he knew exactly what he needed to do.

At work the next day, Kinsey had to confess to Aaron what was really wrong with her. Mainly because she still felt like throwing up. She'd already made two mad dashes to the bathroom only to have Aaron furrow his brow at her when she returned to her desk.

It was best to get this out in the open anyway.

"You're what?"

"You heard me, I'm pregnant."

"What does Logan Donnelly intend to do about this?"

"*We* intend to get through this together and have a baby, that's what. You said it yourself, Ina Crawford never married her Fuller Brush salesman and she had three kids."

"I wouldn't exactly hold that up as an ideal relationship. Young people these days do everything backwards," Aaron grumbled.

"Aaron, we've only known each other a few months. We can't go jumping into marriage just because I'm pregnant. That makes no sense."

"Suit yourself. But you need to protect your heart. Don't go losing it to this guy until you know if he'll stick."

Good advice, Kinsey realized. Too bad her heart had already taken that dive off the cliff. Otherwise she might gladly have followed Aaron's sage advice.

Logan had been antsy all day. He'd barked at every single member of both crews—several times—until finally they managed to stay out of his way.

Since he'd done nothing but toss and turn till the early morning hours, he attributed his bad mood to his restless night. But he wasn't a hundred percent sure that was the problem.

Knudsen was still out there evading capture. That stuck in his craw enough that he intended to do something about it. He'd put in a call to Brent Cody. Even though Brent had yet to call him back, Logan wasn't taking no for an answer. He wanted Brent to approve some sort of protection for Kinsey—even if it was only Deputy Dan sitting in a squad car outside Kinsey's office—at least that might keep him from worrying every single minute she wasn't with him.

Because, holy crap, in eight months he was going to be a father. He'd have a son or a daughter of his own. After knowing for almost twenty-four hours, the shock of it had yet to wear off. That's the reason he wouldn't rest until Knudsen was locked up.

He checked his watch for the twentieth time in half an hour. To hell with this, Logan decided as he headed to his truck. If Brent Cody couldn't return a phone call, he'd go see Ethan personally bend his ear and make his case with one Cody brother.

It took Logan less than five minutes to go the four blocks to Ocean Street. He drove up in the driveway of the Cody house about the same time Garver pulled up to the curb in his squad car. Good, thought Logan. He would convince both men, Kinsey needed protecting.

Having spent better than an hour with Jessie Falcone explaining why it was best not to leave ten thousand dollars to her poodle, Sugar, Kinsey felt worn out. By three-thirty that afternoon she was more than ready to go home.

She allowed herself an image of taking a long soothing shower, getting into a pair of comfy pajamas, and settling back with a good book when the front door burst open.

Carl Knudsen stepped inside the foyer, glanced at Kinsey, and pointed a nine-millimeter pistol at her heart.

From the opposite direction inside his office, Aaron shouted, "What the hell? Carl Knudsen you put that gun down right this minute."

"Shut up old man!" Out of the corner of his eye Carl saw Kinsey reach for the phone on her desk. He turned the gun in Aaron's direction, pulled the trigger. The sound of the shot reverberated off the walls as it hit Aaron in the shoulder. Aaron dropped where he stood.

Carl shifted the barrel of the gun to Kinsey and motioned for her to cross to him. "Come on, sweetheart. You're coming with me."

It crossed Kinsey's mind as she stood up that if she let Carl get her to his car, she'd be a dead woman. This was a serial killer whose body count was in the double digits. She needed to fight not only for herself but for the life growing inside her. Taking her time to walk across the room, she tried to formulate a plan.

"I haven't got all day. Now move your ass over here like a good girl and do it quick or I'll take out this old buzzard here and now for real by putting a bullet in his brain."

The minute she reached him, Carl grabbed her by the hair and tried to drag her out the front door. But Kinsey latched on to the doorframe, holding on with all she had. When he tried to yank her, she gripped the wood with her nails digging into the molding.

She had to fight, to give Aaron time to dial for help.

Inside the house, bleeding and weak, Aaron reached his desk. He punched in numbers on the phone, waited for someone to pick up. When they did, he wheezed into the receiver, "Shooting. Two-six-zero-six Landings Bay. Kinsey's been kidnapped. Knudsen took her. Get Garver!" With that, he slumped onto the hardwood floor.

"Let go, goddamn it!" Carl shouted. With brute force, he yanked hard enough to dislodge Kinsey's hold. He pulled her along across the grass and down the driveway to his SUV.

But Kinsey didn't make it easy for him. With every step, she fought, slapping, hitting at his arm, his face, anything she could reach. "Why are you doing this?" Kinsey cried, her head beginning to ache as he pulled her along by her hair.

"Your boyfriend's gonna pay for opening up this can of worms. You're my ticket out of this town for good." Carl dragged her up to the passenger side of the SUV, threw open the door.

But Kinsey still struggled and kicked. He backhanded her across the face to get her to stop. She went down on all fours onto the pavement. Trying to get her breath back, she tried to roll, but he reached down with the gun and whacked her in the back of the head with it. The thump had her seeing stars. Now on her back, he slapped her again across the face. She put her hands up and started kicking, trying to block his attack. She managed to knock him back a step, and tried to crawl to get away. He caught her by the back of the shirt and threw her down on the ground. The force knocked the breath out of her. This time, he straddled her, closed his hands around her throat.

About that time Dan Garver skidded his police cruiser to a stop. The minute the car stopped moving, Logan shot out of the car with Ethan right behind him. Running full out now to where Kinsey lay beaten, Logan knocked Carl off Kinsey while Ethan put him in a choke hold.

But when Logan spotted Garver just standing there, he barked, "Get an ambulance, she's lost consciousness!" Logan glared at Carl Knudsen. "You bastard! If anything happens to Kinsey, I'll come for you. There won't be any place you'll be able to hide. I'll get you no matter what I have to do or where I have to go! Do you hear me, you son of a bitch?"

Logan didn't think anything or anyone could ever replace his determination to find out what happened to his sister. But right now Kinsey was behind one of the curtains in the ER. She hadn't come around in the ambulance. He'd told the physician on call about her pregnancy. He'd paced and stalked the waiting room. He'd sent angry glares in the direction of the nurses. Nothing had made them move any quicker or gotten him answers. He had just decided to take matters into his own hands and storm the flimsy curtain when the doctor stepped out from behind it. He wore green scrubs and looked no older than thirty.

"I'm Dr. Prather. Are you waiting for Kinsey Wyatt?"

Logan nodded. "How is she? Is she all right?"

"Her vitals are good. She came around briefly, and if you're Logan, she asked for you."

"Damn it! I want to see her."

"You will. We're keeping her here overnight though to make sure we watch her for at least twenty-four hours. She has a concussion and bruising along her face and eyes. The man's attack left her with several contusions on the back of her head and a small gash that took four stitches to close. We think she probably came down hard on the concrete. The palms of her hands are also raw from landing on the gravel." The doctor paused to slap him on the back. "But with all that she's been through she's a young, healthy girl who put up one helluva fight. Give her a few days and she'll be good as new."

Logan wasn't convinced. He wanted to see for himself. So when they moved Kinsey to a private room he followed the gurney into the elevator where he found himself afraid to touch her. Why didn't she wake up and look at him? When the orderlies got to the room, they moved her from the stretcher to her bed. It was then and only then, Logan finally picked up her limp, pale hand, the one with an IV taped to the back.

Her fingers were ice cold.

"Will she be okay?"

Logan jolted a little, at the now familiar voice he had grudgingly learned over the past few weeks to accept. But he wheeled on the man, a showdown long in coming. "What the hell do you care anyway? She trusted you, some fucking spirit she's convinced looks after people. Did you look out for her when it counted? No, you left her dangling on a vine knowing full well it was Knudsen who killed Megan and didn't say a word. You almost got her killed because of it."

The only thing that stopped Logan's rant was the wide-eyed nurse that opened the door a crack, stuck her head in the room. "Sir, if you don't keep it down, I'll have to ask you to leave. Yelling at her isn't going to wake her up any faster."

"I wasn't—" The miscommunication simply made Logan more furious. But he lowered his voice and growled in frustration, "If anything happens to her—"

"You heard the doctor she's going to be all right. You want answers, Logan? Now that Knudsen is in custody, you'll get your answers. I'll see to it. I'm sorry you think I put Kinsey's life in jeopardy. But the story wasn't mine to tell. I understand how you feel though. Believe me. You love Kinsey. Have you told her that by the way?" When Scott saw the deer-in-the-headlights look on Logan's face he had his answer. "Of course not, not Logan Donnelly, man of a thousand different moods and none of them good."

"I'd planned on it." Frustrated, Logan ran a hand through his hair, dropped into one of the plastic chairs. "I even bought a ring. I'm going to be a father. Me of all people? Can you believe that?"

"Why not?

"What if I'm no good at this father thing? My dad certainly wasn't."

"Are you really that screwed up, Logan? Think about it before you answer. You've discovered you're capable of loving the right woman. That's huge. Finding out what happened to Megan, restoring the lighthouse, those things brought you back here. But it's Kinsey who will keep you here."

It was twelve long hours later before Kinsey's came around.

Once her eyes blinked open, Kinsey noticed the pounding in her head first. She did her best to focus through her blurred vision to make out Logan sitting in the chair by her bed. He looked sleepy and irritated. She was beginning to believe that the annoyed thing was his defense mechanism.

As soon as he saw her arm move, Logan shot out of the chair and was at her side in two seconds. Picking up her hand, he placed a kiss on the rough and still-red skin of her palm. "When I saw you on the ground…I've never been so scared in my life."

"How long have I been out?"

"Longest twelve hours of my life."

"Did you get him?"

"Knudsen? Yeah, he's locked up. And he keeps asking to see me."

The next day Brent and Ethan Cody escorted Logan along the corridor at the Santa Cruz jail. As the trio walked, they discussed the reason Logan had been summoned.

"Carl wants to talk—but only to you—and since we all want answers this is our best shot at getting them. From everything the guards tell me Carl Knudsen is on the brink of having a Norman Bates moment. He's been babbling incoherently, going on and on about you, and won't shut up. That might be because he hasn't closed his eyes for longer than fifteen minutes since he got here," Brent explained as he led Logan into the visitor's room.

The guard hadn't brought Knudsen out yet so Logan stood there in the stark white atmosphere having second thoughts. "Maybe I'm not the best one to do this," Logan admitted.

"You're the only one who can to do this," Brent told him.

"Don't be nervous. Just sit down and see what he wants, let him talk, maybe he'll let slip something we can use. When they bring him in, just pick up the black phone there on the wall to talk to him," Ethan directed.

Logan took his seat in front of the glass. If only he'd gotten his hands on Knudsen before now. "I wouldn't say I'm nervous exactly. More like furious. Every time I think of him knocking Kinsey around, I'd like to get him alone for five damn minutes. Maybe that would be time better spent."

"You want him to give up Megan and the other girls? This is the best way to get that," Brent told him.

About that time the door opened. The guard brought a disheveled Knudsen in, cuffed and chained. Logan couldn't believe what he was seeing.

The man on the other side of the Plexiglas didn't resemble the pharmacist Logan had seen around town for the past three months.

This Carl Knudsen had wild eyes that darted around the cubicle like he expected someone to appear out of thin air and knife him. His hair stood up in spiky points. The look might've worked for Brad Pitt. But on Carl, it gave him an air of crazy. He resembled a wild animal waiting for the pack to go for the throat. He had dark circles under his eyes from lack of sleep. In two short days he looked as though he'd aged ten years and gone completely mad.

And that just pissed Logan off. He could just see a judge sending Knudsen to a mental hospital instead of San Quentin.

Brent was right. If he wanted to learn the truth, this might be his one and only chance. He didn't dare blow it now.

When Carl sat down, the guard was the one who picked up the phone and handed it to the inmate, then motioned for Logan to do the same on the other side.

Logan lifted the receiver. The first thing he heard was Knudsen's labored breathing.

And then Logan saw it. Or rather them. All of them.

Scott stood behind Knudsen along with a line of young teen girls of various ages. He recognized some of them by the photos in the police reports. Carly Radigan, Angela Fetterman, Janie Shively, Rebecca Linseed, Aurella Gonzales, Penny Hargrove, Kimmie Pederson, Belinda Truitt, and Sandra Flowers. Behind the glass wall, behind Knudsen, the girls stood staring back at Logan. But the count was off.

There were twelve instead of ten, two Logan didn't recognize.

His breath hitched when his eyes landed on the image of his sister just as she had been in life at the age of seventeen. Megan Donnelly's long chestnut hair was as thick as he remembered. He'd forgotten her green eyes and their fiery gold flecks that turned greener when she lost her temper. Just like his did. She looked exactly the same as she had the morning he'd left with his grandfather for Yosemite.

"You have to make them go away!" Knudsen screamed into Logan's ear. "Make them leave me the hell alone and I'll tell you whatever you want to know. Now!"

Logan swallowed hard, took his eyes off Megan long enough to glance at Scott. He noted the stubborn set of Scott's jaw, the anger simmering in his eyes.

But the moment, Logan saw Scott nod his head, something moved inside him. He fired back, "Knudsen, they'll only rest when you tell me where you buried them. Where are they? We have Carly, she was special. She was your first. Now tell me where you put the rest."

Knudsen started mumbling to himself. "My idea. Kent wanted to dump them in the ocean. But I said my way…my way, it's got to be my way. I wanted to keep them close. Mark wanted to put them with Carly, but I said no…no way…not a good idea. Are you nuts? Put all of them in that root cellar for someone to stumble on her? No way. Someone might come along and want to buy the property one day. Then where would we be? Up shit creek, that's where. Nope…not a good idea to put them with Carly, that's for sure. And look what happened, Logan Donnelly came back, took you twenty years to do it, but you finally came back here. You bought the place. Didn't think you'd find Carly though, did you?" He shook his head. "No, didn't think you'd find Carly," Knudsen repeated.

"When did you add the wall?"

"Kent and Mark did that one weekend. They got scared after we did the fourth girl. Or was it number five? I get them mixed up sometimes. Kent and Mark were always panicking about something, not reliable at all. Should've gotten rid of them both a long time before I actually did. Both were next to useless."

"What do you mean? Kent's gone, he took off?" Logan prompted.

Knudsen started laughing. "Shit. Kent took off all right. That rat-bastard spilled his guts to that slut of a girlfriend, that Sissy Carr. Can you believe Springer told her our secret? Leave it to him to break just because they'd decided to get out of town. But I got the rat bastard back, didn't I? Weeks before they left Sissy came to see me, wanted twenty-five grand to keep her mouth shut. That's why I was waiting on the *Easy Money* that night. I got wind of their plans from Sissy herself. Woman always did have a big mouth. Stupid bitch. I killed them both right there on the deck, took out Kent first with a blow to the head. Sissy started clawing at me right off the bat. I strangled her then and there. Then I headed the boat out to sea."

Ethan passed Logan a piece of paper. Logan skimmed the questions written there and read them off to Knudsen. "How did you get back? What did you do with the money? How is it Sissy's body was found but not Kent's? What happened to *Easy Money*?"

Knudsen looked annoyed at the list of questions for several seconds, and then as if something or someone rattled him again, he picked up the story. "Sunk the damned thing by turning off the bilge pumps, took out the drain plug. Used my gun to put a few more holes in the bottom, but I had to wait damn near all night for it to finally go under. I'd already lowered the dinghy, loaded it up with the bag of money, and headed back inland around four in the morning. I knew I'd have myself a trip in that little boat since I get seasick. But it was worth every minute I spent puking. Only thing I can figure out is that somewhere Sissy's body somehow slipped into the water, maybe before I ever got out of the bay. Bitch must've floated away in the tide. If Harold and Drake Boedecker hadn't gone out fishing that day, you never would've found her. And you'll never find Springer. I guarantee that. He's at the bottom of the ocean. Fish food."

Logan spared a glance at Ethan to see if he was satisfied with the man's story because he needed to get Knudsen back to the girls, specifically his sister. Through gritted teeth, Logan demanded, "Quit stalling. Tell me what happened to Megan. How'd you get access to the car she was driving that night? My grandmother always kept that car in the garage."

Knudsen began rocking back and forth. He dropped the receiver and the guard had to step to the counter to pick it up. When Knudsen finally took it in his fist again, he mumbled, "I remember her. She was so damn pretty, long chestnut hair, big green eyes. Truth be known, I'd had my eye on that girl for a couple of summers back. But that June and July there was something…*special* about her. I'd been watching, waiting. For months, she'd been running around meeting her boyfriend behind everyone's back. Tried to keep track of them both but they were sneaky. Finally made my move that night though when she stopped at the store, saw my opportunity. Murphy's hadn't been opened all that long back then. She couldn't have been inside the store for longer than five minutes because all she came back with was a couple of soft drinks. Anyway, I had to hurry and the lot wasn't that well lit. I remember she was driving her grandmother's blue Chrysler. I opened the hood, took off the oil cap, dumped in the sand. Piece of cake really if you know what you're doing. Car didn't go any farther than three blocks before it started sputtering and stopped right there on Beach Street."

Logan did his best to keep his cool although he wanted to peel back the Plexiglas and lock his hands around the man's throat. Because he didn't have the answer yet, that piece of the puzzle he wanted, he made an effort to keep his voice level when he asked, "Where is she? What did you do with Megan?"

"Gone. Buried. They all are. Give me some paper and a pen, I'll draw you a map. But first, you gotta tell all these girls to go away, make 'em go away. Now! Get that damn Scott Phillips out of here first though. That man's driving me nuts."

Chapter Twenty-Seven

On the last day of August on a bright sunny afternoon, Megan Donnelly's remains were laid to rest next to the graves of her grandparents, Liam and Charlotte. For two decades Logan had known his sister had died the night she'd disappeared.

Knowing for certain was like a weight had lifted.

At fifteen years old he'd left Megan to rot in a field, that grove of trees north of the lighthouse, without ever doing anything to try to find her. Her burial ground for twenty years had yielded twelve sets of bones, bones that one of the monsters kept revisiting year after year. Yes, Logan should've looked for her long before he had. He'd never forgive himself for that, for waiting two decades to do what a brother should have done for his missing sister. Scott had been right about that. He should've manned up a long time ago.

But regrets were a frivolous waste of time now and would do him little good. He couldn't change the past.

As they'd done at Megan's memorial service earlier, the whole town had crowded into the auditorium of the Community Church. Now those same people sat in white chairs lined up at the gravesite for the final goodbye. Even though most of them had never known Megan, it didn't keep the sentiment from reaching Logan's heart.

Flowers in every color and variety adorned the top of Megan's polished bronze casket. Watching them lower it into the ground, Logan knew he would never again leave his sister. He would make Pelican Pointe his home. He'd made friends here, friends he hadn't made in all his worldly travels. He hoped to create here, make a life here with the woman sitting next to him. He prayed she felt the same way.

He would need to find out…and soon.

There would be more funerals, other services to sit through yet. Families in Washington and Oregon right here in Pelican Pointe had answers now. They would finally get to bury their daughters with dignity and respect, to have a place to come to, to put flowers atop a marble marker, and weep.

The town would need to heal from the stigma three monsters had left behind. But heal it would.

Once everyone had gone to their cars and Logan and Kinsey were left to stand over the freshly turned earth, Kinsey turned to him and promised, "The headstone will be ready in a couple of weeks." She slipped her hand out of Logan's to walk a couple of rows back, where Aaron Hartley's headstone stood. Two weeks earlier Aaron had died peacefully in his sleep. His body hadn't been able to recover from the gunshot wound he'd suffered at Carl's hands. To Kinsey, she considered Aaron Hartley to be Carl's last victim.

Now kneeling in the dirt beside the granite stone, Kinsey clutched the remainder of the bouquet of white daisies she held in her hand. When Logan came up behind her, put a hand on her shoulder, she dropped the stems of the daisies she held in the round, metal urn that stood on the base of the headstone. She absently began to arrange the blossoms one at a time. "It's been a rough month for both of us."

Logan helped her to stand. "What do you plan on doing with the house on Landings Bay?"

"Aaron wanted me to have it so I'm keeping it. I'm continuing the law practice right where people know where to come if they need legal help." She slumped against Logan's chest. "I still can't believe he left everything he owned to me. Why would he do that, Logan? I don't understand."

He tucked a strand of her hair behind her ear and lifted her chin. "Aaron had no family, Kinsey. None. I'm convinced he wanted his practice to go on after he was gone. He knew you were his best shot to see that happen. Are you feeling okay?"

She nodded. "The heat's getting to me some. I'll miss Aaron. There's no way around it. He's the reason I'm standing right here. Aaron's the only one who would have given me a chance to become the attorney I've always wanted to be. And I feel fine, Logan, more than fine." Her hand went to her stomach automatically.

Logan pulled her closer, rested a hand over hers on her still-flat belly. He tilted her mouth up for a kiss. "Are you going to stay with me, Kinsey, be with me, here in this town?"

"You're staying in Pelican Pointe?"

"Why would I leave now? I've got a baby on the way. Plus, I'm not leaving Megan again. And I'm damn sure not leaving you. I love you, Kinsey Wyatt, like I've loved no one before you."

She drew in a shaky breath. "I wasn't sure until this moment. You could have said something before now."

He took hold of her chin. "I want to hear you say it."

"I love you, Logan Donnelly with all my heart."

"That's all I need to know."

Epilogue

One month later

Across the street from the Fanning Marine Rescue Center, Logan stood twelve feet off the ground on a scaffold in front of what used to be the old newspaper office. He had his shirt off. The warmth of the September day had the sun beating down on his back. But he couldn't have been more content.

The previous week the entire town had turned out to help prime the exterior of the building with gray paint to cover over all the graffiti-laden brick.

The mural Logan was in the process of working on was in memory of Megan and all the other young girls. It was taking shape gradually like any work of art that took time and patience. Since he only got to work on it in his spare time in between the lighthouse renovations and his own creative process, he knew it would take a while.

Logan didn't mind the wait. He wasn't in a hurry. Not anymore. As long as the weather held, he was pretty sure he could get the mural done by the end of the year.

Sometimes he painted with an audience of twenty or more of the town's most curious. They usually stood around the base of the scaffolding watching as the faces of the girls took shape from the additional photographs the families had sent him over the past few weeks. But occasionally, like today, there was only Troy shadowing and jawing at him.

As Logan had learned, the kid liked to talk.

"It's looking good already," Troy said as he tilted his head to study Logan's work. "You're a much better artist than you are a carpenter."

Logan chuckled. "Smart ass. How are things going at the site? I know you're a man short since Derek got arrested for sexual assault."

Troy lifted one thin shoulder. "Hey, Derek got what he deserved. Like you said, it was only a matter of time before someone filed charges. And once Paul found out what happened to Abby while he was in Afghanistan, Paul didn't mess around waiting to call Dan Garver. Plus, I think Brent is checking out Lilly's mom's death now. The coroner re-opened the case to take another look at how she died." Troy scratched his head. "I hope it doesn't turn out that Derek did something to Lilly's mom." Troy shifted topics. "By the way, thanks for making me foreman. I won't let you down."

"You'll handle it. You like living out at the farm?"

"Oh yeah. It's a great little house. Mona and I get a lot more privacy out there whenever she comes for a visit. In fact, we got us a puppy. Mona named him Silas 'cause that's who gave him to us. How's Kinsey? She still puking?"

"The morning sickness is tapering off some. At least it isn't as bad as it was."

"Do you plan to live in Hartley's house? How's Kinsey adjusting without him?"

"I know she misses him. It still freaks her out a little every time she goes into Aaron's office. But I guess we'll be there until the keeper's cottage is finished. The Landings Bay house at least has plenty of room for the baby."

"Lot of people miss Aaron, will for some time, I guess. Kinsey loses her mom and then loses Aaron. It's gotta be rough." Troy lifted a hip, took an envelope out of his back pocket. "Reason I stopped by was because you got a letter left tacked to the door of the keeper's cottage."

"A what?"

Troy handed it off to Logan. "A letter, sealed up and everything with your name written across it. Maybe it's one of those fan letters. Maybe you have a local admirer since there's no stamp. Kinsey says you get them every now and then from women who land on your website."

This time Logan laughed. "I think Kinsey sends them to me," he joked as he ran a paint-stained finger under the flap. He unfolded the paper, read the first line, blinked in shock.

Relish fatherhood, Logan. It's something I never got to fully enjoy. Every time you hold your son or daughter remember life's too short and precious. If it's a girl name her Megan because life goes on no matter what heartbreak you endure or what tragedies transpire. If it's a boy, go with Liam. It's a good strong name and will make your grandfather proud. Megan sends her love by the way. In fact, look up. Megan wants to thank you for never giving up, for finding her.

When Logan finished reading the last word his head immediately shot up to look around. His eyes lit on an image. There on the corner of Ocean Street stood Scott. He had his arm wrapped around Megan's shoulders. They were young, obviously in love. And they both sported wide, goofy grins as they lifted their hands in salute to wave back at him.

Dear Reader:

If you enjoyed *Lighthouse Reef*, please take the time to leave a review. A review shows others how you feel about my work. By recommending it to your friends and family it helps spread the word. If you have the time, please Tweet/Share that you've finished *Lighthouse Reef*.

If you *do* write a review, by all means let me know via Facebook or my website.
I'd love to hear from you!

For a complete list of the author's other books visit her website.
www.vickiemckeehan.com

Want to connect with the author to leave a comment?
Go to Vickie's Facebook or blog
www.facebook.com/VickieMcKeehan
www.vickiemckeehan.wordpress.com/ blog

Go to the next page for a preview of
Starlight Dunes
Christmas 2013

Starlight Dunes

Three weeks earlier
Santa Cruz, California

A storm churned out at sea. He could smell the rain on its way in. He might not possess the same psychic ability as his brother, Ethan, but Brent Cody recognized a good Pacific squall when he saw one forming on the horizon.

He'd grown up around the ocean, not five miles from the spot where he now walked. Except for the fifteen years he'd given to the military, he'd made this coastal town his home. Now as he left work and crossed the dark parking lot to his truck, he stared up at the ugly-looking, purple clouds moving inland. The heavy low-hanging marine layer had blacked out the stars and more than likely meant before nightfall they'd get wind and rain.

His mother's garden could use it, Brent decided as he climbed into his Dodge Ram pickup to head for home. He placed his briefcase on the passenger side of the bench seat, and started up the engine.

After putting in a fourteen-hour day Brent was more than ready to kick back in front of the flat-screen, heat up the leftover pizza he'd ordered from the night before, grab a cold Steelhead out of the fridge, then catch the last of the hockey game. He was pretty sure the Sharks were on the road tonight in Detroit hitting the ice against the Red Wings. Of course, he'd already missed the first two periods. Good thing, he'd remembered to DVR the game.

His mind on ESPN and sports, he scanned the secure lot out of habit before exiting onto the deserted side street. He hadn't been a member of law enforcement for the better part of a decade not to key in on his surroundings.

Since the people of Santa Cruz had elected him county sheriff six years earlier, most of his days were like today, long and exhausting. He didn't like to admit how much time he spent sitting on his butt plopped in front of his laptop, handling paperwork these days. But because of it he did whatever it took to stay in shape.

Approaching forty, he was mindful his body wasn't the same as it had been when he'd been able to throw a ninety-five mile per hour fastball for his high school baseball team. That's one of the reasons he made sure he jogged at least five miles three times a week. Whenever his schedule permitted, he also tried to hit the state-of-the-art gym down the street from the office to lift weights or work up a cardio sweat on the elliptical. Plus, he'd gotten into the habit of limiting his bacon and egg consumption to a measly twice a week. For all his efforts he still weighed the same as he had when he'd landed in Iraq.

But it sucked getting older, he thought now as he made the four-mile drive to his house. When fat drops of rain began to splat on the windshield, he turned on the wipers and listened as the blades began a back and forth scraping motion. He countered the annoying whap, whap, whap by turning up the volume on the Pearl Jam CD already in the player.

Glancing at his reflection in the rearview mirror, he caught the shadow of a man with Native American features, the straight nose, the strong chin, eyes so brown they were almost black. He audibly sighed at the makings of crow's feet at the corners and the fact that his raven black hair was starting to turn a little gray at the temples. Something his father, Markus Cody, liked to tease him about.

As he drove the streets of the neighborhood where he'd essentially grown up, on impulse he pushed the button to roll down the window several inches on the driver's side in spite of the mist so he could breathe in the cool night air.

Once he'd gotten his bad marriage behind him, he'd finally taken the plunge and bought a little Spanish bungalow with a nice view of the water. The place wasn't large, no more than twelve-hundred-square-feet, but it suited a single guy who had no plans to ever make a family. That's why when he got home tonight, there would be no one waiting for him, no woman, no girlfriend, not even a dog.

It was best that way, he thought, even if he did on occasion dip his toe in the dating pool. After all, he wasn't a loner or anti-social. His mother saw to that because she seemed hell-bent on fixing him up with…someone. Especially since his little brother had settled down in wedded bliss a couple of years back with Hayden and now had a son of his own. Since Ethan's marriage, Lindeen Cody seemed more determined than ever to get her oldest to follow in Ethan's footsteps. Hell she wasn't even subtle about it anymore.

He could chuckle about it—most of the time because the woman thought she was so damn clever whenever she invited him over to supper—as if he hadn't caught on years earlier to her interfering ways when it came to his social life. But what kind of social life did he really have when he was married to his job? He supposed he needed to put his foot down and take a stand with Lindeen Cody, one of these days, tell her to knock it off. Yeah, like that was going to happen. His mother had invented stubborn and patented the formula.

But the truth was without his mother's meddling, he rarely bothered doing anything on his own about it. For one, the long hours made it damn near impossible to sustain a relationship. In his experience women required assurances they were in it for the long-term. The one time he'd walked down the aisle to say 'I do' had been a disaster. While he'd promised to love and cherish, his bride had been the one who couldn't remain faithful for one goddamn tour of duty in Iraq.

But that was ancient history. He'd gotten over the cheating Cindy and never looked back.

Didn't his mother realize that the only women he met on a regular basis and interacted with all day worked for him in some capacity or another? And Brent Cody refused to cross that line at work to mingle anything personal at the office like a liaison. Been there. Done that before, too. It hadn't worked out any better. In his experience office affairs *never* worked out.

Because of that, if Lindeen Cody came across an attractive medical assistant at the doctor's office who she thought her eldest son might like, or a cute saleswoman she happened to run into at the mall who looked like future daughter-in-law material, Brent would hear about it. He'd eventually give in and meet her through his mother.

Which meant Brent went out on a lot of first dates—or met up with women over coffee on Saturday or Sunday mornings—to talk. If the two of them happened to click, they might plan a couple of movie or dinner dates before tumbling in the sheets. They might text during that time hot and heavy. They might even resort to calling each other for a little phone flirting. It might last three weeks or three months. But it never led to anything more permanent or more serious than that.

Brent was aware that at his age it was plenty embarrassing to leave it to his mother to hook up with the opposite sex. But on fourteen-hour days like today, he didn't really see much hope that Mrs. Brent Cody was out there somewhere, waiting in the wings. And at this stage of his life, he didn't spend too much time worrying about it either.

He made the turn onto his street, a nice residential area where young families made children. On automatic, he reached up to hit the remote to open the garage door. The rain had picked up as he pulled along his driveway, inched his truck inside the garage. Grabbing his briefcase, he crawled out of the truck, absent-mindedly wondering whether or not the Sharks were adding a win to their column. When his stomach rumbled with hunger, he remembered he hadn't eaten lunch until four that afternoon and it was now well past eleven. Maybe he'd forego heating up the pizza and opt for a quick bowl of Cheerios instead.

Before he reached the door going into his house, however, he held the clicker for the remote over his shoulder and hit the button to close the garage door. With that one push, the door blew. The force of the explosion blasted him through the air, knocking him back into the wall.

Brent never even had time to reach for his .45 still in its holster strapped to his shoulder. It wouldn't have done any good anyway. The ensuing fire had him trapped.

For a span of several seconds, he couldn't feel his body, didn't remember how he'd slid onto the concrete floor. The blinding light of what seemed like a thousand stars impaired his vision. But then just as quickly, the bright white color leveled out and speared to blazing red. He struggled to move, to lift his arm to dial the cell phone he still gripped in his other hand. He realized then and there he could only move one arm.

Brent heard sirens in the distance. At least he thought he did. It sounded as if two dozen freight trains were roaring through his head. He fought to stay conscious. When his eyes did finally clear enough, he zeroed in on all the blood covering his hands. He realized then how badly he was bleeding. As his strength faded, the blazing hue of red came back threefold.

And then, there was nothing but blackness.

Don't miss these other exciting titles by bestselling author

Vickie McKeehan

The Pelican Pointe Series
PROMISE COVE
HIDDEN MOON BAY
DANCING TIDES
LIGHTHOUSE REEF
STARLIGHT DUNES
LAST CHANCE HARBOR
SEA GLASS COTTAGE
LAVENDER BEACH
SANDCASTLES UNDER THE CHRISTMAS MOON
BENEATH WINTER SAND
KEEPING CAPE SUMMER (2018)

The Evil Secrets Trilogy
JUST EVIL Book One
DEEPER EVIL Book Two
ENDING EVIL Book Three
EVIL SECRETS TRILOGY BOXED SET

The Skye Cree Novels
THE BONES OF OTHERS
THE BONES WILL TELL
THE BOX OF BONES
HIS GARDEN OF BONES
TRUTH IN THE BONES
SEA OF BONES (2018)

The Indigo Brothers Trilogy
INDIGO FIRE
INDIGO HEAT
INDIGO JUSTICE
INDIGO BROTHERS TRILOGY BOXED SET

Coyote Wells Mysteries
MYSTIC FALLS
SHADOW CANYON
SPIRIT LAKE (2018)

ABOUT THE AUTHOR

Vickie McKeehan's novels have consistently appeared on Amazon's Top 100 lists in Contemporary Romance, Romantic Suspense and Mystery / Thriller. She writes what she loves to read—heartwarming romance laced with suspense, heart-pounding thrillers, and riveting mysteries. Vickie loves to write about compelling and down-to-earth characters in settings that stay with her readers long after they've finished her books. She makes her home in Southern California.

Find Vickie online at
https://www.facebook.com/VickieMcKeehan
http://www.vickiemckeehan.com/
https://vickiemckeehan.wordpress.com